DIVIDED

DIVIDED

BILLIE KOWALEWSKI

Billie Kowalewski

Published by Independent Harmony

ISBN: [978-0-692-04643-2]

Typesetting services by BOOKOW.COM

To all of the kids who have ridden in my school bus. From East Haddam, CT, and Old Lyme too. You all know who you are. Thank you for always making me feel like a loved part of your school day. I love you all.

I will never forget surviving "muffin Friday," M&M Mondays, and watching you grow. Follow your dreams, and never let anyone tell you that you can't.

CONTENTS

PROLOGUE

So much happens in a lifetime on Earth. Of course, because of the barrier hidden deep inside our minds, we never think about what might be happening in between those lives. At that point, our life flip upside down and we see everything from a much different perspective. Our stories ending then becomes our beginning, and at other times our middle. We learn so much more at this point, and far too often it is at this time when we realize we could have done so much better.

So why waste this time you were given? The only way to ever fail at anything is to give up, or not try at all. No one is guaranteed a tomorrow on Earth, all we have is today. Seize this time to do all of the things that you know you should. Set goals for yourself, and go after them with everything that you have. Strive to be better every day, and set the ultimate example. Love all of the people in your life, and encourage them to be better too. Most importantly, learn to love yourself.

Your story will someday come to an end, and just like this one, it has only just begun...

CHAPTER 1

BEING crumpled up on the floor in agony made me feel like a hostage. Thanks to our soul mate connection, the searing pain from Kaleb's accident on Earth was rushing straight through me. My head was pounding, and it felt like my left leg and ribs were on fire. I was also in shock, physical pain isn't something we are used to here. It's restricted only to Earth.

I don't think we're properly equipped here to handle this type of situation. Does pain medication even exist up here? If it does, would it work on souls, or is it something only meant to be carried down in our minds to Earth for human bodies? It was crippling, and I was begging the universe for a solution to just make it stop.

My discomfort seemed quite trivial in comparison to what Kaleb was going through. He is on Earth, experiencing a very dark depression, and has the potential of suffering this way for an *entire lifetime*. A fate which, because of the barrier hidden deep inside his mind, he doesn't remember that he has inflicted on himself.

Though it's always our own decision to go to Earth, Kaleb wasn't entirely responsible for this situation we're in. Kaleb was merely following advice from his spirit guide Jack, who doesn't know much about souls like us. Kaleb and I are more than just an eternal couple.

He and I both are extreme souls. An extreme soul is one that has certain characteristics or traits that are far stronger in one direction than the average soul would have. Our trait is that we share a very strong connection to each other. Which is why, I am experiencing Kaleb's pain. Kaleb has yet to learn any of this, due to our one and only rule about learning; that we must learn our lessons on our own. If he had discovered this, we probably wouldn't be in this mess.

If it were at all possible, I would trade places with him in a heartbeat. There's no telling what a human being will do when they're subjected to so much misery. Kaleb's accident wasn't accidental, and I fear the worst is yet to come.

I felt some of the pain finally beginning to dull, and slowly stood up from the floor. The only thing on my mind was peering into the water-filled crater to make sure Kaleb was alright.

When I looked up, I was surprised to discover Zipporah was standing alongside Luke and Jack now. Seeing them standing there with their smiling happy faces was quite upsetting at first, to say the least. It was because of Zipporah's, "Going to Extremes" class, and hearing her tell the story of Charmeine and Zuriel that was where I learned about what Kaleb and I are. I had also learned that Charmeine and Zuriel disappeared from our world because of a predicament quite similar to our current dilemma. Now, Kaleb and I were at risk of meeting the same unknown fate they did.

"Harmony, we have an assignment for you," Luke spoke proudly.

I looked at all of them like they were crazy. There was no way I was doing an assignment knowing Kaleb was suffering like this. I wasn't going anywhere. Not until I knew without a doubt that he would be okay.

"An assignment? I don't think I'm capable of doing an assignment right now. I need to watch Kaleb."

He smiled softly at me, and lightly nudged Jack's shoulder. "Go ahead and tell her," he prompted. Luke seemed smug as he tightened his ponytail.

Jack tugged at his cuffs, smoothing out the creases in the sleeves on his pinstripe suit. "Well, it seems Kaleb is okay physically, and he should make it out of the hospital alright. However, we are concerned he may try to do this again, and possibly be successful."

I shivered at the thought.

He looked over at Zipporah before he continued, and she prompted him with an encouraging smile and a head nod. "Because of yours and Kaleb's," he anxiously cleared his throat, "...unique circumstance.

3

It has been decided, since his actions will affect more than just him, it might be a good idea to send you down to Earth to help him. Hopefully, you can prevent him from doing this again. You must understand though, there are very strict rules that come with what the divine has given permission for you to do."

Some of the agony I was feeling was gradually beginning to fade, as it started to sink in that the divine is allowing me to go down and help Kaleb. I nodded my head, and paid strict attention.

"She'll be fine. She'll follow all of the rules," Luke boasted.

Jack turned to Luke. "Regardless, she needs to understand. There are serious consequences if she does not comply." He then turned back to me. "Do you understand, Harmony? If you do not adhere to the rules, you will be punished."

I nodded. "I understand...I'll follow them."

Zipporah stepped around the crater, her white robe billowing around her gracefully as she moved. She placed her hands on my shoulders, and she had a serious look in her eyes. "You can only affect Kaleb and nothing more. Interfering with anything else there is not allowed and will not be tolerated." Her sweet tone had a serious edge to it.

"I won't," I assured her.

"You and Kaleb are different, and you must help guide him towards this discovery. Make sure he's alright, and ensure that he does not do this kind of thing again. Please be mindful that you cannot tell someone on Earth the answer, they must come to the realization on their own."

"I will."

Zipporah smiled kindly and gave me a hug. Her waist-length silky brown hair draped around me like a curtain. She leaned back to look at me. Her delicate lips were turned up into a warm smile. "Luke will take you to Kaleb's intermediate room. Once you enter, you will be able to control how you would like to interact with him. You can choose whether he can see or hear you." She let go, keeping one arm draped around my shoulder as she continued. "Please be mindful that our interacting this way typically frightens people there, and is why we don't normally do it."

"I will. I'll be very careful," I assured her.

Luke took my hand and led me to what looked like an empty space at first on the far side of the room. Luke waved his hand and a very serious-looking metal door appeared. It reminded me of a bank vault. It was dark grey, and very tall and wide. The perimeter of the door was framed with large heavy-duty bolts, a large hand wheel was in the center.

Luke grabbed ahold of the hand wheel and started to turn it. His muscles, flexing and straining against his snug black tee shirt as he did. Sounds of metal clanking echoed around us as the locks released. He yanked on the handle, and the door let out a loud air hiss. He tugged on the door, walking backwards as he did, slowly swinging open the heavy door.

Luke stepped back from the door and gave me a hug. "I know this is the right thing to do. We'll all be watching."

"Thanks, Lukie."

Smiling proudly, Luke waved his hand, motioning for me to walk inside. I took in a deep breath, and walked in, and I was suddenly standing in Kaleb's hospital room. Luke slowly pushed the heavy door closed behind me.

It's a strange feeling opening a door, and simply walking into a whole other world. Some would argue that this shouldn't be strange to someone like me at all, with our ability to teleport being so commonplace here. But it is. We are not able to teleport between worlds, and we are certainly not allowed to interact with people on Earth. We do, and can, send telepathic messages though, letting loved ones know we are alright after we pass. Those are different.

I held my arms out in front of me to make sure I was not visible, and walked over to stand by Kaleb's bedside. I began carefully checking him over, taking special care that I don't touch or jostle him, revealing myself too soon.

His chin length brown hair was stringy and sticking around his face. Bandages were covering the cuts on his forehead and the brow above his left eye. I glanced around the room quick, before slowly lifting the sheets up to assess the rest of the damage.

I left his hospital gown alone, not wanting to disturb him while he was resting. I'll just have to wait until someone comes into the room to clean him or something to be able to check under that. I was impressed that the doctors had already set his leg.

I looked up and started to glance around Kaleb's hospital room. If it were up to me, I would have chosen a nicer one for him, I thought to myself. The room was simple; it was plain, and dimly lit. The walls were covered in white wallpaper with tiny pink flowers. The bland beige curtain was pulled to one side, revealing the starry night sky.

I stood by the head of his bed, watching him sleep, something I've done countless times, thinking about how I was going to help him. I didn't exactly come in here with a plan in mind. My eyes focused on the cut going across his cheek, and then my mind drifted to our last time on Earth together, and suddenly the plan was there. I knew what I was going to do. Now, I just have to figure out how to approach him. I leaned in close, closing my eyes, breathing in his sweet honey-like scent by his collarbone before moving my lips up to his ear.

"Don't worry my love," I whispered. "I'm here to help you."

CHAPTER 2

Curtis Parker: Born September 14, 1981

May/2005

I'm in the dark. My eyes start to adjust, and I see, I'm standing in a doorway holding a large bouquet of white flowers. Light starts filtering in slowly from the room in front of me, causing my eyes to focus on the exquisite form sitting at a small table. I'm drawn in by her beauty before ever seeing her face. I'm following the way the light reveals hues of pink in her fair skin at each and every curve, right down to her bare bottom. Locks of wild, curly brown hair hang down to the center of her back. A sense of relief washes over me, bringing with it an overwhelming urge to walk towards her. As I start to move, the aroma of the flowers becomes prominent and grows stronger the closer I get to her. As I set the flowers down on the table, I realize I'm not wearing any clothes either, and I turn away quickly, making my escape back towards the open door where I started.

"*Hey!*" she shouts, as she runs after me. I turn around to face her. Our eyes meet and I'm frozen, unable to peel my eyes away from the most beautiful face I have ever seen. Her high rounded cheekbones. Her full lips. Her large, wide brown eyes, lined with long, thick lashes.

We both stand there smiling wide, and I am staring into her eyes, feeling relieved by just her mere presence. Neither one of us, paying any attention to the other's full frontal nudity.

A panel starts to slide down, threatening to close the doorway between us. Both of us are bending with the dropping door, trying to keep the other in sight. The door suddenly slams down hard, making me jump back, and then she's gone.

* * *

"*No way*, I refuse to believe that!"

"Dawn, I don't want to believe it either, but there weren't any skid marks at the scene... What other conclusions could the authorities have drawn?"

"They're wrong, David! There is no way *my son* is suicidal!"

"Let's just be thankful that he only has minor injuries... It obviously could have been much worse than a couple of cracked ribs, a mild concussion, and a broken leg. We won't know what really happened until he wakes up."

My body is sore, and my mind is swirling. Probably from a heavy dose of painkillers, which tells me, it didn't work. I had a moment of weakness and in that last second, I quickly turned the wheel, slamming my car head-on into a giant boulder that was lodged into the side of a hill. My one and only attempt at leaving my miserable existence behind obviously failed▨*stupid airbags.* I was truly hoping that the dream I was having was a sign that I had finally died and gone to Heaven▨*naturally, it wasn't.* So now, I get the pleasure of listening to my parents' debate on whether or not I'm suicidal.

"It's just so hard seeing him lying here, knowing there isn't anything I can do to help him." I could feel someone smoothing down the blanket that's covering me. I assume it's my mother.

"He's in good hands here. The doctor said he'll be back to normal in no time," I heard my father reply.

Normal? *Really*? Because I don't think being this depressed could possibly be defined as normal for anyone. I feel so empty, and hollow. It's as if a small wound has formed where my heart should be that has been steadily growing with each passing day. My whole body aches all the time, and most days I struggle just to breathe. Neither one of my parents are privy to my chronic depression. I didn't want to worry them. I've always been really good at hiding it from everyone.

Please God...don't let me go back to being normal.

"I think he should come home with us for a while once they finally release him."

"That's a good idea. He probably shouldn't be left alone for a while."

"Stop it, *David*! —our son did not try to kill himself!"

Oh God...what have I done? I'm gonna have to make something up before I alert them to the fact that I'm awake, but what? I don't want them to worry about me. What other excuse could there be for me destroying myself and my car? I guess I could just say I fell asleep. That might make some sense to them; it was late at night.

I'm not *suicidal*. I just had a sudden lapse in judgment, and I don't know what I was thinking. It's not like I sit around all day dreaming of ways to off myself. I'm just tired of feeling so miserable all the time.

I can't say that I'm completely sorry for doing it though. Because, the second right before I hit the rock...I heard *her*.

She said my name, and it sounded frantic. "*Curt*!" Clear as day, her beautiful voice shrieking loudly, echoing throughout my car like a tantalizing bell chime. The girl with the bright brown eyes I've been dreaming of every night since I was ten years old. The girl I've been weighing all others against, and they all fail in comparison. The one with the long silky brown curls, and the full lips that I can't seem to find and can't stop searching for. I don't know her name or if she really exists. If she does, I have yet to find her.

I just don't understand why my subconscious would create such a fantasy, and then haunt me with it night after night. I can't even remember why the dreams had started, but I do remember when. It was right after a school fieldtrip I had to a state park. I remember waking up very confused the next morning, but very happy. I also remember feeling quite embarrassed too. That whole first week, I couldn't look my mother straight in the face knowing I was dreaming of a beautiful naked woman every night.

I inhaled through my nose breathing in the faint floral scent of a bouquet of flowers someone must have brought into the room. The smell of flowers has always seemed to relieve the ache in my body in a way that pain medication never could.

"Mom, could you bring the flowers closer to the bed?" I opened my eyes and was surprised when I tried to lift my arm up to point, but the action was cut short. I glanced down at my arms and groaned. Oh, great, *restraints*...I'm such an idiot.

"Oh, thank God!" my mother shouted. She was suddenly hovering over me brushing strands of hair from my eyes. She looked like hell. Her normal, perfectly styled, and heavily sprayed brown hair was pulled up into a messy bun. Loose strains hung around her unmade-up face. "Curt, what were you thinking! Do you have any idea what you put us through?! Don't you know what could have happened?!"

"I'm sorry, Mom... I didn't mean to do that," I sighed, "...it was an accident. I think I must have fallen asleep or something."

My mother turned to look at my father who was standing at the foot of the bed with a smug smile. "I told you it was nothing like they said!" She snapped at him, with a bossy tone. She placed her hands on my cheeks and kissed my forehead. "I'm just so relieved you're alright."

I gently smiled up at her. "Me too."

I turned my attention away from my parents for a moment when I noticed my reflection out of the corner of my eye in the hospital window. The night sky and the dim light in the room had turned the window into a perfect mirror. Only the image I saw wasn't so perfect. I winced when I caught site of myself.

My normal chin length brown hair was messy and tattered looking. I had cuts and scrapes across my left cheek, and a strip of white tape was across my brow with a wide bonus bandage across the length of my forehead. My mind started to drift when my eyes focused on the cut going across my cheek. I was experiencing a strong sense of deja vu, and felt as though I'd seen myself this way before. I closed my eyes, flinching away from my wretched reflection, trying to dismiss that feeling. I could feel the pull of the stiches under the tape when I moved any of the muscles in my face. It took every ounce of strength I had not to cry about my current state. It's my own fault, I did this to my-self. I was in so much pain inside, and now my outside finally reflects exactly how I feel.

I turned away from the horror show that was re-flected in the hospital window. I just couldn't bear looking at it anymore. I started to notice that I could still smell the flowers faintly in the room, and it was bringing some relief to my aching body. I began glanc-ing around the room for them, carefully keeping my eyes away from the window. "Mom, where's that bou-quet of flowers?"

My mother glanced back at me funny. "What bou-quet? Honey, there are no flowers in here."

I was a little confused. I could still smell them. "There's not?"

"No... You're probably just noticing my perfume," she replied.

No, I don't think so. I've smelled her Jean Naté be-fore, and it doesn't smell floral. It smells more like cit-rus. But, just to play it safe, so she doesn't start to think I'm really crazy, I just agreed.

"Yeah, I think you might be right," I said, looking down at my wrists, and then up at her with a puzzled expression. "Why do I have restraints?"

My mother glanced over at my father. Her brown eyes narrowed angrily at him. "Yes David, care to ex-plain to our son why he is restrained?"

My father cleared his throat, and then stuffed his hands inside the pockets of his green Members Only jacket. His stance was stiff from the discomfort he feels from being in a hospital. "The paramedics and the police said your accident seemed," he glanced up at the ceiling as he seemed to be struggling for the right words. "...*intentional.*"

"Intentional?" I repeated trying to sound confused.

"Yes." He sighed. My heart sunk a little knowing he was right. "It was my idea for them to restrain you. I was worried you might try to do something before we could get here."

"Like what?!" I tried to shout, when the air I needed to yell strained against my cracked ribs, making me yelp, and bringing tears to my eyes.

"I don't know." He hung his head down. "I was worried and I wasn't thinking."

I clenched my eyes shut. "I'm not trying to kill myself," I spoke softly through my teeth, trying to avoid upsetting my ribs again. "It was an accident."

My father ran his fingers through his salt and pepper hair before patting my foot. "And I should have known you better than that. Let me go see about getting someone to remove them," he replied sounding guilty. He turned and walked out of the room.

A small part of me feels bad about deceiving them. I did try to end my life. However, both of them are better off believing I had an accident, instead of what really transpired.

"Honey, would you like me to get you anything, or bring you something from home?" my mother asked, still hovering over me.

"No."

"Do you want me to call," a puzzled look came into her eyes as she struggled to remember my girlfriend's name. "Oh, what is her name? Sharon?"

"Shannon," I corrected her.

"Oh, that's right, *Shannon*." She smiled apologetic. "Would you like me to give her a call?"

"What for?" I asked.

"Well, to tell her you're alright. She must be wondering why you haven't called her in three days."

"Three days? I've been here for three days?!" I hadn't realized how long I've been here.

"Yes... So do you want me to call her?"

"No."

"Why not...did you two have a fight?" she asked.

I paused before I answered her. I didn't know how to explain to my mother why I have such apprehensions about calling her. "No, I just don't want her to see me like this." I lied, waving my restrained arms.

"Honey, I'm sure the restraints will be gone by the time..."

"I'll just call her later," I said abruptly, cutting her off.

"*Alright*," she said while fluffing my pillows. "Are you hungry? Would you like me to get you something to eat?"

I know my mother meant well, but her hovering over me like a helicopter was starting to get on my nerves. She gets like that sometimes, very overprotective. I could feel the irritation starting to boil under my skin, and I had to struggle a little to control my voice. "Not right now, I'm tired." I sighed.

"Oh, alright," she said on an exhale. "Why don't you try to get some sleep, while I hunt down your father. I wonder what's taking him so long?"

I sighed in relief at the prospect of being alone. "Okay."

My mother bent down and kissed my cheek. "I'm so glad you're alright," she said stroking my hair with a gentle smile.

I smiled back at her in reply and then I closed my eyes.

CHAPTER 3

I'M in the dark. I'm lying in my bed, and I can feel the coolness from the crisp sheets against my bare skin. My body is aching like I have the flu, and I have to work at pulling the air down into my lungs. Suddenly the pain intensifies. I'm in tears, fighting against the searing pain that is now tormenting my entire body, and I'm struggling to breathe. I'm clutching the sheets, rolling back and forth on the bed, choking and gasping for air, praying and begging for someone to help me.

Unexpectedly, I start to notice the delectable scent of a sweet candy-like flower. Slowly, I begin to feel relief as the aroma becomes stronger, dulling the pain with each intake of breath, and it relaxes my lungs. The scent surrounds me, and I feel myself slowly melting comfortably into my bed. All the pain is now gone, and I'm breathing comfortably.

I can feel warm breath against my lips, and the enticing floral fragrance is powerful as it permeates my nose. I'm drawn in by the delicious scent, tasting it on my tongue, as I feel full lips grazing softly against mine. Something erupts inside my chest making my body come alive once I finally press my lips against the sweetest lips I've ever tasted. Her full lips molding themselves to mine. I reach up, twisting my fingers into her hair, feeling her wild silky curls, reeling in relief that I finally found her.

There's a ringing sound pulsating in the distance. Slowly the ringing grows. Getting louder... and louder ... and louder.

The phone pulled me out of a sound sleep, ruining the best dream I've ever had. I groaned. Sleep is the only relief I ever get from my depression. I rolled to my side opening my eyes briefly to glance at the clock. I groaned again, "Ugh, it's eleven." I rubbed my eyes and I picked my cellphone up off the nightstand to read the caller ID.

"Ugh, of course it's Shannon." I was annoyed, and chucked the phone back up on the nightstand. I don't want to talk to her right now. I pulled my blanket up over my head still thinking about the dream. Since they first started fourteen years ago, I have had the exact same one every night. I was shocked by how different this dream was. And it was so real! I could almost swear it was really happening.

I rolled over grabbing my crutches from the floor leaning them up against the bed. I sat up and grabbed hold of the crutches hoisting myself up onto my feet. In the week I've been home, I've really gotten this whole "crutches thing" down. But I'm sure the eight weeks they said I'd be stuck like this is sure to get old. Thankfully, I don't have to go to work like this, and I was able to talk my parents out of making me go home with them. I love both of my parents very much, and I'm very close with them. My mother tends to go a little overboard at times, and knowing what I just did, I'd rather be alone for a while than have to deal with hiding how I'm feeling all the time around her. She can be very perceptive at times, and I don't want to slip and have her catch on that there is more going on here than I let her know.

I made my way over to my little kitchen and started myself a pot of coffee. Then I went back down the hall to use the bathroom. My apartment is small, but I like it. It's just the right size for one person. The hallway going to the bedroom and bathroom is a little narrow though, which does make getting around with the crutches a little more difficult▢especially when I have to go to the bathroom. It's a small compromise really. The whole apartment is one level, so I'm very relieved right now there are no stairs in here.

When I turned around to brush my teeth, I caught sight of myself in the bathroom mirror. It's hard, but I try not to look. No matter what I do, I can't seem to 100 percent avoid seeing my reflection in something. The windows, and the glass inside the picture frames at night. The side of the shiny toaster, and of course, the bathroom mirror. Seeing the damage I inflicted on myself like I did makes me feel worse than I normally do.

Honestly, I don't need the mirror to remind myself what an idiot I am to have done this. Though the cuts and scrapes on my face have healed some, I have two very constant reminders every day. My cracked ribs, which because of the tight tape job the doctor did, doesn't feel as bad anymore. Then there's my left leg. The doctor said it was pretty much a clean break and it should heal alright. That's the one I truly suffer with. It's not so much the pain of the break anymore, it's the itching. It's constantly itching and I can't reach in to scratch it. It drives me crazy, and at times I wonder if some of this suffering in a way is my punishment. It's the least of what I deserve.

I went back down to the kitchen to scrounge up something to eat. I was *really* hungry now, and needed a cup of coffee. I opened the fridge door trying to decide on what I was going to have for breakfast.

My home phone began ringing. I threw my head back, and started to grumble. *"Oh, for the love of all that is holy!"* I already know who it is, and I don't even have to check the caller ID. I slammed the fridge door and went over to pick up the phone. Sure enough, the caller ID displayed Shannon Hall was on the line.

Shannon is a very nice girl. We met at a party a few months ago. She's blonde and has blue eyes, a nice figure, too. We did hit it off okay at first, and I do find her physically attractive, but there's just something missing and I can't seem to put my finger on what it is. I also find it irritating when she calls me the way she does. She calls me several times throughout the day, even though I've told her many times how much I hate that.

I picked up the phone. "Hello?" I said, trying hard not to sound annoyed.

"Curt, where on Earth have you been?!" she asked sounding very upset.

"I don't know...*around*." I rested one crutch against the counter, and held the phone to my ear with my shoulder while I continued to hunt down something for breakfast.

"Around?" she repeated. "Well, you could have called me."

"I'm sorry. I've just been so tied up lately." I winced at my choice of words because at one point last week I really was.

"So, do you want to do something tonight?" she asked.

I glanced up at the ceiling, groaning internally. "Not tonight Shannon. I'm not feeling very good."

I settled on just having cereal. I grabbed my box of Golden Crisps out of the cabinet next to the fridge, and hobbled over to place it on the table. I then started hobbling back and forth with the one crutch continuing to cradle the phone with my shoulder, putting the rest of what I need on the table. It bothers me some, how natural I am on these crutches. It could be, I was a klutz in a previous life?

"Awe, poor baby, want me to come take care of you?" she asked.

"Na, that's okay. I'm just gonna sleep it off most of the day," I replied, as I hobbled over to the fridge to get the milk.

When I opened the refrigerator door and bent down, a familiar sweet floral scent hit my nose, and I could have sworn I saw something move out of the corner of my eye. Puzzled for a moment, I stood upright glancing around my tiny kitchen, but there was nothing there. I shook my head quick, dismissing what I thought I saw, and then grabbed the milk shutting the door. "I don't want you to catch what I have," I continued—like, broken bones are contagious.

She sighed. "Well, I guess I understand. Will you call me tomorrow?"

"I sure will...*Bye*." I pressed end on the phone and placed it up on the counter. I then hung my head down and sighed.

"You know, you shouldn't lie to her like that."

I whipped around startled by the surprise of someone else being in here, and when I saw who it was, I dropped the milk on the floor. The force caused the cap to pop off and milk splashed up everywhere, including soaking the front of my sweats.

"You know ...normally, I'm quite partial to your sandy blonde hair, but I have to say, I'm *really* digging the dark brown," she added.

I was shocked; it was *her*. There are no words good enough to describe the beauty that is now standing before me. I've never seen brown eyes that glow the way hers do. They're so hypnotic and alluring, lined with those long, thick lashes. Locks of silky curly brown hair framed her face, hanging down past her shoulders, and I couldn't stop staring at her tantalizing full lips. She looked more amazing now than she ever did in my dreams.

She also looked disappointed. She had her arms crossed, and seemed to be anxiously waiting for my reply. I was frozen and confused, with a million questions bouncing around in my head. Plus, I was soaked from the half gallon of milk I just dropped.

Her face softened, going from disappointment to concern. "Are you alright?" she asked.

Hmmm, am I alright? That is a good question. I don't know, I seem to be hallucinating. *Oh God*, maybe from the accident—*How hard did I hit my head*?

"Oh, that's right." She shook her head and glanced down at the floor. "I'm sorry, I forgot for a moment you don't know me right now. I didn't mean to overwhelm you like that." She looked up and smiled wide at me. "I'm Harmony."

24

"Harmony?" I repeated back to her. A funny feeling came over me when I said her name. I almost felt like somehow, I knew that.

"Yes." She glanced down at my feet. "Aren't you gonna clean that up?" she asked pointing at the mess.

I shook my head quick trying to clear away some of the mesmerizing haze. "I know you?" I asked, trying to make sense of what she said.

She smirked. "Of course." My heart started pounding against my chest as she began to walk towards me. "I have just one thing to say to you." She let out a quick chuckle. "I told you so."

She was standing a foot away from me now. My eyes were wide, my heart was pounding, and I was struggling to control my erratic breathing.

She crossed her arms and chuckled again. "You should repeat after me: I will listen to Harmony for the rest of my existence."

I narrowed my eyes at her in confusion, trying to make sense of what she was saying. "I should?"

"Yes...you've always been quite stubborn." She placed her hands on her hips. "Well, more so here than at home."

"Home?" I questioned, still straining to understand. "Where is home?" I asked her.

She smiled wide at me. "We call it Heaven when we are here."

"What do we call it when we're there?" I asked her.

She held her soft smile. "When we're there, we just call it home."

She stood over me while I struggled to clean up the mess on the kitchen floor. Bending down with a cast on your leg is not easy, but I managed.

"I wish I could help you with that but I can't," she said.

I glanced up at her. "Why not?"

"*Hmmm*...how do I explain this?" she replied, placing her delicate fingers to her lips. "Well, I'm not really here."

I pulled myself up onto my feet and tossed the towel in the sink. "Oh great...I am hallucinating."

She giggled. "I can assure you you're not. You can see me, can't you?"

I exhaled, "yes."

"You can obviously hear me, right?" she asked.

"Yes," I replied again.

She reached her hand up and placed it on my arm. A jolt of electricity was suddenly sent surging through my body. My breathing became embarrassingly erratic causing my heart to leap hard against my cracked ribs.

She glanced up at me, and giggled again. "Well, you can definitely feel me."

"Y-y-yes," I stammered.

She walked over to the kitchen table and gasped. "What happened to my Sugar Crisps?!"

"Uh, what?" I replied, still dazed by her touch.

"My Sugar Crisps...now its Golden Crisps? And what happened to the cute little bear?"

I shrugged. "I don't know. They were Super Golden Crisps at one point too, but then they changed it I guess. They still taste the same though."

She sighed. "Well, I guess that's all that matters." She smiled. "Watch." She reached her hand out and tried to grab the box of cereal but her hand went right through the box. "See? I can't pick it up. I can only affect you and nothing more." She walked back over to me. "It's so sweet that you're eating our cereal."

"Our cereal?" I asked her. I was still feeling quite perplexed but I was growing more comfortable with my odd situation. "How exactly do we know each other? Who are you again?"

She smiled fondly at me placing her hand on my cheek, her touch sending shockwaves straight through to my now hammering heart. "I am Harmony, and you are my Kaleb."

"I'm afraid you must be mistaken. My name is not Kaleb."

"Not here," she replied.

"Okay...well then, who are you to me?" I asked her.

"I am your..." She pressed her fingers to her lips while she struggled for the right word. "*Hmmm*, that's hard to describe in Earth terms. I guess, I'm like your wife." She nodded seeming pleased with her description. "Yes, it's like that, only more absolute."

"Really...and how long have we been together?"

"Not very long. We fell in love with each other during the last lifetime we were here together."

"We did?" I replied. I was straining myself, struggling hard trying to remember but I couldn't. "I'm sorry, I wish I could remember."

She smiled at me sympathetically. "It's alright, you're not really meant to right now."

"I'm not?"

"No." She had a soft smile as she gently shook her head in reply. "Why don't you get yourself something to eat and sit down at the table, and we'll talk more. You and I have a lot to discuss."

Since most of the milk ended up on the floor, I settled on having a couple of toaster waffles. Luckily, I had some powdered coffee creamer left over from a meeting at work that I was forced to take home, so I was able to have a decent cup of coffee.

I sat down at the table with my waffles and coffee in the presence of the most beautiful girl that I have ever seen. If this is a hallucination, I don't care. With the exception of the discomfort from my injuries, I haven't felt this good in years. All of my normal anxieties, aches and pains, and my struggle to breathe were gone. She must be Heaven-sent, or a guardian angel. She is certainly beautiful enough to be one.

"Are you an angel?" I asked, after I sat down.

She chuckled. "I wish. Someday you and I will both be. But right now, I'm just a young soul, same as you."

"Oh."

I couldn't stop smiling or staring at her, or marveling over how happy she is. She is the brightest, happiest person I had ever seen in my life. Even her clothes appeared to be happy. She was wearing a brightly colored tie-dye tee shirt. With a mix of reds, blues, and yellows, with a touch of green that swirled outwards from the center. It certainly caught my attention, and it isn't something people usually associate with Heaven.

"Does everyone in Heaven wear tie-dye and blue jeans?" I asked, pointing to her clothes.

She giggled at my question. She glanced down at her shirt and then back up at me and shrugged. "Some do, some don't. This is what I chose to wear to work."

"Oh, so you have a job?" I asked in reply.

"Yes...Curt, before we go any further, I need to ask you for a favor."

"What is the favor?" I replied, smiling.

"I realize what I am about to ask you may be a tall order. My being here in the way that I am is not normal, and I need to ask you to keep all of what we do and discuss while I am here to yourself for the rest of your life."

I started to laugh. "Are you kidding?! That's the last thing you have to worry about!" I replied loudly in between the chuckles. "I'm still not completely convinced right now that you're really here and that I'm not hallucinating. So, trust me, I'm never saying a word! If I ever told anyone about this that would be a one-way speed pass straight to the looney bin!"

She laughed, and then smiled through pursed lips and nodded. She seemed amused and very pleased with my reply. "Yeah, this would certainly do that here."

"Now that we have that understanding, I'm allowed to do a little more," she said. She walked over, pulled out a chair at my table, and sat down. After seeing her hand go through the cereal box I was quite shocked.

"How did you do that?" I asked.

"I'm capable of doing anything that I want. However, I was given very strict rules to only affect you. I would have helped you clean up that mess before, but I am being extremely careful in how much I do, so I don't cause any trouble."

"Oh, well, that's understandable." I smiled at her.

"I was told that sitting would make me appear more human, and you more comfortable."

"Oh."

She looked up at me with a very hopeful and happy expression. "So, are you comfortable with me here?" she asked.

"Very." I smiled at her.

"Good." She held her kind smile, as she reached across the table and placed her hand on mine, sending the shockwaves through me again. "So, how are you?" she asked.

I took a bite of my waffle, and started to chew. "Very good," I replied to her after I swallowed.

"Good," she said again. "I want to make something very clear to you."

The look in her eyes became very serious and her fists were suddenly clenched on the table. "That little *stunt* you pulled..." Her tone changed quickly and she started pointing and shouting at me. "Don't you ever do that again! Do you have any idea what could have happened to *us* if you pulled that off?!" She continued to point and she shook her finger at me. "Thank God your car had those air bags!" she shouted, throwing her hands up. "When I run into the soul who thought that up, I'm gonna kiss them!"

I sat back a little in my chair stunned. Not once did it occur to me that my accident might be the reason she is here. I suddenly felt like my own heart was broken and had to wipe away the tears that were now falling from my eyes.

"You saw that?" I asked her.

"Yes, I saw that," she quickly hurled back at me. "My guide pulled me from my job right before you pulled that stunt. Curt, accidents are one thing; suicide on the other hand, is very serious. A very delicate balance exists between reality and fantasy. Doing that upsets that balance in a soul in such a way that is almost unrepairable. If you had pulled that off, it would've affected not just you, but me as well, and for much longer than an Earth lifetime."

I hung my head down, feeling the weight of my shame. "I'm so sorry."

She exhaled sharply and crossed her arms. "*Now*, I want you to explain to me what was going through your head at that moment that made you think suicide was a good idea."

I wiped away another tear, and slumped back in my chair. "I've just been so miserable. I'm achy all the time, like I have the flu, and I struggle to breathe. I can't even wake up in the morning like normal people do. It's gotten so bad I'm late to work almost every day now. Luckily, my parents own the company so it's not like I have to worry about getting fired. I feel empty and alone, like something's missing in me. I have a girlfriend that I pretend to care about but I just can't connect with. It's been like that for me with all of them. I'm depressed, and it keeps getting worse and I don't know why." I sighed. "I hadn't been planning it or anything, it just popped into my head that night when I was driving home, and I did it."

When I finally glanced up at her, her expression was one of remorse. She felt bad and it showed. "Curt, would you like me to help you understand why you feel this way?" she asked.

I just nodded to her in reply.

She got up from the table and took my hand. "Why don't we go get you more comfortable," she said.

I got up from the table and grabbed my crutches, tucking them under my arms. My heart was pounding as I followed her down the hall, as she knowingly led the way to my bedroom.

"Why don't you lie down," she suggested.

As I sat down on the bed, placing my crutches on the floor, curiosity got the better of me. "Have you been here before?" I asked her.

She smiled as rose colored her cheeks. "Yes."

I smiled at her and just nodded. "I think I knew that."

"I've been here for a while, and I was just trying to figure out how to approach you without startling you. My being here this way is not normal. I was given special permission to come help you."

I took her hand and carefully controlled my voice before I spoke. "How long can you stay?" I didn't want to reveal to her how attached I already was.

"Not too long, I'm afraid. Just long enough to help you understand things. Make sure you're comfortable, and ensure you don't pull anymore Evil Knievel type stunts. I'd like to keep you for the eternity you promised me."

I took in a breath, and exhaled as I sunk back against my pillow. "Okay, tell me everything," I said, placing my hands behind my head.

She sat down on the bed. "Can I ask you a question first?"

I chuckled at her. "You just did."

She smirked. "Wise-ass," she replied. "Are you still feeling achy?" she asked.

"No."

"And the breathing?" she continued.

"I'm fine." I smiled at the realization.

"Curt, lesson one: there is a reason for everything. I promise you there is a reason behind why you ache all the time and can't breathe right. Just like there is a reason for why all of those problems are gone right now. Do you understand?"

"Yes." I smiled at her and nodded. "But what is the reason?"

She smiled at me through pursed lips. "This is where things are gonna get tricky. I cannot just tell you the answer. You must do your very best to try and come to the realization on your own. I do promise you though, I will tell you when you get it right."

I sighed at first. I was feeling a bit worried. What if I can't figure out what she is trying to teach me? I'm thinking this may be one of those occasions where I am gonna have to be very creative and think outside the box. I looked into her eyes with sincerity. "Okay, I will try."

"Excellent." Her cheeks were rounded upwards into a confident smile, lighting up her pretty face. "I need for you to pay close attention. I'm going to tell you the story of how you and I fell in love. You do already know this story, but as of right now, you can't remember it."

I smiled at her. "I would definitely love to hear about that."

"Good." She seemed pleased.

It surprised me when she crawled up onto the bed. She tucked herself under my arm, and snuggled up alongside me. She threaded her fingers with mine, and I pressed my face into her hair, breathing in her sweet floral scent, letting it fill my lungs. I've never felt so at peace or so at home in all of my life. Breathing in her fragrance is like melting into the softest bed, relaxing every limb. I could lay like this with her forever, and a part of me is rejoicing, because I know now that she is mine. Even if that means I can't keep her now.

"Before anyone ever told us anything about our creation, I've always felt a pull towards you. I always thought it was because you and I have known each other since our creation," she began. "Then when we started school you ended up in my class and we've always been friends." She lifted the hand she was holding to her lips and kissed it.

"I never gave much thought as to why I felt that way about you until we started going home early."

I glanced down, giving her a funny look. I wasn't sure what she meant by that. "What?"

"We were dying accidentally before we were meant to," she said.

"Oh." I wasn't sure how to respond. Normally we just think of dying once. "We were?"

"Yes."

"I'm sorry."

She glanced up at me and smiled. "We've already apologized to each other for everything that happened."

"Oh, okay, that's good to know."

"The lifetime we were in together right before the one I'm about to tell you about was very hard for you. Your name was Vinny in that life. I was unaware of what you were going through in your family. You were very angry and mean all of the time, which created a strong aversion for me. You admitted in that life that you loved me, but I was so put off by what was going on between us in school and what happened in this life that I did not return that interest then."

"Did we go home early in that life?" I asked.

She sighed. "Only I did. In that life, you became very jealous when a boy walked me home after a carnival. You followed us, and fought with him. You were about to do something very bad to him, and I tried to stop you. You shoved me back and I ended up hitting my head on something very hard and sharp, which sent me home."

I tightened my arm around her. Even though I couldn't remember, I was shocked at myself. "I'm so sorry I did that."

She glanced up at me and smiled. "You already apologized to me for that." She placed her hand on my cheek. "And I already forgave you." She pulled me closer molding her full sweet lips to mine, sending shockwaves rocketing throughout my body. I twisted my fingers into her hair and pulled myself closer to her, sounds of content were escaping from my lips.

She pulled away smiling, caressing my cheek, and continued. "The last life we were in together, you and I both were in very similar situations, only yours was far worse. You and I met in 1966 when my family moved to Connecticut..."

CHAPTER 4

Veronica Edwards

November/1966

I woke to the sound of a car door slamming shut.

"We're here girls," I heard my mother call out from outside the car. It was a long trip. I was cold, tired, and hungry, but happy to know that the long four-day trip in the car was officially over.

I opened my door, and stepped out of our car to look around at my new home.

I sighed. So, this is Moodus, Connecticut? "*Moodus is a town in East Haddam,*" my mother told us a dozen times in the car. It's cold, and there's no color here, I thought. It's late November so all the color that would be on any of the trees here is now gone. I guess I missed what my mother calls the "spectacular foliage." How could I ever be happy here? I wondered.

* * *

"So, wait a minute...we lived in Moodus?" I interrupted.

"Yes," she replied.

"That's only thirty minutes from here."

"Yes, I know."

"You don't find it weird that I live thirty minutes from the place we met?"

"Not at all. We're naturally drawn to the places and things we are most familiar with."

I combed my fingers into her hair playing tenderly with her curls. "Like each other?" I asked.

"Yes." She smiled.

* * *

I was scared, I never met my grandparents. The only contact I ever had with either of them was the birthday and Christmas cards they sent to me and my sister every year that always contained a ten-dollar bill, and, of course, the occasional phone call⬛when our phone was working.

A tall woman with big brown hair opened the screen door to the enormous white house we were parked in front of and smiled wide. Her hair was so big and was up into one of those beehive hair-dos.

She started to bounce up and down. "Frank they're here!" she shouted. "Frank, get up from that chair and come help them with their bags!"

She was shouting and squealing with delight. She ran over to my mother wrapping her in her arms. "I'm so happy to see you! *Oh*, I've missed you so much!" she excitedly exclaimed, with tears in her eyes. "*Frank!*" she shouted over her shoulder. "If you don't get up from that chair! —*So help me!*"

A man came out the front door. His hair was dark and slicked back with heavy grease. He was wearing a white shirt and his dark pants were held up by brown suspenders.

"I'm up. I'm up," he said rubbing his big belly. "Ah, Donna." He greeted my mother with a gentle hug. "I'm so glad you're finally here. Maybe now your mother will calm down just long enough, so I can get a little peace and quiet."

My mother chuckled.

My grandmother gawked at my grandfather. "Not a chance," she said, crossing her arms. "*Frank*, just get the bags."

My sister and I stood quietly in front of our car. We looked at each other and I could tell what she was thinking. My sister and I have always had a way to tell each other things without even speaking. I could tell neither one of us knew what to make of our grandparents.

"Veronica?" my mother called to me. "Katie? This is your grandma Ruth, and this is your grandpa Frank."

My grandmother walked over to my sister and I, and she bent down looking at us at eye level. "I'm your grandma, but you may call me Mémé." She stood up-right patting her hair. "it's French, and well, I don't look old enough to be called 'grandma'." She winced. "You girls must be hungry. Why don't you both come in, and I'll make you each a sandwich."

Katie and I followed her inside the big white house. As we made our way through to the kitchen, I was amazed by not just the size of the enormous rooms but by the tidiness. My mother was never this good of a housekeeper. Our house was always a mess; dirty laundry was always piled up high in corners of our bedrooms. Stacks of newspapers and magazines were in piles by the couch and the chairs in the living room, which sometimes acted as end tables. Dirty dishes were piled up in the sink most of the time too, and I don't remember the last time anyone in our house used the broom.

This house was so clean. The floors were dark wood and shiny. The walls were white and all the pictures on the walls hung perfectly straight. Pictures of my mother, my sister, and me lined the shiny fireplace mantle. Along the sides of the fireplace were three rows of shelves with little angel figurines lined up per-fectly on each one. The couch and the chairs were pink and had little white flower patterns on them, which were all covered in clear shiny plastic. The coffee ta-ble was a glossy rich brown and had a bowl filled with pink and white flowers in it. I felt like I couldn't touch anything. Everything was so perfect that I was afraid I might mess it up.

My grandmother, or Mémé, as she liked to be called, sat us down at the small table in her clean and fancy kitchen. "Do you girls like peanut butter and jelly?" she asked. Katie just looked at me. I knew that look. It means, you talk, first. I'm too scared.

I turned to answer her. "Yes, we both do," I said.

My grandmother started taking the things she needed out of the cupboard to make our sandwiches. She left the door opened and I was surprised to see how full it was. I never saw so much food stuffed into a cupboard in my life. The inside of the cupboard matched the perfection that was throughout the rest of the house, too. Everything in it was arranged into neat and tidy rows.

It didn't seem to take my grandmother long to assemble our sandwiches, and she put them down on the table in front of us. My sister and I exchanged a long glance and smiled. I picked up the sandwich taking the first bite.

Mmmm...It's been so long since I've had a peanut butter and jelly sandwich. I don't remember it ever tasting this good. The jelly was grape. It was tart and sweet all at the same time. The peanut butter was smooth and creamy, combined with the white bread it stuck a little to the roof of my mouth. My grandmother placed two small glasses down on the table.

"I assume you both like milk?" she asked filling our glasses.

"Yes," I managed to get out through bites. I eagerly grabbed my glass and took a long sip, dislodging some of the sandwich from behind my front teeth.

"You girls be good now. Stay in here and eat your lunch. When you're finished you may help yourself to a cookie from the jar on the counter. I need to talk to your mother for a while in the other room."

We both nodded our heads, and our grandmother left the kitchen.

When Katie and I finished our sandwiches and milk, we just sat at the table. Both of us were quiet. I think we were both deep in thought. I know I was. I was trying to figure out whether I liked my grandmother and what we were supposed to do now. I've always had to do so much on my own and the fact my grandmother made me a sandwich was very unusual to me. I wasn't totally sure what we could do other than we could have a cookie, and that we should stay in here.

Katie turned to me. "I like her," she said softly. She had a gentle smile. "She's nice."

"Katie, it's really too soon to tell," I stated.

I am older than her, I'm eight, and I've been around more adults than her. So, I know them better than she does. Some of them are not good. She's only five. She hasn't even been to school yet.

"Do you want me to get your cookie?" I asked her. Katie smiled and just nodded her head. I got up from the table and walked over to the counter where the cookie jar is and took the lid off. I reached into the jar and grabbed two chocolate chip cookies. I just turned and handed Katie hers because she followed me.

The muffled voices of the adults in the other room became a little more noticeable while I was at the counter and it piqued my curiosity. I looked over at Katie and put my finger to my lips letting her know we need to be quiet. I quietly walked over and stood by the door so I could hear what the adults were saying better.

"So, the deal is, Donna," I heard my grandmother begin. "You and the girls can stay upstairs for now. But in order for you to be able to stay you have to find a job, and you have to enroll them in school right away. Also, no, more, drinking. This is a fresh start for you and the girls. In the meantime, you can help out around here. I know it's the off season, but there's plenty to do."

I could hear my mother weeping. "Mom, I've stopped drinking. Ask the girls, I haven't had a single drop the whole trip here. I'm never drinking again...I'm done, and I'm going to get a great job...I'll turn my life around. I have to...for me, and the girls."

"Have you heard from him at all? Does he know where you are?" I heard my grandmother ask.

"No, I haven't heard a word from him. No phone calls, not even a letter...*nothing*." My mother sobbed.

"How any man could just walk out on not just his wife, but his children?" I heard my grandfather question. He continued, "He's not a real man, not in my book. He had better never show his face around here."

"Don't worry, Dad, I'll show him and he'll be sorry. I'll make something of myself and make him sorry he ever left me."

"When was the last time you girls had a bath?" my grandmother, or Mémé, asked. It was evening now. Katie and I had spent the whole afternoon playing checkers while the adults brought in our things and decided all kinds of things for us.

I had to stop and think. So much had happened that I was having trouble recalling something as small and unimportant as a bath.

"Well, I guess that answers my question," Mémé said. "Who would like to go first?"

Mémé walked into the bathroom and started the water. My sister and I just stood there quietly just outside the bathroom door. "Veronica? How about you? Why don't you go and get your pajamas," she called from the bathroom.

Surely, she can't be serious? She wanted to give me a bath? What am I, two?

"I usually help Katie," I stated, crossing my arms. "And I don't take baths. I take showers...I'm not a baby." A funny look crossed Mémé's face. "Well, surely you are not a baby. I just thought since this is your first night here you might like some help."

"Well, I don't need any," I stated firmly. "And I can help Katie."

"You've been helping to take care of Katie a lot, haven't you?" she asked. A look of concern was in her eyes.

"Yes, I always do."

"It hasn't been easy, has it?" she questioned.

"It's not that hard. She's my sister, I have to."

Mémé tenderly put her hand on my shoulder. "You don't have to do it all by yourself anymore. I'll give Katie her bath tonight. When she's done, you can take your shower. Now, go and get your PJ's."

I stood there for a moment, letting what she said sink in. I'm not used to adults who behave like she does. I wasn't sure what to think. I wanted to believe her more than anything. I'll let her bathe Katie tonight, but I'm going to be watching her.

After Katie and I were bathed and had our teeth and hair brushed, Katie and I climbed into the big bed we would be sharing for now. My mother and Mémé came in to say goodnight to us. Another thing I am not used to. My sister and I usually just go to bed on our own.

Mémé sat on the edge of our bed. "I know you girls have had a big day. I'm so glad you are both here. I just know you will be happy here." She bent down and kissed Katie's forehead, and Katie smiled.

"Thank you, Mémé," Katie said wrapping her arms around her. Mémé leaned over to me and kissed my forehead. That action set off a wave of emotions through me that I held in very tightly. I didn't want to cry in front of her or my mother. I can wait until they all leave the room. I swallowed back the lump that was rising up into my throat and just smiled at her. Mémé got up from the bed and walked to the door placing her hand over the light switch.

My mother bent down and kissed my cheek and then Katie's. "Goodnight girls...I love you." She smiled at both of us and left the room. Mémé turned off the light.

"Mémé?" I called out.

"Yes, Sweetie?" she said.

"Could you leave the door cracked open and the hall light on for Katie? She gets scared sometimes."

"Sure, sweet dreams girls."

I waited until I heard the footsteps fade completely before letting myself cry. I just wanted to go home. I missed my own bed. The comforting sounds of the busy San Francisco streets that existed just outside my window. The street light that shined through the holes in my shade. It's too dark and quiet here. Most of all, I missed my daddy. I still had a hard time believing that he just left us. I knew him. He loved me, and he loved Katie. He had his share of problems too, but he's always been good to us. I turned to my side and let the tears flow a little harder. I didn't try to control them anymore, but I managed to stay quiet. I didn't need

Mémé or anyone else here trying to make me feel better. I didn't want to. I just wanted to be sad.

"Are you alright?" Katie whispered.

"I'm fine Katie, just go to sleep," I whispered back.

"You sound like you're crying. Do you want me to get Mom?" she asked.

I let out a sharp sigh. "No," I whispered back harshly. "Just go to sleep."

I heard Katie turn over. "Okay, night-night Roni."

"Night-night, Katie," I whispered over my shoulder.

The tears continued and they started to make me feel numb. I never felt so alone. I felt like I was in a crowded room screaming but no one could hear me.

I ended up going over the fight I heard between my parents just a few months ago, the one that ended up bringing us here...

"How could you, Donna?!" I heard my father cry out.

My mother was crying. "I'm so sorry Phil, I never meant for it to happen!"

My sister and I were lying in our beds. My parents were shouting at each other, and we could hear every word they were saying.

"He was my best friend. How could you do this to me?!" My father was shouting. "To our daughters?! To his wife?! She was your friend, too. Didn't any of that matter to the two of you?!"

"It was a mistake Phil... a mistake. I never meant for any of it to happen. I wasn't thinking... I was drunk!" My mother was crying and pleading.

"You were drunk?! What kind of excuse is that?! If this was a one-time event maybe I might have bought that. But this has been ongoing for a while."

I could hear my mother continue to sob loudly. "I'm so sorry!"

"And you didn't even have the guts to tell me! I had to hear about it from someone at work! And they all knew! *MY WIFE* was going around behind *MY BACK*!"

I could hear dishes breaking against the walls below.

"Please, Phil...I'll be better...I'll change!"

"No! No more, Donna. I can't do this anymore. You said things would change after the last time. And you betrayed me *again*, and with my best friend! Nope, the two of you can have each other. There is no hope here. I hope you're both happy together!"

I heard stomping up the stairs, and my bedroom door opened.

"Veronica... Katie?" I heard my father whisper.

"What is it Daddy?" I answered back.

My father approached my bed and knelt beside me.

"Sweetie, are you alright? You couldn't hear Mommy and Daddy, could you?"

"Yes, what's the matter Daddy? What's wrong?"

"I have to leave. Your mother and I can't be together anymore."

"Then take me with you," I said starting to cry.

"Shhh...don't cry, don't cry," he said wiping tears from my cheeks. "I can't take you with me. But I will see you, I promise."

"But I don't want to stay with Mommy. I want to go with you."

"I wish you could come with me, you and your sister both."

"Why can't we go with you?" I cried.

"Roni, you're too young to understand, you need to stay strong. You need to stay with your mother, and you need to take care of your sister. Can you do that for me?"

"Yes," I said between the sobs. My sister just sat there crying, she knew something was wrong, but she didn't understand. My father sat on the bed and wrapped me and my sister in his arms, hugging us tightly. His kissed the top of my head and then my sister's. "Don't worry, we will always stay in touch. The only thing that can ever separate us is time. Don't worry; we will see each other again soon. You and Katie will always be my girls. I'll call you, and we'll write to each other. Take care of each other. I love you both so much."

"We love you too Daddy; please don't go!" I begged.

"I don't want to, I have to." My father got up from my bed and walked out the door not bothering to look back. My sister and I just sat there stunned. Neither one of us could move.

"Phil, if you walk out that door, don't think for one second that I'll ever take you back!" my mother shouted.

"Trust me, that thought will *NEVER* cross my mind! Goodbye Donna...have a nice life!"

CHAPTER 5

I wasn't too surprised the next morning when I woke up, and found I had the bed all to myself.

Traitor.

My sister is so predictable. She always gets up earlier than everyone else, and she always gets suckered in by the adults in our lives. Fine. I sighed. At least I have the bed all to myself. I rolled on to my back and got in the middle of the bed. I spread my arms and legs out pretending that I was making snow angels. It will be her own fault. She'll get close with Mémé and Grandpa and then one of them will do something stupid, which of course will make Katie cry. And who will be left to pick up the pieces...*me*. I shook my head just thinking about it. I pulled the covers up over my head. If I block out the light of day, maybe I can just go back to sleep. I'm not ready to go downstairs yet. Just knowing what is waiting for me downstairs makes me feel ill.

My mother slumped over, clutching her cup of coffee in both hands. My sister happily playing, probably with her favorite doll, and the new part I have to get used to, both of my cheerful grandparents smiling, and hoping I'll be happy here.

I doubt it.

I wasn't always like this. There was a time, and it does seem like it was long ago, that I was just a happy kid. A happy kid who just loved her parents and things were simple, and everything was okay.

Looking back through all the things I remember, I think the bad stuff began shortly after I started first grade.

My dad is a fisherman so he was away a lot. So that left mom at home to take care of me and Katie. When I came home from school one day I saw that Mom's car wasn't in the driveway. It didn't bother me at first because I thought she was running late from shopping, she did that sometimes. When I walked into the house, Katie was screaming and crying. I ran into our bedroom and she was curled up on her bed. Her face was purple and she was wet from all the tears.

"Katie, what's wrong?" I said loudly. "Where's Mom?"

Katie sat up and wrapped her arms around me tightly. "When I woke up, I couldn't find her."

I lifted my head up to look her in the eyes. "She probably just went to the store; I bet she'll be right back," I told her.

Around six o'clock our mother still wasn't back yet, so I made Katie and I peanut butter sandwiches. After we ate, Katie and I curled up with a blanket on the couch to wait for Mom to come home. I ended up staying home from school while Mom was missing to take care of Katie. We survived mostly on peanut butter sandwiches and Sugar Crisps cereal. She didn't come home for three days.

When she finally did come home, she tried to make it up to us by giving Katie and me both a new doll and bringing home donuts. I was so mad I just handed the doll my mother gave me right to Katie. I didn't want it. All I really wanted was to know what happened, but she wouldn't tell me. So, for three days after, I wouldn't speak to her. I got myself up for school, made my own lunch, and went to school on my own. When I would come home, I would just walk right past her, not looking at her or speaking one word to her, and go and check on Katie.

She did this a few times while my father was away. I tried to tell my father this many times but he didn't believe me. "Your mother would never do that," he would say. He said this right on up to the day he left.

I turned over and the scent of cinnamon and sugar overwhelmed my nose. Whatever that is smells so good. But, I don't care what it is, I'm not going down there yet, I thought.

Awe! Now I have to pee! I started kicking my feet in protest. Stupid dumb body, why are you betraying me?! Now, my stomach is starting to grumble. I guess I don't have a choice anymore. I was feeling very annoyed at my dumb body for making me have to get up now. Why can't I just stay here and avoid everyone and everything that is down there?

I got up from bed and danced around a little while I pulled the covers up trying to straighten out the mess I made of the bed. Then I slowly made my way out the bedroom door. I went across the hall to the bathroom first. Of course, I *really* had to go now.

I lingered in the bathroom when I was done. I stood in front of the sink on my tippy toes so I could see myself in the mirror.

My eyes are so boring, they're just plain old brown, and *ewe*, full of crusties this morning.

My hair, which once was blonde, now has even more brown strands in it lately than it used to. So, I guess my hair is turning brown. Good, that means I'll look just a little more like my dad and less like, *her*.

I used to hear people say, "You look just like your mother!" all the time when we were out together. I hated that.

I looked around for a hairbrush. My long curly hair was all snarled from sleep and sticking up on one side. I couldn't find one. I'll have to look in my bag later. I ran my fingers through my hair and I tried to smooth down the one side. I looked in the drawer next to the sink and found the washcloths. Washing my face is a good idea, I thought, as I wet the cloth under the warm water. I washed my cheeks and my forehead, and I wiped away the crust from my eyes. It felt good.

I sighed. I didn't have anything left to do in the bathroom, and if I take too long someone was sure to check on me. I turned and faced the door. I know I have to face them all eventually. I just couldn't make myself open the door just yet. The moment I do, my day, my new life, has officially started. Something I'm not ready for, and to be honest, I don't even want. As I stood there with my hand on the doorknob I went over in my mind some of the argument I had with my mom the day we left...

She stood there on our front lawn. Her arms were crossed, her face red in frustration at me. This was the first time I ever really spoke back to my mother. At the time I was desperate, I felt like I had no other choice. I didn't want to leave my friends, my father, and the only home I've ever known, I had to try.

"You'll make new friends," my mother said to me trying to get me into the car.

I crossed my arms and sat on the front steps of my home, crying loudly. "I don't want to make any new friends! I want to go live with Daddy!"

"We went over this! You can't live with your father, he is away too much! There won't be anyone around to take care of you!"

"I don't care! I can take care of myself!" I could feel how red my face was and I could feel all the eyes in our neighborhood watching us at this point, and I didn't care. I was so furious, I didn't want to go, and there was no way I was going to make this easy for her.

"Don't be ridiculous, Veronica! You're only eight years old! You can't take care of yourself!" My mother tried to settle her voice. "Please!" she begged. "Just get in the car. You're really gonna love living in Moodus. You'll make a lot of new friends; you'll see. You will be so happy there."

"I'll never be happy there! You're the worst mother in the world! *And*, if you make me go, I promise you I won't even try to make any new friends! I'll be mean to everyone there!" I was serious.

"Is that supposed to scare me, Veronica? You don't have a choice; now get your butt in the car or I'm gonna pick you up and throw you in! Your only choice is the easy way or the hard way!" She crossed her arms and looked at me very sternly. "Either way, *you* are going young lady!"

As I sat on the steps, I remember studying my mother's face trying to figure out if there was any hope at all I could possibly win this fight. I remember now, I saw no hope. I stood up and stomped over to the car and opened the door. "You're the worst mother *EVER*! I'm never speaking to you again!" I shouted at her as loud as I could. I got in the car and slammed the door shut.

My mother got into the driver's seat with a smug smile. "*Well*, at least the ride there will be peaceful."

I meant what I said. I'm not speaking to her ever again. I didn't speak a word to her the whole ride here, and I certainly intend on continuing to give her the silent treatment forever. All of this, all the problems we had at home, their divorce, and the move here is all her fault. I don't know if I'll ever be able to forgive her.

My stomach growled. I guess, I'll have to ask Mémé for some breakfast. I know I'm not asking Mom.

I walked out of the bathroom and down the stairs on my tippy toes. I wanted to listen to what was going on before just entering the kitchen. This is a habit I developed growing up. I have found it's always best to know what's going on in a room that adults are in before just walking in. That way, you can avoid a lot of problems you didn't see coming.

I stood outside the kitchen door and I could hear a tea kettle whistling, followed by the sound of footsteps crossing the room and the clicking sound the knob makes when you turn the stove off. I could hear someone tapping their spoon against their cup and then the tinging sound it makes when they place it on the table. I could hear the rustling of a newspaper's page being turned, and the sound of a bowl being filled with cereal.

"Katie?" Mémé called. "Are you sure Veronica likes this kind of cereal?"

"Yes, she eats it all the time," I heard Katie reply.

"I'll wait until she's in here before pouring the milk in. I think this weekend I'll take you both with me to the grocery store, so you can pick out the things you like to eat."

"Okay, Mémé. Can I help you with the turkey?"

I heard an oven door opening. "Nope, it's all set at the moment, but you can help me in a little while when it's time to baste it, alright?" I heard the oven door shut.

"Yay," I heard Katie reply.

"Where is she?" I heard Mémé wonder out loud. I heard footsteps approaching. "I thought I heard your sister get up..." Mémé came out of the kitchen door and gasped. "Oh, Veronica! You scared me! What are you doing standing out here?"

I didn't want to tell her exactly what I was doing so I gave her a half truth. "I was just about to go into the kitchen."

"Oh, well, I poured you a bowl of Sugar Crisps. You do like those, right?"

Actually, they're my favorite, but I kept my answer simple. "Yes," I replied.

"Well then, we're off to a good start today. I didn't pour any milk in yet. The bowl is on the table, along with the milk; you can go ahead and help yourself. I'll be right back."

I walked into the kitchen and looked around the room. My sister was sitting at the table with our grandfather who was reading his newspaper. I couldn't help wondering where *she* was.

"Where's Mom?" I asked.

My grandfather looked up from his paper. "I guess she decided to sleep in today."

I just shook my head as I went to sit down at the table where my cereal was. It's obvious that my grandpa doesn't know my mother at all. I don't really understand why, but, I've noticed right after she stops drinking she sleeps a lot. Sometimes it would be for days. There were a lot of days Katie and I would just take care of ourselves because we couldn't get her up. I'm sure this is something Mémé and Grandpa wouldn't know.

I poured the milk in my bowl, scooped up a heaping spoonful of my favorite sweet cereal, and shoved it in my mouth. The bite was so big, as I was trying to chew I could hardly keep my mouth closed, and some milk was dribbling out. I heard Katie giggle, and since my mouth was so full and I couldn't speak yet, I gave her a light nudge on her shoulder with my elbow. Grandpa peered at us over his paper, smiled, turned the page, and went right back to reading.

After what seemed like forever chewing I finally swallowed, and I started to remember the sweet cinnamon smell from earlier.

"Grandpa," I began shyly.

"What can I help you with?" he asked me, not bothering to look away from the newspaper. "Well," I said continuing carefully. "I smelled cinnamon before, and I was wondering what it was."

Grandpa put down his paper to look at me. "So, you smelled those, *didja*?" he asked, with a playful smirk.

"Yes."

"Your grandmother made cinnamon rolls this morning. Do you like those?"

"Yes."

"So, I guess it's safe to assume then that Katie likes them too?"

"Yes."

"Would you both like to split one then?"

Katie and I looked at each other and then turned to nod our heads at Grandpa. He set down his paper and walked over to the counter next to the stove where a cloth-covered dish sat on top. He put the cloth to the side and put a big roll on a plate and placed it between Katie and I on the table.

"Your grandmother wasn't sure if you would like these," he said, as he went back over to the rolls. He put one on a plate and sat back down at the table. "I told her she was crazy. Of course, you both would like them. She can get a little worked up over things sometimes."

"Who gets worked up?" Mémé asked as she entered the kitchen. "You weren't saying this about *me*, now were you?"

I watched Grandpa quickly place his newspaper over his roll. "Of course not, dear," Grandpa said. He winked at both me and Katie.

That made me laugh. I stopped and put my hand over my mouth catching myself. But then I thought, why did I stop laughing? It doesn't mean I like them or anything.

Mémé stopped at the table in front of Katie and me eyeing the plate in between us. "So, which one of you is eating that cinnamon roll?" Mémé asked. Katie and I just sat there frozen. I don't know about Katie, but I sure didn't know what to say, and that gave me butter-flies in my belly.

"Well?" she said crossing her arms. Both Katie and I slowly lifted a hand up. Suspicion crossed Mémé's face. "Did Grandpa give you that?" she asked us.

My eyes shifted to Grandpa for a moment, and then right back to Mémé's. In that brief moment, I saw him look down at his hidden dish and slowly shake his head side to side. I'm not totally sure but I guess he doesn't want Mémé to know about his roll.

Katie was the one that ended up breaking the si-lence. "Yes, Roni and I are sharing it," she said happily.

Mémé still looked suspicious. "Really?" she said keeping her arms crossed. She looked over at Grandpa as she continued to speak. "That was so nice of Grandpa, to give you one to share like that."

Grandpa cleared his throat. "Veronica was still in the middle of her bowl of cereal, and Katie had already finished a bowl. I thought giving them one each would be too much."

"So clearly, you're just being responsible and caring."

"Yes, of course," he replied.

"So, it has nothing to do with your love of sweets and baked goods?" she asked, still sounding suspicious.

"Nope, just thinking of the girls," he said coolly.

"Well then, why is there only six rolls left?"

Katie, Grandpa, and I looked over to where the dish was. The dish with the rolls was left uncovered. Grandpa sighed, and lifted his newspaper. Mémé grabbed the plate and set it down in front of me. "There, you don't have to split a roll. Frank, you know you can't have those. You know what the doctor said. Those are for Donna and the girls."

"I know what the doctor said, but I didn't think one small little cinnamon roll was gonna hurt."

"Frank, you always get too excited. It's never just one with you. You have to lose a few pounds. Now, finish your grapefruit."

I watched Grandpa slouch back in his chair in defeat. I took a bite of the roll Mémé gave me, and I actually felt a little bad about eating it. Would one cinnamon roll really have hurt him? Who knows? What I do know though, is that this cinnamon roll is delicious. I think if I was Grandpa, I would have taken the risk eating these too.

"So, are you girls looking forward to starting school here?" Mémé asked changing the subject.

"I can't wait," said Katie. "I hope I make a lot of friends."

Mémé smiled. "That's so good Katie, I hope you do too. In fact, I know you both will," she said. She turned to face me. "What about you Veronica, are you looking forward to starting school here?"

I took another bite of my cinnamon roll and as I chewed I was deciding on what answer to give her. I could just lie and say that I am looking forward to it. But then I thought, why lie? Why start off that way? I said I was going to be mean to everyone here, not lie to them.

I swallowed and looked up at Mémé. "No, not really," I stated.

Mémé looked a little sad. "Oh, I'm so sorry you feel that way. Maybe over time your feelings will change."

I crossed my arms. "Nope, never."

I could hear the sound of my mother's feet dragging down the hall into the kitchen. My suspicions were confirmed when she entered saying, "Don't waste your time, Mom," as she ran her fingers through her snarled hair and looked up at me with her grumpy before coffee face and forced a smile. "She's determined to be miserable here."

I got up from my chair and walked over and put my plate in the sink. Not wanting to talk to my mother directly, I looked up at Mémé. "I'm not determined," I stated firmly. "I just know that I'll never be happy here."

My mother didn't say anything in response. She just took her coffee and sat down at the table. What could she say, really? She knew she messed up. All of this is her fault. She knew she was the one who made the mistake that made us move here. She knew how angry I was at her, and how much I blame her.

If only she could have just been like all those other kids' moms like I've seen at school and on TV. The kind of mom that likes to make their kids' lunches, and kisses boo-boos. The kind who will stay with you when you're sick, and be there in the mornings when you wake up. The kind of mom you can count on. I really wish she was like that. Maybe she'll be different living here, I thought. Maybe she'll change? I really hope so.

It was Mémé who ended up responding. "You know you could be happy here if you tried, if you really wanted to be."

"Nope," I said simply.

"Well...I guess that's it then," she replied with a light shrug of her shoulders. "It's really too bad you'll never be happy here. There are so many great things about living here. I won't try to force you to see them."

I just stood there at first. I wasn't sure how to re-spond. It almost didn't make any sense what she was saying. Really, she's not gonna try to make me like it here? My mother wouldn't shut up about it for week's right up to the day we left. All I could think to say was, "Thank you."

"You're welcome. Now, why don't you go and get yourself dressed for the day; it is a holiday," Mémé said.

This took me by surprise. "It is?"

"Yes Veronica, it's Thanksgiving. Now please, go and get dressed."

All of our toys and games are still packed away so there wasn't much for us to do. Mémé had suggested we try going outside to play for a while. Katie and I did try, but found it to be just too cold outside here to play. Katie and I ended up sitting at the kitchen table playing checkers again for most of the day, while Mémé buzzed about making our Thanksgiving feast.

Mémé was smiling and humming joyfully to herself. She moved through the kitchen like a ballet dancer moves across the stage, and I found it strange that I felt very soothed by what she was doing.

My mother burns pretty much everything, and makes such a big mess when she tries to cook. The only thing she ever really made for us was sandwiches. My father was the cook in our house. He was the one that always cooked the turkey on Thanksgiving. So maybe that's why I'm feeling very comforted by Mémé cooking happily in the kitchen. Maybe it reminds me of my father? Well whatever the case may be, at least I know the food will be good later.

Shortly after breakfast, my mother went back to bed. So, I have to say, my day so far has been good. Sure, I'm not in San Francisco, but not having to deal with my mother much today has been nice. The more time I spend with Mémé and Grandpa the more I'm finding that I'm actually warming up to them. I'm still not completely sure if I like them yet, but so far, they are alright.

I wonder if Katie and I could just live here, and then *she* could live somewhere else.

When Mémé was finished, she called everyone to the table. When I sat down at the table, I made sure that someone was sitting on both sides of me to avoid sitting next to my mother.

Everyone but my mother was sitting at the table. Mémé said we had to wait for Mom before we can start eating. All I could think about was how dumb that was, and that we would probably be waiting all night. Mémé tried many times to wake her and get her to come to the table, but she wouldn't budge.

After a half hour of waiting, Mémé finally gave up. "Well that's it!" She threw her hands in the air on her way to the table. "Go ahead and dig in, I guess, she's not coming!"

I looked up at Mémé. "I could have told you that," I said softly.

Mémé sat down. "Is she always like that?" she asked.

"She's only like that when she stops drinking," I told her.

Mémé sat there looking stunned. She didn't speak right away. "When she stops drinking?" she questioned in reply.

"Yes."

"Has she stopped drinking before?"

"Yes."

"Does she stop drinking a lot?"

"Yes."

Mémé sat there with a look on her face like she was deep in thought. She wiped a tear from her cheek with the back of her hand. "Well let's not waste any more time today on things we cannot control." She took in a deep breath and shook her head a little, forcing a smile. "Today is Thanksgiving and I see two reasons here to be thankful for." She held out her hand for my plate. "White or dark meat, Veronica?"

"It doesn't matter, I like both," I said smiling back at her. It was at that moment that I knew my grandmother, my Mémé, was good, and how things might be different from now on.

CHAPTER 6

Not only did my mother miss Thanksgiving, she ended up sleeping most of the weekend too, and since Mémé wasn't sure how long she was going to be like this, she took it upon herself Monday morning to sign up Katie and me for school.

Great.

So now Katie and I are enrolled at the elementary school, and we start on Wednesday. I can't say I'm happy about that.

It was early Tuesday morning when Mom decided to finally get up for good. I thought I was the first one up, but she was sitting at the kitchen table drinking a cup of coffee when I walked in. I froze at first; I had been happily avoiding her for days. What do I do now?

My mother looked up from her coffee and gazed at me with apologies in her eyes. "Good morning, Veronica," she started softly. "Why don't you sit down and I'll get you your cereal this morning."

I slowly walked over and sat down at the table not saying anything. Honestly, I didn't really know what to say to her. The fight we had before we left was the biggest fight we ever had.

She put a bowl and spoon on the table in front of me and started filling it with my Sugar Crisps and milk. "Sweetie," she started as she sat down. "I was hoping you would get up first today. I wanted a chance to speak to you alone." I took a bite of my cereal, and looked up at her allowing her to continue. "I want to apologize to you, Veronica. Between the time in the car on the way here, and the time I spent in bed, I've had a lot of time to think about the way I have been, and I'm ashamed of myself. I have not behaved the way a good mom should have. I was being very selfish, and I'm so sorry. I realize that maybe if I had behaved differently that we would probably still be in San Francisco, and you have every right to be mad at me for it …it's all my fault. I can't change what I did in the past, but I hope over time you can forgive me."

I took another bite of my cereal and while I chewed I thought about what my mother was saying.

"Things will be better now," she said. "You'll see. I'm going job hunting starting today. I'm going to get a great job, and we're gonna get our own little place, you, me, and your sister. I'll take you girls to school and I'll join up in one of those PTA things. It will be so great here." She leaned down so she could look me straight in the eyes. "Veronica, I'm never drinking again, I promise." I started to cry and I threw my arms around her neck.

There were two different emotions that were going through me at that moment. The first was relief. The only thing I really want in the whole world is for my mother to be happy with us.

The other feeling I have is doubt. I feel so guilty for even thinking it. But there is a part of me that doesn't fully believe what she is saying. She has said things like this before. But she's never really admitted she had done anything wrong before, so there was a small difference here.

My mother pulled back so she could wipe my tears with her hand and she kissed my cheek. "Things will be different here. It will be a fresh start for us. This is a good place to start over, and do things right." Her eyes welled up with tears. She wiped under her eyes with her hands and took a deep breath. "What do you think about me taking you and Katie out shopping today for an outfit for school?" she asked.

I forced myself to smile. "That sounds like fun, Mom."

"Well then, we can all go after breakfast. I'm gonna go wake Katie." My mother was smiling and she pranced on her tippy toes out of the kitchen.

I just sat at the table and continued to finish my cereal. I held my smile until she was out of the room.

I groaned, *shopping*. I hate shopping. Especially shopping for clothes. My mother is fully aware of how I feel about it. I've kicked up a fit about this on more than one occasion. Did she think I was kidding? Or that maybe, over the course of the move here, this feeling may have changed. *Hmmm*...let me think... Nope, still hate it.

I just couldn't give her grief over something as small as my dislike of shopping when I know she's dealing with something much harder; I know she's trying.

When I was finished, I just sat there in the chair. A part of me was afraid to move or even breathe. If I were to get up right now I might do something to mess up this potentially good morning. It kind of reminded me of walking on glass. I felt like I'd have to walk very carefully, on my tippy toes to avoid making any cracks, or break it entirely. At any moment I could step wrong in this fragile place and the whole thing would just shatter, and who knows how long this might last.

Everyone ended up going shopping. Mom, Katie, Mémé, Grandpa, and me all crammed into our little Chevy. This will be a long day, and I now know this shopping trip is guaranteed to be torture.

In the past when my mother would finally wake up after quitting drinking she would become very energetic. She would end up making big plans, like taking Katie and me to the zoo or to the beach. Or she would go out and buy paint and paint the living room or the kitchen. She would end up going all day long —cleaning, painting, shopping, whatever activity she could think up. I don't know where she gets all this energy from. Maybe it's from all that sleep she gets from being in bed for so long? I don't know, but she can be so hard to keep up with!

She ran around the department store gushing over clothes and shoes with Katie running right alongside her. Katie shares her excitement about clothes and shopping. I normally end up being dragged around the store because I just want to get in, get what I need, or want, and just get out.

Like I've said before, I don't enjoy shopping. And since I didn't want to upset my mother, I thought I would just try to make things easy on her today by keeping my mouth shut. I won't complain, I swore to myself. I'll just keep pace with Mémé and Grandpa who were just browsing, and try to behave myself.

A small part of me wishes I could enjoy it the way they do, but I just can't.

It's just so much work! All the walking around, then having to try everything on to make sure it all fits, and you have to lug it all to the car, then into the house, blah, blah, blah! Too much hassle if you ask me. There are much better ways for me to spend my time.

My mother grabbed a couple of dresses for Katie and me to try on, (of course they are matching, gag!) and headed straight for the dressing rooms. She pointed me towards a stall and gave me my dresses to try on. Then she went into the next stall with Katie to help her try on hers. The dresses my mother gave me were both jumpers. One was a dark red with crisscross black and white stripes that met in the center. And the other was bright green with large white daisies on it.

I sighed; my mother and I have very different taste in clothes normally. She's one of those moms who likes the frills. She likes wearing skirts and dresses, and she likes to dress us like her.

I'm not one of those girls that likes to wear dresses and skirts. I find them very uncomfortable actually.

I've always been the type of kid who likes to play outside. I ride my bike. I play kick ball and tag. Sometimes, I even play baseball. These kinds of things are not easy to do in a dress or skirt.

When you wear dresses and skirts you have to worry about keeping clean. Which, I don't really want to care about when I'm playing. Sometimes, you have to worry about keeping it out of the wheels of your bike, or having it fly up when you ride fast. Then how do you slide home and keep the sand out of your butt? Sandboxes are no fun in a dress either. I remember in kindergarten playing in the sandbox in a dress, then the mess I had up my rear after. I had sand in my butt until I got home.

Also, it's November, almost December, and it is very cold outside. More so than I'm used to. There is just no way I'm wearing something that is wide open on one end and lets in big drafts! I like to be comfortable, I'm not crazy!

To make this easy on myself, I'm going to have to agree to one of these. The red one really isn't me at all, and the stripes on it are a little too weird. The green one is weird too, but it is a bright green which I like, and at lease the daisies have yellow centers. Yellow is my favorite color. I could probably wear my black Mary-Janes with this, and living here I'll definitely need some tights or something under this so I don't get cold.

I put on the green jumper over my shirt and it fit well. I leaned out the door. "Mom, I like this one."

Mémé heard me and wandered over to see. "Oh, Veronica! Don't you look beautiful," she gushed.

I smiled at her, but inside I winced, because I'm pretty sure everyone in the whole store heard her.

I felt like my face was redder than that other dress. "Thank you, Mémé."

My mother stuck her head out of the stall to check on me. "Oh, you like that one?" She paused as she walked out of the stall pulling it shut. "Well, Katie likes the red one." She stiffened up a little and she pressed her lips into a line. I knew by her expression and her tone that she would rather I get the red one.

I know I already accepted the fact I was going to end up with something I didn't like just to make her day easier, but I still felt a little disappointed.

I should be used to this though. It's always Katie who gets to choose.

If wearing that dumb red dress makes her happy, and it helps her in some small way, then I guess I have no choice. What kind of daughter would I be if I kicked up a tantrum now? What if I did and she changed her mind and decided to start drinking again? Then it would be all my fault and Katie would end up hating me forever. I couldn't do that.

I walked back into the stall and changed back into my clothes, and I put the green dress back on the hanger. I didn't bother trying on the red dress in hopes that tomorrow a small miracle would occur and it suddenly wouldn't fit, so I could just wear what I really wanted, which is my red and white striped cotton pullover, and my red pants. They are the most comfortable clothes I have, so of course they're my favorite.

I sighed on the inside as I hung the green dress back on the rack where it belonged. When I turned around I was surprised to find Mémé standing right behind me.

She stood there gazing at me with her arms crossed, and her brows were creased. "Did you pick out what you wanted?" she asked.

I looked at the new red dress I held in my hands. "Yes, I did," I replied.

She bent down so she was at eye level with me and looked me right in the eyes, which made me a little uncomfortable. "Really?" She sounded suspicious. "Because I could have sworn you liked the green one."

"I did."

"Then why are you getting the red one?"

I shrugged my shoulders. "I like the red one."

"That's not what you said when you came out of the dressing room before," she argued.

I started getting annoyed with her. "Well, I changed my mind," I huffed at her. "I'm gonna go find Mom and Katie."

I started to walk away from her and she put her hand on my shoulder stopping me. "Veronica, I was watching. I saw what happened. You can't honestly tell me you just changed your mind."

I shrugged her hand off. "Well, I did." I turned and walked away looking for Mom and Katie over by the dressing rooms. As I walked, I fumed. Who does this lady think she is? Does she think she knows me? Knows everything about me, Mom, and Katie? So what I wanted the green dress. Who cares, really? I didn't really want a dress anyway, and I'll probably only have to wear this maybe one time—never if I get my miracle. It doesn't even matter what I want right now anyway. I really didn't want a dress at all, or to go shopping for that matter. Nope, all that really matters today is that Mom's day was nice, and it was easy for her. Too bad Mémé doesn't know this. How helpful I am being to my mother. I really am on my best behavior.

Later, at the restaurant, the subject of the dumb dresses got brought up again.

We were halfway through dinner when Mémé started. "Donna," she began very calmly. "I was wondering about a little something I noticed when we were at the dress shop earlier."

My mother looked up from her plate. "And what is that?" she asked.

"Well it seemed to me Veronica really liked that green dress with the flowers on it."

I sat there at the table frozen in shock, watching Mémé's face, and then my mother's.

"For some strange reason after saying out loud that she liked the green dress, she decided to get the same one that Katie was getting." Mémé was looking my mother straight in the eyes and continued. "It seemed clear to me that she didn't really like the red dress. She liked the green one. She was allowed to get the dress she wanted, right?"

It was the weirdest thing to hear my mother stutter just a little before she answered her. "O-o-of course she was allowed to," she paused. "The girls just like to wear matching clothes."

"Oh, so the girls still like to wear matching clothes?" Mémé looked at Katie first, who appeared to be not really paying attention to anything except for her cheeseburger, and then she stopped to watch my face. I'm not sure what she saw there, horror probably. She only made one last comment before dropping the subject. "Oh, that's cute. You're lucky that Veronica still likes that sort of thing. You would have kicked up quite the fuss when you were her age. Veronica's a very good girl."

"Yes, I know," my mother replied.

The next morning my mother came in with Katie and they both woke me up for school. "Veronica, time to get up, it's your first day of school," my mother said abruptly turning on the light. Katie jumped up and down on the bed with excitement. "Veronica, come on! Get up! Get up! I get to go to school with you!"

I pulled the sheets up over my head and rolled over. "Ugh, I know! Just give me five more minutes Mom, please. I'm tired."

"No Veronica, I can't let you. You need time to get ready and eat your breakfast."

"Please Mom, just five more minutes," I begged.

"No Veronica! It is time to get up!" she yelled.

"Fine!" I snapped. "I'm up! Are you, *happy*?!" I shouted.

"Yes, see you downstairs." I glared at her until she left the room. Katie followed quietly after her.

I hate getting up early, and I especially hate getting up while it's still dark outside, and my mother knows it. Why she's got to wake me up the way she does really annoys me. Dad always let me have five extra minutes when he was home. And he never just turned on the light like that. He was always gentle about how he got me up for school. Maybe he figured out that I'm not a morning person. It sure would be nice if Mom would.

My new clothes were laid out on the hope chest that was at the foot of the bed along with my Mary-Janes.

I sighed. Today was going to be a long day. I don't know anyone at this school. What if everyone does hate me? What if I do end up with no friends here?

As I put my clothes on (no miracles today) I considered what that might be like, having no friends. I thought it could be kind of lonely depending on how you looked at it. I never really feel lonely though, even when I am alone. It could be nice, no one to argue with except myself. No one to worry about either. I would only have to worry about myself. After a while I bet it would get old though.

I went downstairs to have my breakfast. I cringed a little when I entered the kitchen. I don't know why but for some reason seeing everyone sitting around the kitchen annoyed me this morning. I began thinking about being alone again, and how nice it would be. At least mornings would be pleasant.

Katie was the one to interrupt my daydream. "Mom's driving us to school today Roni!" she exclaimed.

"So!" I snapped at her. I wasn't really trying to be mean to her, it just came out that way.

Mémé put her hands on top of Katie's shoulders and quickly started turning her around. "Katie, why don't you wait to tell Veronica anything else this morning until after she's had her breakfast," she suggested.

Smart lady, I thought.

Mom drove us to school like Katie said she would. She even went as far as walking us into the building! I have to admit, I was a bit surprised to see her do that. The last time I saw her do that was my first day of kindergarten. It must just be because it's Katie's first day of kindergarten.

Because of Mom's behavior in California, Katie was never enrolled in school when she was supposed to, so she's starting a little late. I wonder if Katie will end up having to stay back.

Mom walked us into the main office.

The office reminded me a little of my old school's office. The walls were a dull gray color. It looks like it might be some kind of paneling. It has two desks in the far corner where the office ladies (as I like to call them) sat and answered the phones.

One thing that was different from my old school was the wall of colorful drawings and paintings done by students to the right of the long, bright orange desk that divided the room. My mother sat us both down on the bench that was against the wall and went to talk to the woman who was standing at the long desk.

She was an older woman. Probably the same age as Mémé. Her hair was short and curly and she wore glasses that made her look like she had cat eyes.

She smiled at Katie and me, and looked up at my mother. "Hello, how can I help you?" she asked.

"My daughters are starting school here today," my mother replied.

"Oh, these must be the Edwards girls!" she exclaimed. She seemed a little too excited. They must not get new students very often, I thought to myself.

"I'm Mrs. Gibson. I've been expecting you." She smiled as she grabbed two folders from one of the desks in the corner and pulled a paper from each one.

The office lady turned to me. "You must be Veronica. You have Mrs. Coleman, and your room number is 305. I'll walk you down. She's an excellent third-grade teacher, you're gonna love her."

She then looked at Katie. "And you must be Katherine. Your teacher is Mrs. Warren. Your mother can walk you down to your class." She looked up at my mother. "It's room 202, which is straight down the hall on the left."

My mother patted my shoulder. "I hope you have a good first day. You'll take the bus home this afternoon."

Mrs. Gibson handed my mother a paper. "Please give this to Katherine's teacher." Mrs. Gibson turned to me. "Are you ready to walk down and meet your new class?"

I watched my mother and Katie walk down the hall and disappear into a classroom. Suddenly, my throat felt like it was dry and sticky.

I tried swallowing to clear it, "Okay," was all I could get out. I hope we pass a water fountain on the way to the classroom. I don't know what's wrong with me. I didn't think I was really this scared. Maybe because it wasn't really real before now.

I slowly followed Mrs. Gibson down the hall. It took everything I had to keep putting one foot in front of the other. My heart pounded loudly the closer we got to the classroom. I felt like I was about to get a shot at the doctor's office.

We stopped at room 305, and Mrs. Gibson opened the door. I held my breath as I walked in.

The very first thing I noticed was there were only twelve kids, so I would make thirteen. Whoa, I thought. There were nineteen kids in my class back home. At least it will be easy to remember all the kids' names. The desks were all set up in neat and tidy rows. The room had a strong scent of construction paper and paste. Just like my old classroom did.

The teacher got up from her desk and walked over to greet me and Mrs. Gibson. Her high heel shoes made her footsteps loud and it echoed as she crossed the room. She was young and slender. Her hair was blonde, shoulder length, teased at the top, and curled up at the ends, probably with a lot of hairspray.

"Mrs. Coleman, this is Veronica Edwards. Today is her first day."

Mrs. Coleman smiled. "Hi Veronica, welcome!" She pointed to an empty desk near the back. "Why don't you put your things in the closet over by the window, your spot is marked with your name, then you can sit in the empty desk next to Mary."

I could feel all the eyes watching me as I hung up my coat and put my lunch pail in the bin under my hook. I turned and went to sit down in the only empty desk I saw. I assumed the girl with the long red braids and freckles I sat next to must be Mary.

About ten seconds after I sat down the teacher called on me to introduce myself.

"Veronica, why don't you tell us a little about yourself?"

"You already know my name," I stated.

She chuckled. "Yes, that's true. Then why don't you tell us where you're from?"

"I'm from San Francisco."

"*Ahhh*...California!" she exclaimed, happily. "So exciting, and why did your family move here?"

"Because, my parents got divorced."

Those words rang out across my new class like a loud bell. The shock I witnessed on my new classmates' faces confirmed it. It was the first time I had actually said this out loud to anyone and I regretted saying the words shortly after I said them, especially to a room full of strangers. Not because I felt bad for my mother. It was because I was still sad about it. I guess it's a good thing it's such a small class.

After that, the day went along like any other school day. Mrs. Coleman took attendance and the hot lunch count. Then we all said the pledge of allegiance.

I found that most of the things they're just starting to learn about in this class, I already learned about back home. It feels good to have a head start. I hope that means I might get better grades here.

When the teacher told us that it was time to go to lunch I was ready for it, I was so hungry.

I wasn't completely sure what to do so I just watched what the other kids were doing and I did the same.

I was in a hurry trying to keep up with the rest of the kids (I was afraid I was gonna get lost) and it all happened so fast. I grabbed my pail from the bin, swung myself around, and slammed right into someone and we both landed on the floor.

When I landed on the floor I had the wind knocked out of me and felt a sharp pain in my tailbone. "Owe!" I yelled.

I looked up and saw a chubby boy with dark jet-black hair sitting on the floor across from me. "I'm so sorry, I didn't see you," I said to him.

"Awe, that's okay," he said smiling. His cheeks were red with embarrassment. "I shouldn't have been standing so close behind you."

I'm not normally clumsy, but this odd feeling came over me that told me I should be careful when getting up⊠like the boy has something to do with it.

The boy got to his feet before I did, and held out his hand to help me up. "I'm Jackson Wright. My family calls me Seth. Well, mostly my mom does. Most of the kids here call me Jackson."

I hesitated for a moment before I took Jackson's hand. I wondered briefly if taking it might result in more injuries. But I ended up taking it anyway and let him help me.

"I'm really sorry by the way. I didn't mean to do that," I said.

"It's okay, really. It was an accident," he said with a grin.

It took me a few minutes before I knew what to say, because I was suddenly confused. Did he want me to call him Jackson or Seth?

"It is nice to meet you," I started. "I am confused though. Did you want me to call you Jackson or Seth?" I said shaking his hand.

"Oh, it doesn't matter. Either one is fine," he said. His green eyes creased when he smiled because of his chubby cheeks.

I giggled. "Okay then, how about I call you Jeth, then. See, Jackson and Seth put together."

"I like that." He chuckled.

I raised an eyebrow. "Or, I can call you *Sackson*?" I suggested. I think, I like that one better.

Jackson laughed. "Do you know how to get to the cafeteria?" He asked.

"No."

"Do you have anyone to sit with at lunch yet?" He asked.

"No, I don't."

"Do you want to sit with me?" His green eyes lit up, and his voice shot up just a little at the end of his question. "I have cookies. I'll share them with you."

I can tell he's the kind of kid who gets excited easy. He seemed nice enough, "Sure that sounds nice." I said. Why not, I added in thought.

Jackson walked me to the cafeteria. He chattered on the whole way about how great it was to go to school here, and how nice everyone is. How he and his family had moved around a lot, and how he moved here about a year ago with his mother and father. So he understood what it's like being the new kid.

Jackson led the way to the table where our class sits. When Jackson and I sat down, the girl on the other side of him made a face and then moved herself and her lunch to the other side of the table.

I was a little stunned to see someone do that, and was wondering why. I looked over at Jackson. I thought he'd be upset by that. But he was too busy taking his lunch out of his pail. I don't think he even noticed. I did notice and it angered me. Jackson was nice enough to not only introduce himself, but he helped me find my way to the cafeteria. I don't know who that girl is, but I'm giving her the evil eye for the rest of the day.

When lunch was over I was shocked to learn we had to go outside for recess.

"So, you guys actually play outside in the cold?" I really wasn't expecting it, and I had left my coat in the closet inside the classroom.

He chuckled. "Every day, unless it's raining," Jackson replied.

He thought I was being funny, but I was serious. What kind of people would send young kids outside in the cold? I was standing in the doorway. I wasn't exactly sure what I was going to do but there was no way I was going out there.

A teacher on lunch duty was watching me and Jackson and came to see what the problem was. "Is there something wrong?" she asked.

Jackson was the one to answer first. "Well, Mrs. Walker, Veronica is from California, so the cold weather bothers her. She's not used to it yet."

I was surprised how quick little Jackson here understood why I might not want to go out there.

"Oh, I see." The teacher looked at me. "Well, all the kids have to play outside for recess here every day, weather permitting, no exceptions." She spoke like she was reading. "Where's your coat?" she asked me.

"It's in the classroom closet," I answered shyly.

"Why did you leave it in there?" Mrs. Walker asked making a face.

"Because I thought it was too cold to play outside. I didn't think we would have to."

"Well, it will do you no good in there. Why don't you go down and get it. It will be much easier to play out there if you have a coat."

I hung my head down. This lady was mean. Why on Earth would she make me go out there, knowing the cold bothered me?

Jackson looked at me and then turned to the teacher. "Mrs. Walker?"

"What is it Jackson?"

"I thought maybe since Veronica's new, I should walk her down to the classroom so she could find her way easier. I'll make sure she gets outside."

"Alright, but don't take too long."

Jackson and I started back down the hall to the classroom. When we turned the corner, Jackson started to snicker.

"What's so funny?" I asked him.

"If we take our time getting your coat, we should just miss recess."

"Thank you," I said sighing relief. "I really didn't want to go out there."

"It's my pleasure. Honestly, I really didn't want to go out there either, I'm still not quite used to the cold yet myself."

"Not used to it?" I questioned. "Why aren't you used to it?"

"My family lived in Florida before we came here. It's where I was born."

"Why did your family decide to move here?" I asked him.

"We were always moving around a lot when we lived in Florida. I hated it. As soon as I would make new friends we would all of a sudden have to move. When

I would ask why my mom would just say it was because of money. I guess we don't really have a lot. Anyway, my mom is from here. We were living with my grandpa, until he moved upstate. Now we live in a new house, and we've been here for a whole year! I hope we never have to move again."

"Whoa, I was whining about just this one move, you had to do it over and over?"

"Yep, I think I counted twelve times."

"Twelve! Wow, well it sounds to me like you're done if you've been here for a year."

"I hope so," he said letting out a sigh.

We reached the classroom and I retrieved my coat from the closet. I pulled my arms through the sleeves and thought briefly about how the coat made me feel so weighed down and trapped, I can barely move. It's one of those long coats that hung down past my knees, with the big buttons that go all the way down and has a strap in the middle so you can tie it shut. I wonder if I'll ever get used to the cold or wearing coats.

I turned and saw Jackson waiting for me by the door. As I walked over I thought it was a little odd how comfortable I felt around him already. I've only known Jackson for about an hour now, but it felt like I've known him a long time. I felt so comfortable that I decided to ask him about the girl at lunch on our walk back from the classroom.

"Hey, Sackson?" He chuckled when I called him by the nickname I made for him.

"What?" he said smiling.

"I was wondering about that girl at the lunch table."

He seemed a little confused at first, and then he became kinda quiet. "What girl?" he asked softly.

"There was a girl already sitting at the table when we went to sit. As soon as we sat down she moved to the other side of the table."

He made a face. "Oh, her. What about her?" He seemed to be hesitating a little.

"I didn't think you noticed her. She picked up her stuff and moved when you sat down."

"So," he shrugged.

"So, weren't you offended by that?" I watched for his reaction.

"Does it really matter?" He shrugged again.

"Um, yeah it matters." I could feel myself starting to get upset. "What she did was rude. Who is she?"

"That's Claudette Stanwood, she's never nice. What she did at lunch today actually wasn't that bad."

"What do you mean, not that bad?" If this was not that bad, I hate to think what she's like to him normally.

When we got to the door to go out to the playground the bell rang, meaning recess was over and it was time to go in. Thank God! I wonder if I could do something like this every day. I was so happy, Jackson and I had walked slow enough that we did miss recess.

Since Jackson and I never made it outside, we ended up being the first ones back to the classroom. I whistled to myself as I happily hung my coat back up, and went to sit down at my desk. Which I now know is right behind Jackson's desk.

While I waited for class to start, I watched the other kids as they started to come in. I started zoning out a little, and began to examine each face carefully as they came in through the door, looking for similarities to the kids in my class back in San Francisco.

Most of the kids in my class are very different looking. Except, one boy here kinda reminds me of a boy named David back home. They both have the same shape around the eyes. His eyes are set wide apart making the space between his eyes seem pretty big, which does make him look very similar. It makes me wonder if they are related. Their hair was cut similar too. They both have that buzz cut. I remember, David has red hair and this boy has dirty blonde hair.

I noticed that Jackson's haircut is different from the rest of the kids. It looks like it was cut around his face and his ears, and it's cut so straight across the back of his neck. He looks like he must have just gotten a haircut not too long ago. I bet his mom cuts it.

I continued to stare off into space, wondering about the kids in my class back home. I was thinking about how they were probably starting gym right now when my thoughts were suddenly interrupted...

"What are you looking at?" I heard a girl ask. The voice was coming from a girl with long dark brown hair that was pulled up into a tight ponytail with feathery bangs. I was surprised. I didn't see her sitting there before since she was now sitting at the desk diagonal from mine, which was blocking my view of the door. I didn't even see her sit down.

I noticed it was that rude girl Claudette from lunch.

"I *said*...what are you looking at?!" she spoke again, this time with a snotty tone. She was staring me down now. I hadn't answered her at first because I didn't realize she was talking to me.

Now, she was sitting up tall in her seat. Her whole body turned and was facing my direction. She was sitting like a princess on her throne, staring me down with her wide blue eyes.

"Um, what?" I said sounding confused.

"Why are you staring at me?" she asked. This question confused me even more. I wasn't looking at her at all. What's wrong with her? All I could think to say to her was, "I wasn't staring." I replied sounding very confused.

"Yes, you were!" she snapped suddenly. "I saw you. You were staring right at me!"

I shook my head trying to clear it a little. She just wasn't making any sense.

"I was looking at the door," I stated firmly.

"No, I saw you! You were staring right at me!" Her tone was very bossy, and then she looked over my shoulder. "She was staring at me. Patricia? Karen? Did you see that? She was staring." I turned to look to see two blonde girls smiling and nodding their heads. I didn't know which one Karen or Patricia was, but only one of them spoke. "I saw her...she was staring."

"Do you have a staring problem?" Claudette asked.

"No," I said glowering at her in confusion. I was frustrated by this whole conversation.

A sly smile slowly crossed her face. "Then why are you doing it now?" she asked.

I slumped back in my chair, feeling a little stunned. I couldn't take anymore conversation with this girl. Are all the girls in Moodus this ridiculous?

"And what are you looking at, *freak?!*" she suddenly barked. I looked up to see if she was still talking to me and became very upset because she was staring down poor Jackson who was stuck sitting next to her.

"And what have I told you?!" she snapped at him. "Maybe I didn't make myself clear enough. You are a freak, and freaks like you are not allowed to look at me."

Jackson turned and slumped over his desk looking down. I couldn't see his face but it looked like he was wiping away tears.

Claudette's words towards me were stupid, and childish, they didn't upset me much. I was really kind of amused at first. I've never met anyone like her before. But when I heard her call Jackson a freak, I started shaking.

My breath became short, and my heart thumped against my rib cage twice before I could speak.

"Hey!" I managed to get out between the breaths, "don't you call him a freak!" I struggled to get control of my breathing. I wasn't really scared of this girl, why was my body reacting this way?

She took her eyes off Jackson and turned to look at me. "I can do whatever I want," she stated sounding superior. She was looking me straight in the eyes now. "I'm not listening to a loser like you who has divorced parents, and a staring problem."

I was really mad. I had thoughts of jumping out of my seat and pulling every perfect hair from that ponytail. I wanted to slap her across her stupid face so much, and I think I would have. But, the teacher walked in just after she spoke, forcing this crazy conversation to end, and Princess Claudette quietly turned to face the blackboard.

CHAPTER 7

THE walk home from the bus stop was horrible! I was so right about wearing dresses in the cold weather. I was shivering and my teeth chattered the whole way. I seriously thought my butt was gonna freeze and fall off. Thank God, I don't have as far a walk as I did when we lived in San Francisco.

I'm never wearing a dress in the cold again!

The walk home made me really notice my grandparents' house for the first time. The house stands so tall. It's much bigger than my old house. It's white and has a big front porch with chairs to sit in, and a small roof that overhangs it. Along the edge of the porch's roof and the main big one are fancy carvings that remind me of lace, and every window in the front of the house has black shutters. Even the bushes in the front are fancy and perfect looking.

I also noticed a lot of small houses in the back that resemble the big house with its black shutters and fancy lace trim. There is a playground on the side with swings, a jungle gym, a big slide, and two seesaws. In the front of the house right next to the slick, black mailbox is a small sign that said: Sunset Hills Resort.

When I walked in the front door, I was greeted by sweet music. Grandpa was in the living room playing the piano with Katie sitting on the bench watching by his side. The song was soft and almost delicate somehow. I quietly shut the door behind me and just stood there listening. As I stood there, I felt an overwhelming urge to just close my eyes. The song was soothing, and familiar. I had such a bad day and it actually made me feel better. I listened quietly with my eyes closed allowing the song to relax me and soothe away all my frustrations from my day at school.

It took me a moment before I realized the song had ended.

"Oh Veronica, you're home," Grandpa said. "How was school?" he asked.

I kept my answer simple. "Fine."

I really didn't feel like talking about my day yet. I really just wanted to forget about it for a while. I was still thinking about those weird girls. I'm not sure I can explain it right.

"Grandpa, what song is that?" I asked.

Grandpa smiled. "'Que Sera, Sera.' Did you like it?"

"Yes, it was pretty."

"Thank you." Grandpa smiled, and then changed the subject. "Do you have any homework?" His tone was warm and light.

I sighed. "Yes."

"Well, you can sit at the coffee table to work on it," he suggested.

"Okay." I knelt at the coffee table and started to spread out my things so I could do my homework. I noticed Mémé and my mother weren't around.

"Where are Mom and Mémé?" I asked.

"Your mother went to a job interview today." He leaned back to glance at the clock on the wall. "I thought she'd be back by now, she left at nine this morning." He looked puzzled.

"And Mémé?" I asked.

"She went to the market to pick up a few things, she'll be back soon."

"Oh." I opened my bag and put my books on the coffee table. "Grandpa, why does it say Sunset Hills Resort, outside in the front of the house?"

"Because this is a resort, and that's the name of it. People come here in the summertime for their vacations."

"Really?" I didn't know that.

"Didn't you see the small cabins in the back? Or the playground, or the swimming pool?" he asked. He sounded surprised.

"Yes, but I didn't know what they were for."

"People come from all over just to stay here. In fact, Moodus is home to many more resorts like ours as well." He smiled proudly. "It's so much fun here in the summertime. We have lots of activities that we do with the guests, and sometimes we have live music. But for the most part we just leave them be. They like to come here for the peace and quiet, and to relax. When you get older you can work here like some of the local kids do for the summer, Katie too." He tousled Katie's hair. Grandpa beamed and a light came into his eyes. "I think a lot of the guests come for your Mémé's cooking. On Saturday nights, we do a big feast. Mémé and I roast a pig for the Fourth of July, and all the guests bring a dish. We have a big bonfire, with marshmallows, and tons of deserts..."

"*Frank*!" I heard Mémé yell as she marched through the kitchen, and into the living room. "You need to calm down! You get too carried away when you start talking about food, and then you're raiding the kitchen looking for sweets that you know you can't have!"

Grandpa sighed and sulked at the piano. "Yes, dear."

Mémé pinched the bridge of her nose with her fingers out of frustration.

She sighed. "Frank, you have to stop doing this to yourself!" She shook her pointer finger at him. "You're making things so much harder than they need to be!"

Grandpa was slumped over as he rose from the piano and wandered over to the couch. He made a low thud when he sat. "I know." He sighed. His face was so sad. He picked up a book from the coffee table with an odd-looking spaceship on the cover and started to read it.

I feel so bad for Grandpa. It's too bad he can't have any sweets and it makes me sad watching Mémé yell at him for even just thinking about them.

Mémé looked at me and Katie. "Your mother still isn't back yet?" she asked.

Katie and I glanced at each other, and when I looked back up at Mémé I just shrugged. I didn't even know she had a job interview today. Mémé just sighed and left the room.

I wonder how long a job interview is supposed to take. As I took my pencil out to start on my homework, a thought occurred to me, and my hand slowly started to tremble. I glanced over at the clock.

"Grandpa, did Mom say she was doing anything else today?" I kept my eyes down on my work. I couldn't look up at Grandpa.

"No, she didn't. Maybe she stopped to visit some friends; she hasn't been home in a long while. That's certainly possible, I'm sure she'll be home really soon."

Oh, how little Grandpa knows my mother, I thought. This just felt so familiar, this couldn't be happening again.

Could it?

My breathing became difficult, and I could feel my chest starting to heave as my heart pounded against my ribs, and I was gasping for air. I had to struggle to gain control before I could speak.

"Oh," was the only word I could get out.

It hadn't occurred to me until now how scared I really was. I thought about getting up to hide myself in the bathroom. I had to close my eyes and work really hard at making myself calm down. I didn't want anyone to know how I was feeling.

She has left us and come back so many times. You would think I'd learn by now not to trust anything adults say, especially her. Why did I think she might actually be different now? That she might change since we moved here.

Then something suddenly occurred to me, causing even more panic. What if the real reason she moved us here was to leave us? I feel so bad for thinking it.

But, would that be such a bad thing? Mémé and Grandpa are really nice. There's lots of food here and their house is warm and cozy. Sure, school here is different than what I'm used to, and the girls in it seem to be crazy. But I'm safe here, and so is Katie. That's all that really matters. I think we would be okay.

Well, if she did leave us, this time we wouldn't be alone.

What I never could understand and I still don't, is why she can't just be happy with us? Did we do something wrong?

Did I? I sometimes wonder if it's me. I know I'm probably being silly but sometimes I get the feeling she doesn't even like me.

Whatever is happening, I have no choice but to wait and see. So, I'll just sit here and work on my homework, and just not think about this anymore until I'm finished. It's not like I have a lot anyway, just math and spelling. It will be nice to have it done and out of the way so I don't have to worry about it at all for the rest of the day.

When I was finished with my homework, I was actually mad. Normally, when I have homework it feels like it takes me hours to do it. Today it felt like ten minutes. I ended up searching my bag to see if there was any more in there, of course, there was none.

After my homework was finished, Mémé let Katie and I sit in the kitchen and have chocolate chip cookies and some milk. As we ate our snack I watched Mémé. She seemed like she was busy cleaning the already clean kitchen, but she kept looking up at the clock. Every so often she would stop to look out the window. She didn't say anything, but it's almost five now and I could tell she was worried about where Mom is.

I sat back in my chair and looked around the clean kitchen. I like living here, I thought to myself. Mémé and Grandpa are nice and they give us treats all the time. I think the last time I had an after-school snack was before Dad left.

Mémé may be worried about where Mom is but I'm not. I hope she did leave us here, then that means we get to stay.

"Veronica," Mémé interrupted my thoughts.

"What?"

"Isn't Tuesday your birthday?" She smiled.

Her question surprised me. "Y-y-yes," I stammered.

"Well why didn't you say anything?"

"I forgot."

I couldn't think of a better excuse, and I didn't really know how to explain it yet.

When any adults ask me anything, I normally give the simplest answer possible. Yes, no, or fine, work well. Oh, and I like I forgot, and I don't know, they work great too.

Depending on the person, telling a grownup I forgot is an easy answer to give when there are just way too many details. Most don't really care enough to listen for the full answer anyway. Or they don't believe you so it's an easy out. You have to be careful though, because sometimes, I don't know and I forgot get you yelled at.

I did remember my birthday. But I didn't think about celebrating it this year because honestly with everything that has happened I didn't feel like it. And I'm only turning nine, it's not like I'm turning ten or thirteen or something.

"You forgot?" She chuckled. "What kind of kid forgets their birthday?"

I just shrugged. I still had no real explanation for her.

"You can have a birthday party here. You can invite the girls from your..."

"No!" I shouted, cutting her off.

Mémé flinched. "*Alright*...No birthday party then." She paused. She looked like she was thinking about what to ask me next. "Didn't you make any friends today at school?" she asked.

"Yes."

"Well?" she prompted.

"Well what?"

"Who is it? What is her name?" She crossed her arms.

"His name is Jackson."

"His?"

"Yes."

"Didn't you make friends with any of the girls?"

"No."

"Why not? What happened?"

I sighed. I don't know if I can explain it right, or if she'll believe me. What happened with those girls today was so weird that I couldn't believe it myself.

I took a breath. "The girls here are crazy." I sighed and continued. "This girl in my class said I was staring at her, when I wasn't. I was just daydreaming. Then she said that I have a staring problem, and these other girls said I did too...It was stupid."

Mémé looked puzzled. "Who were these girls?"

"Claudette Stanwood and these other two girls, Karen and Patricia," I told her.

"Claudette Stanwood?" Mémé looked stunned. "Are you sure? It couldn't be Claudette, she's such a sweetheart. Her father owns Stanwood's Market where we get our groceries."

I knew she wouldn't believe me. Maybe I should tell her what she did to Jackson.

"At lunch, when Jackson sat down next to her, she just got up and went to sit somewhere else. And then in class when she said I had the staring problem, she called him a freak. She said he wasn't allowed to look at her...she's mean."

"Let's go," she ordered. "Get in the car."

I was a bit stunned. "Where are we going?" I asked.

"We are going to Stanwood's Market. We're going to talk with Mr. Stanwood right now and straighten this out."

I was in such shock. I tried so hard to talk her out of it, but Mémé put Katie and I in the car, drove us down, and marched us right into Stanwood's Market.

I've never seen anyone like Mémé before. With no fear, I watched her look around the store, pause briefly just inside the doorway, and then make a beeline straight for the meat counter, where a very tall, slender man with dark hair was standing.

He smiled. "Hello, Ruth. How can I help you today?" he asked.

Mémé crossed her arms. "Well, I'm not here for any groceries. Apparently, your daughter and my granddaughter here had a problem today in school."

Mr. Stanwood stiffened and he looked at me. "Oh? What happened?"

Mémé turned to me. "Veronica, you need to explain to Mr. Stanwood what happened."

Me? I thought.

Not one time has my mother or my father made me confront a problem this way; I was suddenly frozen. I know Mémé means well but I have a feeling nothing good will come from this.

I began to answer Mr. Stanwood, but the shock I was feeling was making the words come out jumbled and so soft that I don't think they could hear me. Mémé saw the panic on my face and she just started to tell Mr. Stanwood what I told her.

She did fine of course. She didn't leave anything out. I was really hoping to be done with this quickly. That maybe Mr. Stanwood would just say something simple like, I'll have a talk with her.

Sigh...Nope.

Instead, Mr. Stanwood turned and called her out to talk with us. "Claudette, can you come out here please?" I guess she was just in the back room. Oh, good.

Claudette walked out from behind the meat counter⊠strolled out was more like it. The look on her face was perfectly formed into a sweet smile, and her hands were tucked behind her back. She looked at all of us. Her eyes were shifting from face to face. But her eyes seemed to rest on mine the longest. I could almost hear her screaming at me through her thoughts.

She looked up at her father with innocent eyes. "Yes, Daddy."

"Mrs. Morrel is here with her granddaughter, Veronica. She's in your class. She told me you said some mean things to Veronica at school today and to a boy named Jackson. Is that true?"

Claudette was still looking up at her father and answered him flawlessly. "No, Daddy." Her voice was so sweet that if I wasn't the one she had been mean to, I would have believed her as well. I watched as her eyes shifted quickly to me then back to him. I swear I could almost feel the bullseye she was now drawing forming on my forehead.

Mr. Stanwood asked her again in a stern fatherly voice. "Claudette, you know how I feel about lying, young lady. I want you to swear to me right now that you are telling me the God's honest truth."

"I didn't say anything mean to her at all," she said coolly. "She was staring at me and I asked her to stop. That's all." She turned and faced me. "I'm sorry if you thought I was being mean."

"Oh," I just nodded. I didn't know what else to say to her. I was still in shock from Mémé forcing me to come here. I ended up just standing there like a dope.

A satisfied look came into Mémé's eyes. "See, it was all a misunderstanding." She patted my shoulders.

"I'm glad we could straighten this out." She sounded relieved. "Why don't we go home." She looked up at Mr. Stanwood. "Thank you for your help."

Mr. Stanwood smiled. "It was my pleasure. It was so nice to meet you, Veronica." He turned and went back behind the meat counter.

We started to leave. Mémé took Katie's hand and started leading her down the aisle and I slowly followed. We didn't get very far before I heard a familiar voice calling⊠more like taunting me.

"Bye, Veronica." Of course, I was the only one who turned to look at her, so no one else saw her. She stood there with her hands behind her back. Her stare sent chills through me, and a sly smile crept slowly across her face. "See you tomorrow at school."

When I woke up it was still dark. The clock on the nightstand said it was ten past twelve. I had to go to the bathroom. Katie was still fast asleep snoring next to me. I hate having to get up in the middle of the night. I always try to avoid it by *going* before I go to bed. Sometimes that doesn't always work, so of course I'm annoyed with myself. I quietly wandered out into the hall and on my way to the bathroom I noticed the light coming from downstairs, and I could hear talking. It sounded more like furious whispering. I crept quietly down the stairs, it sounded like the talking was coming from the kitchen. I stopped about halfway down because I could now hear what was being said.

"And you didn't think any of us deserved a phone call?" It sounded like Mémé and she sounded angry.

"Mom, I'm not a kid anymore. I didn't do anything wrong!"

"We were all worried, and you have responsibilities, Donna."

"I'm well aware that I have responsibilities, thank you very much, and there was nothing to worry about. I'm a big girl now. I just don't get why you're so upset."

"You left this morning for a job interview. A job interview doesn't last that long, and you stayed out until almost midnight."

"So."

"*So*...You never said you were doing anything else today, and it was the girls' first day at school. You should have been there for them when they got home."

"You were here." I heard someone gasp.

"Yeah, I was, and so was your father. But what if we had plans, Donna? What if the girls came home to an empty house?"

"They would have been fine, Mom. You're overreacting."

"You just left them. They are five and eight. They can't be left alone yet."

There was a pause in their conversation.

"So, where were you?" I heard Mémé ask. "Have you been drinking?"

"I had my job interview. I got the job by the way, thanks for asking⬜I felt like celebrating a little."

"I told you no drinking."

"So, what if I did? It was just a little. Like I told you, I was just celebrating. I'm fine, don't worry, I can handle it."

"Like I haven't heard that one from you before."

I had to go bad now, and I was too tired to listen anymore. This conversation between my mother and Mémé is just making me upset.

The rest of my school week went the way I thought it would. The next day my mother wouldn't get up so Mémé walked us to the bus stop. Thank God, I wore pants today. It seems to have gotten colder.

While we were waiting for the bus Mémé asked me about my birthday again.

"So, are you sure you wouldn't want a party? I can make you a nice cake."

"No, I don't want a party." I smiled. "I like the cake idea though." Mémé chuckled.

"Well then, how about I take you and your friend, what was his name again?"

"Jackson," I reminded her.

"Jackson what?" she prompted.

"His name is Jackson Wright."

"Oh." She thought for a moment. "I don't think I know that family, they must be new."

"He said he just moved here, too," I replied.

"Oh. How about I take you both roller skating. There's a new roller rink that just opened up. The kids here seem to love it. It looks like a lot of fun."

Katie looked up at Mémé; she put both her hands up above her eyes shielding them from the sun. "Can I come too?" she asked.

"Of course you can. Oh look, the bus is coming." Mémé turned to me. "When you see Jackson at school today ask him if he would like to come. We're going to go Saturday afternoon. Ask him for his phone number so I can call his mother."

"I will."

With the exception of the usual chatter that accompanies a school bus, the ride to school was fairly quiet. I sat in a seat close to the front with Katie, and just sat back and stared out the window. As much as I always loved sitting with my friends back home for the ride to and from school chatting away, I really do appreciate the quiet ride. And well, it's not like I have any friends on this bus yet anyway.

When we pulled into the parking lot of the school I realized I wasn't sure what I was supposed to do. In my old school, you just went into the cafeteria. Then when the bell rang, you would line up and then your teacher would come to walk you down to your class. I wasn't sure if it was the same.

As we were pulling up to the building I watched the kids getting off the bus ahead of ours. The kids were running towards the playground, putting their school things on the ground by the edge of the sidewalk, and scattering to different parts of the playground.

I leaned over to Katie. "I guess we just go to the playground for a while until they call us in?" My statement came out like a question.

Katie shrugged. "I guess."

When it was our turn and we started to unload, I let Katie go ahead of me. I started to wonder if maybe she would need my help finding her classroom.

"Do you need me to walk you to your classroom when we have to go in?" I asked her as we stepped off the bus.

Just as soon as I asked her, a little girl with brown hair came up shouting, "Katie!"

Katie's face lit up and she started waving her hand above her head. "Diane!"

"Roni, I'll go in with Diane, she's in my class," she said in a hurry. Her and Diane took off running, tossing their belongings on the ground just like the other kids, and were climbing up the jungle gym.

Oh well, I guess Katie doesn't need my help today, I thought.

I took my time walking over to the playground. It was very cold this morning. My teeth were chattering and I could see my own breath. I crossed my arms trying to hold in a little warmth. How can these kids play out here like it's warm out? I just don't get it. And how is it that Katie and I both moved here from the same place and she doesn't appear to be suffering in the cold the way I am? She looks just as comfortable as they do.

"Snitch," I heard a familiar voice say, followed by a lot of what sounded like evil snickering. Claudette was walking by along with Karen and Patricia. As she walked past and our eyes met I could see the anger in her eyes. It was clear to me that going to talk with her father yesterday wasn't the best idea. This girl is seriously becoming a thorn in my side. I'm going to have to keep any future problems I have with Claudette to myself.

"Veronica!" I heard a much nicer voice call to me. It was my new friend Jackson, he was running over, and I felt so relieved to see him.

"Hi, Sackson!" I waved.

"And how are you this morning?" he asked.

"I'm good today. How are you?" I asked in return in my happiest tone.

"I'm good today, too. I'm so happy to be in school," he replied, sounding relieved.

"You're happy to be in school?" That puzzled me, most kids don't like school. What an odd thing to say, I thought. "Why?"

Jackson just sighed. "Awe, my parents were fighting this morning when I left for the bus stop."

"Oh," I said quietly. I can certainly understand that one.

"I'm sorry to hear that." I patted his shoulder. "I always hated when my parents were fighting. But, that's all over now."

He turned and was staring off into the trees. "I wish my parents would get divorced," he said.

That surprised me. Most kids don't want that at all. I know I didn't.

"Why would you say that?" I asked him. He sighed again, and looked down at his shoes.

"They fight a lot. Sometimes, really bad. I just want it to stop."

"Oh. That makes sense," I told him. I couldn't take seeing my new friend so sad. I was suddenly thinking about what Mémé said about going roller skating on Saturday and decided to change the subject.

"Hey, you know what might cheer you up?" I asked, trying hard to control my excitement.

He looked up. "What?"

"My birthday is Tuesday, and I'm not having a birthday party this year. So, my grandmother is taking me roller skating and she said I can bring a friend." I clasped my hands together. "So, do you want to come with me on Saturday?" I asked him in my sweetest voice.

Jackson's eyes widened. "Do you mean Moodus Family Fun Center?"

"Um, I guess. Mémé never said the name. Do you want to come?"

"Yes!" He smiled wide. "I'll have to ask my mom, though."

That reminded me. "Mémé said I need to get your phone number so she could talk to your mom about Saturday."

"We don't have a phone," he said. "But my mom works at Stanwood's Market while we're in school, she can talk to her there."

The bell rang, meaning we could all finally enter the warm school building. I bent down to pick up my bag and when I stood up I felt someone bump into me, stepping on the toe of my shoe at the same time. "Owe!" I said loudly.

"Watch where you're going!" Claudette shouted with a snotty tone as she walked by. Jackson and I stood there and watched her walk past us. She had her nose in the air clutching her books like she was guarding them from us.

I still can't make heads or tails of this girl, what is her problem?

"Snitch!" she called over her shoulder. I could safely assume that insult was towards me, based on the fact she called me that earlier, and she seems to like calling Jackson a freak.

I shook my head, I better stop looking at her, I thought to myself. Otherwise the staring problem thing might start again!

Thursday and Friday, held more of the same from her.

In class, when the teacher was present, Princess Claudette appeared to be a perfect little angel. But as soon as Mrs. Coleman's back was turned or she was out of the room, the trouble would start. Calling me a snitch, tripping me on my way to my seat, flicking my pencil or my books off my desk. It amazed me how much she could think up just to try to annoy me. With the exception of Mémé dragging us into her dad's store the other day to talk to her and her dad, I'm not sure why she has such a problem with me. It's not like I did anything to her. It's never been my style to make trouble for myself or to be mean to others. So, why this girl was picking on me was such a mystery.

And when Claudette wasn't tormenting me, she was torturing poor Jackson.

This angered me more than her picking on me, and I think she could tell, because she would glance in my direction after she said or did anything to him. But every time she did anything to me or Jackson, I would just take a deep breath and bite my tongue. That's one thing my father had taught me. Kids like Claudette, who like to pick on other kids and cause trouble do it for the attention. He always said I should ignore them, and that reacting to someone like that would only make the problem bigger, and would solve nothing, possibly getting me into trouble. I will be good and do what my father taught me. The brighter part of my week was when two girls came up to me at recess and introduced themselves, Evelyn Sanders and her friend Leslie-Ann Clark. Evelyn is in my class and

Leslie is in another third-grade class down the hall. They don't seem as crazy as Claudette, but I'm not trusting either one of them yet—just in case.

CHAPTER 8

SATURDAY morning, I bounced down the stairs and skipped over to the kitchen table. I was so excited about going roller skating with Jackson. I've never roller skated before, I hope I don't fall down a lot!

I think Katie was excited too because the second I sat down and started pouring my cereal she asked, "What time are we going roller skating?"

"We're picking up Jackson at his mother's work at one, and then we're going to the roller rink," Mémé replied.

Having to go to Stanwood's Market wasn't appealing. I hope we don't see Claudette. I shivered at the thought.

"Why aren't we picking him up at his house?" I asked.

Mémé shrugged. "I don't know, his mother just said it would be easier."

When I finished my breakfast, I decided to go get ready. "Mémé, can I take a shower this morning?"

"Of course you can, Veronica, you live here now. You don't need to ask me every time you want to take a shower. Just go ahead."

"Oh, okay." I wasn't sure what else to say. "Thank you."

"You're welcome." She smiled. "I'll be right back in. I'm just going out to the mailbox."

Katie tugged on her sleeve. "Can I play with the piano in the living room?" she asked.

"As long as you are very gentle," Mémé replied to her.

One of the last things my father bought me (actually for my birthday last year) was a pair of bell-bottom blue jeans. I remember my father telling me how popular they were, and that all the kids were wearing them. I also remember my mother saying that she didn't care what the other kids were wearing and that she didn't like them. Between my father and me bugging her a ton we convinced her to let me keep the pants. I haven't worn them much because, at the time he bought them the pants were just a little too big. Okay, like two sizes too big. I remember when I put them on they were falling down and I had to hold up the legs so I could walk without tripping.

Luckily, they fit me well now. Not that I ever cared. I always wore them anyway and I'm wearing them today! Because I love those pants, and they go great with my purple shirt!

As I was toweling my hair, I could hear someone playing the piano and a bunch of excited voices.

I started to panic, because I thought Mémé ignored what I said and threw me a party after I said I didn't want one. I started to wonder who exactly was down there. Please God, don't let Claudette be down there!

I opened the bathroom door just a crack so I could listen. With the door cracked open the piano was a lot louder and clearer. It was that pretty song Grandpa was playing the other day, "Que Sera, Sera."

As I listened to the music I could also hear Mémé. "That is just remarkable!"

Then I heard my mother exclaim, "I always knew she was special!"

I closed the door and finished getting myself dressed. There's definitely something going on down there. It doesn't totally sound like a party though, thank God!

It's not that I don't like parties, because normally I do. It's just the thought of having to deal with the girls from my class in my home for a few hours scares me.

When I came downstairs and into the living room, I was ambushed by my mother. "Veronica!" She pulled me by the arm, dragging me over to the piano. "Look at what your sister can do!"

My sister sat poised on the edge of the piano bench. She had her head tilted slightly to the left as she listened to each note, swaying her tiny legs back and forth. She looked so natural, the way she was moving her small fingers across the keys as though she has been playing her whole life.

Katie being able to play the piano wasn't news to me. I've seen her do this once before, the last time Mom left us alone.

I had gotten a toy piano for Christmas. It was something I played with all the time. Normally during our time alone, I would do things with Katie so she wouldn't be scared about being alone, or worry about when Mom would come back.

The last time we were making up songs. We had so much fun, I was playing the toy piano just pressing on keys making noise and I made Katie sing, letting her be the one to make up the song. We were being silly.

I remember getting up to go to the bathroom, and while I was in there I could hear her pressing each key from high to low, then low to high. I remember, I was going to yell at her for touching my toy. But by the time I went back into our room Katie was playing "Twinkle, Twinkle Little Star." I have to admit I was surprised when I saw that. I had asked her to play something else and she played "Rock-A-Bye Baby." She played all kinds of songs after that. For some reason, the piano comes easy for her. If Mom wasn't ignoring us like she was she would have seen this then.

She did the exact same thing then that she's doing now. I had asked her then why she turns her head like that and she had told me that she can hear the piano better that way.

So, when Mom told me, "look what your sister can do," I couldn't react the way she wanted me to because I already knew this, it was of no surprise.

I just shrugged and went to sit on the couch. This seemed to make her upset with me, since she was expecting a very different reaction.

"Veronica, what's wrong with you?" she asked, with her hands on her hips. She sounded upset.

"Nothing," I replied back.

"Aren't you going to say anything?" she prompted.

"About what?" I asked.

"Your sister can play the piano without ever having a single lesson, or anything, and you can't say something nice?" She sounded annoyed.

"Um...Good job, Katie."

My mother just huffed a little, and went back to watching Katie. Mémé came and sat down next to me.

She looked up at my mother, sighed, and then she leaned in to speak in my ear. "Have you seen Katie do this before?" she asked quietly.

I just nodded my head in reply.

Mémé smiled and patted my knee. "You have mail on the kitchen table."

This surprised me. I didn't expect to get mail here. I smiled and jumped up from the couch, running to the kitchen table. There was a big brown box. The post mark said San Francisco, Calif. There was no other name on it except for my own.

I was so excited. I've gotten mail before, but I never got a package!

I spent several minutes struggling with the tape. Whoever taped this box up went crazy with it! I was pulling long ribbons of it off over and over. Once I finally got the package open I had to dig through a ton of newspaper. Buried under all that paper was another box, only this one was giftwrapped with party balloon wrapping paper and a card was taped to the top.

My name was printed on the envelope in all capitals, which led me to my first clue who this was from. I took the present and curled up with it in my lap on the kitchen floor. It felt just a little heavy. I opened the card first, unsealing the envelope and gently pulling the card out.

The card's cover was decorated in a rainbow of different colored party balloons with a big yellow nine in the center.

I opened up the card and began to read it:

Dear Veronica, Happy Birthday!

I hope you're having a very special day, I miss you, tons! You'll have to write to me and tell me how you like your new school, and how everything is going. I hope you like the present.

I love you! Tell Katie I love her and miss her too!

Happy birthday, Sweetie!

Love, Dad

I was so excited. I've missed him so much, and this present made me feel like he missed me too. I ripped off the wrapping paper and opened the box. This box was stuffed with newspaper too, but not as much. In the middle of the crumpled paper was something wrapped in one of his old blue handkerchiefs. I pulled it out and pushed the box to the side. I took off the handkerchief and gasped.

My father gave me my grandmother's music box! He always knew how much I loved it. He always told me someday he would give it to me, but I never expected now! The music box is oval shaped, silver, and shiny. It has two roses on the front and vines that wrap around the sides. On the lid, there are two hearts linked together that I always traced with my fingers.

Excitedly, I turned over the box and carefully turned the key for my favorite part. I turned the box back over and lifted the lid. The inside was the soft purple velvet that I remembered, and when the music began it all started to come back to me. How I did know that song Grandpa and Katie played. It was the one from when I was very little. The one my father would play to me at night before bed sometimes, or when I had a bad dream, "Que, Sera, Sera."

I was so full of happiness in this moment. All from this small box my father gave me. I didn't even realize I was crying at first, until I felt the tear that flowed down my cheek hit my arm. I wiped my cheek with the back of my hand and continued to sit on the floor enjoying the gift my dad sent me.

* * *

I was suddenly surprised by the description of the music box. I had purchased one not too long ago at a flea market that fit that same description. "You said the music box was silver and oval shaped?" I asked her, interrupting her story.

"Yes, and it has two roses on the front with hearts on the lid," she said.

I got up from the bed and quickly grabbed my crutches and went over to my dresser. I pulled open the top drawer and pulled out the music box I had purchased to show her. When I turned around she gasped.

"Curt, that's it! Wind it up and open it. The inside is purple."

If there had been any doubt in my mind at all about her story before, it was gone now. I gently wound the key on the bottom and then carefully lifted the lid. The music box's song hung heavily in the air and I was in awe.

I smiled at her. "I bought this at a flea market a while ago. I was just so intrigued by the designs on it."

"You got this for me before we left for the last life and you gave it to me when I came home," she replied.

"And I wish I could give it to you again." I set the box down on top of my dresser and turned to face her. The small box continued to play and I set down my crutches leaning them against my bed. I took her hand in mine and wrapped my other arm around her waist, pulling her in closely. I pressed my cheek against hers and placed her hand over my heart and began swaying her carefully trying to keep the weight off my broken leg. "I wish I could move better, but I'm a little limited at the moment," I spoke softly in her ear.

She kissed my cheek. "I love you too."

* * *

"Veronica, what is that?" my mother asked.

I didn't bother to turn to look at her. "Dad sent me a birthday gift," I replied.

My mother was standing over me now. "He, gave, you, that?" Her tone sounded like she was stunned.

"Yes," I said.

"Why?" my mother asked.

"For! My! Birthday!" I cheerfully announced. Mom sat down on the floor beside me⊠flopped down is more like it.

"He wouldn't let anyone touch that...had it hidden ...." She was babbling but I wasn't really paying much attention. "He said that box is about thirty years old...
"

"Veronica what is it you have there?" Mémé interrupted my mother's rambling.

"Dad sent me my grandmother's music box for my birthday!" I practically sang it at her.

"Wow, it's really beautiful." Mémé crouched down between me and my mother. "How did he know where to send it?"

"The last time I saw him I told him Mom said we were moving to Moodus," I told her.

"Ah, I see. That was very nice of him."

"Of course, it was nice of him. I just don't get why he would give a family heirloom like that to a nine-year-old," my mother said.

"Does it really matter why he did it? She is his daughter, and that box belonged to him. He is free to do what he wants with the box," Mémé replied.

"But she's a little kid," my mother argued.

Mémé stood up. "Donna, may I see you in the other room please."

I watched my mother and Mémé leave the room.

I gently closed the lid and I traced the hearts with my finger. I should call Dad and say thank you to him. It's the least I could do.

Holding onto my gift, I got up from the floor and went towards the living room, so I could ask about calling him. Out of habit I paused just outside the doorway. Good thing I did because I could hear Mémé and my mother arguing.

"What is the matter with you?" I heard Mémé say.

"There's nothing wrong with me, I'm not the one who's stupid!" my mother replied.

"You're upset that Phil gave her that music box."

"No, I'm not."

"Yes, you are! I'm your mother and I can tell. I don't know why you continue to try to lie all the time! You've always been such a terrible liar!"

"I'm not lying! I just don't get it! I was his wife! He knew how much I loved that box! He could have given me that box a long time ago, but he never did, and I could never understand why!" My mother was getting louder now. "Then he just goes and gives that box to Veronica! A little kid! Why didn't he just give that box to Katie then if he wanted to see it destroyed!"

"I think you're completely overreacting, Donna! And acting like a total spoiled brat! Are you actually jealous that Veronica got that?"

"I'm not jealous!" my mother huffed.

"You are! I can't believe you're behaving like this! It's her birthday! You're supposed to be her mother!"

"That music box is valuable! She'll just end up destroying it!"

"Donna, you couldn't possibly know that," Mémé barked back at her, sounding frustrated.

I couldn't take listening to this argument anymore, so I walked into the living room. "Mom," I said, my voice sounded shaky.

My mother whipped around. "*WHAT*!" she snapped loudly.

Mémé and I both flinched.

"I promise nothing bad will happen to this music box. I'll go put it on my dresser," I told her.

I did as I said I would, just like I always do.

I went upstairs to my room, and put my birthday gift on top of the dresser and propped up the card my dad sent with it right next to it. I ran my fingers across the roses on the front of the box. I'll have to wait for everyone to cool down before asking about calling him. I couldn't help feeling a little guilty for getting this gift. I never knew how my mother felt about it. I wonder if Dad knew how upset she would get by giving me this. And I also wonder now if that was the point.

When we pulled into Stanwood's Market, Jackson and his mother were waiting outside. Even though Mémé was still furious with my mother, she followed through with taking me, Jackson, and Katie skating. That's something my mother wouldn't have done.

Whenever there were plans to go anywhere and my mom and dad had a fight, my mother would end up closing herself up in her room and then our plans would be canceled.

I do remember one time we had plans to go to the zoo. Mom and Dad had a fight, and then Mom locked herself in her room. Dad told us to get in the car, and that he had had it. We were going anyway.

Me, Dad, and Katie, spent the whole afternoon at the zoo. I remember we had more fun that afternoon just the three of us, than we ever did when all of us went. That night when we got home, Mom and Dad had an even bigger fight, which had Dad sleeping on the couch for a week! I suppose since Mémé is her mother, she probably won't have to sleep on the couch.

Mémé beeped the horn, and I rolled down my window and waved. Jackson smiled and waved back.

Mémé opened the door. "Veronica, stay in the car and keep an eye on your sister. I'll go and talk with Jackson's mother."

I watched as Mémé and Mrs. Wright talked. Jackson was leaning back against his mother squinting from the sun. She had her arms wrapped around his shoulders. Every so often she would reach up and tuck a loose strand of hair behind her ear, never once letting go of Jackson.

Jackson's mother is so beautiful. She's thin and she is short for an adult. She has the same straight jet-black hair like her son, and they share the same shape in their eyes. I wonder if they share the same color? I watched her rustle his hair, and kiss his cheek, then lick her thumb to wipe away a smudge from his chin while he made a face. Watching them made me feel the same way I always felt seeing other mothers with their kids, a little jealous.

I hope Jackson knows how lucky he is.

Jackson and his mother followed Mémé to the car.

"So, you must be Veronica?" Jackson's mother stuck her hand through the window. I did what I assumed I should do and shook her hand. Her hand was so warm.

"It's so nice to finally meet you. Jackson's been going on and on about you, since you started school. It was so nice of you to invite him skating with you today."

She smiled, and until now, I don't think I've ever seen a smile more genuine, and I can see her eyes are blue. I wonder, where Jackson gets the green from?

"It's nice to meet you too, Mrs. *Wrig*..." I started to say.

Jackson's mother cut me off. "Please call me Joan." She turned to her son. "You remember to be polite now. I'll come by Veronica's house after work and pick you up. Love you." She kissed Jackson's cheek, and he flushed with embarrassment as he opened the car door. "I'll be good, Mom." He was looking down at his shoes. "Love you, too," he replied.

I tried to hide my smile as I scooted over, and he quickly got into the car.

"Jackson honey, don't forget to give Veronica the birthday gift you made for her."

"Awe, Mom, I didn't forget! It was supposed to be a surprise!" He sounded even more embarrassed.

"Oops! Sorry, honey. I'll shut up now. I have to go in now anyhow. You kids have a good time!"

"Bye Mom!" Jackson called out.

Jackson, Katie, and I all waved to her as we left the parking lot.

It didn't take us too long to get to Moodus Family Fun Center. I was excited, I've always wanted to try roller skating my whole life!

"Jackson, do you know how to roller skate?" I asked him as we were getting out of the car.

"Yes. I'm not very good though. Last time I came here I fell a lot." Oh good, I thought. We're already clumsy, this ought to be fun.

When we went in, Mémé took Katie up to the counter to pay, and Jackson and I went and sat at one of the booths on the side of the main rink.

"This place is loud and huge!" I shouted.

"Yeah, it is! Look, there's the pinball machines!" Jackson shouted. "I love pinball. Look, there's the main skating area there." He pointed. "See, on that side they have an area just for beginners. We should probably go over there, so we don't get trampled."

"Good Idea!" I had to agree that was a good idea. "Oh look! They have hot pretzels! I love those! Maybe we can get one of those after!"

"What size are your feet?" Mémé yelled over to us.

I put my foot up on the bench to check the tongue but the size was rubbed off. Last I knew, my size was a nine and a half. "Mémé! It's nine and a half, I think!" I yelled. I was already having fun. Any place that you have to yell over the noise is always fun! "Jackson, what's your shoe size?"

"I think mine is ten," he said.

I happily yelled again. "Mémé! He thinks his is ten!" I like this place already, I thought.

Mémé walked over to us with the gentleman from the counter. "Sam here is going to measure your feet for the skates. It will be a lot easier than guessing!" Sam bent down and measured my foot and then Jackson's and hurried behind the counter.

Katie looked up at Mémé. "Mémé, I don't want to skate," she told her.

Mémé placed her hand on Katie's shoulder and looked at her with a sympathetic smile. "Awe, why don't you want to try skating?"

"Because it looks, too scary," she said.

Mémé looked up and watched some of the bigger kids flying by fast on their skates. Two kids knocked into the dividing wall right in front of us and fell on the floor.

She flinched. "You know Katie, I think I'll call your grandpa to see if he can come get you." Mémé patted her shoulder. "I think, you my dear, may be slightly too young for this."

"Jackson, Veronica, I'll be right back. I have to go use the pay phone."

Sam the roller skate guy brought Jackson and me our skates and was nice enough to help us put them on.

The skates felt heavy on my feet, I wasn't sure how I was going to stand up in them.

"Do you want help getting up?" Jackson asked. He was already on his feet. Show off.

Help? That might be a good idea, I thought.

"Yes, please. You've done this before?"

"Yes, Mom and I came here once, and when we lived in Florida my mom took me a few times. It's hard at first, but once you learn how to skate, it's a lot of fun." Jackson grabbed my hand to help me up.

When he grabbed my hand and pulled me up, it brought me back to the first time we met on the classroom floor.

"What if I fall?" I said.

"You might. You can't worry about that. Just hang on to the wall with one hand until we get over to the beginner's area. I'll be right next to you to catch you if you need it."

Mémé and Katie came and sat down at the table. "Grandpa is coming to get Katie soon, and I'll be sitting right here." She pulled a book from her bag, and her Polaroid camera. "Go have fun."

I took a deep breath and got to my feet, holding on to the table for support. I just have to get from here to the beginner's area, I thought. I can do that. I took a step and I suddenly grabbed on to Jackson because I thought I would have to right myself. I surprised myself a little I wasn't falling the way I thought I would.

I let go of Jackson. "Hey, this isn't so bad," I said.

"That's because this area's carpeted. It doesn't let you roll the way the wood floor does."

I swallowed down the small lump that rose up in my throat. In just a few short steps I will be stepping out onto the wood floor. I was a little scared. What if I do fall?

When we got to the entrance for the beginner's area, I stopped and took a deep breath.

"Don't worry, I'll help you. Just hold on to the railing that's on the wall, and I'll hold your other hand." I'm so glad Jackson was with me here. I could tell he's a good teacher. He held my hand and my elbow as I took my first step onto the shiny hardwood floor.

I could immediately tell the difference between the carpet and the wood. The moment I put my foot onto the wood my foot slid right out from under me, and I landed on my butt. "Whoops!" I grabbed the rail with both hands, and struggled to get onto my feet. It was hard to get my feet to stay in one place so I could get up.

Jackson held his hands out. "Do you want me to help you?"

"Not yet." I was trying to figure out a way to get up onto my feet. "If I need it I will ask."

He held his hands up. "Okay."

While I was still hanging onto the rail an idea occurred to me. I let go of the railing and picked up my left foot with my hands and placed the wheels right on the floor. That one was the easiest to get to since I was sitting funny on my right foot. I grabbed hold of the railing, and used it to help me pull myself up slowly and carefully. I carefully dragged my right foot forward as I got up placing the wheels flat on the floor. I let out a sigh of relief. I was up on my feet.

"Good, Veronica. Now watch me." Jackson took off around the circle. It looked like he was just sliding his feet. He stopped next to me. "Put your feet like this." He parted his feet just a little. "Now, I'm going to tell you the same thing my mom told me. You're gonna hold one foot steady while you push off with the other. Then you do the same with the other side. Watch me." He demonstrated, while I watched him, and circled around again. "Now it's your turn." He made it look so easy. I let go one hand off the railing and I tried copying what Jackson showed me by placing my feet apart a little. "Good. Now you're gonna have to let go of the railing."

I was nervous, but I let go. Well so far so good. I didn't fall yet. Jackson stayed by my side. "Now, do what I showed you. Push off with one foot, and then the other." I almost did it and then I wondered, how do you stop? "What do I do when I want to stop?"

"Oh, that's easy, you just drag your toe. See that rubber stopper on your toe? That's your brake."

"Ahh, I think I got this. Here I go!" I pushed off with my foot. I rolled forward a little and then came to a stop. I was so excited. "I did it! And I didn't fall!"

Jackson stopped next to me. "That was really great, Veronica! Let's skate more!"

I really pushed off this time. One foot, and then the other, it really was fun. I got half way around the circle before I lost my balance spinning myself around, and falling right on my butt. "Owe!"

"Veronica, are you okay?!"

"Uh, yes, but I think I may have put a dent in their floor." That was something my father always asked me whenever I hurt myself. "Did you put a dent in that?" It always made me giggle. And saying it certainly made me feel a little better, it kept me from crying.

"You're not gonna give up, are you?" Jackson asked.

"Nope, if you can do this, then I can!" I pulled myself up off the floor. "Let's try that again!"

The whole time we were skating I fell so much! I know I'm gonna have bruises on my butt tomorrow, and I think I may have actually left a few marks on their floor. Jackson fell a few times too, but not as much as I did. I did manage to make it around the circle a few times, which I am proud of. I waved and called over to Mémé every time. "Mémé look at me!"

Mémé took a few pictures. Once I slammed right into Jackson, which reminded me even more of my first day at school because we both landed on our butts on the floor that day, too. The other accident we had was me tripping over him right after he fell in front of me.

After every accident, Mémé would look up from her book, check to see if we were okay, and then once we were up she would go back to reading her book.

Mémé spoiled us while we were there, letting us play a few games of pinball and buying us pizza and each a hot pretzel! I don't think I can remember ever having this much fun, or eating this much junk for my birthday. The best part (at lease to me) was walking right after I took the skates off. My legs felt like jelly.

We got home around five, I think. I was hoping maybe Mom was still here when we got home so she could meet Jackson, but of course she wasn't. Maybe next time, I thought. Jackson did get to meet my grandpa, though.

We all came into the house through the kitchen.

We had stopped at Stanwood's Market on the way home so Mémé could pick up something for Grandpa for dinner, which was nice because we got to tell Jackson's mom all about our afternoon.

Mémé was taking his dinner out of the bag and putting it on the counter when Grandpa came in. "So didja kids have fun?"

"Yeah, it was so much fun," I told him. I walked over to Mémé and put my arms around her. "Thank you for taking me and Jackson skating today. That was so much fun. That was the best birthday ever!"

She patted my back. "I'm glad you had a good birthday, Sweetie."

Grandpa smiled, rubbing his big belly. "And who is this fella?" he asked.

I pointed with my thumb. "Oh, that's my friend Jackson. He's in my class at school."

Grandpa held his hand out to Jackson. "It's nice to meet you. Are you staying for dinner?"

"Grandpa! We just had pizza at the roller skating rink!"

"Didja bring me any leftovers?"

"Oh, for the love of all that is holy!" Mémé shouted. "I'm making your dinner right now!"

Grandpa flinched. "What are we having?" he asked shyly.

"Well, I ate with the kids. Katie is getting the leftover pizza. You're having chicken breast and vegetables!"

"Alright! *jeez*." He held his hands up. "I didn't think one piece of pizza would derail my diet," Grandpa said.

"I don't care what you think!" she huffed. "You're not going to have anything you're not supposed to until the doctor says you can. Do you hear me?!"

Grandpa sighed. "Yes."

"Good. Then let me finish fixing your supper. Why don't you go into the living room and read one of your science fiction novels. You have that new one on the coffee table."

"Okay." Grandpa sulked his way out of the kitchen.

I started thinking about the gift my father sent me, and how I wanted to show Jackson. "Mémé?"

"What is it, Sweetie?"

"Can I take Jackson upstairs so I can show him what my dad sent me for my birthday?"

"Sure, go ahead."

"C'mon Jackson." I grabbed his hand yanking him with me. "Wait until you see it!" I ran up the stairs dragging him by the arm. I opened my bedroom door and ran over to my dresser.

The spot where I left my new music box and the card was empty.

"That's weird," I said. I looked behind the dresser, under the bed, in the closet, and I couldn't find it.

"I left it right here." I pointed to the top of my dresser. "The music box and the card. C'mon Jackson, we have to go tell Mémé."

I ran down the stairs and into the kitchen. "Mémé, I can't find the music box, or the birthday card my dad sent."

Mémé furrowed her brow. "Where did you leave it?"

"I put it right on top of my dresser just like I said I would. I put it there right before we left." Mom and Mémé's argument was slowly starting to enter my mind. Mémé wiped her hands off on a dish towel and started up the stairs. "Are you sure it's gone?"

"Yes Mémé, I looked everywhere."

Mémé searched my room coming up empty. "That daughter of mine," she said under her breath. "She just never thinks. I don't know what is ever going on inside that head of hers." She grabbed both my shoulders bending down to look me in the eyes. "I will get that box back; do you hear me? And your card too, alright? Then we will hide it from her, so she can't find it. It's yours, not hers." I just nodded my head, agreeing with her. "If only she could just see what she's doing," she said shaking her head.

Jackson just stood quietly by the door watching.

My mother has done a lot of selfish mean things to me in the past. But I didn't want to think that my mother took my music box. Because if she did take it, a family heirloom that my father gave to *me*, because he loves *me*, and I am part of *his* family, things between my mother and me will never be the same. How would I ever be able to trust her with anything again?

Not that things between us were ever very good anyways. I always hoped that one day, things between my mother and me would change and everything would get better.

Sometimes, I feel like my mother gets some enjoyment from making me sad. This isn't the first time she's done something like this to me. Although this is the first time I really cared for what she took. One thing that I haven't told anyone is that I have noticed, she never does any of these things to Katie, if she has I've missed it.

"Veronica, why don't you and Jackson play some checkers? His mother will be coming by soon to pick him up," Mémé suggested.

"Okay, we can do that." I smiled. "Jackson, do you want to play checkers?"

"Sure," he said, finding a seat on the floor of my room. I couldn't tell if he was at all uncomfortable having to be in this situation with me, if he was, he didn't show it.

"Okay, I'll get the game out," I said.

Mémé smiled, and finally left the room. I crossed my legs and sat down crisscross in one fluid movement holding onto the checker board. I heard Mémé's footsteps fade down the stairs just as I started taking the board and the pieces out. I let out a heavy sigh. I hadn't realized I was holding my breath.

"Are you alright?" he asked.

"Yeah." I was putting the pieces on the board. "Do you want to be red or black?"

"Are you sure?" he asked me again.

"I'm okay. This is nothing new. My mother has always been like this. She's always been mean. You're lucky your mom is so nice."

"My mom is very nice. Too bad my dad isn't."

"So, I have a mean mom, and you have a mean dad. Maybe they should get together and have a party," I said.

We both giggled.

"If you ever want to talk about stuff…you can talk to me," Jackson said. He took my hand in his. "I swear if you tell me anything, you can trust me, and I will never tell a soul."

I smiled. "So, you'll be my secret keeper?" I asked.

"Yes."

"Like a best friend?"

"Yes," he said with a wide grin.

The more I thought about what he said, the more I liked it. I did have friends back in San Francisco before, but none of them were my best friend. I've never had one of those. It would be nice to have someone I could trust, and tell all my secrets to. It would be nice to be able to talk to someone about stuff that bothers me. It's not like I can just go talk to Katie, Mémé, or Grandpa. Katie is too young to understand anything, and well, Mémé and Grandpa are adults, so they can't always be trusted.

I probably should make the same promise to him too, I thought. I can't expect him to just keep all my secrets without telling him he can trust me with his.

With my hand still in his, I leaned in. "I promise to be your secret keeper too. Anything you tell me I swear I will never tell a soul either *and* I will be your best friend." I smiled at him too.

"So, best friends for life?" he asked.

"Yep."

"You want to be red this turn?" he asked, still smiling.

"Yeah sure. We can switch next game." We started playing and it was fun. It was the first time in a long time I felt like I could just be myself. I felt so free.

"Ah! I almost forgot!" he suddenly yelled, digging into his front pocket.

I sat up startled. "Forgot what?"

He smiled. "Your birthday gift, silly."

I giggled, clapping my hands over my mouth.

"Give me your hand," he said.

I held out my hand like he asked, and he placed a thin woven bracelet into my hand. The bracelet was blue and red and had small white beads threaded through in a few random spots. I loved it. "Thank you. It's really pretty."

"You're welcome. I had started making it when I went to camp when we were living in Florida, and I finished the rest after we moved here, it took me a while."

I ran my finger across the bracelet feeling the beads and the weave.

"It's a friendship bracelet. I was saving it, for my first real friend," he said.

"Can you help me put it on?" I asked him.

I held out my arm and he tied on the bracelet for me. The bracelet was a little too big, but I didn't complain. I loved it, and I will wear it. We're best friends now. Too bad I don't have one to give him.

"I wish I had a friendship bracelet for you."

He looked at me puzzled. "Why?"

"Because we're best friends! You need one too."

"Nope," he stated.

"Why not," I asked him. Now I was the puzzled one.

"Because boys don't wear bracelets. Only you get one."

"That's dumb. Here, give me your wrist." I held out my hand, and he placed his in mine. He had a puzzled look on his face. I traced his wrist with my finger going all the way around, and I made silly sound effects. "There," I said. I was satisfied with my idea. He looked at me funny.

"Now you have a friendship bracelet too, just no one will ever know, except for me and you."

Jackson smiled. "Thank you, Veronica. I'll never take it off."

"Me neither," I replied. "I promise."

Jackson and I played five games of checkers before we became bored of it. It was dark out so it's not like we could go outside to play; not that either one of us would want to anyways. It's too cold.

"Want to go downstairs and see if we can watch some TV?" I asked him.

"Sure," he replied.

I was about to ask Mémé if we could watch TV when we went downstairs, but someone was sitting in the kitchen talking to Mémé.

They both looked up at us from their cups of coffee. It was Jackson's mother sitting with Mémé.

"Hi kids!" she said. "Did you have a nice time today?" she asked Jackson.

"I had the best time," he said with a big smile.

She reached over and he just went straight into her arms. She kissed the top of his head. "I'm so glad you had such a good day," she said as she rubbed his back. "Mrs. Morrel and I have been talking. I have to work Saturdays now for a while, and I thought maybe you could play here while I work."

Jackson's face lit up. "*Really*, can I?"

I was standing on my tippy toes waiting for an answer.

"It's alright with me," Mémé said. "Veronica, it's really up to you. You're the one who will be spending time with him."

"Uh, yeah, he can play here!" I replied.

Mémé and Joan laughed at me. Joan took a sip of her coffee. "Jackson, we have to go now. It's late, and your father will be upset if we don't get home soon."

Jackson hugged me. "See you Monday."

"See you," I said hugging him back.

On Monday morning, I was eager to get to school. I couldn't wait to talk to my new best friend! I got dressed quickly, and brushed my hair and teeth fast, and then I ran down the stairs. I almost ran right into Mémé who was standing in the kitchen doorway.

"*Whoa*! Slow down! Why are you in such a hurry today?" She smiled.

"I don't know." It was morning and I didn't want to go into a big thing about how I couldn't wait to see my friend.

"Well, there's someone in the kitchen who would like to talk to you."

Awe, right now? I thought to myself. I looked around Mémé and saw my mother sitting at the kitchen table, and placed right in front of her was my music box and the card my dad gave me. I was so annoyed. Why couldn't we have done this yesterday? Oh yeah, I remember, because she didn't come home Saturday night, and all day yesterday. Not that I missed her.

Mémé pushed me backwards out of the kitchen and into the living room. "I know how upset you must be with her. She feels terrible about what she did, and she is your mother. Please be kind and just listen to her. I know you can do that. Be a good girl and give her a chance."

A chance? I thought to myself. Is Mémé out of her mind? I've given her tons of chances, and she just does what she wants anyway. She doesn't really care about me, only herself and Katie. Saturday when Katie left with Grandpa she ended up going shopping with Mom. Not that I really care. I hate shopping and she knows that. Mom bought her new shoes and a new doll. Then she came home before Jackson and I got there, dropped Katie off, took my stuff, and left.

Mémé was all for me forgiving my mother, and I wasn't really ready to do that. So instead of saying how I really felt I just said, "Fine," but I crossed my fingers, so I didn't really mean it.

I went back into the kitchen so I could get this apology over with so I could just leave for the bus. Suddenly, I wasn't very hungry anymore.

"Oh, Veronica!" my mother started. Of course, she was crying. What do those tears really mean? I wondered. Is she sad because she hurt me or is she upset because she has to give back the music box?

"I'm so sorry for how I acted on Saturday! Daddy had every right to give this to you. I don't know why I got so upset. I don't know if you're going to fully understand, but I think it's because I'm not completely over him. It hurt me that he gave this to you. Because I know now he must be over me." She handed me the box and the card, then wiped her nose with her tissue.

"I promise to never take this from you again, and if you keep it on your dresser that's exactly where it will stay. Your things are yours," she said.

I sighed. "Okay." I forced a smile. What I really wanted to say was, 'and I should believe you why?'

My mother hugged me, and being the good girl that I am I hugged her back.

"I start my new job today," she added. "I start the day before your birthday. I think it's a good omen."

"Yeah, I think so too," I said, not that I really care right now.

I went back upstairs to put my music box and my card back on my dresser, and then I suddenly had an idea. I went back into the kitchen to test it out.

"Mom?" I began softly.

"What is it Veronica?" She was still wiping her tears with the tissues.

"Do you think I can call Dad after school today? I didn't get a chance yet and I would like to thank him for his gift."

My mother didn't say anything right away, but she made a funny face. I could tell she was choosing her words very carefully, because Mémé was in the room.

"Sure, honey. Of course, you can."

To continue my test, I went up and hugged her. "Thanks, Mom!" I smiled really big so Mémé could see. I looked up at the clock. "Whoa! Is Katie ready? We have to get out to the bus stop."

My mother was the one who answered. "Katie has an appointment that I have to take her to before school. So, I'm dropping her off."

I hugged Mom and then I hugged Mémé. "See you all later, thanks Mom!" I shouted as I left the house.

Dealing with Mom this morning almost made me miss the bus. Thank God, I didn't. I really didn't want to go back to the house again. I couldn't help feeling like she's lying about letting me call my dad. If she refuses to give me his number then I will get it myself. I'll just call information.

When I finally got to school, Jackson was waiting for me by the edge of the school building. I smiled and waved to him from the bus window.

I still find it funny how comfortable I feel around Jackson already. He makes me feel better. I'm thankful he's in school today, because after the morning I had if he wasn't here I'd probably cry.

I went up and hugged Jackson, I was so happy to see him.

"Hi, Veronica!"

"Hey, Sackson!" We both laughed.

"So how are you this morning? Did you get your music box back yet?" he asked.

I sat on the ground near the edge of the building and hugged my knees to my chest, and he sat down next to me. Boy the ground here is cold this time of year!

"Yes, I got it back. She gave it to me this morning. She did take it, and I'm still mad. Mémé told me I had to be nice about it because she feels bad."

"So, you had to be nice to her?" he asked.

"Yeah, not that I wanted to be." I paused for a moment; I was trying to decide on telling him a secret. "Can I tell you a secret?" I asked quietly.

Jackson leaned in. "Of course. That's what best friends are for."

I smiled at first and then my smile faded. "I don't think my mother likes me."

Jackson's expression became puzzled. "Why do you think that?" he asked.

"Because, Mom and I fight a lot, and she seems to do more things with Katie than she does with me. I'm sure it's probably because Katie believes every single thing she says no matter what she does, and I don't."

The bell rang. "We have to go in," he said. "You can tell me the rest at lunch."

When we stood up Katie came skipping by us. "Hey, how was your appointment?" I asked her.

She looked confused. "What appointment?" she asked in back reply.

"The one Mom took you to on her way to work."

She still seemed confused, so I tried to make it sound simpler.

"Where did Mom take you before she went to work?"

Katie's face lit up, and I could tell she now understood. "Oh! She took me for pancakes."

"See, Jackson." I threw my hands in the air. "Do you see what I mean?" I said and then we headed in.

I walked with Jackson to our classroom. I said good morning to Evelyn, put my stuff in my bin, and hung up my coat. Mrs. Coleman wasn't here yet so Jackson turned around and we both started talking. Mostly about how much fun Saturday was and what we were going to do next Saturday.

While we were in the middle of talking about our plans, Claudette took her seat. I pretended not to notice her, and it seemed like Jackson was doing the same thing. He had his back to her so he couldn't see anything she was doing. But unfortunately, I could, because she sits right next to him.

She was turned and she was watching us.

I swear I tried not looking at her. But, it is so hard not to look at someone when you can see them looking right at you. I think Jackson could tell because the harder I tried to keep my eyes from drifting to stare back at her the more he hunched over. Like, he could feel her eyes drilling a hole into the back of his head.

"Are you two boyfriend and girlfriend now?" she suddenly asked. Jackson and I snapped our heads around to look at her.

"Well, are you? ⊠It's a simple question."

Jackson's face was pale and frozen. He looked scared, and so I don't think he was able to answer her. In the few seconds I had to think, I realized no matter what answer I give her, Claudette would find a way to make fun of us.

"You know, Claudette," I began as smooth as I could manage. I even folded my hands on the top of my desk and leaned back in my chair. I really tried hard to make her see Jackson may be scared. But I wasn't. "It's really none of your business." Okay, I was a little nervous.

"So, you are aren't you?" she asked.

"Again, *none* of your business," I said flatly. I watched Jackson thaw out some.

"How nice, the freak has a girlfriend." Her tone was mean.

"Don't call him that," I said. I was trying so hard to just stay calm. I know the teacher will be here soon.

"Don't call him what? Freak? You're not the boss of me. I can call him anything I want to." She looked over at him. "Hey, freak!" She laughed.

I was getting so mad. I can't stand when she calls him that. How dare she call him that!

"You know, I just told you, quit calling him that!" I barked at her.

That just egged her on more.

"Jackson is a fat freak, a freak who cries all the time⊠what a loser!"

"Stop calling Jackson a freak!" I shouted.

"*Awe*...how sweet.   The freak's little girlfriend is sticking up for him⊠isn't that cute, girls?"

Patricia and Karen both nodded, their smiles were taunting. I still don't know which one is which.

"For your information, Jackson is my friend. And I already told you none of it is your business!"

"*OH*! So, the freak *is* your boyfriend!" she taunted. "I *see*!"

Jackson could have stopped me or butted in at any time but he didn't. He just let me go letting me decide what to say.

I was suddenly so mad. "Yeah, so what!" I snapped at her. I stood up from my desk, staring her straight in the face. "STOP CALLING HIM A FREAK AND LEAVE

HIM ALONE! *HE'S MINE!*" I shouted loudly pounding both my fists on the desk.

She flinched back in her seat, in shock. I shocked Jackson too, his eyes were wide. I even shocked myself. I don't really know why I said it like that. I just wanted her to shut up. Once it was out there like that though, I became worried about what Jackson was thinking. I'll be nine tomorrow, I'm not ready for a boyfriend yet. I'm gonna have to talk to him at lunch or something. I don't want to hurt his feelings. He's my best friend.

Mrs. Coleman came in, and the class became quiet. I spent the day up until lunch trying to figure out what I was going to say to him.

When we went to lunch I still had my guard up. I'm not sure why, but for some reason I'm feeling very protective of Jackson. I didn't want anybody making fun of him. I hovered over him at the lunch table, sitting right next to him the whole time.

I'm confused about this. I can't understand where this feeling that I have to defend him is coming from. I know we're best friends now, but I still haven't known him for very long.

I was a little nervous too, because we still had to talk about what I said to Claudette.

When I brought the subject up at recess, Jackson was very cool about the whole thing.

"It's alright Veronica, I understand, we're just friends," he said. Then he just dropped the subject saying we don't have to talk about it.

I corrected him. "You and I are more than just friends, we're best friends!" I said this trying to make him feel better, but I fear it didn't help.

When I got home after school my mother wasn't home yet. I tried asking Mémé when Mom was coming home but she said she didn't know. Then I asked her if my mother left a phone number for me so I can call my dad and she hadn't. I figured I'd just wait until she came home to ask her but she didn't come home until eight. She said her boss asked her to stay late, and there was no point in her giving me the number now because I have to go to bed. I don't know what she's thinking. Does she think if she avoids giving me the number I'll just forget about it and stop asking? Well I won't forget, I love my father and I will be asking her for the number again. If that doesn't work, I'll just call information when no one is looking. I do know how to use the phone.

Mémé tried so hard to convince me I needed to bring cupcakes to school for my birthday on Tuesday, but no matter how hard she tried, I refused. There was no way I was gonna give that girl or her little so-called friends cupcakes. They can live without them. Maybe I'll bring cupcakes next year if they're not in my class.

Mémé did make a nice dinner for me for my birthday. I asked for spaghetti for dinner and that's exactly what I got. She made me a cake, too. I'm bringing some in for lunch tomorrow to share with Jackson.

Mom came home and actually ate dinner with us. She gave me a card with twenty dollars in it. "Veronica, you can be so difficult to shop for, so I thought you might like to buy yourself something instead this year," she said. I was so surprised.

As time went on, I began to notice a few things about Jackson. The first thing I noticed was that a lot of the kids at school don't talk to him.

Pretty much no one. I watch, and I can see, they avoid him. The ones that do talk to him never say or do anything nice. I have found that it's not just Claudette calling him freak. A lot of the boys are doing it too. The kids here don't seem to like me much either (not that I care) but they don't pick on me the same way they pick on Jackson.

The second thing I noticed is that Jackson never sticks up for himself. Whenever anyone does things to Jackson he just takes it. I've seen kids trip him in the hall, they push him, flick him in the head, they knock stuff out of his hands, call him names, and he never does anything about it. I saw one kid take his snack, and I was the one who had to yell at that kid.

The day I first met Jackson, he had told me how nice everyone was here. I wonder now, who was he talking about? He couldn't have been talking about any of these kids. Because from what I can see, he had no friends until I came.

The third thing that I noticed, (and this is the one thing that really bothers me) is that he seems so scared all the time. The look that comes into his eyes when the kids here say or do anything to him is the look of real fear. He just freezes and shuts down, taking whatever mean thing the kids are doing to him. I worry about where this comes from.

When he comes over to my house on Saturdays, Jackson is a totally different kid then when he is at school. He plays all kinds of games. He loves to roller skate, and has a wild imagination. One day over the winter Mémé talked us into playing in the snow. That lasted for about ten minutes for the both of us.

He brings over spaceships, his GI Joes, his toy cars; last weekend he brought over his Legos. He never cares if we play with any of my toys or his. He's just a bright and happy kid.

And he's so smart, too. I have found that school work is easy for him. He gets A's and B's on everything. A lot of times we will sit and do homework together. He helps me anytime I get stuck on anything.

I really wish the other kids at school could see what I see in Jackson.

I've also noticed he doesn't talk to me about much. I've told him secret after secret. I've told him everything about me, about my father, all the stuff that happened in San Francisco with my mother, the way I feel and see things, and so far, he's told me very little about his home life. I've tried to get him to tell me about some of the bullying that happens at school, but he never does, he never talks. He just changes the subject trying to avoid talking about it.

The worst part is that I'm worrying about him all the time and I can't stop. After he goes home after playing with me all day on Saturdays, or he's not in school, that's when it's the worst. I can hardly eat, and I've been losing a lot of sleep worrying that he will be okay. When I do finally see him it's such a relief. Because it feels like I've been holding my breath the whole time, and I can finally breathe.

CHAPTER 9

I was still swaying with Harmony long after the music box stopped. I stood back to look at her. "I was a fat geek!" I chuckled.

She smiled kindly, and caressed my cheek. "I never saw you that way."

"Thank you. I'm more than grateful. I'm still in awe that I could ever be this lucky to be with someone as beautiful as you are," I replied.

"You are just as wonderful to me, inside and out."

"That Claudette girl sounds like she was horrible."

Harmony chuckled. "She bordered on difficult."

I tightened my arm around her and smiled, gently and carefully leaning her back to dip her. I pulled her in close pressing her up against me. Her eyes were glowing. I was impressed with myself how well I managed to do that with my current handicap.

"You know it's funny," I began. "It seems so natural to be doing this. Dancing with you like this, I mean."

"That's because you do this all the time. You're always dancing with me, even when there is no music."

She chuckled. "I'm always wondering what's going on inside your mind while we dance. If maybe you have songs in your head or something."

I leaned in and pressed my lips to hers, breathing in her intoxicating floral scent. I could feel it traveling through my entire body awakening my soul. I pulled away slightly hovering just above her lips so I could speak when the answer to that suddenly entered my mind.

"There isn't a song. You are my Harmony," I replied softly.

The doorbell rang and I groaned. "There hasn't been a single person here all week, and they pick today of all days to show up!" I complained.

"It's alright. I'm not going to interfere with anything. I'll be like a flower on the wall," she replied.

"You, my dear, can interfere with anything you like," I assured her.

She affectionately kissed my lips. "I can't, I'm not supposed to."

"Well, how do I introduce you then?" I asked.

"You don't. They won't be able to hear or see me. Only you can."

I sighed when the doorbell rang again. "Hang on, I'm coming!" I yelled out. I smiled at her. "I hope I can get rid of whoever that is quickly. I don't want to waste any time I have with you." I grabbed my crutches and started making my way to the door.

"Curt, I'll be right back," Harmony said quickly, before vanishing into thin air.

When I opened the door, my sister came barging in. "Mom and Dad are on their way here."

I quickly shut the door behind her. "Why? What did I do?"

Mary moved her sunglasses from her eyes to the top of her head. "Nothing, you know how Mom is. She's worried you can't take care of yourself."

I narrowed my brows at her. "I can take care of myself just fine," I stated.

"Really? Then why are your dishes all over the table still?" She smirked.

"Because the crutches and the cast slow me down. Quick, help me clear the table before they get here." Mary and I got to work clearing the table and loading the dishwasher. I sighed in relief that we cleaned up before our parents got here and were finally able to sit down.

"So, what's up with you?" Mary asked when we sat down at the table.

I glanced back at her funny. "Nothing, why?"

"You just seem happy today," she commented.

"Can't a guy be happy?" I asked back.

"Not you. You're never this happy." She waved a dismissive hand at me. "Don't go acting all surprised like you don't know what I'm talking about either. I've noticed how miserable you've been. You can hide it from

Mom and Dad, but you know you can't hide it from me."

"You've always been perceptive. You're right, I was pretty miserable for a while." I smiled and shook my head a bit. "Let's just say, the accident has brought a little 'harmony' into my life." I chuckled to myself on the inside about my reply. If she only knew how true that statement was.

She glanced back at me funny. "Well, I guess that's good." She sighed. "So, Mom and Dad have me filling in for you at work," she began, changing the subject.

I love my little sister, all five feet two inches of her. Unlike most brother and sisters, she and I have always gotten along. I can tell her things and she doesn't judge me. Of course, I've always done the same for her, and we have come to each other's defense a few times at school. She and I share the same color dark brown hair, only she likes to lighten hers. And unlike the other people in my life, she knows, just ask me about something once and then leave it alone. Dwelling on stuff just gets on my nerves.

"That's good. How's that going?"

"I have some bad news. Don't get mad at me, okay," she started.

"Okay..." I prompted.

She ducked a little before she spoke. "I had to fire your receptionist."

"What?! Why?!" I was shocked. Okay, not really. My receptionist has always been great, but she did have a tendency to not show up every once in a while. I know I should have fired her long ago, but I was just way too depressed to even care. Besides, she made decent coffee.

"Because, she barely did anything, and then she didn't show up for two days. What choice did I have?" Mary replied.

I sighed. "So, who's answering the phones now?"

"I've been doing it, but don't worry, I hired a temp agency. They are sending someone in starting next week."

"Okay, good."

My doorbell rang and my sister and I exchanged a glance.

"Do me a favor," I started. "Help me make this visit brief."

"What do I get for helping you?" she asked.

"What do you want?"

"*Hmmm…*" She was drumming her fingers on the table and glanced up at the ceiling thinking for a moment. "…how about your new MP3?"

I groaned. I just bought that but I was desperate to make this visit go quickly. "Fine, it's yours, just get them out of here."

"Why? Gotta hot date?" she teased.

"Mary, shut up, and just help me," I barked back.

"Don't worry, I'll do it."

"Thank you." I sighed in relief.

"Love ya, big brother," she said, as she got up to answer my door.

"Yeah, love you too."

My mother came charging in with her arms full of grocery bags. My father trailed behind carrying some too.

My mother set down the bags on the counter. "I figured since you're a little handicapped at the moment you probably needed some things from the store."

I smiled at her. "Thanks Mom, you didn't have to do that."

She walked over to me and grabbed me by my cheeks. "Yes, I did. I can't let one of my babies starve." She kissed my cheek. I saw my sister smirking and rolling her eyes behind her back. I had a hard time holding back the laughter.

I'm sure I was beet red. "Mom, I'm twenty-four. I haven't been a baby in quite a while."

"You and your sister will always be my babies," she replied happily. "Want me to cook you some dinner?" She started taking food out of the bags.

"Mom, he already ate," my sister commented trying to earn her new MP3 player.

"Oh, you did?" My mother looked a little disappointed.

"Yeah, sorry, Mom. If I had realized you were coming over I would have waited," I added. I even tried pouting a little.

"I know I should have called and checked first. I just thought you might be having a hard time taking care of yourself with that cast and the crutches."

"I'm doing okay, Mom. Showering is a pain, but everything else isn't that bad."

"Are you sure you're alright?" she asked.

I smiled at her. "Yes I'm sure. But if I need anything I'll make sure I call you first, okay?"

"Dawn, give the boy some credit. He's a grown man for crying out loud," my father butted in.

"I can at lease put away the groceries we bought for him," she said sounding defeated.

"Go ahead," my father replied waving her off. "Did your sister tell you, she fired Brenda?" he continued, as he sat down at the table.

"Yeah, and I'm a little disappointed. Who's gonna make my coffee now?" I said trying to make a joke. "Thanks to Mary, I have to make it myself."

My father narrowed his eyes at me. "Did you just make a joke?" he asked sounding surprised.

His question struck me kind of funny. "Yeah, why?"

"I'm not complaining. You just don't usually."

"Well, I felt like joking. I was trying to make light of the fact I'll have to put up with temps for a while." I glared over at my sister.

"Curt, I did you a favor. That girl was useless. When you come back to work just hire someone permanent if you want. Only this time, hire someone who actually does work."

"You're funny," I replied sarcastically. When my father turned around, I glared at my sister and nodded my head towards our parents. I then quickly put my fingers up to my ears swaying a little reminding her of the prize. Then as soon as my father started to turn back around, I quickly dropped my hands down.

Mary cleared her throat. "You know, Mom, I haven't eaten yet. How about since Curt already ate the three of us go out to eat tonight?"

My mother perked up. "What would you suggest? Italian or Chinese? There is that little place in town your dad's been wanting to go to. You know, that little steak place."

"*Oooh*...steak sounds good," Mary replied happily. She took my father's hand. "Dad, you wanna go get steak tonight?"

"Sounds good to me," he replied. "Curt are you sure you're not hungry or anything? You know you can come with us."

"I'm good, Dad, really. I'm totally stuffed from earlier, thanks anyway."

My mother leaned over and gave me a hug and kissed my cheek. "I love you honey. I'll see you in a couple of days."

"Okay, I love you too, Mom," I replied. "Bye, Dad." I watched as both of my parents headed out the door.

Mary walked over with a smug smile and leaned in a little. "I believe that is a new record for me." She chuckled. "You can hand over the player at any time."

"I'll give it to you soon. I owe you." Mary and I bumped knuckles before she followed out the door after our parents.

I sat back in the kitchen chair sighing relief when the door finally shut. As soon as I did, I felt someone's fingers combing through my hair tilting my head back. Her lips met mine and I moaned in relief.

How will I get through the rest of my life without this?

She pulled away slightly. "Did you miss me?" she asked.

"Duh." I smiled at her. "Where did you go?"

"My guide asked me to step out for a moment. So, I went home quick to change my clothes."

I took her hand and pulled her around in front of me so I could see. She was wearing a bright yellow snug-fitting cotton top that hugged her body and outlined her bust nicely, and a pair of black denim jeans.

"I was rather fond of the tie-dye, but you look beautiful."

"Thank you," she said smiling.

"So why did your guide ask you to step out?"

"He was afraid I might interfere while your guests were here."

"I can't see how you would."

"He was afraid that if I recognized any of them I might slip and say so."

"Oh, you can't do that?"

"No."

"Why not?"

"Because it would ruin the lessons you're here to learn," she replied.

"Oh."

She sat down on my lap and placed her arms around my neck. "You know what I can tell you though?"

I wound my arms around her waist. "What?"

"How happy I am to see you." She pressed her lips against my neck and was slowly running them up and down to my collarbone. That action set the shockwaves off, sending them surging throughout my body, making my breathing ragged and my body crave her.

I suddenly realized I was in an odd predicament and I wasn't sure what to do about it. I want her. I *need* her. I don't know how long this life might be, and just the thought of going fifty plus years waiting for her is a painful thought. She is supposed to be more to me than just my wife, right? She also seems to have some limitations on what she's allowed to do while she's here. *Oh God*, I wonder if that's something that's only done on Earth? How do I even approach this?

She stopped running her lips along my collarbone and looked up at my face. "Are you alright?" she asked.

I choked a little before I could speak. "I'm fine," I replied.

She raised an eyebrow. "You're awfully quiet."

I decided to suck it up and just ask her. "I was wondering about something."

She was casually running her fingers up and down my arms and my chest driving me crazy.

She smiled at me. "Wondering about what?" she asked.

I began stuttering a little. "D-d-do we ever… A-a-are we allowed to? …up there?"

She had a coy smile and was playfully kicking her feet. "What do you think the answer to that is?" she asked. She leaned in molding her soft full lips to mine intensely, forcing my brain into a meltdown. She slowly moved her lips, kissing me right up under my ear. I could feel her warm breath against my neck making my heart pound loudly. Her kisses were twisting and turning my nerves, putting them on edge. I almost couldn't form coherent thoughts smart enough sounding to even answer that. I took in a deep breath and let it out slowly before trying to answer her.

I held my eyes closed so I could speak. "I'm thinking we do." I opened one eye to peek at her.

"Duh," she replied grinning.

I laughed and let out a sigh of relief when I heard her reply. "Good."

"Why don't we go back to your room and I'll tell you more of our story," she suggested. She got up from my lap and started heading down the hall towards my bedroom. I grabbed my crutches and got to my feet quickly trailing after her.

"Harmony," I began when we entered my room. I was trying to continue our conversation from the kitchen.

She turned around. "Yes, my love?" she replied. I felt my heart thump against my ribs when she said that.

"I was wondering something else." She stood there smiling at me patiently waiting for me to continue. "Is there any limits on what you can do with me?" Wow, I can't remember the last time I felt so nervous.

She narrowed her brows at me. "Limits?" She seemed confused.

I moved in a little closer. "Well, yeah... Are we... *limited*? Would doing anything with me interfere?" I spoke very softly trying to hide how nervous I was.

"Oh." Rose colored her cheeks and a soft smile spread across her beautiful face as she caught up to where I was. "I can only affect you and nothing more. Making love is okay."

I sighed in relief quickly moving in closer to her. I dropped the crutches hastily, both of them making a low thud when they hit the carpeted floor. I took her tightly in my arms molding my lips to hers, kissing her passionately, breathing in her heavenly floral scent. I was combing my fingers into her hair pressing myself against her, pushing her backwards toward the bed.

I moved my hands down from her hair, trailing my fingers down her frame to her waist and I felt her quiver. I could feel her tracing her fingers along the skin on my arms. I ran my fingers just under the hem of her shirt feeling the soft smooth skin along her back. I pulled away slightly and waited a moment for her to open her eyes. When she finally looked up, my breath caught. I was trembling, staring deep into the depth of her alluring wide brown eyes. I lifted her shirt up over her head and tossed it gently to the floor.

"I love you, Harmony," I told her.

"I love you too," she replied.

* * *

Jack and I watched as Harmony reached over and turned off the bedside lamp. The lighting in the room we were watching them in from the waterfilled crater became dim. Jack waved his hand over the pool to turn down the sound and give them a bit of privacy. No, we don't watch *everything*.

He looked up at me. His brows narrowed with doubt. "I'm not so sure this was the best idea anymore."

I crossed my arms in anticipation of the argument that typically comes from him. We differ greatly in our guiding methods, and since Harmony and Kaleb interact on a regular basis we bump heads often.

"Why, not?" I asked him. My tone was a bit defensive.

Jack raised a brow and pointed towards the crater. "Look at what they're doing right now. How will doing *that* guide Kaleb to learn why they are different?"

"She has already made progress. Haven't you been paying attention? He's been hanging on every word she has spoken. We're gonna have to trust that Harmony knows what she's doing with him and give her some time."

"Perhaps we should have given this a time limit," he suggested.

"Maybe." I couldn't completely disagree. "For now, we'll keep an eye on them, and in the meantime, we'll try to come up with a solution in the off chance he doesn't learn what he and Harmony are. I have faith in her when it comes to him though. Can't you see it? Their connection is quite strong."

Jack let out an awkward chuckle. "They're definitely different." He became quiet, pausing for a moment as he glanced down at the water. He seemed to be deep in thought and then he let out a noticeable sigh. "I'm sorry, Luke," he said suddenly before glancing back up at me with remorse in his eyes. "I should have taken your advice about Kaleb. I always thought the existence of extreme souls like them was a myth. I can see it in him now and I'm embarrassed that I missed it. If I had listened, none of this would have been necessary."

I smiled and gave him a firm pat on his shoulder, with a tad too much force judging by the way he launched forward suddenly, so it ended up being more of a shove. *Whoops.* "You're forgiven, buddy."

* * *

She was laughing. "You were so funny... *Do we have limits.*"

It was evening now. We were lying intertwined in my cozy bed, warmed by our body heat after the best night of my life. Being with Harmony was unlike anything I've ever experienced before. Once we began I couldn't focus on anything else except for loving her. The way my body was reacting against her skin was extraordinary. It was as if time had stopped and we were in a whole other dimension. It's no wonder I've been so miserable. My subconscious knew what my brain didn't. I was missing my other half.

I tightened my arms around her pulling her snug up against me. I couldn't help laughing along with her. "I didn't know. It's not like I know all of the rules or anything. I didn't want to do anything wrong."

"Like us doing that is wrong," she replied. I could hear her smiling.

"Some people would disagree."

"It's not wrong if you are in love and you are committed to each other," she said.

"Good." I sighed in relief. "I feel like you and I do this a lot at home."

She was tracing the plains of my chests with her finger before she spoke. "Yes."

My whole body tingled when she said that. "Harmony, what is our home like?" I asked her, changing the subject a little. "Do we have a house?"

"We have a home, but it is not a house," she said.

I was intrigued. "What kind of home do we have then?"

"You and I live in a forest," she replied.

I was a bit baffled. I was trying to understand how exactly we live there. "A forest? How does that work?"

"What do you mean?"

"How do we shower? Do we have a bed? Do other souls come hiking through at times? I'll bet that would be a little awkward."

She laughed. "No one walks through. Do people walk through your apartment?"

"No."

"Our place has all of the privacy your apartment does, plus it's pretty."

"It sounds nice. What about showering? Do we bathe in a creek?"

She laughed at me again. "No, we have a washroom, and before you ask, yes we have a bed. It's a hammock strung between two pine trees."

"That sounds nice. I'll bet you and I are in that a lot."

"No, I wouldn't say that."

"We're not?" With what we were just talking about before, I couldn't help sounding surprised.

"No."

"Then where are we usually?"

"There is a large flat rock that is up against a big oak tree by our stream. We are usually there. We rarely bother with the bed."

I was kind of in awe at myself. The freedom we must feel from making love that way must be incredible. I pressed my face into her hair breathing her in. "I wish I could remember," I whispered.

"You will, when you get home," she said.

I took in a breath, deciding to change the subject. There is no use in dwelling on things we cannot control. "So, are you going to tell me more about that last life or are you just gonna keep me hanging?"

"I told you I would. I was just spending some much-needed quality time with you before I have to go home."

I gently kissed her lips breathing her in. "And I love you for it."

Chapter 10

"It was just another typical Saturday," she began.

It's April, and the weatherman had said it was supposed to be warm today. Yay! I was excited. Jackson and I can finally play outside. His mom normally drops him off around eleven, and I couldn't wait.

My mother does seem to be trying to change. I haven't noticed her drinking, and her job seems to be going well. She's a receptionist at an insurance office. She said she answers the phones and she does all the filing. She has been working a lot and saving her money. She's staying late a lot at work and she's even been working on the weekends! She keeps talking about us getting our own place. I don't understand why we can't just stay here with Mémé and Grandpa. I didn't think they minded us being here.

In her free time, Mom has been taking Katie to piano lessons and she even took her to a few talent agencies. She says a kid with a gift like Katie has should be in the spotlight. That's where Mom and Katie went this morning, to meet with an agent. Katie had an interview in New Haven. Then, I guess Mom has to work tonight.

I'm so proud of her.

Because of the nice weather, I was in such a great mood, and I was eager for Jackson to come over. The closer it got to eleven, the more often I was checking outside to see if he was here yet.

"You know, a watched pot never boils," Grandpa said. He was sitting at the kitchen table putting his shoes on. The resort employees were starting today, getting everything ready for the tourist season, which starts next weekend.

"Uh, what?" I said, I was a little distracted. I didn't hear what he had said.

"I said, a watched pot never boils. It's an expression. It means the more you keep watching for something, the longer it will take for it to happen."

"Oh." I thought about what Grandpa just said. "I'm bored, Grandpa. I just want Jackson to hurry up and get here so we can play outside."

"He'll be here soon, so try to be patient. Why don't you go find something to do for now, while you wait for him."

I left the kitchen frustrated. "Ugh!" I stomped my way into the living room and turned on the TV. *Journey to the Center of the Earth* was still on, so I just plopped myself down on the plastic covered couch and pretended to watch it. About halfway through *King Kong*,

I looked over at the clock. It was quarter after; I went and looked out the window and still no Jackson. He's always here by now, and I became even more restless. I turned off the TV and went upstairs to my room. I tossed myself backwards on my bed. Where is he? I wondered.

I grabbed my jump rope from my toy box, and decided to just go play outside anyway. That way we can get right to playing when he shows up.

I went outside and the sun was bright and warm. I looked up at the sky, closed my eyes, and faced the sun, just like I used to do all the time when I lived in California. I love doing that, the sunlight shines through your lids and all you can see is red.

I skipped rope for a while. I like doing that. I'm pretty good at it. I can jump for a long time without tripping up on the rope. I can even cross my arms. I think it's a talent.

Mémé walked by with the wheelbarrow and smiled at me. "It's nice to finally see you playing outside," she said.

"I'm waiting for Jackson still, what time is it?"

Mémé looked at her watch. "It's five after twelve," she said. "Maybe his mother didn't have to work today."

"Maybe," I sighed. I was disappointed.

"If that was the case, it would have been nice of her to let us know." She patted my shoulder. "They're probably just running late today," she added before walking away.

I know she just said that trying to make me feel better.

Just then a car pulled up in front. It was old and rusty, dark smoke was pouring from the tailpipe. Jackson was sitting in the front seat next to a man. I've never actually seen him before, so I could only assume that it was his father. I became so excited I ran towards the car. I stopped suddenly when I caught sight of Jackson's dad.

Jackson's father was ragged and dirty. I'm not sure he's heard of soap, or a toothbrush. When he smiled his teeth were the color of coffee. I couldn't tell exactly what color his hair was either because of how dirty he was, but it seems to be a light brown.

He turned to face Jackson, leaning back against the door, and he lit a cigarette. He looked up at me and smiled wide. "*So...this must be your little girlfriend,*" he said loudly.

Jackson sat there in the front seat in that familiar frozen pose that I was used to. He didn't move, and he didn't speak.

"Now, Jackson, you never told me how pretty your girlfriend is." He started to laugh, and he slapped Jackson on the shoulder. It didn't seem like he hit him that hard, but I saw Jackson wince like it really hurt, but he never made a sound.

"Your mother will be by to pick you up when she's done with work." Jackson still didn't move yet. "Well go on now, go play with your little girlfriend. Don't keep her waiting." He winked at me.

Jackson finally stepped out of the car, and closed the door. "Bye, Dad."

"Have fun with your little girlfriend, *son*." He spoke loudly again, his body shaking with laughter.

We both stood there quietly as he put the car in gear and we watched him drive away.

I didn't know what to say at first. I just stood there and I didn't say anything. Jackson took a deep breath and exhaled, and then he turned around to face me. "So, what do you want to play today?" he asked. His smile was forced.

"Um, we can go in the back and play on the playground," I suggested.

"Okay."

We started walking around to the back of the house. I noticed right away that Jackson wasn't his usual upbeat self. I could plainly see that something was bothering him but I didn't push. I figured he would talk to me when he was ready to.

We did play on the playground for a while. He didn't seem to want to do much, and whenever we climbed anything he kept making funny noises like he was having a hard time.

We were climbing on the jungle gym, and I had let him go down first. When I was looking down watching him, I noticed something dark colored under his shirt by his collar. I suddenly had this nagging feeling that something was very wrong, and I needed to find out what that is on his back.

This kid never talks about anything, and if I want to have any kind of real chance to get anything out of him, I need to make sure there are no adults nearby, just in case I have to yell.

After we had climbed down from the jungle gym, Jackson wandered over to the swings and just sat down. I went over and sat down on the swing next to him, and I had a small plan.

"Do you want to take a walk with me?" I began. "There's a stream in the back of the resort and we could go exploring."

Jackson was staring at his feet and he was kicking the dirt. "I don't know if I feel like going exploring," he said.

"C'mon Jackson," I smiled and nudged his shoulder, "...you know you want to." I was pouring on the charm and he started to smile. "It will be lots of fun. You can make up the game." I leaned my head on his shoulder. "*Please*...go for a walk with me, I'll be your bestest friend forever."

He glanced at me and smiled. "I thought you already were?" he asked.

"Yes, but then I will love you, even more!" I took his hand, and was gently taunting him, pulling his arm. "C'mon, Sackson... Let's go walking down by the stream." He got up from the swing smiling, but I could tell he really didn't want to. "*You know you want to.*"

I held his hand as we started to walk down to the stream.

We passed by Grandpa on the way. "Hey, where are you two going?" Grandpa asked.

"We're just going for a walk Grandpa, we won't go too far," I replied.

He chuckled. "Just stay out of trouble."

On the way down to the stream, I was trying to figure out what I was going to say to him. As far as I was concerned this kid was gonna spill his guts to me whether he liked it or not.

I let go of his hand when we reached the water's edge. When Jackson sat down I got another glimpse down the back of his shirt, this time it was a better one and I gasped. I went ahead and lifted up the back of his shirt. His back was covered in dark blue and yellowing blotches.

"Jackson what happened?!" Something inside me felt like it just burst. Jackson yanked his shirt back down.

"Don't do that!" he snapped at me, and I flinched.

I knelt down beside him. "What happened to your back?!" I demanded.

He turned his head away from me. "I fell."

"You fell? I fall all the time and my back doesn't look like that."

"Well, I did."

"Jackson, aren't we best friends?" I asked him.

"Yes."

"Didn't we swear to tell each other everything, and keep each other's secrets?"

He sighed. "Yes."

"Well so far I've told you everything about me. I've even told you about things no one else knows. Do you know why I did?"

"Why?"

"I did it because you are my best friend, and I love you. I trust you with my secrets, you swore on your soul, and I know you keep them." I put my hand on his shoulder. "You know I swore on my soul too. I promised to keep all your secrets and you haven't told me any. I know there are things bothering you, I can tell. No one else knows you like I do, and I'm worrying about you. You really can trust me. I promise you, I will never tell anyone what you tell me, and I will never make fun of you."

He curled his knees in and laid his head down. "You're the only one," he said.

"I'm sorry about that, Jackson," I told him. I felt so bad for him. I didn't know what else to say.

"I've just been afraid that after a while, you would just end up being like the rest of the kids," he admitted.

"Well as you can plainly see, I am nothing like the rest of the kids. I think for myself, and do my own thing. I always have."

"You certainly do."

"That's another thing I want to talk to you about. When the kids at school pick on you, why don't you ever stick up for yourself?" I asked.

"I don't know."

"You know, you can't always ignore them. That doesn't always work. You need to stop letting kids push you around all the time. You need to fight them back."

"I can't."

"Why not?"

"Because I'm scared," he whispered.

"What are you so scared of?" I asked him. I shrugged. "They're just kids like us."

"That's easy for you to say."

"Why do think that?" I asked him.

"Because you're braver than me, and you're not scared of the other kids like I am."

"Wait a minute... You think I'm not scared?"

"You are?" he questioned. He sounded surprised.

"Uh, yeah, of course I am."

"Then how do you do it? How can you just yell back at them?" he asked.

"I use it. I take the panic that I start to feel, and instead of letting it win, I breathe it in. Then I use it to push out of my mouth whatever comes to my mind. I don't really know how else to describe how I do that."

He looked like he was deep in thought. "I think I understand you."

I smiled at him. "Plus, most of the stuff with the kids happens at school. How much can they possibly do back to me there if I stick up for myself?"

"They can beat you up."

"True, they could. But most of them won't, most of the kids are all talk. You've seen me yell at them, do they try to beat me up?"

"No."

"See, Jackson. My father used to say, you should never make fun of others or start fights and that I should always try to be the better person and try to walk away every chance I get. But that isn't always possible, and if I do get into a situation that I can't walk away from, that I should defend myself however I have to, and to make that other kid sorry they ever messed with me. He said I'll never feel bad about myself if I go down fighting." Jackson was quiet. I could tell he was thinking about what I had said.

"Now quit stalling, and tell me what happened to your back."

A tear trickled down his cheek and he turned away from me resting his head on his knees. "My dad was mad at me, and he hit me with the kitchen chair, and then he threw it at me."

I clenched my fists. It took me a moment before I could answer. "Why?" I didn't want to reveal to him how upset I was.

"He was supposed to bring me here today for Mom, because she had to go to work and he needed the car. After he dropped her off, we went home. He forgot to bring me here. I asked him if he could, and he got upset because I didn't remind him when we were in the car still."

"Is that all?" I asked him through my teeth.

"That's what happened today. He's always mad at me, I can't ever do anything right. He hits my mom too, they're always fighting. She's trying to save up money to get us away from him. I don't know what's wrong with me."

I couldn't believe what I was hearing, and I thought I had it bad. I wish there was something I could do to help him. All I wanted to do was scoop him up and hide him away somewhere where no one could find him.

How do I protect him from this?

"Maybe we could talk to Mémé and your mom, and see if you can sleep over," I suggested. I put my arms around him, and I rested my head against his. I would sleep better tonight if he was here.

"I want you to listen to me right now. Promise me you will hear every word I say."

He just nodded his head.

"You are very good. I've never met another person in this world better than you are. There is absolutely nothing wrong with you, and I know this for a fact. I will always be your friend. And you're not quite the scaredy cat you claim to be. Do I really need to remind you that you were the one who introduced yourself to me before any of the other kids did? You were very brave my first day."

I went on. "I've learned most adults are stupid and mean, and you can't trust them. If your mom can't get the money to get you guys out of there, you and I can just run away."

He looked up at me. "You would run away with me?" He sounded surprised. How could he really be surprised at this point?

"Of course, I would. Just say when, and we'll go. We can go tonight if you want. I told you, we're best friends and I love you."

"You do?" He looked surprised.

I smiled at him. "Yeah."

"I love you too, Veronica."

"No more being afraid at school. That is certainly one place you don't have to be." I started chuckling. "Do you know how funny it would be to see the look on Claudette's face if you yelled back at her? She'd probably wet her pants." We both giggled.

"Wanna go see if Mémé will let us have a few cookies?" I suggested trying to cheer him up.

"That sounds good." He smiled.

We got up and walked back towards the house. "Mémé, can we have cookies?" I asked her on the way in.

"Go ahead and help yourself," she said.

"Can Jackson sleep over tonight?" I asked.

Mémé gave me a funny look and shook her head. "No."

"Can I go sleep over at his house?" I tried a different path.

"No, that's not allowed either," she said.

I was confused. "Why?"

"Because, boys and girls can't have sleepovers," she replied.

"Why not?" I asked. I was still very confused by this.

"Veronica, they just don't. I'm sorry, it's just not proper for boys and girls to have sleepovers."

I grabbed Jackson's hand and sulked all the way into the house, stomping my feet. I was so mad. How am I gonna watch over him tonight if he can't sleep over? And I don't get what the big deal is. Why can't Jackson and I have a sleepover? It doesn't make any sense.

Jackson and I went back outside to play after our snack. We went back to the playground, and this time we just played on the swings. I could tell he was feeling better because he was laughing, and because he now had a light in his green eyes.

This did make me feel better in a way. It was good to see him like this. He's definitely a lot more fun. But that nagging feeling in my gut that something was wrong here just wouldn't stop, and the closer it got to the time his mother usually picks him up the worse it got.

When Jackson's mother pulled into the driveway I panicked, and I grabbed his hand. "C'mon Jackson!" I pulled him hard and we ran down to the stream and ducked behind a tree.

Mémé was calling us. "Veronica! Jackson!" she called out. "Joan is here! You need to come in now! It's time for Jackson to go home!"

I was really freaking out now, and I started to cry. I squeezed Jackson's hand. "I don't want you to go."

"I don't want to go either, but I have to."

I stomped my foot. "It's really stupid that you can't sleep over," I told him.

"I know, but don't worry, I'll see you Monday at school."

I just nodded, and hung my head down.

"Veronica?"

I looked up at him. Without warning he kissed me right on my lips. It wasn't like the kisses adults do, it was just a peck. It surprised me though, and I wasn't sure what to do. For once, I was the frozen one.

"It's time for me to go home now," he said softly.

His mother stood there patiently by the car. We walked hand in hand, neither of us saying anything.

"Hello, Veronica. Did you two have a nice afternoon?" she asked.

I just nodded my head. I was still a little dazed. She held her arms out to Jackson and as always, he went straight into her arms.

"Friday, I don't have to work. So how about I take both of you skating, and then to a movie. As long as it's alright with your mother."

Jackson was the first to speak. "That sounds like a great idea. Veronica, do you think it will be okay with your mom?"

"I'd kick up a fit if it wasn't," I said seriously.

Joan laughed and cupped my chin. "Veronica, you're always so funny."

How is that funny? I thought to myself. It's true.

She turned to Jackson. "Go get in the car, Sweetie, it's time to go."

Jackson hugged me.

"See you Monday," I said, as I hugged him back.

"I'll wait for you on the blacktop," he replied.

It was so hard to wake up Monday morning. Mom came in to wake me up, and she flicked on the lights. "Time to get up!" she yelled.

I saw how dark it was through the crack in the shade, and I wanted to slap her. I turned over throwing the sheets over my head. "It's not time to get up yet!" I yelled.

My mother came back in. "Yes, it is. It's dark because it's raining. Now get up, Veronica!"

I felt like I was dressing in my sleep, I was still so tired. Why is it always so hard to wake up when it's raining? And why won't it rain like this on days that I don't have to wake up so early?

Mémé was nice enough to get up a little bit early this morning (I can't tell you how she did it) to make pancakes. They were so delicious, I ate three.

Katie and I put on our rain boots. I grabbed my umbrella and then I handed her hers as we were heading out the door.

"You know what they say?" I asked Katie as we put our hoods up. "April showers, bring May flowers." She didn't seem very amused by the rhyme. Katie and I walked by ourselves to the bus stop, and we splashed in a few puddles on the way. We were soaked by the time the bus arrived.

On the way to school, I began to think about what had happened on Saturday right before Jackson left. I had butterflies in my stomach and a million questions on my mind.

What did that kiss mean? Why did he do it? Are we still best friends? Are we boyfriend and girlfriend now? Does he like me that way? What do I do when I see him? What will I say? I guess I won't know any of those answers until I get to school. I wasn't sure what to think or even worse, what I really wanted.

Because of the rain we would be having indoor recess today, which was fine by me; it was still a little chilly in the mornings here. When I got inside the cafeteria, I looked around for Jackson, but I didn't see him. I spent that whole time before the bell rang walking around the cafeteria looking for my friend. When the bell rang I spent the walk down to the classroom arguing with myself about where he might be, and what will I say when I see him. Maybe he's already down in our classroom? But he waits for me every morning. Maybe he's sick? I wondered. But he seemed okay on Saturday.

When I entered the classroom, I saw Jackson's seat was empty and I sighed. Where is he? I need to talk to him, I thought to myself. I put my stuff in the closet and went to sit down at my desk. Maybe he'll come in late, he's done that before. That's probably it! He's running late. I'm sure he'll be here soon then.

Claudette interrupted my worrying. "So, where's your boyfriend?"

I rolled my eyes and sighed. "I don't know."

"Shouldn't a girlfriend know where her boyfriend is?"

"Why can't you just shut up?" I snapped at her.

"*Wow*. You're grouchy this morning," she replied with her snotty tone.

Claudette shut up when Mrs. Coleman came in. She wrote the date on the blackboard: Monday April 17, 1967, and then sat down at her desk and began to take attendance.

"Mary?"

"Here."

"Charles?"

"Here."

"James?"

"Here."

"Jackson?" She looked up from her paper. "Okay, so no Jackson this morning."

She went through the rest of the class, and took the hot lunch count. Usually, if he was running late he would have been here by now. After Mrs. Coleman got the attendance and the hot lunch count she called my name. "Veronica?"

"Yes, Mrs. Coleman?" I answered.

"It would have been Jackson's turn today to take the lunch count down to the cafeteria and hand in the attendance sheet to the office, but since he's not here, why don't you do it today."

"Okay." I got up from my seat and took the papers from Mrs. Coleman.

"Make sure you hand in the lunch count first," she said.

"Alright," I replied.

I walked out of the classroom and went down the hall to the cafeteria. I had to pass by the front entrance to the school to get there. When I looked out the doors I saw two police cars parked out front, but I didn't see any policemen in them.

I handed in the lunch count and passed by the doors again. Again, I noticed the police cars, but I still didn't see the policemen until I looked up and saw them through the office window.

The two policemen were standing at the office desk. One had placed his hat on the counter. Out of habit I listened outside the door of the office before I went in.

"Is he going to be alright?" I heard one office lady ask.

"It's too soon to tell, ma'am. He's been taken by ambulance to the hospital, he has sustained serious injuries. The EMT says he is in critical condition," I heard one policeman say.

"And, his mother?"

"She was dead on scene. The paramedics did everything they could."

"What's going to happen to him?"

"He'll be taken into state custody for now. We're trying to locate any family members who are able to take him."

"Oh, that poor thing! To think we had a criminal like that just living among us!"

"Don't worry, the situation is under control now, we have him in custody. Thank you for your help."

"Poor little Jackson!" I heard one of the office lady's cry out.

I stood there outside the door frozen in shock. I knew what I heard, and I knew I had to go into the office but I couldn't make myself move. The policemen left, they walked right by me, and didn't see me.

"I can't believe it!" I heard one office lady say. "How could any father do that? If that poor boy lives he will be without his mother," I heard her continue.

"That boy must have angels watching him! You heard what that policeman said, he missed his heart and lungs by an inch!" I heard another say.

"Cut up his face, too!" I heard someone else say.

"They won't really know how bad his injuries really are until they get him to the hospital."

I made myself walk into the office then. I needed them to stop talking about him. I couldn't take it anymore.

I started shaking uncontrollably and when I walked in my legs stopped working, and I dropped down to the floor, still clutching the attendance sheet. I was suddenly gasping for air and I couldn't breathe. I curled up against the wall. I couldn't stop the pain that now ached through my entire body, and I began to cry.

The ladies in the office tried hard to talk to me, and they called my teacher down. But I just covered my ears, and began screaming. I didn't want to hear anything anymore, and I refused to talk to them.

They called home for me, and soon Mémé and Grandpa both came to take me home. Grandpa scooped me up from the office floor, and Mémé wiped my tears. Both of them were saying, "It will be okay, Veronica," over and over, as they carried me out of the school, and on the ride home.

Grandpa laid me on the couch when we got home, and Mémé put a blanket on me. They just let me lay there and cry. I didn't want to do anything else.

Occasionally at first, everyone was coming in to check on me. But the second anyone laid a hand on me, I couldn't stand the feeling, and I would start screaming and crying again.

They just left me alone after a while, and I just laid there silent.

I spent the rest of the day drifting in and out of sleep. Every time I woke, the pain would start again, and I would cry myself back to sleep. Someone left a tray with a bowl of soup and a sandwich on the coffee table for me. I suspect it was Mémé.

I faced the back of the couch, and I just laid there with my eyes shut. I had my face buried in the cushions. I never wanted to wake again.

It was sometime later that I became aware of muffled voices around me. It was dark now, and I didn't know what time it was. I felt numb, and empty. Even though I had slept for what seemed like an eternity, I still felt tired. What's wrong with me? Was I sick? Did I get hit by a bus or something? I felt odd and out of sorts.

I had been laying there crying on the couch for so long I wasn't sure if I was awake or if I was asleep. Maybe I'm dreaming?

I heard the click of the TV being turned on, and the sound of someone turning the knob to change the channel. I opened my eyes a little, the only light in the room was coming from the television.

"Good evening, and welcome to Action News Eight...
.and we begin with today's top story:

Murder shook the land of the little noises early this
morning....a woman in Moodus is dead tonight and her
son was brutally injured, after police attempted to ap-
prehend a man wanted on weapons and murder charges
from Tampa, Florida...

Police surrounded the home of Jackson Wright, also
known as "The Slug," early this morning... Wright brutally
stabbed his wife and son, while the police were trying to
enter the home... The police apprehended him while he
was trying to turn the knife on himself... Police tell Ac-
tion News Eight the woman was found first upon enter-
ing the home, the little boy was found hiding in his closet
...he has suffered multiple lacerations and is in serious
condition at this hour... Tonight...Wright is being held on
five hundred thousand dollars bond, pending charges...
"

I started to cry again, and I covered my head with
my hands. I closed my eyes tight...*Help*! I'm having a
nightmare and I can't wake up!

I stayed on the couch for the rest of the week. I didn't
want to go to school. I didn't want to go outside, or
play anything. I just couldn't. Mom and Katie left me
alone, and didn't bother me, which was good, because
I would have screamed at them if they did. Those two
know how to get on my nerves.

Mémé was the one who began really bugging me
on Friday. "Veronica, you have to eat more than just

a few bites... Veronica, you have to get up sometime ... Veronica, you can't just live your life on the couch," Blah, blah, blah!

On Saturday, she was like a broken record. "Veronica, you can't do this to yourself... Veronica you have to brush your teeth... Veronica, what do you think Jackson would say if he saw you like this?" That comment made me throw a cup at her. What is wrong with this woman? Does she want to be on the same list as my mom?

Sunday morning, she snapped.

"THAT'S IT!!!" she yelled, storming into the living room. She scooped me up and threw me over her shoulder. That did it! She's on the list now! I was kicking and screaming, but that didn't matter. She held me up on her shoulder all the way up the stairs and planted me in the bathtub. She turned the cold water on me. I was still in my clothes from Monday. I screamed at the top of my lungs at her, and then she startled me—she screamed back. The water was spraying in my face and soaking through my clothes. It was freezing and I was shaking from it, my teeth were chattering.

"Do you think you're the first person in the world that this sort of thing has happened to?!" she shouted with clenched fists. "I know it's horrible...no wait, it's beyond horrible for something like that to happen to your friend! But Sweetie, he's okay. The news said he wasn't dead. So that's a good thing. It's something to be happy about, and isn't that something worth living for?!"

I shook and shivered trying to answer. "Y-y-yes-s."

"Don't you think Jackson would be disappointed if he came back here to visit you and you were a zombie on the couch?"

I sucked in a jagged breath. "Y-y-yes-s."

"Then quit lying around feeling sorry for yourself." She turned the cold water off. "Now, how about you get out of those clothes and take a real shower. I'll go get you your PJ's. When you're done, come and see me, and I'll brush your hair for you."

After I took the hot shower I did feel better. I still felt kind of hollow and numb, but better. I changed into my jammies, grabbed the hair brush, and went downstairs. I found Mémé in the living room.

"I thought you might like some hot cocoa." She pointed to the mugs on the coffee table. She took the brush from me. "Have a seat," she said.

Mémé put my hair behind my shoulders and began pulling the brush through, and it felt nice. I don't remember the last time Mom did this for me. I usually brush my own hair.

"Do you want to talk about anything?" she asked me.

"I don't know."

"Okay," Mémé said. She just stayed quiet, and brushed my hair.

"Jackson's Mom is dead," I said softly. My question came out more like a statement.

Mémé sighed. "Yes," she replied tenderly.

"But Jackson's not?"

"As far as I know he is okay. He was just hurt."

"Is Jackson's father dead?"

Mémé sighed again. "No."

"Where is he?" I held my breath for the answer.

"Oh, he's in jail. That man will be in jail for the rest of his life."

I exhaled. "Good." I was so relieved. Mémé kissed the top of my head. "There, all the knots are out," she said.

I turned and Mémé handed me my cup of cocoa.

"You were a great friend to Jackson," she said. "I honestly believe he will never forget you for that." I sipped my cocoa, and Mémé tucked my wet hair behind my ear. "You'll see him again, Veronica." She lifted my chin up. "So, no more lying around feeling sad. When bad things happen, you cry, you let your feelings out. Then you get up, dust yourself off, and keep going. Life goes on."

I thought about what Mémé said, and it did make a little sense. I've never been the kind of kid to just roll over and die. If that was the case I would have died long ago the first time my mother left us, or when my parents got divorced. I'm tough and I'm a fighter. I went to take a sip of my cocoa and then I noticed my bracelet. I put my cocoa down on the table and ran my finger across the weave feeling the beads. "I'll miss him," I said softly.

Mémé rubbed my back. "He'll miss you too."

When Monday morning finally rolled around, I can't say I was eager to go to school, but I was ready for it. I used some of my time on Sunday night to do my make-up work that Katie was nice enough to bring home for me. I got my book bag together, got my sister, and headed out to the bus stop. It was a nice day today; the sun was bright and glistening off the dew-covered grass, and it was warming up already. I strolled to the bus stop this morning, I was in no rush. The school will still be there. I'm gonna just keep going like Mémé said.

School seemed to be buzzing in the same way it always does when I arrived. The kids were scattering off to the various parts of the playground from their busses, the usual teachers on bus duty.

Everything was the same, life does go on.

As I slowly made my way to the playground I began thinking that things would be just a little different for me this morning.

I won't see him waving by the usual spot he waits for me in the morning. I'll miss that. I'll miss seeing him smile when he would finally spot me in the crowd. I'll miss tripping over and bumping into him on the jungle gym. I'll miss his laugh. Most of all, I'll miss having my best friend.

* * *

"Wow...all of that happened to me?" I asked her.

She was quiet at first. "Yes."

"You weren't kidding when you said my family was worse. I'm glad I can't remember any of it."

"That time was incredibly hard for both of us. But we learned so much from that experience, and thankfully, we don't have to repeat those lessons."

"Why would we have to repeat lessons?" I asked her.

"Sometimes we mess up or we somehow avoid doing what we are supposed to."

"I know this seems like an obvious question, but how can I make sure I don't have to repeat a lesson?"

She placed her hand on my cheek. "Make sure you rise up to meet each challenge life hands you and see them through. And don't try to avoid any problems, face them head on. That's the only way."

"I can do that."

"I know you can. I've seen you do it before." She chuckled. "So do you want to hear a more humorous part to this part of our story?"

"Sure."

"I remember, I was forced to write...."

* * *

Dear Diary,

This is stupid! I don't know how I let anyone talk me into doing this! I can't believe I just wrote dear

diary like one of those stupid weirdo girls! Hopefully this is the only diary entry I'll ever write, I hate this.

Mémé is making me write this, as my punishment for getting suspended from school for two days for fighting. She said this part isn't my whole punishment, but is required if I want to keep this from my mother. "She's never here anyway. She'll never even realize you've missed any school." I was beginning to doubt Mémé after that whole music box thing, and her telling me I had to be nice to my mother because she felt bad. I guess, I can't really argue with her. She thinks she can keep my mother from knowing about my suspension... *okay*. Did she forget about Katie?

I love that girl but sometimes she has a big mouth.

Mémé just thinks that after what happened to Jackson, and then after what happened today at school, I should have a place to "vent my feelings." She thinks I'm angry.

"Maybe if you do this you won't feel the need to beat up anyone else in school and you'll have fewer suspensions," she said.

So now I have to write about my first day back to school.

I got through the morning without anyone saying a word to me about what had happened to Jackson. Everyone in my class was quiet, including Princess Claudette. Mémé must have called them—I know it wouldn't have been my mother.

We got through the pledge of allegiance. Mrs. Coleman carefully took attendance and the hot lunch count, taking special care not to even look at Jackson's empty seat. She had Charles bring them down this morning.

We took a spelling test. I'm not too sure how I really did, and I don't care. We went through class like it was just a normal, average, run-of-the-mill school day. She didn't even comment on my absence.

I ate lunch alone at our table. I really wasn't up for trying to make any real small talk with anyone just yet. Like my mother would say after one of her AA meetings she used to go to. One step at a time.

When we went out to recess, as usual, all the kids ran out to the playground. Not me, I wasn't really in the mood yet. I strolled out, just taking my time letting life go on around me.

I sat in our spot next to the building, hugging my knees up to my chest. I caught sight of my friendship bracelet and just spaced out looking at it for a while.

"Veronica?" I heard someone say. The sun was high in the sky now, and when I looked up it made me squint my eyes.

Evelyn and Leslie were standing in front of me. I have to say I was a little surprised.

"Yeah?" I answered them.

"We're sorry about what happened to Jackson," Evelyn said.

"He was always so nice to us," Leslie said.

I smiled at both of them. "Thanks."

"We were going over to play hopscotch," Evelyn said. "You can play with us if you want to."

I sighed inside. Keep going, I reminded myself. I stood up from our spot and brushed the back of my pants off. "Okay, that sounds like fun."

As we were walking over to the part of the black-top where the hopscotch was laid out, we crossed paths with Claudette and her friends, Karen, Mary, and Patricia.

"I know it sounds a little mean, but honestly Karen, we already had enough freaks here before he came, and I'm glad he's not here anymore." She turned her head following me with her eyes. "Well, I guess we'll never be *completely* freak free," she said loud enough for me to hear.

I stopped dead in my tracks and turned around. "Did you say something?" I asked her as casually as I could. I felt my pulse quicken just a little.

Princess Claudette looked at me. "I wasn't talking to *you*," she huffed. "I was talking with my friends!" She turned to face her group and began talking again, this time she was louder. "As I was *saying* before I was so rudely interrupted! I'm glad were down one freak! They should just go back where they came from!"

"Don't you talk about him like that!" I ordered.

"I can talk about whoever, and whatever, I want to, it's a free country!"

I was trying to be a good girl, I turned to walk away. I didn't hear whatever Patricia may have said, but I certainly heard Claudette.

"Patricia, that kid was such a loser! He was fat and he cried all the time like a big baby!" She laughed out loud. "Jackson was a freak!" When I turned around Claudette was turned and facing me.

I was so mad, I walked right over and punched her right in the face. I'm pretty sure I hit her eye. When she fell to the ground, I jumped on top of her, hitting her as much as I could. I was shouting at the top of my lungs, "I HATE YOU! DON'T YOU EVER TALK ABOUT HIM! DON'T YOU EVER CALL HIM A FREAK! YOU ARE NEVER ALLOWED TO TALK ABOUT HIM AGAIN! IF YOU DO, I'LL BEAT YOU SO BAD, YOU'LL BE THE FREAK!"

It took two lunch aids to pull me off of her, and they carried me off to the principal's office to call my parents. I kicked and screamed the whole way. Claudette went to the nurse's office. I guess she needed ice for her dumb face! Not that ice will help that mess! I can't say I feel that bad about hitting her. Is that wrong?

The other part of my punishment is that I have to work for the next four weekends at the resort. We're telling Mom I volunteered. She said she'll find me work I can do.

So yeah that was it, I got busted for fighting, and I never thought that would happen. I will try harder to not lose my temper anymore, no matter how much someone tries to make me mad. Yes...that includes Claudette.

CHAPTER 11

I burst out laughing. "You beat up that Claudette girl because she called me a freak?!"

"Yes, of course I did," she said matter of fact. "Every one of us has a limit of what they can take. I had already reached mine long before she started with the comments that day. Poor thing never saw it coming."

"I love you so much," I told her chuckling still. I tightened my arms around her and kissed her cheek. "I'll bet she never said anything like that again."

She smiled at me. "She avoided me for quite some time after that."

My stomach growled loudly and Harmony chuckled. "I am sorry, I'm keeping you from eating," she said.

I tenderly kissed her lips. "I haven't minded one bit. In fact, I would give it up entirely if I found out that was the key to keeping you."

"I love you too," she replied. "Come on, let's go out to the kitchen and feed you. Then after you eat, I'll tell you a little more."

She got up from the bed, and I rolled to my side to watch her. I was following her curves with my eyes, and watching the way her long wild curls swayed across her back as she moved. I couldn't help marveling at the flawless beauty of her skin, trying to commit every part of this image to memory as she walked across the room. I never want to forget a single thing about her. I watched as she quietly got herself dressed and then she turned to look at me.

She had a playful smirk. "What?"

"I'm gonna miss you when you have to leave," I admitted.

"I'm never that far away, and I'll be waiting for you when it's time for you to come home," she assured me.

"I know. It's just gonna be so long from now."

"It's not really. It just feels that way. That's an effect Earth has."

I sighed as I sat up, and started to get myself dressed. She walked over and placed her hand on my cheek. I closed my eyes and held her hand to my face breathing in the sweet floral scent from her wrist. "I know it's hard," she said. "But you're strong. So much stronger than you ever give yourself credit for."

I just nodded at her in reply. I couldn't open my eyes at first. I didn't want her to know how scared I was at the thought of her going home and having to survive the rest of my life not seeing her. I wonder how badly I might suffer when she finally has to go. Just the thought of going back to the aches and pains, the struggle to breathe, along with the rest of my misery makes me shudder. I grabbed my crutches and got up, starting down the hall to the kitchen. I'll just have to deal with what comes after, when that time comes. I'm not going to let that minor concern ruin the best moment of my life.

I decided to keep it simple, and started taking stuff out of the fridge to make a ham and cheese sandwich, placing it all on the table.

"Would you like me to make you something?" I asked her.

She smiled at me from the table. "I would love that, but I couldn't eat it if you did."

"Oh yeah, sorry, I just remembered."

"It was sweet of you to offer," she replied.

"Don't you need to eat though?" I asked.

"I can if I want to, but I don't have to," she said.

"So, you don't need to eat?" I asked clarifying.

"Nope."

"So, you never feel hungry?"

She smiled. "Only when I'm on Earth."

"Wow, that must be nice."

I sat down at the table and assembled my sandwich quickly. I hadn't realized how hungry I really was until I smelled the sweet maple honey ham and the mayo. When I began eating, I was taking large bites and she started laughing.

"Wow, I'm gonna have to make sure we pause a little more often so you can eat. I forget what being hungry is like," she said.

I had to swallow before I could reply. "Yeah, it can be a little overwhelming."

"So, what do you do for work?" she asked suddenly, it sounded like she was just making conversation.

I smiled at her. "I run my parents' factory. Well, my sister and I both do."

Her eyes widened. "You run a whole factory? What do you make?"

"We make furniture," I replied.

"What kind of furniture?" She seemed intrigued.

"All kinds; bed sets, dressers, tables, couches, rockers. Whatever my father thinks up."

"Oh." She pressed her fingers to her lips, seeming distracted by her thoughts a little. "So, I assume your father builds it?"

"He just designs it now, but yeah he used to. The factory workers build it."

She chuckled a little to herself and shook her head quick. "That's great...and your mother? What does she do there?"

"She handles the upholstery part and her and my sister oversee the stores. My parents started the company from nothing, and now have not just the factory, but ten factory stores as well."

She sat back in her chair grinning. "Wow, I'm impressed. That's amazing."

"It is," I agreed.

"Do you like running the factory?" she asked.

I shrugged. "I don't mind. It's a job. It will be a pain when I go back to work though."

"Why is that?" she asked.

"Because my sister just fired my receptionist. I'm gonna have to deal with temps for the time being, while I look for a permanent one."

She looked confused. "What's a temp?"

"It's just a temporary worker. We can hire a company to send us someone to fill in right away so we are not short staffed."

"Oh. Why don't you just hire one of them to be there permanent?"

"I might offer whoever they send me the job if I like them," I replied.

"Oh, well, I guess that's good. Why did your sister fire the one you had?"

"She was lazy, and she didn't show up for two days. She did occasionally do that, but I was so depressed before that I didn't care. Plus, I didn't want to go through the hassle of finding a new one. I was being a bit lazy, too." I chuckled and shook my head. "My sister on the other hand, is the exact opposite of me and tends to run away with her mouth quite a bit. I knew it was only a matter of time before she did that."

Harmony had a funny look in her eyes and she chuckled. "I think I like your sister," she replied and smiled kindly. "So, are you full?" she asked, when I finished my sandwich.

"Yeah, I'm good," I replied leaning back in my chair a little. "So, what would you like to do now?" I asked her.

She pressed her delicate fingers to her lips like she does when she's deep in thought. "Why don't you tell me a little about your girlfriend."

I sat there in stunned silence. I could feel the blood draining from my face. I'm sitting with my quote un-quote *wife* who I just made love with, who just asked me about my girlfriend. I had no clue on how to pro-ceed. Under normal circumstances this should be a sign that I should escape quickly by any means neces-sary, but this situation is far from normal. "Uh...what do you want to know?" I asked her.

"Wow, look at your face." She giggled. "You look like I've got you locked down in an electric chair with my hand on the switch." She giggled again. "You don't have to feel bad about having a girlfriend here or a wife even. This is Earth, and you're supposed to live your life, which includes having all kinds of relationships. We all know this, and it's nothing to feel bad about."

I hadn't realized I was holding my breath until I let out my sigh of relief. "Okay," I replied still tip-toeing a little.

She smirked. "I've had relationships on Earth before I fell in love with you, you know."

I sat back a little thinking about what she just said, along with our story and that little bit from a lifetime she told me about where she said my name was Vinny. "Really?" I replied. Until now, it hadn't really sunk in that we may have had more lives than the one she was currently telling me about. "How many?" I asked.

"How many what? How many relationships?" she asked me, trying to clarify.

"How many lives have you lived?"

"Oh, about a hundred and fifty, more or less," she said.

"Do you know how many I have lived?"

"Well, about a hundred and fifty...and a half."

"Wow, I never thought about it like that before," I replied.

"It does shed a different light on things, now doesn't it?" she said. "It's sweet you were worried about upsetting me by telling me about your girlfriend, but you don't have to be. This is all a part of who we are."

She truly is magnificent. Try to have this same conversation with Shannon or any other girl on Earth and it would be World War III. I know guys who would kill for a woman like this. It's quite a nice feeling being able to be so open like this, and not be criticized for it.

"Her name is Shannon. She is twenty-four and she works as a personal trainer," I said.

She smiled at me kindly before she spoke. "How did you meet her?" she asked.

"A friend at work was having a party and he set us up."

"How long have you been seeing her?"

"About four months," I replied.

"Do you love her?" she asked suddenly. My heart stopped, and I felt fear quickly rocketing through me like jet fuel. It took me a moment before I could speak. "I don't know."

"Why, not?" she asked.

"I don't know," I shrugged, "it's just not that simple," I replied.

She narrowed her brows at me. "Curt, it is that simple. You either love her or you don't," she said flatly.

"But I don't know if I do," I replied. "That's been most of my problem all along. I don't know what it's supposed to feel like. I don't seem to be able to feel anything towards them. Shannon is nice, and she's very pretty, but I don't know if I love her."

"You told me that you love me. Why is that?" she asked.

"Because I felt it," I said quickly and I was suddenly awestruck. I knew I said it, but I didn't realize that I did until she pointed it out. I didn't even realize what I was feeling towards Harmony was love. I never made the connection, and I never even thought about it. I said it without thinking, which is new for me, because the only girls I've ever said that to are my mother and my sister.

"So, let me ask you again. Do you love Shannon?" she asked.

I sighed before admitting what I now know. "No."

"It's not good to try and keep the relationship going if you don't love her. It's not fair to her. She has feelings and deserves better than that, don't you think?" She reached her hand across the table and held mine. "How would you feel to be in a relationship with someone who didn't love you?"

I sighed. "I know, I have to talk with her...and I will." I sighed again. "Harmony, what if I can't find happiness in a relationship down here?"

"That's something you want, don't you?" Her reply was more of a question.

"Yeah, I do. I want to settle down at some point and share my life with someone and have a family. But I obviously can't live a lie, look where that got me," I said pointing down to my leg.

She became quiet and her face grew long. "Is that why you did it?"

"It was a huge part of it. The depression, the ache in my body, the struggle to breathe, was all manageable depending on the day. It was the part where I just couldn't fall in love with any of them. A lot of the time I just couldn't even get near them. It just felt wrong, like putting your shoes on the wrong feet. I thought maybe this falling in love thing was something of fiction writers. When I met Shannon, I forced myself to really try. She's very pretty and nice, but that's it. I just can't make myself fall in love with her. It's embarrassing, but I tend to forget about her most days."

I anxiously ran my fingers through my hair combing it back. "It was late, I was coming back from Shannon's and I was angry with myself. No matter what I did that night it just felt wrong. The harder I tried to get close to her the more it seemed to hurt. It was actually making the ache and the struggle to breathe worse. I got through it but I told her I was feeling sick so I could get out of there and go home. I freaked out on the ride home."

She got up from the table and walked around stopping in front of me. She ran her fingers across my cheek, wiping away one of the tears I let spill out like a weakling. I don't know what it is about this beautiful creature that seems to make me crumble this way. She held out her hand and I placed mine in hers. She smiled kindly. "I can relate to what you went through. I've felt that before."

I sucked in a jagged breath before I spoke, "Really?"

"Yes. Why don't you and I go back to your room and I'll tell you more of our story," she suggested.

I grabbed my crutches and stood up from the table leaving my dinner mess behind. I know I should clean it up but I don't care right now. It's a trivial thing in reality, when I know my time with her will be running out. I need to spend every second I can with her.

Maybe by sacrificing everything else, I can hold on to her in my mind and in my heart for the rest of my time here until her and I meet again. Maybe this will be enough to get me through the rest of my life.

She was crawling across my bed when I entered. She turned lying down on her back and held her arms open to me and smiled wide. "Come lay with me, Curt."

I set my crutches on the floor and crawled onto the bed placing my head on her chest. She curled her arms around me holding me tightly and I felt relief. No one has ever made me feel this way ever. Lying here in her arms surrounded by her sweet candy-like floral scent is pure bliss. I don't remember the decision, but I wish I never came here without her. I will never do this again.

I placed my free arm around her waist and smiled. "This is something I know you and I must do often. I can feel it."

She rubbed my back and kissed the top of my head. "Yes, of course."

"Are you comfortable?" she asked me.

"Very," I replied.

"Good. The next part I'm gonna tell you about is my side of our time apart. You and I haven't discussed everything that had happened during that time yet, so I don't know all of what happened to you. I only know what I was dealing with."

"Okay," I said glancing up at her. "Will that be something I'll remember when I get home?" I asked.

"Yes."

"Well then, I promise to tell you about it when I get home," I assured her.

She placed her hand on my cheek and gently held my head back to kiss my lips. The moment her lips met mine my head began swirling like it did when I was on those painkillers and I couldn't control the sounds of delight escaping my lips.

She pulled away smiling kindly, her big brown eyes full of light. She began caressing my cheek. "We will start with my thirteenth birthday...."

CHAPTER 12

December 5, 1971

Today is my thirteenth birthday. (Well, technically it's tomorrow.) It's Saturday, December fifth, and Mémé has surprised me by taking me and my friends, Evelyn and Leslie, to Moodus Family Fun Center to do a little roller skating.

For obvious reasons, I just couldn't come here. I wasn't ready, so I've been avoiding it for the last four years.

I've come to learn that my Mémé can be quite devious at times when it comes to getting what she wants, or getting people to do things that she wants them to. Even when they insist they don't want to. She has been known to actually claim that she really does know everything.

She has tried on several occasions to make me go to Moodus Family Fun Center, but I just couldn't do it.

Normally, for my birthday she comes over to my house for dinner, or we go over to hers. Then after dinner she gives me my gift. This time she's done things a little different. Today she went as far as picking up my friends this morning, and then driving them to my house just to give me my gift. When they all stood around me insisting I open the darn thing right then and there, I knew something was up. When I opened the gift, I discovered a brand new shiny pair of white roller skates with yellow wheels. A small part of me wanted to chuck the skates at all of them.

But instead, I controlled my anger and I surrendered. I give up. There really is no winning a tug-o-war with my Mémé, especially when she brings an army.

Mom, Katie, and I are no longer living with my Mémé and Grandpa. We haven't been living there for a little over two years. Mom has rented us a quaint three bedroom cape in a small neighborhood right next to Moodus reservoir. The place is okay, I guess. I do like having my own room. I can't say I miss sharing a bed with my sister⊠she steals the covers. But I did think it was a little unfair that she gave Katie the bigger bedroom. "*She needs the extra space for her upright,*" Mom told me.

I miss living there. I've grown very close to both of my grandparents. It can be hard at times, living with Mom and Katie. Mom has never been easy for me to live with, and the older Katie gets the more like my mother she seems to become.

Nowadays, my mother dotes on my sister's every wish. If Katie wants something, my mother gets it for her. If Katie doesn't want to do something, she doesn't have to. Often enough (pretty much every day), I'm stuck doing Katie's chores because she's *special*. My sister's musical talent has really become a thorn in my side. When I'm not doing all the chores in the house, I'm in my room, with the door closed. I have to say it may be small, but it's my own personal heaven.

Moodus Family Fun Center hasn't changed much. I thought it would be a lot harder to come here than it is. They still have the same pinball machines as they did the last time I was here, but now there are two pool tables. That might be fun.

Evelyn and Leslie have proven to be great friends. They're trustworthy and a lot of fun, especially Evelyn. Evelyn and I seem to be a lot alike. She has light brown hair like I do (yep, no more blonde for me!). The only difference is that she likes to wear things like head-bands and barrettes in her hair and I don't. I find wearing things like that in my hair very uncomfortable.

Leslie is the one with the dark brown hair. When I first met Leslie, her hair was long and wavy and it hung down to her waist. Then about six months ago she had a gum incident, and then her mother cut all her hair up to her shoulders; it does look nice though.

Leslie tends to be more competitive than Evelyn. If I have an opinion on anything, nine times out of ten, Evelyn will agree with me, whereas Leslie won't. That doesn't seem to hurt our relationship though, Leslie's a blast.

I also find (with Evelyn especially) between the three of us that we usually end up finishing each other's sentences, like Katie and I used to do.

While I was lacing up my new skates I caught sight of my friendship bracelet. I ran my finger over the weave feeling the beads the way I always do when I think of him. I thought about how he came with me my first time coming here for my birthday. I smiled. It used to be very painful to think about him, but now I don't mind so much anymore. I hope he's okay and happy wherever he may be.

I stood up from the booth. "God, I hope I can still remember how to do this."

Evelyn patted my shoulder. "Don't worry! It's just like riding a bike!"

Leslie took off on her skates. "C'mon you guys, they're playing my song!"

"I still swear I've heard this one year's ago!" I shouted over to Leslie.

"Veronica, Venus has only been out just a few months, not years!" she shouted back.

"Hey, does anyone want a piece of bubble gum?" Evelyn asked.

I waved. "Yeah, I do!" I took my piece of bubble gum, un-wrapped it, and popped it into my mouth. Leslie skated over and I handed her a piece.

Bubble gum is one of the many essentials whenever Evelyn, Leslie, and I hang out. The others are chocolate and Coca-Cola. We love pizza too, but that one tends to be mostly a sleepover thing. We're a quirky group.

Evelyn and Leslie took off around the rink. "Come on, Veronica!" Evelyn shouted.

"Hey, I'll race ya!" Leslie shouted.

"Maybe we should wait to see how she skates first," Evelyn suggested loudly.

I took a deep breath and exhaled. "I am sure I can still do this!"

I slowly entered the rink and rolled out onto the shiny hardwood. I pushed off without really thinking too hard about it and I was skating. Right away Evelyn and Leslie started clapping dramatically. It was so embarrassing!

We skated around and around the rink. I was starting to remember why I love skating so much, because the speed makes me feel so free.

As we made our way around the rink I noticed Mémé had her Polaroid out and was taking pictures.

My Mémé has changed some over time. Her hair now has wisps of gray in it, and she's let go of that beehive hairdo for a more natural look. Her hair hangs down past her shoulders now and is very curly. I have to say she looks great and I do prefer it. She and my grandfather are well and happy.

I was watching my wonderful Mémé and I was feeling spunky, so when we passed by her I blew the biggest bubble I could and did a silly pose for her. She snapped the picture, with a huge smile across her face. For once, I'm doing what she thinks I should be—skating, being a kid, and having fun.

I can't say fun is a regular occurrence in my life right now. With my schedule the way it is, I just don't have time for it. My days consist of school, homework, chores, and sleep.

When we first moved into the new house, Katie and I had a fairly even amount of chores we were doing. I did understand she is a bit younger than me, so at the time we started doing chores, I had to take the harder stuff.

Every Sunday my mom leaves a list of chores she wants us to do every day during the week. It has stuff on it like doing the dishes, vacuuming, dusting, cleaning the bathroom, loads of laundry, etc.

Mom had said we had to do chores because our house in San Francisco was a pigsty and she won't go back to living that way. Which she said was all my father's fault.

We were both told that the chores are for both of us. One half of the list is for me, the other half is supposed to be for Katie. On days when Katie has piano or dance, I was told I had to take her part of the list since I don't have any extracurricular activities yet.

When this started, Katie had piano on Mondays and dance on Wednesdays. Both of these classes were one-hour sessions. Over time this schedule has increased, and now Katie goes to piano on Mondays still but has an extra piano lesson on Thursday for two hours instead of the normal one-hour session, and she goes to dance on Tuesdays and Wednesdays. So, you'd think she'd help with the chores on Fridays? Nope. She never gets in trouble for it either. If I'm lucky I can get her to help fold the laundry but it's only her own clothes. She won't touch anyone else's. I try to organize my time as well as I can after school so I can get everything on the list done, do my homework, eat, and sleep, but that isn't always easy. If I don't do something on the list then I can't go anywhere or do anything on the weekends until I make up whatever chore I missed. That seems to be a lot lately. Most of the time I don't even notice I've missed something; I swear sometimes Mom adds things when I'm not looking. I think I'm losing my mind sometimes.

I've tried complaining many times about the way the chores are. My complaints only got me grounded anytime I say anything. It really isn't fair. Mom and Katie don't have to do anything, while I have to do them all? So, I've given up complaining. There's nothing I can do about it.

Things wouldn't be this way if we were still living with Mémé and Grandpa. I did have chores there too. But, so did Mom and Katie. So, it wasn't the insane, unfair amount that I have now.

Mémé called us over to the table for pizza and Cokes, which was great. She even had the staff bring out a cake, and everyone sang happy birthday to me, which embarrassed me to high heaven!

I do have other plans tonight, too. I'm sleeping over at Evelyn's house, and Leslie is too. I love sleeping over at Evelyn's house. Her mom is the coolest! She's spunky and energetic, which explains where Evelyn gets it from. She lets us stay up late, eat popcorn, and watch TV.

There is one thing on my agenda tonight that I'm a little nervous about, and I'm trying not to think about it. While I'm at Evelyn's house tonight I'm going to call my father. I've been trying to get my mother to give me his phone number to let me call him for a long time now, and I've had zero luck with that. Every time I ask, my mother throws a big fit about how I don't appreciate anything she does for me, and how she doesn't understand why I would want to talk to someone who never even writes to me. Then she storms off crying and locks herself in her room.

Evelyn was kind enough to call information for me and get his phone number, and I already gave her mother twenty bucks for the long-distance call. Mémé has been nice enough over the last few years to let me work at the resort for a little pocket money. She pays me ten bucks a week to entertain some of the kids there and I've been saving. I would have tried calling from my house but I knew if my mother ever found out she'd go crazy.

It's not fair, I miss him. I dream of seeing him again. I know Katie's memories of our father are a bit faded, but mine are not. I just want to talk to him.

Mémé drove me and my friends back to my house when we were done skating. I had so much fun I really didn't want to leave.

"Do I really have to go home already?" I asked, as I stared out the window.

"Yes, you do. Don't you and your friends have plans tonight? I wouldn't want you to miss out on those," she replied. She patted my knee.

When we went inside my house, Katie was sitting at the kitchen table looking at a picture book. I could hear my mother yelling from upstairs.

"Where were you?" Katie asked.

"Mémé took me skating," I replied.

"Mom's mad, you didn't finish the laundry."

"Katie, there isn't even that much left."

"Yeah, well, you left before you were done with it."

"Does it mean anything to her that it's my birthday this weekend?" I asked.

"Oh...I don't know," she replied.

"Where's Mom?" I asked. I needed to change the subject. I was starting to get mad.

"She's on the phone with Arnold," Katie replied.

My mother's been keeping secrets. It came to light about two months ago that my mother had been having an affair with her boss, Arnold Fletcher, who is (or was, not sure what's going on with that) a married man. He fired her. She spent many nights crying on the phone with him, and I guess she still is. I can only assume that this was his way of dumping her. She never actually told me what had happened. I just put two and two together listening to her on the phone, and from the one encounter we had when we stopped for gas one afternoon at our town's only gas station.

We were parked at one of the gas pumps. My mother rolled down the window and handed the attendant a ten-dollar bill. Another car pulled in on the other side of the pump. There were two people in the car, a young blonde girl in the passenger seat and in the driver's seat was an older woman that I recognized.

"Isn't that Mrs. Fletcher?" I asked.

I had met both Mr. and Mrs. Fletcher before when I had to go to the company picnic that they have every Fourth of July, so I was sure it was her. My mother glanced over and then quickly turned away looking straight ahead.

"*HOMEWRECKER*!" Mrs. Fletcher yelled out her window.

I was sitting in the back seat and I watched my mother's face change suddenly in the rearview mirror. She became angry and stepped out of the car then, slamming the door. She faced Mrs. Fletcher down and began shouting, "He loves *me*, not *you*! You're just jealous because you're a dried up old hag, and he prefers a *REAL WOMAN*!"

Mrs. Fletcher huffed, and was so outraged that she drove off out of the gas station in a huge hurry. She never even got her gas. It was a few days later that Mom got fired. My mother has since then gotten a new job as a receptionist in a dentist's office. But I guess she still has something for this Arnold guy, which I'll never really understand. Mr. Fletcher is an older heavy-set man with a greasy comb over, ewe! My mother is a very pretty lady when she takes care of herself. To me she could do so much better than that guy.

Mémé scowled at Katie and folded her arms. "And what exactly were you two doing this morning that you couldn't be the ones to finish the load of laundry?"

Katie looked up at her with an innocent expression "Mom took me for my hair appointment."

"You couldn't get your hair done later or maybe on a different day?" Mémé asked, she sounded annoyed.

"I have my recital this afternoon," she stated this like it was obviously important.

"Katie, where is your mother?"

"She's upstairs."

Mémé marched out of the kitchen and went upstairs. Me, Evelyn, and Leslie just stayed in the kitchen. I went over to check the list on the wall, Evelyn came up behind me. "We could help you with the laundry, and then we can go to my house sooner," she suggested.

"That would be nice, but you know you don't have to." I sighed. "My chores are my responsibility."

"Veronica, what are friends for?" Evelyn patted my back.

I went into the bathroom and grabbed the hamper. It was heavy. I swear this thing was not this full before we left this morning for the rink. I went over by the back door where the washer and dryer is and started loading the washing machine. When I couldn't fit anymore laundry in, I put in a scoop of powder and turned on the washer. Sometimes I wonder if Mom and Katie find this complicated, they are of simple mind.

We turned our heads in the direction of the voices yelling from upstairs.

"Do you think she'll still let you go?" Leslie asked.

I shrugged. "I don't know. The rule is as long as I finish the chores then I'm free after. But who knows, she's in one of her moods."

"I don't know how you put up with this," Evelyn whispered harshly. "I would have lost it with her a long time ago."

Leslie leaned in. "Yeah, Veronica, I don't know how you put up with it either. She treats you like a slave," she whispered.

I just shrugged again, and sighed. "What choice do I have?" I whispered back. "It's not like I can do anything about it."

Evelyn and Leslie put their arms over my shoulders. "We'll think of something; I can't stand watching this all the time," Evelyn said.

"Yeah, it's not right," Leslie added.

Katie walked in just then. "What are you three doing?" she asked.

Evelyn looked up at Katie. "We're helping Veronica with the laundry, what's it to you?"

"I was just asking," Katie said sounding innocent.

"Why? So you can run and tell Mom?" I accused.

"No, I was just going out to the car for something." Katie left out the back door.

"So, what should we do while we wait for the laundry?" I asked the girls. I was trying to make light of my situation.

"We could help you get your stuff ready to come to my house," Evelyn suggested.

"I'm already ready to go, I packed my bag yesterday," I admitted. "We could just hang out in my room."

The girls and I headed for the stairs to go up to my room. We stopped when we saw my mother and Mémé were on their way down.

"Hello girls." My mother sounded cheerful. "And where are the three of you off to?"

My mother could have been an actress. She uses this cheery happy tone whenever things are not going her way or she doesn't like someone, and I could tell she was definitely using it now. She can flip like a switch. One second she'd be screaming about something, and in the next she can look and sound like everything is fine. I'm disappointed that she thinks I'm this stupid. I wonder if she thinks I'm fooled like my friends. Or maybe she doesn't care and the act isn't for me, it's for them. I wonder what is gonna happen to me when I come home tomorrow.

"Hello, Miss Edwards." Both of my friends were extra polite.

"We're just going up to my room for a while," I told her. "I started a load of laundry, when the washer stops I'll come down and put it in the dryer."

My mother's face was unreadable. "Nonsense, Veronica! It's your birthday!" She embraced me. "I wouldn't make you do chores this weekend!"

Good Lord! What did Mémé say to her?! Because this wasn't the case last year. She was scaring me. Who is this woman?

"Oh, well, there's a load started anyway." I did my best to not sound so surprised.

My mom cupped my chin. "You are such a good girl! I'll take care of the rest of the laundry. You don't have to worry about a thing."

She looked over at my friends. "Would you girls like a soda? There are Cokes in the fridge. I know how much you girls like those."

"Of course, we do!" Evelyn said.

The three of us, Evelyn, Leslie, and I sat around our small kitchen table drinking our Cokes. My mother acting like she's nice was really making me feel on edge. I felt like the floor was gonna drop out from under my feet or something. Mémé just stood in the doorway watching us, arms crossed, with a very satisfied look on her face. My mother just stood by the counter and continued to sound cheerful.

"So, are you girls excited about your big sleepover tonight?" my mother asked trying to sound interested.

"Yeah," Leslie said.

"Are you girls going to stay up real late and talk about boys?" she asked.

That question made us all snicker.

"Don't be shy, girls! That's what me and my friends did at our sleepovers."

"*Maybe...*" Evelyn answered.

"Veronica, since I have to take your sister to her recital this afternoon, your Mémé is going to take you to Evelyn's house."

"Okay."

"This recital is very important for your sister. Don't forget to wish her luck before you go."

"I won't, I'll go tell her right now."

"Are you ready to go yet?" Mémé asked.

I stood up from the table. "I just have to get my overnight bag."

When I went upstairs to get my bag, I stuck my head into my sister's room. "Hey, good luck at your recital Katie."

"Thank you, Roni," she said.

I went into my room and grabbed my bag off my bed. There was no need to pack because I had packed it yesterday. I stopped by the bathroom to grab my toothbrush and stuffed it in my bag. There, all set, I thought.

I paused when I caught my reflection in the mirror. I haven't changed too much. My hair is longer now and my bangs have grown out some. I stood there wondering for a moment how much do I look like her? Or do I look like my father? I still just see the same girl, only with much darker hair than I used to have. I leaned in closer to the mirror examining my face looking for a small amount of my dad. I couldn't see it. I wish I could. It's been so long since I've seen him, I wasn't really sure anymore. Thankfully, I couldn't really see my mother either.

Sometimes I wonder about Katie. She's nine now and she spends a large amount of her time with Mom, and she takes after her too. I'd like to think I take after my father, and I know I don't take after her. I wonder sometimes if that's the reason Mom gets so upset with me, because I'm like him, or maybe because I look like him?

When Mémé dropped us off at Evelyn's house I made sure I gave her a huge hug. "Thank you, Mémé!" I sang in her ear. I'm so happy to have an adult who seems to be normal, and on my side. "Thank you for giving me such a great birthday!"

Mémé smiled. "Oh, you're welcome, Sweetie. I'm glad you had such a good day." She patted my back. "Have a wonderful time with your friends."

I grabbed my bag, and the girls and I started up towards the house. Evelyn's older brother Greg and two of his friends, Kevin and Paul, were in the driveway playing the radio loud and had their heads under the hood of a car. Greg is a sophomore in high school, his friends Kevin and Paul are both freshmen. Greg always says Paul's on the five-year plan...whatever that means.

I like when Evelyn's brother is around. They play cool music and he and his friends are funny, and it doesn't hurt that Kevin's kind of cute.

The boys looked up from the car's engine. "Hey, girls!" Greg greeted us. "Are you two here for the night?"

I let Leslie answer. "Yep, I hope we're not cramping your style."

The boys chuckled. "Nope, doesn't bother us one bit," Paul replied with a wide grin.

We started walking to the door when I suddenly heard my name being called.

"Hey, Veronica." I turned around and Kevin was standing alone away from the car smiling. I felt my cheeks flush. I looked down at my feet, I was so embarrassed. I brought my eyes up and looked back at him again, and he was still standing there smiling. All

I could do was smile too and then I went inside the house.

Evelyn, Leslie, and I spent the afternoon hanging out in Evelyn's room listening to the radio, and a few records.

We gossiped about some of the kids at school. I learned that Claudette has been going steady with a boy named Steven. But she has been talking on the phone with Mark, the boy from my third-grade class, behind Steven's back. Mark just so happens to be going out with Claudette's friend Karen. I'll just have to save that little gem for a later date.

After the fight Claudette and I had where I landed in the principal's office (and she went to the nurse), I have very little problems with her anymore. She pretty much avoids me now; it's been nice.

We ate dinner late because the three of us were fooling around too much up in Evelyn's room. Because of the boys, we almost didn't get anything. Luckily, Evelyn's mother saved us a few slices of pizza. After our pizza dinner, Leslie and I rolled out our sleeping bags on Evelyn's floor. I got my PJ's out of my bag and went to change in the bathroom across the hall, and I brushed my teeth. While I was brushing my teeth, I was trying to decide about whether or not I was really going to call my father, and then what do I say to him if I do? What if he doesn't remember me? What if he has a new family now and he really doesn't care about me anymore? I had some serious jitters. When I got back into Evelyn's room she already had the piece of paper out that had his phone number and had the telephone ready.

"So, are you going to call him?" Evelyn asked me the second I closed her door.

I took a breath trying to calm myself. "What if he's not home?" I said.

"Then try calling him later, there is a three hour time difference," she suggested.

I sighed. "What if it's the wrong Phil Edwards?" I asked.

"Then we'll call information again. Veronica, quit stalling and just dial the stupid number!"

"Veronica, don't worry, we're here for you if you need us," Leslie said.

I took the piece of paper from Evelyn and grabbed the phone. I put the receiver to my ear and I put my finger in the dial hole and turned it for each number. The only noise in the room was the soft clicking the dial makes on the return. The phone started to ring on the other end and my stomach started doing twists and turns.

I heard a gentlemen answer. "Hello?"

"Hello is Phil there?" I asked quietly.

A man cleared his throat. "Speaking."

"I'm not sure if I have the right Phil Edwards..." I started. "But, my name is Veronica."

"*Veronica...?*" He sounded startled, but then he began shouting. "Veronica! Oh my God! Oh honey! How are you?!"

"I'm okay."

"Oh, I've missed you!" he told me, and I began to cry. I felt like I'd been suffocating for too long and could finally breathe.

"What's wrong, why are you crying?"

"I've missed you too, Daddy. Why haven't you written to me?" I managed to get out between sobs.

"Veronica, I've been writing to you, and your sister. Haven't you been getting my letters? Did you get the music box?"

"I got the music box. That was the first and last thing I got. I haven't gotten any letters. Where have you been sending them?"

"I've been sending them to your grandparents' house. I didn't know where else. No one told me where you were living exactly."

"I wanted to call you after I got the music box but Mom wouldn't let me. Thank you for giving me that, I love it."

"You're welcome, honey. It was always meant for you."

I then proceeded to tell him everything that has been happening at home. The stuff with the chores, the stuff with my mother and Katie, and the fact that I feel my mother doesn't like me, and why I feel that way. How my mother reacts every time I even try to ask about calling or writing him.

"Does your mother know you are talking to me now?" he asked.

"No, I had to call you from my friend's house. I gave her mother money so I could."

"Please thank her for me. I'm glad you have such good friends. I'm so happy you called me. I didn't know what happened to you, or your sister. I've been so worried."

"Dad, can I come live with you?"

"Sweetie, I wish you could. But I still live alone and I'm still working on the boat, you would be alone too much."

"I'm alone all the time, Dad. Mom and Katie leave me alone all the time, I'm used to it."

"Yes, but it's for just a few hours. This would be for weeks at a time. At lease living there you have your grandparents to help. However, I am seeing someone ..."

"Really? Is she nice?" I interrupted.

"Yes, maybe if things work out between us you can move back out here. But I won't make you a promise that I can't keep. So, this is a maybe...do you understand me?"

"Yes."

"Would your friends mind if I send you mail to their address?"

"I don't know, let me ask them." I pulled the receiver away from my ear a little. "Evelyn, my father wants to know if he can send me mail here. Do you think your mother would mind?"

Evelyn gave me a funny look. "Of course not, silly! Why'd you even ask!"

"It's fine, Dad."

"Good, give me the address." I told him where to send the mail. "You and I are going to stay in touch, no matter what. I always knew *you* would call me." He sighed. "Veronica, what would happen if your mother found out you were talking to me?"

"She would probably run screaming into her room like a big baby, and then later she'd ground me."

"Well then, I guess me calling to yell at her won't help you, will it?" he asked.

"Probably not," I replied.

"Wow, I really thought she might change after our divorce but I guess she didn't. I am so sorry you're going through all of this. And I really am surprised at your grandmother. She always seemed so level headed. When is the next time you'll see your grand-mother?"

"She's the one picking me up tomorrow at one."

"When you see her ask her if you've gotten any mail from me there, see what she says."

"I will."

"Veronica, we should probably hang up now. I wouldn't want your friend's phone bill to be outrageous. You and I will stay in touch now. I love you sweetheart...happy birthday."

"I love you too, Dad. Bye."

"Bye, talk to you soon."

When I hung up the phone I was still crying. Evelyn and Leslie were, too.

"So, I wonder what your grandmother did with your letters?" Evelyn asked.

I shook my head. "I don't know. But tomorrow, I'm gonna find out."

When Mémé pulled into the driveway I was ready to go. Not in the sense like my bags were packed, which they were. But in the sense that I was ready to deal with this deception, and yell at or scream at whoever's fault it is.

"I'm not taking any more crap from anyone in this joke of a family anymore!" I shouted in the kitchen. I made both Evelyn and Leslie jump.

"I'm so sick of the way everything is all the time! Having to tip toe around my mother, doing all the chores, and getting trampled on. From now on, I'm fighting back!"

"Hear, hear!" Evelyn shouted. "Don't take anymore crap!"

"We're behind you Veronica," Leslie added.

I grabbed my bag and marched out of the house ready for battle. No more crap! I reminded myself as I opened the car door.

"Hi Sweetie, happy birthday!" she said. She smiled at me and it looked genuine. "Did you and your friends have a good time?"

"Yes, it was very...enlightening." I tried to control my tone, but I sounded irritated.

Mémé gave me a funny look, as she backed down the driveway. "Well then...I guess that's good."

I took a few minutes preparing myself. I was trying to think of the calmest way I could begin this conversation.

"Mémé?" Control your temper Veronica, I reminded myself.

"What is it, Sweetie? Is there something bothering you?" She patted my shoulder.

"Have I gotten any mail at your house?" I folded my arms, and watched her face.

She looked puzzled. "Not lately, why?"

I felt my pulse quicken. "So, I've gotten mail at your house?"

"Yes, you know you do," she trailed off, shaking her head. "Wait...don't you?"

"I don't know, you tell me," I barked back at her.

"Veronica, what is going on? What are you asking me exactly?"

Do I need to spell it out for this woman? She must know where these questions are leading. "Have I gotten any mail from my father in the last four years?"

Her answer was simple. "Yes."

I couldn't quite read the look on her face. So, I couldn't tell what she was thinking.

"So where is all my mail?" I asked her.

Mémé was stopped at a stop sign. She was staring out the window, and spoke like she was distracted. "I've been giving it to your mother."

I was so angry, I opened the door and jumped out of the car. I slammed the door shut, and screamed as loud as I could and just started walking; I needed air. I felt like I was suffocating.

Mémé pulled the car over and shut off the engine. She stepped out of the car. "Honey, come back! I didn't know she wasn't giving them to you!" she was shouting. I turned back and faced Mémé, clenched my fist, and screamed as loud as I could, "I just don't get it! What the hell did I ever do to that woman?!"

"Veronica, you watch your language!"

"I don't care right now!" I yelled at her. "What did I ever do to her that she can't do a single nice thing for me?! Why can't she just let me be happy? Or care that I even *EXIST*?!" Then I angrily shook my finger at her. "And *you*!" I shouted. "I was starting to trust you; how could you just hand *MY MAIL to HER*?!" I was growling through my teeth.

"Veronica, if I knew she would do that, or if I thought she was doing it, I would have stopped! I swear, I'm on your side. I can *SEE*! Now *please*, come back and get in the car, we'll figure it out."

I was out of breath and we we're in the middle of nowhere. I was out of options. Only this town has everything and everyone so spread out, so walking home really was out of the question. I receded, and got back in the car. But I was in no way feeling better.

"Veronica, I can see that there is a problem between you and your mother. I'm not blind. I didn't think that things were this bad, I never imagined. I'm so sorry I gave her your letters. I won't make that mistake again. I've been trying to help you all along. But, I can't help as well unless you open up to me. You have to open up to someone. You can trust me."

I crossed my arms and didn't look at her. "I called my father."

A part of me can't believe I just told her that. The other part hopes she does squeal on me and tells my mother, that would probably be like a slap in the face to her.

"Oh," Mémé stayed very calm. "So that's how you found out about the letters then?"

"Yes," I snapped.

"Does your mother know you called him?"

"No."

"She hasn't let you has she?" She was soft spoken.

"No."

Mémé sighed and sat back against her seat. "Why don't you and I go back to the house. You can have some ice cream and we will talk for a while." Mémé reached over and rubbed my shoulder. "Really, you can trust me."

We went into the house through the kitchen door. My grandpa greeted me. "Hi, Veronica. Come for a visit?"

Mémé patted my shoulder and answered him before I could. "She's here for dessert. I have to call Donna quick to let her know that Veronica will be here for a little while." I took a seat at the kitchen table.

Mémé called Mom and told her that she was keeping me with her for the afternoon, and that she'd have me back by around six. Mom didn't object at all. You'd think she might a little bit since it is my birthday. That's what normal moms would do.

It did help me relax a little knowing I wouldn't have to spend that much time with her tonight. I don't know if I can hold onto my cool if I have to deal with her a whole lot anyway.

Mémé took a tub of chocolate ice cream out of the freezer and grabbed two bowls. Grandpa watched me and Mémé with suspicious eyes. "So, what's going on?" he asked, he sounded concerned.

"If I give you a bowl of ice cream will you go into the other room with it and keep your mouth shut?"

"It's okay Mémé, he can stay," I told her. Grandpa smiled and sat down next to me at the table, his expression was smug.

Mémé surprised me, when she gave me my ice cream she gave a small bowl to Grandpa as well. Grandpa's diet must be going well. Mémé sat down across from me with her bowl. "Okay kiddo, tell me everything."

I took a deep breath and exhaled, and proceeded to tell Mémé everything. About how she treats me, about how she is with Katie, along with all the stuff that happened in San Francisco, and the drinking. I even told her about Mom and Dad's fight. The one I heard the night he left. When I told her about the times she left us alone her eyes bugged out wide.

"That's why I think she hates me. Because I don't believe her the way Katie does. Oh, and I'm not talented like Katie is either, or like shopping, and getting all dressed up. I'm not a normal girl."

"Veronica, there's nothing wrong with you," Mémé assured me.

"I know that."

"Are you sure?"

"Yes, I know it's all her."

"Sweetie, I'm sorry you've had to go through so much."

Grandpa sighed. "I just don't know where we went wrong with her."

"I can tell you right now where all of the problems started." Mémé sounded bossy. "It was that Hank guy she was with. Don't you remember, Frank? That guy was nothing but trouble from day one!" She looked at me. "She followed him out to California, we tried to stop her. But she just wouldn't listen to us. She always seemed to have a problem with listening to what others tell her. She was always rebellious, has to learn everything the hard way. Shortly after she moved out there, he dumped her for someone else, or so she says. She met your father just after."

Grandpa hung his head down. "We spoiled her too much, Ruth. She was our only child, we were always too lenient."

Mémé just crossed her arms and scowled at him. "Frank, we did nothing wrong. Donna is her own person, a very selfish one. We didn't teach her that. You know we didn't."

Mémé checked her watch. "Veronica, it's time to take you home."

I really didn't want to go. "Can't I stay here with you? Can't I just live here? I won't be a bother and I'll help out around here," I begged.

Mémé put her arms around me. "I would keep you if I could, but I can't. You're not our child. You have to live with her. We can't just take you from her, the law won't allow that."

"That's so stupid!" I said.

"Veronica, you can't just ignore her. You have to face her and what she did. It's the right thing to do."

That's a load of crap, I thought to myself. And why can't I ignore her? I've done that before. Ignoring Donna is something I'm good at.

"Fine." I huffed. I let my Mémé win. The last thing I need right now is to anger the one adult who seems to be on my side.

Later when Mémé and I pulled into the driveway of my house my nerves were on edge. I was really hoping Mom was out somewhere tonight. Nope, lucky me, she's home.

I gave my Mémé a big hug before I opened the door. When I stepped out, I turned back to face her. "I love you Mémé," I told her, right before I shut the door.

As I walked up towards the house something occurred to me. My mother may have given birth to me but she's not my mother. She hasn't behaved as such for as long as I can remember. Since I moved here, Mémé has been more of a mother to me than my own, and as far as I'm concerned, she is my mother now.

My mother doesn't love me and I'm okay with that. There doesn't seem to be anything I can do to change it. None of that matters to me anymore anyhow. I know I have people in my life who do love me and that's enough.

CHAPTER 13

THE living room was empty, and the lights were dim when I walked into the house. The gentle hum from Katie's piano flowed down from upstairs. I hung my jacket up on the hook, taking great care to not make any noise. Maybe, if I'm quiet, I can get to my room without having to deal with anyone tonight.

My mother walked out of the kitchen and paused briefly when she saw me, her expression was unreadable. She then walked over to the sofa and sat down. She grabbed a nail file off the coffee table, sat back, put her feet up, and began filing her nails.

I didn't say anything to her. I couldn't just start yelling and confront her the way I wanted to. Once I saw her, my stage fright kicked in and it was making my stomach turn. I tried to walk past her and just go to my room. I really didn't want to do this with her right now. I almost made it, I had one foot on the stairs, but she stopped me.

"*So*...did you have fun this weekend?" she asked, her tone was accusing.

I ducked down a little like I just avoided a slap. I could feel the weight of her words on my shoulders.

"Uh, yes," was all I could get out between my now panicked breaths.

"Don't worry. I saved the rest of that laundry for you...oh yeah, and there's a mess in the kitchen." She sounded bored.

I was taking slow deep breaths in, struggling to gain some kind of control so I could speak. There was no way I could let her just keep talking to me like this. I closed my eyes for just a second, and found a small amount of control that way. "I thought you were going to finish the laundry?" I opened my eyes so I could watch her face.

She held her cool composure. "And why would I do that?"

I took another slow breath in and let it out. "Because you said you would take care of it." I could feel myself slowly starting to gain control of my nerves. I felt myself become stronger and more confident with each breath I took in.

My mother lightly chuckled. "Tell me, why on earth would I do your job for you?"

I was starting to get angry. "Uh, cause it's my birthday today," I said. I was getting louder now.

"It's a lot of people's birthdays today," she replied. I gasped.

"You told me, in front of my friends, and Mémé, that you would never make me do chores on my birthday."

"What?" She sounded surprised and folded her arms. "Do you actually think you deserve special treatment just because it's your birthday? Don't you think your being selfish, Veronica?"

This woman was giving me a headache. "How am I being the selfish one... *Mom*?! I do all the chores all the time!" I yelled.

She got up from the sofa, and began shaking her finger at me. "You think I get a day off of work because it's my birthday? I don't get any special treatment! Why should you?! It's not like your anything special!"

I gasped, I was insulted and I'm sure it showed. "Like Katie?!" I yelled back. It was at that point when I noticed Katie was still playing her piano, only now she seemed to be playing faster. As my mother and I went around and around arguing about how Katie's better than I am, the louder we got, and the faster Katie seemed to be playing.

"I'll bet when Katie's a famous musician she's gonna tell you to shove it!" I yelled at her. My mother flinched.

"She would never do that!" she yelled at me.

"If she's smart she will!" I yelled back.

My mother and I were out of breath, frustrated and staring each other down. I decided to go for it.

I had both fists clenched hard. "Where's... My... Letters?" My chest heaved in and out between each word. I tried very hard not to just yell that.

My mother's face went blank. "What letters?" she said calmly.

"The ones from Dad," I said.

"He never sent you any letters," she said very coolly, but I saw a shift in her eyes, and I knew right there she was lying.

"Liar!" I stated this with confidence, and this time she was the one who ducked.

"Don't you talk to me that way! He doesn't write to you! —He doesn't even love you!"

"Liar!" I said again. "He does love me, he always has! *MY FATHER TOLD ME HE HAS SENT ME MAIL!*" I yelled as loud as I could and shook my finger at her. "*NOW WHERE IS IT?!*" I demanded with clenched fists.

"YOU UNGRATEFUL LITTLE BITCH!" she yelled, and then slapped me right across my face.

I was stunned, she slapped me hard. Instinct made me immediately cover my slapped cheek with my hand, the pain lingered.

"How dare you speak to me that way!" She stood over me with clenched fists. "After all I've done for you!" She was shouting just inches from my face.

I ran up the stairs to my room and slammed the door shut, locking the door.

"DON'T YOU RUN AWAY FROM ME!" she screamed. She was like a wild animal as she flew up the stairs behind me, and began pounding on the door.

I opened the door and faced her down getting inches from her face.

"HE SENT ME MAIL! WHAT DID YOU DO WITH IT?!" I screamed at her.

She crossed her arms with a crazed look in her eyes. "I threw it in the garbage." She was smug.

"I HATE YOU!" I screamed in her face. "I want to go live with Dad!"

"Well you can't." She kept her arms crossed and her face was smug. "You can't even live with your Mémé. I would never allow that. What would people think? You have to live with me." She chuckled darkly. "You have no choice."

I went back into my room slamming the door again right in her face and I turned the lock. I was beyond mad now.

Birthdays suck! I'm skipping over the whole stupid thing next year!

My mother tapped lightly against the door. "I want you to get a little something straight. You live in my house, and you're *my* child. So, you will do every single thing I tell you to do or there will be hell to pay." She paused for a moment. "Get used to that room honey, because you'll be in there for a while." She was sounding so casual and satisfied because she thought she won. "Oh, and guess whose chores just increased tenfold. And you can forget about seeing your little friends for a long time," she said through the door. "Oh yeah, if I ever find out you went behind my back again talking to your father, I'll make you wish you were never born."

I laid down on my bed and listened to my mother's footsteps fade down the stairs before I let myself start breaking down.

I hate her.

If she thinks she's gonna keep me locked up in this place like a prisoner, she's wrong. I heard the front door slam and I went to the window. I watched my mother get into her car and pull out of the driveway. Cool, maybe she won't come back! I laughed out loud. Too bad I didn't see any suitcases, because then I could really celebrate!

There was a soft knock on my door. "Veronica? Can I come in?"

I sighed. "Yeah." I went and unlocked my door for Katie. I'm not mad at her. Katie came in and sat on my bed, her face wet with tears. "Are you alright?" she asked.

"Katie, do I look alright?" I was crying too, I'm sure my face was a mess.

"No," she said quietly. "You guys really scared me. Why did you have to yell at her like that?"

"Katie, she makes me do *all* of the chores, and she treats me different then she treats you. Not that I think you don't deserve it. But, it would be nice if she treated me the same as you."

She just nodded. Even she couldn't deny that.

"You know Daddy has been writing to us, and Mom has just been taking our letters and throwing them in the garbage. That's the one I'm most angry about. I don't care anymore whether or not she likes or loves me. But she needs to leave my relationship with the one parent who does alone. She could have just continued to ignore me like usual and just given me my mail and this fight would never have happened."

"Daddy's been writing to us?" She seemed surprised.

"Yes."

"But Mom told me he doesn't love us anymore, and that's why he left us."

"Open your eyes *Katie*, she lied to you!" I sighed. "That's all she does, lies, lies, *lies!* You can't believe anything she says. Dad does love us."

Katie sat on the edge of my bed and curled her legs in.

"Mom left you know," she said quietly.

"Yeah I know."

"What if she doesn't come back?"

"Katie, we'll be alright. You and I were always okay, remember?"

"Yeah." She smiled a little.

"This time we can call Mémé, she's right down the street. She's not stuck out on a boat like Dad was."

"Can I sleep in here tonight?" she asked.

"Sure, but don't expect me to be pleasant company tonight," I warned her.

Katie smiled and hopped across my bed and crawled in. "Thanks, Roni."

"Just don't hog all the covers." I poked her belly making her laugh.

When I woke up in the morning it was quiet. The sun was shining through the window hitting the wall in a funny direction. I felt well rested. A little too well rested. I looked over at my alarm clock and it said it was eight fifteen.

"Crap! Katie come on, we missed the bus!" I shouted jumping out of bed. I started rummaging through my bureau looking for something to wear. Katie was standing quietly by the window. "Katie come on, we have to hurry up!"

"Is she dead?" Katie quietly asked.

I stopped and snapped my head around. "What?"

"Is she dead?" Katie asked again.

I made my way to the window and peered through my curtain, and I gasped. I started dressing in a hurry while running down the stairs.

"Call Mémé!" I shouted at Katie. "She'll know what to do."

I threw my shoes on fast and grabbed my jacket. I flung the door open and ran outside. Everything was a blur. My mother was lying on the lawn half out of her car, covered in vomit. In the seconds it took me to get to my mother, a torrent of thoughts was flooding my mind. Oh God, what if she is dead? What if the fight we had last night was our last conversation? I was so angry, and full of hatred towards her, but I didn't want

to end things with her that way. Because, I would forever have to live with the fact that it was our fight that
caused her to leave the way she did last night.

Please, let her be alright.

"MOM!" I yelled. I knelt down next to her and put my
hands on her face and her neck. She was still warm,
and still had a pulse. Thank God! I thought. I was
shaking her and slapping her face trying to get her to
wake up.

She was obviously very drunk, and she smelled horrible. How she can be passed out on the lawn in December baffled me. Doesn't she feel the cold?

Katie came outside. "Is she okay?" she asked.

"Yeah I think so." I turned to look at her. "She's just
drunk."

Mémé pulled into the driveway and flung herself out
of the car, rushing over to my mom. "You girls go inside now and get ready for school." Katie complied, but
I hesitated.

"Do you want me to help you with her?" I asked. I
was feeling so guilty, if we didn't have that big fight last
night she wouldn't be like this now.

Mémé dragged my mother onto her feet and slung
her arm over her shoulder. "Veronica, just get the
door."

She lugged my mother into the house and laid her
on the couch.

My mother suddenly burst into laughter, and was
rolling around. "Katie, go up to the bathroom and get

me a wet washcloth," Mémé said. "Veronica, you go get the aspirin and a glass of water."

I went into the kitchen and got what she asked for, and I grabbed the pail from under the sink. I knew from past experience that she was probably gonna need it.

I put the pills and the water on the coffee table, and placed the pail on the side of the couch.

"What's so funny?" Mémé asked her, she sounded annoyed.

Mémé grabbed the wet washcloth from Katie and began trying to clean my mother's face. My mother then went from the hysterical laughter to crying and clutching her head.

"Now, what's the matter?" Mémé sighed.

My mother leaned over the couch and started heaving into the bucket. Mémé began rubbing my mother's back, and held her hair. "How you can keep doing this to yourself, I'll never understand."

My mother laid back on the couch moaning, clutching her head again. "Could you not be so loud," she whispered. "My head is pounding."

"I'll bet it is," Mémé replied. "Girls, why don't you get your stuff together, and I'll give you a ride to school this morning." She handed two aspirins to my mother and handed her the glass of water. "You take these and sleep this off. I'll be back after I take the girls to school. Would you like me to make you some breakfast?"

My mother groaned. "No food."

I grabbed my book bag. I was thankful that I was going to school. Watching my mother like this made me feel so horrible. Especially knowing everything was all my fault.

On the way to school Katie and I were quiet in the car. I don't know what was going through Katie's mind, but I know I was feeling guilty for the way my mother was this morning.

"This is all my fault," I whispered.

Mémé glanced over at me. "What's your fault?" she asked.

"Mom leaving last night, and coming home drunk." I hung my head down.

"Veronica, how is any of that your fault?" she asked.

"Because, I had a fight with Mom last night. I made her so angry with me. I asked her about the letters. I shouldn't have done that."

Mémé glanced at me with furrowed brows. "You were not wrong in asking her about the letters. Asking her was the right thing. Your mother is an adult, and she made the decision to go out, and she made the decision to drink. She is responsible for herself. Don't let your mother's behavior make you feel bad. You're facing your problems, she's not. Every time she takes a drink she is drowning them not facing them."

I looked over at Mémé. "Then what should I do? I feel like I should apologize, or something."

"I'm not sure that you should try to do anything just yet. She's in no shape at the moment anyway."

We pulled into my school and Mémé pulled up to the front door and parked. "I know you girls have been through so much this morning," she started. "But for the rest of the day, I don't want either of you to think about any of it. So, the moment you step outside this car and shut the door, Veronica, case closed. Your mother is gonna be my problem for the rest of the day. I'll be spending the day at your house, so I'll see you both when you come home."

I got out of the car and shut the door. I heard Mémé yell, "Case closed, Veronica!" I turned back, nodded and forced a smile, then walked into the middle school.

I did my best as I always do, to try not to think about what happened this morning, and last night, but it was hard to do. Especially when your friends know you and can tell when something is bothering you.

When Evelyn, Leslie, and I sat down at our lunch table, Evelyn just about burst. "So, what happened? And why were you so late this morning?"

"A lot happened...really, there's too much to talk about right now. Can we talk about this later?" I begged.

Evelyn sat up in her chair. "Veronica, we care about you. We can tell something's bothering you, now tell us!"

"You know we'd never tell anyone," Leslie added.

"I know. I just didn't want to talk about any of it yet," I replied.

"Did you ask her about the letters?" Evelyn asked.

"Yes," I sighed. I might as well just get it over with, I thought to myself. "We had a big fight, too. I think it was our biggest. She admitted to throwing out my letters from my dad, and then she grounded me to kingdom come."

Evelyn shook her head. "I can't believe she was just throwing out your letters like that, and she grounded you for even asking, that's bull!"

I nodded. "I know, I'm still pretty mad about that," I said.

"I agree, Veronica. She's always grounding you, she treats you so unfairly," Leslie added.

"I know, and that will probably never change." I sighed. "There really isn't that much I can do about any of it right now anyway."

"Don't tell me you're just gonna take that crap," Evelyn replied.

"What choice do I really have? I'm stuck, I can't just go live with Mémé, I already asked. And Dad said I can't live with him right now either. He still lives alone and he's still working on the boat. I'm just going to have to deal with Donna for now."

"I bet you could live at my house, my mom loves you," Evelyn suggested.

"I would if I could," I told her. "But I'm only thirteen. I don't think my mother will just let me go without making a really big deal right now, and do you blame her? She has a live-in maid and a babysitter so she is free to do whatever she wants."

I was in no hurry when I was walking home from the bus stop. Can you really blame me? When I left this morning, my mother was a vomiting, moaning, wreck on the couch. I can only imagine what she's like now.

When I walked into the house the living room was dark, and all the curtains were closed. Mom was snoring on the couch, with a washcloth across her face. Katie wouldn't be home for about another hour. If I'm quiet enough, I can make my way across the living room to the kitchen, then I can probably get my homework done. I don't know what my night will be like and I would like to have one less thing to worry about tonight.

I wonder what time Mémé left or if she's coming back anytime soon? She said she'd be here when we came home. Maybe I should think about dinner for Katie and me tonight as well.

I've come a long way from the peanut butter sandwiches of long ago. I find cooking to be quite easy, and it does help to have someone like my Mémé teaching me how. The only problem I run into living here and having to make dinner is the lack of ingredients. My mother might be a regular at the dress shops, but grocery stores are a foreign land to her. I looked through the cabinets and in our freezer, and sighed. The only thing I can come up with for tonight is spaghetti and meat sauce. The hamburger is frozen solid so there aren't too many options. I'll just have to brown the hamburger in the pan to thaw it for the sauce. I put the hamburger on the counter and sat down as quietly as I could to start my homework.

I sat down and opened up my social studies book to the page we are currently on, but then I got interrupted.

"Is somebody here?" I heard my mother whimper from the living room.

I got up from the table and went into the living room so I wouldn't have to yell (I know better). "What's the matter, Mom?"

"Oh." She moaned, and turned to her side. "I need my ice pack."

"Okay." I went back into the kitchen and grabbed the ice pack from the top of the refrigerator and the ice cube tray from the freezer, and I put them on the kitchen table. I grabbed a glass bowl from the cupboard, and put it on the table.

I hate our ice cube tray, lifting that handle to get the ice cubes out can be quite the pain in the butt. I forced the ice cubes out of the tray and filled the ice pack then screwed on the top. I put the remaining ice cubes in the bowl and stuck them back in the freezer. I then made sure I refilled the ice cube tray and stuck that back into the freezer too, and it all just barely fit.

I went back out to the living room and handed my mother the ice pack. "Here."

I hesitated before just going back into the kitchen. "Mom?" I spoke softly.

"What is it?" she whispered.

"I just wanted to say that I'm sorry about yesterday."

"Uh, huh." She placed the ice pack on her head and turned over. I sighed and went back into the kitchen.

Well that seemed useless. I know Mémé said I have nothing to apologize for, but I still felt bad and I thought apologizing might make me feel better.

It didn't really. I felt the same. Why don't I feel better? Actually, it almost felt wrong to apologize to her. That kind of bothers me. Am I a bad person? No, I don't think that's it. I'm generous and giving, and I'm never mean or rude to anyone. Well, unless they deserve it.

I didn't have that much homework. I got through it pretty quick, just social studies and math. I got up and quietly began some of my chores. I washed all the dishes that were in the sink, and wiped down the counters and the table. Then I took out the broom and swept the already tidy floor.

I didn't know what to do next, so I just sat down at the table. I folded my arms on the table and rested my head, chin down. Well, this is different, I thought. I would start the rest of the chores I normally do but most of them would make way too much noise and I don't want to wake my mom.

Hmmm, why do I call her that? I wondered.

Mom.

It does feel kinda strange sometimes when I call her that. It almost doesn't fit. She's not really a mom. A mom is someone who takes care of their children. Mine does not. Well, she takes care of Katie⊠just not me. Maybe I'm not her kid? Maybe she found me on the doorstep one morning, and took me in because she thought animals might eat me, and was just nice enough to keep me inside expecting my real mother would return. But my real mother was struck down by a bus and killed, so then Donna was stuck with me.

I sighed, the chance of that being true is very slim.

Maybe the maternal instinct that most of the other mothers have was never triggered in Donna Edwards. That's it! God forgot to flip her switch! Or maybe he just flipped the wrong one? You know, the one marked *crazy*!

I laughed quietly to myself. I wondered randomly if she would get mad if I started calling her Donna, or Miss Edwards.

I flexed my arms out stretching and I caught sight of my bracelet. I ran my fingers across the top feeling the beads the way I always do. I know this sounds a little odd (and I would never admit this to anyone), but sometimes when I do that it feels like I'm connected to him. Like maybe he's thinking about me, too.

I continued to just sit there at the table. I was enjoying the peace and quiet, along with my random thoughts. I just let myself zone out, staring at my bracelet for a while. I wonder where he is? He did mention a few times he had a grandfather. Maybe he went to live with him? I hope so. Why hasn't he written to me? I would have written to him, but I didn't know where to send anything to. Then I had a horrible realization. What if Jackson wrote to me and she threw out those letters, too? I could actually feel my blood starting to boil, and I wanted to run out in the living room and demand to know right now. I would hate her for all eternity. Wait, let me think about that ...yes, yes, I would!

"Okay, just calm down. You don't know if he even sent you anything. You'll just have to wait for Mémé so you can ask her," I had to tell myself. Now I was talking to myself like I was talking to another person. Maybe I'm crazy now?

Maybe Jackson didn't know our actual address? His mom always dropped him off all the time. It's not like we we're writing to each other all the time then. Oh, now see, Jackson was so lucky to have Joan for his mom, even if it was only a short while. *Oh*, and how she adored him! I used to love to watch her with him. The way she would casually put her arm around him, or just fix his hair. She would smile wide every single time she saw him! Who could blame her though, Jackson's the best.

I heard the back door open, and I sat up quickly, drying my eyes. I had let a few tears escape while I was daydreaming about my friend, and his beautiful mother.

"Veronica?" I heard Mémé call out.

"In here," I choked a little. I had to cough to clear my throat.

Mémé came into the kitchen through the back door, her arms were full. "What are you doing just sitting in here?" she asked.

"Oh, nothing. I just cleaned up and I did my homework. What did you bring?"

"I picked up a bucket of chicken for dinner tonight. I hope you're hungry."

"Yeah, I am. That's good, I guess I can just put that hamburger in the refrigerator to thaw and I'll cook it tomorrow."

"Were you planning on cooking dinner?" Mémé asked.

"Sort of. I didn't know what was going on tonight so I took the hamburger out of the freezer just in case. It was a good thing I did that, I had to make room for the bowl of ice anyway."

"Why? Did she need the ice pack?"

"Yeah..." I trailed off a little because the ice pack didn't have anything to do with the topic it ended up reminding me of.

"Mémé," I spoke softly, I didn't want Mom to overhear. "Has Jackson ever sent me any letters to your house?"

"No, I'm sorry he hasn't... You still think about him, don't you?"

"Sometimes. I just wish I knew where he was so I could write to him or something."

"I'm sure he's fine. That poor boy went through a lot. You have to try to remember that everybody has their own way of coping or dealing with tragedy and loss. You just never know how something like that will affect you until you go through it. He may not be ready to write to you. He might be afraid to."

That seemed silly to me, Jackson afraid of me? Yeah right. "Why would he be afraid of me?"

"Well most of the times he came to the house he was with his mother. Maybe he's afraid he'll end up thinking about her when he's not ready to."

"Oh." I guess that made sense. "So, trying to find out his address somehow so I can write him might be bad then?"

Mémé put her arm around me and gave me a hug. "It might, I don't really know. You have to give people space sometimes. For now, you're just gonna have to learn to be patient in matters such as these."

I nodded. I know she's probably right. It's just hard sometimes. I miss my friend.

Mémé and I both turned when we heard the front door open.

"Mom?" we heard Katie call out.

"Oh, I'm right here honey," I heard Mom reply. She wasn't whimpering the way she was just an hour earlier. Mémé was just about to walk out into the living room but I put my hand on her shoulder to stop her.

"Are you alright?" Katie asked Mom.

"Yes, I'm fine, Sweetie," she said.

"What happened?"

"I was just really upset last night, that's all."

"Why were you so upset?"

"Your sister upset me. She really hurt Mommy's feelings. She yelled at me. All I ever ask her to do is to help us out around the house, it's the least she could do. I work so hard for the both of you every day, and she just doesn't appreciate anything I do for her."

"I appreciate you, Mommy."

"I know you do, Sweetie, I love you. You're the good girl."

I just slumped down in a chair at the kitchen table. I didn't want to go out into the living room. I was a little stunned. Mémé just stood there quiet, and held her hand on my shoulder. Why? Was all that went through my mind. Why is she like this? Why am I here? What purpose is there for me being here in this house? If I'm such a freaking disappointment then why doesn't she just send me to live with Dad? Or let me live with Mémé?

I got up from the table and walked right into the living room. I glanced over at both my mother and my sister giving them both the meanest stare I could muster up, and went upstairs to my room.

I shut and locked the door, and then curled up on the floor next to my bed pulling my knees up to my chest. I was angry, and I have every right to be. I always feel so alone here. Mom and Katie have each other and I have no one. I do everything for them, and they still treat me like crap! I'm so sick and tired of being mad and miserable all the time! I've come to realize that I'll never really be a part of this family. Sucker is no longer stenciled on this girl's forehead.

The only way I'm ever gonna be happy is if I get out of here.

I leaned over and reached my arm under my bed and grabbed my music box from its hiding spot behind my nightstand.

When we lived with Mémé and Grandpa I had no problems keeping this on top of my dresser. But, once we moved here I had some anxiety about just leaving it out like I did there. It was probably some sort of survival instinct I had telling me to protect it, and with obvious good reason.

I opened up the box and took out the money that I had stashed there and counted it. I still have one hundred and fifty dollars saved up from birthdays and from working at the resort. It wasn't hard to save this up at all, and I bet I can save up more. I wonder if Mémé will let me work extra this summer. Oh! And on April vacation! A plan started to form in my mind. I'll work and save every penny I get. I'll get my driver's license, too. I'll bet Mémé and Grandpa will help me with that. As soon as I have enough saved up, I'll buy myself a car, and I'm out of here! I'll go back to San Francisco, and I'll find a job. I wonder how much it costs to rent a small apartment out there. It's not like I need much.

I just have to make sure starting now that I stay on track. No fooling around, just working and saving. Those are now my top priorities, if I ever want to be happy again.

* * *

"Your mother was, horrible!" I told her, interrupting her story.

She laughed. "True, it was not easy living with her."

"Why would anyone have to live like that? Or the way I did in that life?" I couldn't help wondering out loud.

I felt her shrug. "I'm not too sure. Perhaps some of us have behaved like that before in previous lives, and the universe is trying to teach us what it feels like to be on the receiving end? I'm just guessing really. I don't really know."

I leaned my head back to glance up at her. "I guess that does make some sense," I replied. I placed my head back in my spot against her chest and tightened my arm around her so she could continue. She kissed the top of my head.

"I spent most of my time after that working hard, and saving every penny. The fighting between my mother and I continued, and really began to escalate after I turned seventeen..."

CHAPTER 14

March/1975

I pulled my arms through the sleeves of my jean jacket pulling it on over my favorite concert tee. I ran my fingers along my neck to pull my hair out from under the collar. I did the final check of my overnight bag, making sure I have everything I need for a night like this one. Tee-shirt, a pair of pants, underwear, comfy socks, and of course, my toothbrush. My heart pounded loudly as I pulled the zipper shut.

"Psst! Veronica! ⊠*VER-O-NI-CA*!" Evelyn whispered loudly.

I quickly got to my bedroom window pulling it open, and leaned out before Evelyn could alert the entire house to the fact that I'm sneaking out.

"Shut up!" I whispered loudly. "*This is serious!*" I leaned back in to listen just in case.

I reached out and I dropped my overnight bag into Evelyn's arms.

I leaned back in listening very carefully for any sign that I might be getting caught. All was quiet so I leaned back out. "Okay! Chuck it!" I whispered down to Evelyn.

Evelyn tossed up a bundle of rope I had asked her to get from her dad's garage. I caught it and got to work quickly tying it as tight as I could around the bottom of my bed post. I tossed the remaining part of the rope out the window and prepared myself. I stuck a leg out and straddled the window. I took the rope into one hand and grabbed the edge of the window with the other. I slowly started lowering myself down, and then used the rope to climb down the side of the house like Spiderman. Once I was close enough to the ground I let go of the rope and landed on my feet.

Evelyn and I both laughed. "Where did you park?" I asked her.

"Down the street a little...let's go!"

We ran down the street into the night, giggling as we did.

In a normal family, this sort of thing might not be necessary. Unfortunately, this is how my life is now. And when I want a little freedom these are the kinds of drastic measures I'm being forced to.

I was going to drive myself tonight. But my mother was so kind to let the air out of two of my tires while I was in the shower getting ready to go out. *Bitch*.

See, she insisted that I was to go nowhere this evening (she said I was grounded), like flattening my tires would somehow stop me.

Donna and I are no longer seeing eye-to-eye anymore. She continues to try to ground me for all sorts of things that she feels I did wrong. She screams and yells, and I simply ignore every single thing she says, and keep going on about my business.

It was inevitable really. Did she really think that I would just continue to be something she stomped on like a door mat? Um, I think not. I'm almost out of here anyway. I've saved up quite a bit of money and when this school year is up I'm leaving for California, and I've only got four months to go.

I'm planning on finishing school there. I could probably get away with saying I live with my dad until I'm officially eighteen, which will be halfway through my senior year. I'm seventeen now anyway, she wouldn't be able to stop me. Heck, I dare her to try.

Donna has a new boyfriend nowadays, too. His name is Ray Phillips, and she has him living with us. He's a freeloading, annoying jerk, who doesn't work and just sweats and drools all over our couch all day, and I can't stand him. With him around, I can't trust my mother with anything, or put anything past her either.

It's no surprise that she's always made my life difficult. But when my seventeenth birthday rolled around and Mémé and Grandpa surprised me with a 1970 blue Plymouth Cricket, *well*...she lost it. It seems now her main mission is to make my life as miserable as possible every day, as opposed to the occasional misery I had grown accustomed to. I had been saving up to buy a car on my own, but my wonderful grandparents took it upon themselves to give me one instead, which has put me even closer to my goal⬛getting the hell out of here.

I'll have to deal with the two flat tires later. Mémé is going to be so pissed when I tell her. I hate just leaving my car unguarded like that but there was absolutely no way I was gonna miss out on tonight's plans.

Evelyn's brother, Greg, is working at this bar called Wicked Riff's. It's right on the edge of town. Okay, technically it's not even in Moodus. It's in Colchester, but who really cares. The place is so cool. Greg's a bartender there, and he knows about mine and Evelyn's crazy obsession with hard rock music. Bands like Led Zeppelin, Aerosmith, Black Sabbath, and Deep Purple are the best. Of course, the louder they are, the better.

Tonight, there happens to be a great live hard rock band playing, and Greg was nice enough to talk his boss into getting the bouncer to let us in tonight. He had to make a promise to his boss that neither of us would be drinking, and would be on our best behavior. Evelyn and I fully intend to keep up our end of Greg's promise.

Also, Evelyn said Greg's friend Kevin will be there tonight, and according to Evelyn, this would be the reason we were even invited.

Kevin likes me, and we've gone out a couple of times. He is cute. He has wavy, sandy blonde hair and blue eyes. But I have found I seem to be kinda picky about little things when it comes to guys. For example, Kevin makes this funny sucking noise sometimes when he eats (and every once in a while, when we're making out) and it can be kind of a turn off for me. I do try hard to ignore it because he's such a sweet guy, but sometimes, I just can't.

Plus, I always thought that when you meet the right person there would be sparks or some sort of feeling that you've found the one, and I just don't get any sort of feelings like that when I'm with him.

I'm not looking to get serious with anyone right now anyhow. I tell him this on a regular basis, and sometimes I'm not so sure he takes what I say seriously. I'm four months away from my freedom. I've worked so hard towards my goal, and the last thing I want is to get sidetracked.

We got into Evelyn's car and I threw my bag in the back.

"How soon do you think they'll notice you're gone?" she asked.

"Well it's March, and I left the window wide open. I'd say the odds are good that one of them will discover it pretty soon." I chuckled.

"I felt like I was helping someone escape from prison!"

"You were, living there is my own personal prison."

We pulled into the bar's parking lot, and the place was packed. There were cars everywhere, and we ended up having to park in the rear of the lot.

When we walked up to the door I could hear the band from outside, and I became excited. I felt like I was at a concert and I couldn't wait to go in.

Evelyn was the one who spoke to the bouncer. "Hey, Lou!"

"Hey, Evelyn! I was just starting to wonder about you. Greg said you and your friend were coming tonight. I was expecting you a little earlier than nine thirty."

"Yeah sorry, we ran into a slight snag on our way, but we're here now."

"Good, go on in. You girls have a good time!"

"Thanks, Lou." Evelyn winked and patted his shoulder.

Evelyn opened the door and the band's volume soared to a crazy level. The bar was packed wall to wall with people everywhere.

"This place is crazy!" I had to yell over the band.

Evelyn smiled. "Yeah it is!" she yelled back. "C'mon, let's go say hi to Greg and the boys, and we can stash our stuff behind the bar!"

"Okay," I yelled.

We began trying to make our way through the tightly packed bar, but it was very difficult. Evelyn and I started off trying to be polite as we made our way towards the bar.

"Excuse me," Evelyn and I kept repeating over and over as we tried to make our way through.

I was getting really annoyed because a lot of the people were ignoring us, and we got stuck a few times. Then when someone stepped on my toe that's when my annoyance turned to total aggravation.

I threw my hands up. "Okay, that's it!" I pushed my way in front of Evelyn, and I grabbed her hand.

"Make way, coming through!" I shouted pulling my friend's arm, while pushing, squeezing, and shoving my way through the crowd towards the boys. I was feeling very pleased with myself once we finally reached the bar.

Kevin and Paul were on the far end of the bar talking to Greg who was working behind it. Greg waved calling us over. "Hey, girls!"

"What took you guys so long?" Kevin asked. "We were starting to wonder if you were coming."

Evelyn handed Greg our jackets. "Sorry, we had to perform a prison break," Evelyn shouted over the music.

"A prison break, and who was the criminal?" Paul asked shouting back.

I put my hand up. "That would be me," I shouted. "Donna felt I should be punished for not attending Katie's dance recital the other day."

"Didn't you have to work?" Paul questioned.

"Yeah, but apparently Donna felt I should skip that and go to Katie's recital with her and Ray like a family because that's way more important."

Kevin came and stood next to me. "So why didn't you just leave like usual?" Kevin asked.

"Because earlier while I was in the shower, Donna let the air out of two of my tires. Then her and Ray sat downstairs in the living room, thinking they were blocking my only exit." A sly and proud smile crossed my face.

"So, how'd you get out?" Kevin asked.

"I called Evelyn from my mother's room. She brought me rope and I went out my bedroom window."

"Whoa...you're crazy! You could have gotten hurt," Kevin said.

"Na, I knew what I was doing. Getting by Donna is something I'm good at."

"I'm just glad you made it. Can I buy you a Coke?"

"Sure, that would be nice," I blushed.

"Hey Greg, can you get Veronica a Coke?"

"Coming up." Greg handed Kevin my Coke. Kevin smiled and handed it to me.

I leaned back against the bar and took a sip. "Thank you."

"You're welcome."

There was an awkward silence for a moment between us. So, I just sipped my Coke and began looking around at the crowd, and taking in the bar's scenery.

This place is so cool. The walls are painted red and they have bizarre things hanging from them. Things you wouldn't normally think to hang up. The walls are covered in motorcycle parts and gear, handlebars, seats, wheels, and helmets. Suspended from the ceiling is a complete motorcycle, it's shiny red and covered in chrome. I started thinking about how much it would really suck for the person standing under it if it ever fell...

"I could help you," Kevin said interrupting my thoughts.

"Um, what?" I said sounding distracted.

"With your tires, I have a tire pump in my car. I could fill them, as long as your mother didn't cut them."

"She didn't, she's not that smart," I said.

"When were you planning on going home?"

"I'm not. I'm going to my grandparents' house."

"When are you going to get your car?" That was a good question, I hadn't really thought about that yet.

"I didn't really think that far ahead yet," I admitted.

"Well, if you want, I could give you a ride home later, and I'll pump up your tires for you. Then I'll follow you to your grandparents' house."

"Is it gonna make a lot of noise? Because I'm not interested if it's gonna wake up Donna."

"No, we'll be real quiet. She'll never know anything."

"Thanks Kevin, that sounds like a great plan."

Evelyn grabbed my arm. "They're playing 'Immigrant Song!' Let's go!" She dragged me and we pushed our way to the front of the crowd where the band was playing.

Evelyn and I started dancing. We always get so carried away when we listen to hard rock music. We never have any sort of real rhyme or reason when we're dancing. We mostly just jump up and down, throw our arms up, and turn. We probably look ridiculous, but we're having so much fun that neither of us ever care.

It's really too bad Leslie doesn't share our love of hard rock. She prefers R&B and she's not hanging out with us as often anymore. She's really into running track now, and she's obsessed with training, exercise, and her competitions. Sometimes, Evelyn and I go to her track meets to cheer her on, and we still all sit together at lunch.

Evelyn and I danced to five songs before we were even tired. I was the one who had to stop. It was so hot in there, and I needed a drink.

"C'mon, Evelyn." I had to lean in and talk in her ear. "Let's go see your brother and get a drink," I panted.

Evelyn nodded. "Yeah, good idea!"

The crowd around the bar was a lot bigger than it was before. We had to really squeeze and push to go back to the end of the bar where we were.

"You girls looked like you were having fun," Kevin shouted.

"Yeah, it's hot though. I need a Coke."

"One Coke, coming right up!" Kevin shouted.

I stood there leaning against the bar waiting for Kevin to return with my Coke. Suddenly, I got shoved from the side, and I felt something ice cold soak my back. "*Ahh!*" It was such a huge shock, and I turned around quick. A guy with jet-black hair sitting at the bar got shoved off his stool and spilled his beer all down my back, and boy was I mad!

"*Hey*!" I shouted at the man. "Watch what you're doing!"

The man glanced over his shoulder. "Sorry."

I barely caught a glimpse of his face. He was no one I knew, and he didn't look much older than I was. He must go to school in Colchester or something. I think he might be crazy. His hair was hanging in his face and he was wearing dark black sunglasses. Who wears sunglasses at night? And in a dark bar? He stood up from his stool, nodded, and walked away going towards the pool tables.

Kevin returned with my Coke and I was still quite pissed.

"Here you go." He handed me my drink. "Whoa, why are you all wet?"

"Some dumbass just spilled his beer all down my back! Now I'm gonna be wet and stink like beer the rest of the night!"

"We should let Greg know so no one thinks you girls were drinking tonight. I'd like to see you be able to come back in here again."

I nodded at him. "Good idea."

I told Greg and his boss what happened and I described the guy. I pointed in the direction I saw him go. They both went looking for him but ended up not finding him, which was just fine by me. With a guy like that, who knows what could have happened!

Around twelve thirty I had had enough. "Hey Evelyn, is your car unlocked?"

"Yeah, why, do you want to go?"

"Yeah, Kevin's gonna give me a ride home and help me get my car, then he's gonna follow me to Mémé's."

She raised her eyebrow and smirked. "Cool, make sure you call me tomorrow." She winked.

I just rolled my eyes at her, and gave her a hug. "See ya."

I was quiet on the ride home, for a lot of reasons. Mostly because I was still grouchy from that guy who spilled his drink on me. I was still all wet and now sitting in it, and all I could smell was beer. The other reason was I wasn't sure how quiet Kevin could really be, and if he wakes my mother it will be World War III on the front lawn, which I know the neighbors will love listening to in the middle of the night.

"Kevin, would you mind not pulling right up to my house? I want to make sure I don't wake anyone."

"Veronica, I already planned on doing that. Have a little faith."

"Sorry, I'm just paranoid."

We pulled over about three houses down from mine, and Kevin turned off the car. We both got out; I grabbed my bag out of the back seat and he went over to his trunk and took out the air pump. We started walking to my house and the neighborhood was quiet. The sky was so clear tonight, there were a million stars in the sky. "Have you ever noticed how much clearer you can see the stars in the winter as compared to the summer?" I asked him. "I wonder why that is?"

"Hmm, I don't know. Speaking of winter, aren't you cold?"

"Yeah, I'm still not totally dry yet. I can't believe that happened to me. I swear, I have all the luck!"

Kevin chuckled. "Here...why don't you take my jacket."

"Awe Kevin." I felt awkward. I didn't want to take his jacket. He'll start thinking this is serious, and I can't deal with that right now. "You don't have to do that. I'm fine, really."

"Veronica, I insist." He smiled and took it off and held it up for me.

I tried one more attempt at dodging wearing his jacket. "Are you sure you want me to wear it? I stink like beer."

"Of course." He held the jacket open for me and bounced it a little until I finally slipped my arms in. I have to admit it was definitely warmer.

When we got to my house, I was thankful that all the lights were off, which means no one is expecting me to come home tonight. I always wonder if they ever really miss me when I go out, or if they give me the hard time that they do in hopes that maybe I'll decide not to return. There's always questions, and sometimes there really is no answer to them.

Kevin got to work right away pumping up my tires. I was thankful, but even more thankful that I had thought to grab my keys before I left.

"I still can't believe she did this," I said to him quietly.

"Yeah, it is a little screwy that a mom would let the air out of her daughter's tires like that." He stood up and brushed his pants off. "All finished. Do you want me to push your car out of the driveway so you don't wake anyone by starting it?"

"Na, I don't care if she hears me. It's not like I'm coming home until tomorrow...or maybe the next day."

Kevin chuckled.

"Are you warm enough with just the flannel?" I asked him.

"Sure. Besides, I wouldn't want you to be cold and uncomfortable," he replied.

"Well then, when would you like your jacket back?"

"You can give it to me Monday in school." He smiled. "You know, Veronica, you deserve so much better than the way she treats you."

I sighed. "Yeah, I'm aware of that."

"Then why do you put up with it?" he asked.

"I didn't really have a choice before, but I've been saving, and I'll be moving at the end of the school year."

"Really? Where are you moving to?"

"Back out to California to be near my father."

"Are you serious?" he asked, he seemed surprised.

"Yes, I'm not happy here. I have no reason to stay."

Kevin's face went long, and then his expression became serious. "You know, you do have reasons to stay here."

"Really? And what are they?" I crossed my arms. "Enlighten me."

"Well, you have your grandparents. They obviously love you. They did buy you a car."

"Yes, but my Mémé said I can't live there because Donna would never allow that."

"Well, what about your friends?"

"My friends?" I asked.

"Yeah, what about Evelyn? You two are joined at the hip, aren't you?"

"True, we are most days. She knows about my plan and is completely supportive. I was considering asking her to join me."

"Oh, I didn't know that." He sighed, and moved in a little closer.

"What about me?" he asked softly.

"You?" I could feel where this might be going. "And what about you?"

"Yes me. I could make you happy. I think you deserve so much better than this." He waved his hand towards the house. "If you'd just let me, I could give you so much. I'd do anything for you."

He leaned in closer, and he was inches away from my face. I froze holding my breath. "Anything?" I spoke softly. It came out like a question.

"Yes, anything." He held my face in his hands and swept some hair out of my face. "We could get our own place together," he whispered. "Just you and me. I would take care of you the way you deserve." He slowly leaned in, coming closer, and I could feel his warm breath as he gently caressed my lips with his, and it made me shiver. When he finally pressed his lips to mine, my will crumbled, and I was kissing him.

Kevin always seems to know just what to say to make me kiss him. A part of me doesn't really mind, I like making out with Kevin. I do get a small thrill from it. But I still don't get that feeling that I think I should when I kiss him and it bothers me. Maybe that's something that only happens in movies?

I started to wonder if I could be happy living with Kevin. But there was this part of me that was shouting, *You don't even know if you love him! Don't let him sidetrack you! Stick to the plan, Veronica!*

Kevin did follow through with what he said about following me to Mémé's house, which was nice of him. I pulled my car around to the back where the cabins are and parked in front of one of the heated cabins Mémé leaves unlocked for me in case I need it, which lately seems to be pretty often.

Ahhh, the cabin, or my second home as I like to call it. It has everything I need on a night like this—heat, a hot shower, and a bed.

I owe my Mémé and Grandpa a ton. If it wasn't for them, I wouldn't have gotten the job I have now at the nursery school. Mémé noticed how much I loved working with the kids here in the summers, and I guess some of the parents commented on how good I was with them, so she got me a job at ABC's & 123's Nursery School and Daycare. I work part time every day after school until six, working with preschool-aged children. At first, I was only assisting, but now I am doing some teaching as well. The director found I have a gift for working with children that have special needs and who have difficulty learning. I'm not totally sure how I do it exactly, but I can relate to young kids in a way most adults can't. Maybe it was my strong aversion I've always had towards most adults that fuels this talent. I'm not really sure what it is. I love working with the little kids, and when I get out to California I plan on going to school to become a full-time preschool teacher.

Then they helped me get my license. My Grandpa was nice enough to teach me how to drive and he took me down to get my license. Driving is so easy. I was surprised at myself how fast I learned.

Then they went above and beyond with getting me my car. I really am grateful, and I don't know how I'll ever repay them.

Then they let me stay here whenever I need to, no questions asked.

Well, it is Mémé. She can't really resist asking me something like, "So what happened this time?" or "what did my daughter do now?"

I turned on the lights and the heat when I walked in shutting the door behind me, and headed straight for the bathroom. I couldn't wait to wash off the stink from the bar. I can't believe that guy spilled his entire beer down my back and then just left the way he did⊠what a jerk!

I took a nice hot shower, brushed my teeth, and crawled into bed. *Ahhh*, I didn't realize how tired and achy I really was until I laid down. I started thinking about Kevin and some of the things he was saying. He couldn't be serious. He doesn't even know me. So, I can't take any of that at face value. Plus, while we were kissing he made that sucking noise he makes when he eats. I shivered, I really don't know how much farther this is gonna go.

When I woke in the morning, I did what I always do.

I got up, I got dressed, and I changed the sheets. I turned the heat off, and I picked up all my stuff making sure the cabin was the way I found it.

I tossed my stuff in my car, and walked up towards the house to get some breakfast. When I got to the door Grandpa opened it before I could.

"Good morning!" he said, smiling wide. "So, didja sleep in the cabin last night?" he asked.

I smiled back. "Good morning, Grandpa. Yes, I slept out there."

"Did you want a little breakfast?" he asked.

"Yeah, sure," I replied.

"Well go ahead and help yourself. You know where everything is."

I grabbed a bowl and a spoon from the strainer, grabbed the box of Sugar Crisps and the milk, and sat down with Grandpa at the table. I put my breakfast together and started eating.

"So, what happened this time?" Mémé asked when she came into the kitchen.

I had to finish chewing and swallowing before I could answer. "She was mad at me because I missed Katie's recital the other day."

"Why did you miss Katie's recital?" she asked.

"I had to work. I thought I was being responsible," I said.

"You were. I'm just not getting it though, so just explain the whole thing."

I sighed. "Mom wanted me to go with her and Ray to Katie's recital as a family. I had to work and I told her that. She wanted me to call out. She said the recital was more important. I chose to go to work instead. She then told me I was grounded and that I couldn't go anywhere this weekend. But as you know, she says that every weekend. Then while I was in the shower getting ready to go out, she let the air out of two of my tires!"

"She did what?!" I knew my Mémé would react that way. "So, wait a minute, if she did that how did you drive here in it?"

"I was getting to that part." I took a breath. "Don't get mad, Mem... I called Evelyn and she brought over some rope and she helped me escape out of my bedroom window..."

Mémé and Grandpa's eyes went wide when I told them that.

"Then another friend of mine, Kevin, pumped up my tires for me, and followed me here to make sure I got here alright."

I looked over at Grandpa. "You might want to just check my tires for me. I got here okay but I'm not sure if she did any damage."

Grandpa patted my knee. "I'll take a look after breakfast."

Mémé crossed her arms. "All of this is because of this Ray character?"

I nodded my head coolly. "Pretty much. Has she called here yet looking for me?"

"Not yet, why?"

"That's what I thought. I figured it out a while ago, most of this drama is for him. She doesn't really care if I actually go to Katie's recital, or if I fall off the face of the planet. Just as long as *he* thinks she does."

"Well, Grandpa and I didn't get you that car so she can trash it! It's yours, not hers." Mémé said. "I'll be sure to call her this morning and give her a piece of my mind!"

I chuckled. I love my Mémé. "I figured you'd do something like that."

"Well I can't just sit here and ignore what she did. I'll make sure she knows to keep her hands off your car."

"Thanks, Mémé."

"Oh Veronica, do you remember me telling you a while ago about that beautiful log cabin someone started building up in Devil's Hopyard?" Mémé asked, changing the subject.

"Yeah, I remember."

"The rumor around town is that whoever was building it finally finished with the inside, and that they just finished moving in there a couple of days ago. Have you gone up and seen it yet like I told you to?"

I ducked a little before I answered her. "Not yet."

Mémé hit me with a dish towel. "Veronica, you don't know what you're missing, it's beautiful!"

"I'm sorry; I've just been so busy," I replied.

"I know, you work too much. Well, you and I should take a ride this morning and go check it out."

Since moving here, I've only been to Devil's Hopyard a handful of times. It's a shame really, it is truly one of the most breathtaking places I have ever seen. It's a heavily wooded area on a winding road with stone bridges and hiking trails. My favorite part of Devil's Hopyard is Chapman Falls. It's a beautiful waterfall with a wood bridge that crosses over the top so you can look over and watch the water cascade down. One of the last times I came here was with Grandpa. He gave me a penny and told me to toss it in and make a wish. I wish I could remember what I wished for.

Mémé turned the wheel of her Town Car, turning onto the road that runs over the falls. "I know I'm driving very slowly, I just don't want you to miss anything about it," she said.

I turned to look at her and smirked. "Just as long as the people who live there don't call the cops because they think you're some weird crazy lady, who keeps driving by really slow."

Mémé nudged my shoulder and chuckled. "I've only come up here a few times, it's not like I drive up here every day."

She pointed up ahead. "Look right there, up on the left."

At first glance, it just looked like a typical log cabin. It was a deep rich brown color and resembled my old Lincoln Logs. But once we got up a little closer, I started seeing some of the finer details that she had described to me before. Like how the covered porch wraps around the entire house. The unique way the porch railings and slats curve and bend the way a tree would, making the house seem like it grew up from the ground. Two large picture windows framed the large dark-stained door. It truly was beautiful, and one of a kind. I'd never seen anything like it before, and of course my Mémé was right, it totally fits the Devil's Hopyard setting.

"Wow Mem, you were right. It's really beautiful," I told her.

"I usually am." She sounded smug.

"I think it needs a little something though." A funny tingling sensation came over me when I spoke.

"That house is perfect," she sounded surprised. "What on Earth could that house possibly need?" she asked.

"Plants, it needs flowers along the front porch, and maybe a couple of lilac bushes on the far corners." I suddenly had a weird case of deja-vu. "That's so weird." I shook my head.

"What's weird?" she asked.

"I just felt like I've said that before." I shook my head again. "Whoa, that was strange," I replied.

"It sounds it."

CHAPTER 15

" AND just where were you all weekend, little girl?"
Ray asked.

He was sitting at the kitchen table having his coffee. As I came down the stairs I started gagging when I caught sight of him. He was dressed in his normal morning bum attire—his boxers, dirty tee-shirt, and his wide-open hunter green bathrobe.

I kept my answer simple. "Out." I really hate talking to him.

He narrowed his eyes at me. "Your mother is very upset with you, young lady! You snuck out the window?!"

I rushed to get my book bag together, making sure to grab Kevin's jacket. "Yep."

"You know, you're just carelessly destroying your relationship with her!"

I sighed. "That ship set sail long ago." I didn't bother looking up at him.

"You're awfully ungrateful young lady. Your mother does everything for you, and you don't even care...it upsets her."

I glanced up at the ceiling for a moment, and I thought about answering him back with a few gems about my past relationship with Donna. He has no idea what I've put up with from her over the years. He should really just shut up and mind his own business, but that would involve actually looking at him and talking to him in length, and I might vomit if I do that. I sighed. "I don't really give a shit."

I did glance back over my shoulder just in time to catch the shock that crossed his face before I left though, that was funny.

I picked up Evelyn at her house for school like I do most mornings.

"Good morning, Veronica," Evelyn greeted me with a smile as she got into my car.

"Hey, Evelyn."

"And you didn't call me *why*?" Evelyn asked.

"Because I was busy helping Mem and Grandpa the rest of the weekend. Oh, and avoiding Donna."

"Oh yeah...how much trouble did she give you about sneaking out the window?"

"When I got home last night Katie was already in bed, and I never even saw her or Ray. But Ray did inform me this morning how upset she was, and how I'm ungrateful because my mom does everything for me, or whatever." I shrugged.

"What did you tell him?"

"I told him that I don't really give a shit." I chuckled. "You should have seen his face."

"That's okay Veronica, I like keeping my breakfast down." I laughed, and we both high-fived each other.

Evelyn put her feet up on the dashboard. "I still don't get what your mom sees in that guy. She could totally do so much better."

"I know, she dates beneath her, really. I think they met at the bar she goes to. I think he's her drinking buddy." I chuckled. "There's no way she's in it for the money."

Evelyn glanced over and raised an eyebrow. "You think she's in it for the sex?"

"EWE, EVELYN!" We both shuddered hard, and I shook my head. "Thanks for that mental image! Let's talk about something else now so I don't vomit inside my car this morning!"

Evelyn reached inside her bag. "You got a letter from your dad on Saturday." She handed it to me.

I smiled. "Thanks, Evelyn." I leaned forward and tucked it into my back pocket.

She smiled back. "No, problem."

"*Okay… So…*did you and Kevin have a good time the other night?" she asked.

"It was fine."

"Veronica! You left the bar at like twelve thirty, and you were alone with Kevin until God knows when, and it was just fine?!"

"Not much happened. He pumped up my tires for me…and we talked a little."

I pulled into the school's parking lot and I found a parking spot next to a nice shiny black Ford Mustang convertible.

"Whoa, whose car is that?" I asked Evelyn when we got out.

Evelyn shook her head. "I haven't got a clue. I don't know of anyone getting a new car."

Kevin walked over greeting me by my car and I handed him his jacket. "Thanks for lending me your jacket the other night, and for pumping up my tires," I told him.

"No problem, *anything* for you." He emphasized the word "anything" and winked.

That made me think about the other night, and I blushed.

"There's a dance coming up in three weeks. Do you want to be my date?" he asked.

I'm always up for any plans that get me out of the house. "Sure, sounds like fun."

"Great!" He sounded excited. "I'll see ya later!"

We walked into the school, Evelyn and I headed for my locker.

I hate the way they assign the lockers. They do it alphabetically by last names, and so of course, my locker is in the busiest hall. In the mornings, this hall is almost as bad as the bar. It's always so crowded and a big pain in the butt. Especially when I'm in a bad mood, which ends up being most days.

I opened up my locker and put my bag in it and started grabbing what I needed for first period. Evelyn leaned back against the locker next to mine. "So, didn't anything happen?"

I closed my locker and leaned next to her. I knew what she really wanted to know. "We made out a little."

She raised an eyebrow. "That's it?"

I shrugged. "What more do you want?"

She threw her hands up. "I don't know... Don't you like him?"

I tapped the back of my head against the locker, and I looked up at the ceiling. "I don't know. He's a nice guy, but..."

She sighed. "But, what?"

"I just don't get that feeling when I'm with him, or even when we kiss."

She looked confused. "So?"

"*So*, shouldn't there be something more? Shouldn't I feel something towards him?"

"But he's hot," she argued.

"Yes, but there's just something missing," I replied.

She gave me a playful shove. "Who cares?! He's a hot guy and you get to make out with him!" It's nice to know where my friend's priorities are.

"Who cares? I do," I sighed. "Oh yeah, there's one more small problem with Kevin."

She seemed shocked. "What?"

"You know that gross sucking noise he makes when he eats?"

"Yeah," she prompted.

"Well try listening to that while you're making out!"

Evelyn laughed. "Only you, Veronica, can find the oddest flaws."

Just then, we noticed everyone in the hall moving out of the way of something big, like a tornado was coming. Kids started to part down the middle of the hall, and were backing up into us, blocking our view.

"What the heck?" Evelyn started to say. Both of us squeezed in between two kids that were standing in front of us so we could see.

He moved through the packed hall as if it were empty. His overwhelming presence parted the crowd, and seemed to make every jaw drop. Not once did he stop to move out of someone's way, they all moved for him.

He was wearing a leather jacket, blue jeans, and a black tee-shirt. His jet-black hair was overgrown around his eyes down past his chin, and it hung around his face like a stringy mop. He wore dark black sunglasses, and his face had two overlapping purple marks that ran the length of his left cheek. He had a very menacing expression, and judging by the reaction he was getting, people surrounding him seemed very intimidated.

He stopped in the center of the hall, and was closely examining a piece of paper; most likely his locker assignment or his class schedule. He turned and snapped his head up quickly at a kid who was staring at him, and I watched that kid suddenly flinch, and take an automatic step back.

The bell rang and the hall began to empty as kids headed off to their first-period class.

"*Well*...you don't see that every day," I said to Evelyn.

"Did you at least check out his butt?" She smiled, and put her thumbs up. "Nice."

"God you're rotten," I smiled. "You my dear, are going to hell for all your dirty thoughts." I chuckled.

"In a hand basket." She grinned and nodded. "See you at lunch!"

I reached into my back pocket and took out the letter my dad sent. I stopped briefly on my way to my first-period class to read it.

Dear Veronica,

How's my girl? Are you staying out of trouble? I just wanted to tell you I have some exciting news. Linda and I are going to Las Vegas and we're getting married! Isn't that great?! She's going to be your new stepmom! I've told her all about you and your sister. She's looking forward to meeting you. Maybe I can try calling your mother and talking to her about having you and your sister out here for the summer? Thanks for sending the pictures; you're growing into such a beautiful young woman. I love you, hope to see you soon.

⊠Dad.

It's so nice to know that my father finally found someone. He deserves some happiness after dealing with my mother. I'm a little nervous about him calling her though. I hope he changes his mind on that one. I have enough problems with her. Maybe I should let him know about my plans to move out there? If he's getting married, I could probably just live with him. Linda will be around so I wouldn't be alone when he's on the boat. I know I don't know her but I'm betting she's probably way nicer than Donna.

My first-period class is English, with Ms. Mcgrath. That old bitch hates me, and believe me, the feeling is mutual. She picks on me all the time. It would be nice to get through one class with her where she doesn't call my name for something, or try to give me a detention.

I went and took my seat and put my books down on my desk. Kids were still piling in, and the old bat wasn't here yet. Good, maybe we'll get lucky today and have a sub.

I took out a pen and started doodling while I was waiting; just my usual loops and stars. The pen slipped from my fingers and rolled onto the floor. I bent down to pick it up, and I knocked my head hard into someone who was reaching for it at the same time. "Damn it!" I snapped.

When I looked up, the guy with the jet-black hair and the dark sunglasses was standing over me, handing me my pen.

"Thanks," I said.

He nodded quickly then sat down at an empty desk.

I looked around wondering if anyone was going to be nice and tell him we have assigned seats in this class. Everyone was looking in opposite directions, and no one was making any eye contact with him. I quickly realized no one in this class was gonna be brave enough. I sighed and rolled my eyes and I leaned over. "Hey, you know, we have assigned seats in this class."

He stood up. "Thanks. Where should I sit then?"

His voice was so much deeper than I was expecting and a funny feeling suddenly came over me as he spoke, causing my vision to go slightly askew for a moment. I shook my head a little clearing away the odd sensation. "Well, I wouldn't sit there. That seat is contaminated," I told him.

He narrowed his brows. "Contaminated?" he questioned.

"Yes...a horrid, wretched girl sits there." Claudette Stanwood came in just then, and sat down in the now empty seat.

He chuckled. "So, are you going to tell me where I can sit?"

"Oh yeah, there's an empty seat over there." I pointed to the empty desk towards the back, and smiled at him.

"Thanks."

By the time lunch rolled around, it seemed like the new kid was all anyone could talk about. "What's his name? That kid looks like trouble. I wonder why he moved here? I wonder where he got that scar? Where did he come from?"

It seemed the main focus on most minds was, how scary looking he was. The mysterious dark sunglasses he wore all day, the black leather jacket, the angry look in his eyes⊠or so they say. He's in my first two classes, and I didn't see him take off those sunglasses once. So how can anyone say his eyes looked a certain way? I heard a few kids on the way to my third-period class speculate on whether or not he just got out of jail. I had my doubts.

I sat down at the lunch table next to Evelyn and Leslie with my sandwich and Coke.

Evelyn was already animated. "His name is Seth Chase! He moved here with his grandfather, they used to live in Waterbury."

"How'd you find that out? He hasn't talked to anyone all day," Leslie asked.

"Charles assists in the guidance office, and I got the information from him," she said.

I laughed. "And how did you manage that?" I asked. Though, knowing Evelyn, I could only imagine.

She smirked. "I have my ways."

"You know everyone here is too scared to talk to him," Leslie commented.

I glanced down at the table. "I talked to him," I said casually. I took a sip of my Coke.

Leslie and Evelyn both looked up at me, they seemed surprised.

"You talked to him? What did you talk about?" Evelyn asked.

"Nothing really. We have assigned seats in English class, and he had sat down in Claudette's seat." I winced. "So, I just told him we have assigned seats and I pointed to where he can sit."

"Is that all?" Leslie asked.

"Pretty much, he seems nice enough."

Evelyn and Leslie's eyes were wide.

"Veronica, you don't know. I'm sure Jack the Ripper was pleasant to talk to as well," Leslie replied.

I just raised an eyebrow. "Be serious, he's not Jack the Ripper." I chuckled.

"Maybe he's not Jack the Ripper, but he could be just as dangerous," Leslie commented.

They're all being so stupid, I thought to myself. I think everyone's active imaginations have certainly gone wild. I took a bite of my sandwich and glanced around the cafeteria until I found him.

He was sitting at the far end of one of the tables in a folding chair. He was leaning back in the chair with one foot across his knee, and his arms were crossed.

He wasn't eating anything and he looked bored. Didn't he get a lunch? I wondered.

There were three boys sitting at the same table as him. I could tell they were all sitting as far away from him as they could. Every so often one of the boys would glance over at him and then glance back and begin talking. How rude, I thought, it looked to me as though they were talking about him.

He hung his head back and stretched, looking up at the ceiling, and then sat back up. I watched him reach into his jacket and pull something out. He flipped it around fast and I quickly realized it was a butterfly knife when he cut a string off of his pant leg. He stared at the three boys for a long moment, as if he were deep in thought. Suddenly, he sat up and reached over, stabbing his knife through an apple that was on one of the boys' lunch tray, making them all jump.

I have to admit, it was so unexpected, I jumped too.

He pulled the apple off the knife, licked both sides, and flipped it around to close it. He tucked the knife back into his jacket, then took a huge bite of the apple; never taking his eyes off the three boys, a satisfied smile across his face.

I guess at first glance he does look dangerous⬛especially with the scar. But, I'm kind of wondering if that's the point. Maybe he wants people here to fear him. I can't say that I'm afraid of him, though. I think it's safe to say that I'm the only one so far besides any teachers who have actually talked to him.

After the incident with the apple, the rumor mill was churning out some real doozies...

"Did you hear that Seth kid got that scar in a bar fight? I heard he got arrested for stabbing a guy and he did time in juvie! I heard he had to move here because he knocked up some other guy's girl! Did you hear that Seth kid has a fake ID and he goes drinking at the bar every weekend?"

Two weeks of that crap I had to listen to!

I was so sick of hearing all the wild gossip going around about this kid, and I'm sad to say, Evelyn and Leslie were the worst ones. It was Friday morning, and they were already very animated.

"I heard he has a tattoo," Evelyn said as she checked around and leaned over to Leslie and pointed downward. "You know where!"

We were hanging around my locker waiting for the bell to ring, and I was already in a bad mood. Mostly, because Donna and Ray were badgering me about the chores I neglected to do and my irresponsible behavior before I left. But even more than that, this obsession everyone has with talking about this kid was wearing heavily on my nerves.

"You've got to be kidding!" Leslie shouted. "Who in their right mind would get a tattoo there?"

"Veronica, can you believe that?" Evelyn shouted. I was so desperate for the bell to ring. All of this was giving me such a huge headache.

"Whoa, really?" I replied. I was trying to sound interested, but it came out like I was bored.

"Veronica, what's the matter with you this morning?" Evelyn asked.

"Nothing, I have a headache, and I'm just sick to death of hearing all the wildly untrue rumors about that Seth kid."

"Veronica, how can they be untrue⊠just look at him," Leslie chimed in.

I looked down the hall, and he was just hanging up his leather jacket in his locker. He had his sunglasses on top of his head today, and was wearing a grey tee-shirt and holy blue jeans. His facial expression this morning didn't make him look half as scary as he did on his first day.

"Yes, I see. Because it's always a good idea to judge a book by its cover." I was really annoyed. I immediately started walking down the hall heading towards first-period English before I said something really mean to Leslie. The bell hasn't even rung yet, and I don't care. I had to get away from this mind-numbing chatter before I just lose it.

I sat on the floor outside the classroom door. I went through my bag and grabbed a piece of gum and popped it into my mouth. I just sat there chewing on it while I rested my head against the wall and I closed my eyes.

I was alone, and it was quiet for a moment, and I was happy. No badgering from the so-called family, no excessive mindless chatter, and no rumors about that Seth kid.

Just a few minutes of Zen before class, that's all I need.

The bell rang and I sighed.

Crap.

I got up from the floor and brushed off the back of my pants. When I looked up, that Seth kid was leaning against the opposite wall waiting to go in too. Of course! I thought. I wanted to hit my head against the wall! Can't swing a dead cat without hitting this kid!

I went into the classroom and took my seat even more aggravated than I was before. I have two classes with this kid, and they're both first thing in the morning—*great!*

When class began Ms. Mcgrath seemed to be in rare form. We just started reading George Orwell's *1984* yesterday, and she called on me to read first. "Miss Edwards?"

"Yeah," I replied. Of course, the old bat is picking me first today of all days! I really wasn't in the mood for this crap, and I was cursing her straight into the fiery pits of hades in my head.

"Stand up, and read pages twenty, to twenty-one." I stood up and sighed and then began reading.

I got about halfway through the first paragraph. "Veronica, do you have gum?!" she asked.

Whoops. "What?"

"You know I don't allow gum in my classroom, Miss Edwards! Now come spit it out!" she demanded, holding up the trash can.

I didn't really mean to, but I was so irritated that when I walked up to her desk and tried to spit my gum out towards the trash can, I missed, and it landed on her shoe.

She huffed and grabbed a tissue from her desk to clean the gum off. She scribbled across her yellow pad. "DETENTION! You're staying after school young lady!" She handed me the yellow slip.

"Good luck making me serve that!" I snapped back at her. I turned around to go back to my seat and I paused for a second, when I saw that Seth kid was gawking at me. He had an odd look on his face and followed me to my seat with his eyes. I snapped my head around and looked back at him with narrow angry eyes, and he quickly turned and faced the blackboard.

"Well, Miss Edwards?" Ms. Mcgrath folded her arms.

"Well, what?!" I demanded, hitting my hands on the desk.

"Read pages twenty to twenty-one."

"No!" I was way too aggravated to read anything anymore.

"Out! Go to the office young lady!"

"Fine!" I snapped. I gathered up my books and stormed out of the room, slamming the door. God, I hate it here. I hate this school. I hate this town. I hate living with Donna and that scumbag.

Maybe I should just leave ahead of schedule. I don't know what I'm waiting for. Everything about this place angers me to no end and I have no reason to stay here. Besides, I have enough money now. I wonder how many state lines I could get across before people notice I'm gone!

My after-school job put me in a much better mood. As soon as I walk through the door, I have five kids that run over all excited to see me and they grab ahold of my legs.

I love working with the kids. They're cute, and they always make me laugh. Today, I worked with a little boy who is autistic named Stephen; I helped him relate words with pictures. Then I got to read a story to the kids about barnyard animals, and I let them make the animal sounds.

By the time it was six, I felt so much better. It's nice to be able to come to work and just leave all my problems behind for a while. I think I'd be so messed up if I didn't have this job to go to every day.

Once I got home from work everyone was out including Ray. Whoa, I thought. This is a rare treat. I wonder what's up? Today did start off kinda crappy, but it seems to be ending quite nicely. I can live with that.

Oooh, since no one is here, I think I'll take advantage of that fact and take a swim in the bathtub for a while.

While I was getting what I needed for my bath I decided to call Evelyn real quick and apologize for my behavior this morning. She of all people should know how I feel about that kind of stuff. All the gossiping and petty crap most kids our age thrive on, I can't stand. So, it gets on my nerves way faster than others.

The phone rang twice before someone picked up.

"Hello?" I heard a guy say.

"Hello...is Evelyn there?" I asked.

"Oh, hey Veronica, it's Greg."

"Hi Greg, is Evelyn home?" I could hear some rustling and some whispering in the background, but I couldn't make out what was going on completely.

"No, I'm sorry, she's out at the moment. Did you want to leave her a message?"

"Na, that's okay." I suddenly had a feeling that maybe I shouldn't bother.

"Okay, bye," he said, and I could hear some shushing and giggles in the background right before the phone disconnected.

I decided to just let that go before I end up all pissed off again, and go hop in the bathtub. As I grabbed my stuff off my bed I had noticed that my room seemed a little neater than usual. I just shrugged it off, and went over to the bathroom.

I ran the water as hot as I could stand it, and then I made it just a tad hotter. This way, I can stay in it just a little longer before I get cold. I added some Mr. Bubble to the running water and then I stepped into the tub.

Ahhh, this is good. I leaned back closing my eyes. This right here is exactly what I needed. Maybe my guardian angel finally came back from that long vacation she took away from my life and is finally trying to help.

I stayed in and soaked until my fingers became all pruny. Then I wandered over to my room and put on my pajamas and lounged on my bed for a while listening to my Aerosmith record. I guess I might actually be staying home on a Friday night. Wonders never cease.

Oh yeah, I got paid today. I should put my money in my hiding spot. I really should get a bank account, but there's no point now that I'm leaving.

I pulled back the covers on my bed and pulled out my mattress a little. When I went to lift up the fitted sheet, I realized someone had changed them.

I felt my heart thump against my rib cage in fear as I pulled back my fitted sheet. I reached into the hole I made in my mattress for my zipper pouch, and my heart sank into my stomach, because it wasn't there. I pulled my bed out from the wall and looked around. Maybe it was on the floor where I keep my music box? Thankfully, the music box was still here, but my zipper pouch, which contained over two thousand dollars, was gone. I felt sick to my stomach. I ran across the hall to my mother and Ray's room throwing open the door. I quickly began rummaging through their things looking for my zipper pouch.

"If it's in here, it had *better* contain every dime!" I said out loud to myself.

I pulled open the bottom drawer of her dresser and saw the pouch tucked in between the folded clothes. As soon as I saw it, *I knew*. I picked it up and opened it, but I didn't really have to. I could feel it was empty.

I was so mad; tears were spilling hard and fast down my cheeks. I marched into my room and slammed the door as hard as I could. I was pacing the room, and I felt like I couldn't breathe. I was definitely suffocating.

"SO THAT'S WHERE THEY ALL ARE! THEY'RE OUT SPENDING MY HARD-EARNED MONEY!" I yelled out, and then I screamed. I went into my closet and grabbed my duffle bag throwing it on my bed.

"THAT IS IT!" I yelled.

I changed out of my pajamas, and I started filling the duffle bag with my clothes. I grabbed my music box and packed that, too.

I grabbed my keys and my overnight bag off my nightstand and then I grabbed the duffle bag. I ran down the stairs and out of the house not bothering to look back. I have seventy dollars in my wallet right now. I'm betting I can get pretty far on that, and if I need it, I'm sure my father will wire me the rest.

I was still very livid when I pulled into our town's only gas station. I wouldn't have stopped if I wasn't on E. Thank God, this place stays open past eight on Fridays. Otherwise, I might not get as far tonight.

When I pulled up to the pump and got out, I realized that I parked too far away from the pump. I groaned, and got back into the car and fixed it so the hose would reach.

Then, when I unscrewed the gas cap, I was really mad still and I slammed it on the trunk of my car. Well then it bounced off and rolled across the parking lot. So, I had to go chase after it, swearing and grumbling under my breath.

I impatiently pumped my gas, tapping my foot hard the whole time.

I realized while I was pumping my gas that I forgot my toothbrush and I was cursing myself up and down. Well, too late now! I thought to myself. I'm not going back there!

I hung the nozzle back up and forced myself to carefully screw the cap back on so I wouldn't have to chase it again.

I marched up to the gas station to pay. I yanked open the door hard, slamming it like an idiot into my own face.

I stomped my foot and rubbed my nose. "*Mother*⊠!" I shouted. I heard someone stifling a laugh from behind the counter. "Shut up!" I snapped over my shoulder.

I marched to the back of the store, grabbed a Coke, and I began searching around for a toothbrush. I was hoping that maybe I just might get lucky here. I couldn't find one and I was frustrated. I looked up towards the counter and leaning over it, flipping the pages of a magazine, was that Seth kid.

Great! This day just keeps piling on the shit! It's official now, I think my guardian angel finally quit.

I took in a breath trying very hard to control my temper. "Excuse me; do you sell toothbrushes in here?" I asked him, as pleasant as possible.

"Oh, yeah." He kinda sounded like he was being sarcastic.

"*Really*?" I raised an eyebrow. "And where might they be?"

"Oh, we keep them behind the counter." He stood up and leaned back against the wall.

I sighed. I really wasn't in the mood for this kind of shit. "And why is that?" I crossed my arms.

He smirked. "Because they're special, these toothbrushes have been approved by the American Dental Association."

I looked at him with my brows narrowed in frustration. Why can't people around here just be normal?

"*Look*...stop messing with me. Do you sell toothbrushes or not?" I huffed at him.

"Nope, just gas, car crap, and Cokes," he said smoothly. I really wanted to just slap this guy.

I exhaled sharp. "Fine, I just need to pay for my gas and my Coke then."

I reached over and handed him a ten. He paused while grabbing it for a moment and then looked up at my face. "You're that girl that got kicked out of English class today... Veronica, right?"

"Yeah."

"I'm Seth."

"I know."

"That's an interesting bracelet you have there," he said to me as he was giving me my change.

"Thanks."

"Where did you get it?" he asked.

"I don't want to talk about that."

"Why not?" he asked.

"Because, I don't like talking about that!" I snapped at him.

He crossed his arms and bent down a little to look me in the eyes. "You're not scared of me, are you?" he questioned.

I chuckled. "Why would I be?"

"Everyone else is," he stated.

"Well, I'm not everyone else, I think for myself."

"Why don't you like talking about your bracelet?" he questioned.

I sighed, and ran my fingers across the weave feeling the beads. "Because, it hurts to think about him."

Why the hell did I just tell him that?! God, I'm so stupid! I thought. I've had the worst day ever. I already felt like I was injured and bleeding, and this kid was nice enough to pour a little lemon all over it.

I'm out of here.

I turned and started to walk out the door and he ran around the counter and grabbed my arm. "Veronica, wait!" he shouted.

I turned around trying to pull my arm out of his hand. "Let go of me!"

"Can you keep a secret?" he spoke softly. "Do you swear on your soul?"

My anger slowly started to fade as each word he spoke clicked into place one by one. I closely studied his face and looked deep into his eyes, which until now, I hadn't noticed that they were green.

"Jackson?" I managed to choke out.

He just nodded and a tear spilled down his cheek. My head started spinning and I gasped. "Holy, shit!" I yelled. I threw myself at him hugging him as tightly as I could, and I was suddenly crying.

I was filled with so much relief. I felt like I'd been holding my breath for years and I could finally breathe again.

I stood back and wiped under my eyes and smiled at him. Then I was suddenly so mad, I narrowed my eyes and punched him in the arm.

"*Owe*...what was that for?!" he asked, rubbing his arm.

I was pointing at him. "That's for not writing to me or calling!" I shouted at him, staring him down. My hands were balled into tight fists. "Then you had the nerve to wait until now to tell me you're here!"

"I know, and I'm sorry... Can we just sit and talk for a while? I'll explain everything." He turned over the sign and locked the door.

CHAPTER 16

WE sat on the floor behind the counter. The only light we had was coming from the lamppost across the street. I was sitting right up against him resting my head on his shoulder. My arm wound around his, and I was holding his hand.

We were laughing. "I still can't believe you're really here," I told him.

He squeezed my hand. "It's been a long time."

"So, were you ever going to tell me?" I asked.

"I did tell you."

"I mean, if I hadn't come in tonight like I did, would you have told me?"

"I was getting around to it." He paused. "I hadn't seen you in so long, I wasn't sure I'd recognize you. Then on my first day I saw this familiar face when I walked into English, but I still wasn't completely sure. Then lucky me, you dropped your pen. I picked it up just so I could look a little closer."

"Yeah thanks, I still have the lump." I rubbed my head.

He chuckled. "You know it's funny. On your first day, I was the first one who talked to you, and then on mine, you were the first one to talk to me."

"That's because everyone else was too scared." I laughed.

"It figures you wouldn't be." He rubbed my hand. "After that, I was just making sure it was you. I didn't want to take a chance and find out I was wrong. Then you had that squabble with Ms. Mcgrath earlier..."

"I know, that old bitch hates me," I interrupted. He chuckled again.

"Then I started wondering if you were still the same; if you were still the same girl that promised to keep my secrets. I wasn't sure how I was gonna tell you." He started laughing. "Then you came storming in here tonight all bent out of shape over something, and I saw you were still wearing that bracelet I made years ago. I knew right then I could tell you."

"You know you're lucky, if you hadn't stopped me, I would be on my way to California tonight."

He looked over at me surprised. "Really, why?"

"Well as you may or may not remember, my mother doesn't like me. I've been saving up for a long time now to move out to California to be near my father and was planning on leaving at the end of this school year. Well, when I got home from work today I discovered that Donna had found my money stash and took all of it. I had just gotten paid today and I had a little in my wallet from last week so I was just gonna leave with that. I figured, if I got stuck I would just call my father and he could wire me the rest."

"Whoa, how much did she take?"

"I had a little over two thousand dollars saved up."

"You had two thousand dollars saved up, and you didn't have it in the bank?"

"It was supposed to be a secret. Evelyn knows, but no one at home knew what I was planning, and I mean no one. Plus, I'm underage, there was no way I would have been able to save up all of that in a bank and take it out without some serious explaining."

I shrugged. "I didn't want anyone to stop me."

"Are you still leaving?" he asked.

"Not tonight." I heard him exhale like he was holding his breath. I turned to him. "Can I ask you a question?"

"Sure."

"So, is Seth your legal name now?" I asked. I felt funny about asking him that. The last thing I wanted was to upset him.

"Yes."

"When did you change it?"

"When I was twelve."

"Can I ask why?"

"Because Jackson Wright was my father's name, and I didn't want to hear that name ever again."

"Understandable," I agreed. "But now I can't call you Sackson anymore."

He laughed. "I used to like it when you called me that. But I would really appreciate it if you didn't call me anything close to Jackson ever again."

"Again, totally understandable. I promise, I won't."

"Promise me you won't tell anyone about me either. I don't want anyone here to know that I'm *that kid*." He winced.

"Of course, I promise. I would never tell anyone. We're best friends, remember?"

"Yes." He smiled. He seemed to relax a little, and I just relaxed with him, enjoying the quiet moment.

"So, why did you pick Seth Chase?"

"Seth was my middle name and Chase was my mother's maiden name."

"Oh." We were quiet for a moment.

"I owe you my life," he suddenly said.

"What?" That statement took me by surprise.

"Do you remember all those things you told me the last time we were together?" he asked.

"Yes." Of course, I do. I've played that day over and over in my mind for years.

"*Well*, while my father was on his," he sucked in a huge breath, "rampage, all I could think about was what you said about not letting anyone push me around, and about fighting back."

My heart was twisting while I listened, and I couldn't control the tears that were now falling from my eyes.

"My father had just finished with my mother and he was coming for me with the knife..."

I felt like I was gonna be sick. "Seth, you don't have to tell me about this."

"Am I scaring you?" he asked.

"No," I lied. "I just didn't want you to be upset, that's all."

"I've been waiting to tell you this for a long time."

I sucked in a breath. "Okay, continue." I closed my eyes and braced myself for the rest.

"He chased after me and knocked me down waving the knife. He obviously cut me, but I never felt any of it, and I fought him back. I kicked him really hard in the stomach and then really hard," he cleared his throat, "'somewhere else, and he fell to the floor. I got to my feet and ran to my room closing myself in my closet. He banged on the door, shouting and screaming at me to come out. I held the knob tight with all my strength until the police found me."

I was sobbing. I used my free hand to wipe my cheeks.

"Then I ended up living with my grandfather in Waterbury, and that school was tough, much tougher than the school here. I never would have survived everything I went through, and going to school there, if it wasn't for you and what you said to me. Thank you."

"You're welcome." I put my free arm around him and gave him a squeeze. I wasn't totally sure what to say. I was in uncharted waters. It's not every day that I get a compliment that big. "I always wanted to tell you how sorry I was about your mom, I loved her."

"Yeah, I loved her too." I saw him reach up and wipe his cheek. Then he took in a breath.

"I was so thankful that you were alright, and still am. I've missed you," I told him.

"I missed you too, and I'm sorry I didn't write to you …I had a lot of adjusting to do."

"I wanted to write to you, too. I tried asking Mémé if she knew where you were but she didn't."

We sat there quiet for a while. Seth was the one who broke the silence.

"You know, you were my first kiss."

I chuckled. "So that's what you were just thinking about?"

"Yeah."

I glanced over. "Was I any good?" I was teasing.

"The best." I could hear him smiling.

I playfully smacked his arm. "You're just saying that." I sat back.

"We were young… What else do you want me to say?" He chuckled.

"I was so surprised when you did that," I admitted.

"You weren't upset that I did that were you?" he asked.

"No. A little confused at the time, yes, but I wasn't upset."

Curiosity got the better of me. "Have you kissed other girls after me?"

I heard him exhale. "Yes."

"A lot of other girls?" I pressed.

"I don't know...my fair share." He shrugged. I was quiet while I processed that.

"Does that bother you?" he asked.

"No."

"Then why did you ask?"

"I was just curious." I paused for a moment. "Can I ask you something else?"

"Sure."

"Have you done anything...*else*?"

"No." He was quiet. "Have you?" he asked.

"Have I what?"

"Well, have you kissed anyone else after me?"

"Yes, and I haven't done anything *else*, either." I figured I'd save him the trouble of asking.

"Really?" His tone had a teasing edge to it.

I turned and looked at him with narrow brows. "Yes, really."

He chuckled. "*That's not what I heard...*" he sang teasing.

I was sitting straight up now looking at his face. "What exactly did you hear?"

"I heard you and that senior Kevin Mitchel are hot and heavy!"

I crossed my arms. "Explain," I demanded.

"I was in the locker room the other day changing for gym when I overheard your name. That Kevin kid was bragging about how hot and heavy you both were. He said that you let him get to third base all the time and that you told him after the dance he would be *sliding home.*"

I was livid. "Would you mind if I confront him about that on Monday? I won't mention where I heard it," I asked. I tried hard to control my voice.

He chuckled. "Go right ahead."

"Kevin and I have gone out a few times. We've made out, but that's it. That's as far as I've ever gone with him."

"There's been no one else?" Now he was the one pressing.

"Nope, just that jerk," I sighed. "See this just proves to me you can't believe everything you hear."

"Why, what have you heard?" he asked.

"Oh, all sorts of things about you..." I was taunting him.

"Like what?"

"Like... You were stabbed in a bar fight."

"Funny. What else?"

"Stabbed a guy and did six months in juvie."

"Go on."

"You knocked up some guy's girlfriend and *had* to move here."

He laughed, and shook his head. "Wow."

"You have a fake ID and you go drinking every Friday night."

"That one's half true."

"Half true?" I questioned.

"Veronica, I'm eighteen. I'm older than you remember."

"So, you go to a bar on Fridays, which one?"

"Wicked Riff's," he replied.

"Oh!" Right there it clicked. "You were that jerk that drenched me with his beer, weren't you?"

"Were you the girl in the Aerosmith tee-shirt?"

"Yes!"

"Then yes, that was me. Some drunk jerk pushed me off the stool. I'm sorry I did that."

"I was so pissed. I stunk the rest of the night."

"I really am sorry," he said.

"I forgive you." I smiled at him.

"Hey, wait, how'd you get in there?" he asked.

"Do you remember Evelyn?" I asked him.

"Vaguely," he admitted.

"Her older brother works at the bar and he got us in that night so Evelyn and I could watch the band."

"Oh."

"So, do you want to hear another rumor?" I asked him.

"Yeah, sure."

"My personal favorite came from Evelyn this morning." I turned to look at him smirking and raised an eyebrow. "Do you have any tattoos?"

"Tattoos?" He shook his head. "No."

"Well, apparently you do have one on your," I looked down at his pants.

His eyes went wide. "I don't have any tattoos there." A sly smile crossed his face as he reached for his button. "I could show you, if you like."

"Um, that's okay! I believe you!" I shouted waving my hands. I was glad it was so dark in here. It helped hide how red my face just got.

I changed the subject. "So where are you living exactly?" There was no way I was leaving here tonight without that information.

"My grandfather just finished building his dream house here."

"It's not the log cabin up in the Hopyard is it?" I asked.

"Yes, why? Have you seen it?"

"Mémé took me up there last Saturday to see it. She has a thing for houses, and she's a little nosy."

"So, you're still close with your grandparents?"

"Yes, they treat me more like their daughter than my own mother does."

"That's good you have them then."

"Speaking of which," I grabbed his arm and checked his watch. It was three a.m. "I should get going."

I stood up and stretched. I was stiff from sitting on the floor for so long.

"Where are you going tonight?" he asked.

"Well, looks like my plans have changed some." I shrugged. "Mémé and Grandpa leave a cabin open for me, just in case I need it. I'll be heading there tonight."

"So, you're not going to California?" He asked.

"Not tonight."

"What are you doing tomorrow?"

"Hmmm…will you be home tomorrow?" I asked him with a big smile.

"Yes."

"Well then, I guess I'll be coming up to see your house…if that's okay?"

"Sure."

He walked me out to my car, which was still parked at the gas pump. I smiled and gave him a hug. "I'm so happy you're here. Good night, Seth."

He hugged me back. "Good night, Veronica."

I drove to Mémé and Grandpa's in a daze. This whole day has been quite the ride and my head was still spinning. I was so euphoric now⊠my best friend's back!

I grabbed my bags and happily danced my way into the cabin. Then I danced around the cabin turning on the lights, and the heat, and while I was getting my pajamas on, which caused me to fall onto the floor while I was trying to pull my legs into my shorts.

Instead of the raging fit I would normally throw over such things, I found myself laughing. It totally hurt when I fell, but I was way too happy to care.

I turned off the lights and got into bed and I pulled the covers up. I turned to my side and tried closing my eyes for a while but I couldn't sleep. I was way too excited. I tossed and turned trying to find my sweet spot so I could just fall asleep but I just couldn't. My mind was racing at full speed, and all I could think about was seeing Seth tomorrow. Okay, technically it's today. I couldn't wait.

I turned over and checked the alarm clock. Ugh, it's only five! If I don't get any sleep I'm gonna be useless all day. I wonder what time I should go there? *Ahhh*, why can't I sleep! An hour went by and I started flailing my arms and legs tossing the blankets onto the floor. I was arguing back and forth with myself.

I abruptly sat up. What is wrong with me?! I've got to calm down. I should be sleeping, not wide awake!

I got up and went into the bathroom, and I looked in the mirror. God, I look horrible! My hair was sticking up on one side and the circles around my eyes are huge! I'm so gonna look like crap all day! There's no point in trying to sleep anymore, anyway. I should just take a shower and get dressed, I thought to myself.

It didn't take me very long to take the shower, but it did take me a while to figure out what I was gonna wear. I dug through my duffle bag, and I then agonized over two different tops, something I don't normally do. By the time I was finally done getting myself dressed and turned around, I was horrified to discover that in my pursuit to find something perfect to wear and not getting any sleep that I had destroyed the entire cabin. The blankets from the bed were all over the floor, and so was every piece of clothing from my duffle bag.

It took me a good hour to clean up the cabin and make the bed, which was good. I wasn't totally sure what I was gonna do to kill time before trying to go up to the house for breakfast. I didn't want anyone to realize how eager I was to leave and so I didn't want to go up there too early.

I put all my stuff in my car and started the walk up to the house that I've done so many times before. I started thinking about what I was gonna do tonight. I don't really want to go back home. I decided not to worry about it now.

I walked into the house through the kitchen. Mémé and Grandpa were already up having breakfast.

"Good morning, Sweetie," Mémé greeted me. I walked over and kissed Mémé's cheek and then Grandpa's.

"Good morning," I sang. I waltzed around the kitchen grabbing everything I need for my breakfast and put it on the table.

"Well, you're in a good mood this morning," Mémé said smiling at me.

"Yes," I replied.

"Didn't you have a fight at home?" Mémé questioned.

"Sort of."

"Sort of? Then why did you sleep in the cabin?"

I sat down at the table and told Mémé about the money I had saved up and how when I got home yesterday it was gone, and how I found my empty pouch in Mom's dresser.

"How much did you have saved up?" she asked.

"A little over two thousand dollars." Mémé's eyes bugged when I told her.

"Why on earth would you have that much saved up in your room like that?" she asked.

"I was saving for a car, originally. But then you gave me one, so I just kept saving. I figured maybe I would just use it to get my own place or something." I just left out how far I was planning on going.

"You were planning on moving out by yourself?" Grandpa asked.

"Eventually, I'm not happy living with them."

"Well I guess that's understandable," Mémé said with a heavy sigh. "What are you gonna do now?" she asked.

"I'm not sure, I can't figure out the right way to handle any of this yet," I told her.

"You'll do the right thing. You always do," Grandpa added.

I got up from the table and put my bowl in the sink. I leaned against the counter and glanced at the clock.

"Do you have somewhere to be this morning?" Mémé asked.

I smiled. "Yeah I have plans."

"That explains it." She leaned over to Grandpa. "Look at how she's blushing, I'm betting she has plans with a boy."

"Mem!" I looked down, I was so embarrassed.

"Well, who do you have plans with?" she asked.

I sighed. "His name is Seth. But it's not what you think."

"Really, that's not what it looks like to me. You should see your face."

"Really, we are just friends," I assured her.

"I think you would like to be more than friends," she said.

"I think it's about time I got going," I replied.

Mémé got up from the table all smiles and put her arms around me. "I didn't mean to embarrass you this morning. You say you're just friends with this Seth and I believe you. But it wouldn't surprise me at all if he's smitten with you." She kissed my head. "What boy wouldn't be?"

I'm sure I was ten shades of red now. "Thanks Mem, I'm leaving now."

It was about ten when I finally left my grandparents' house. I was grumbling on the whole way about what Mémé was saying. I can't believe she thinks I like him like that, I thought. I then started to worry about if I was showing up too early. Maybe he likes to sleep in on the weekends. Oh God, I never met his grandfather.

What if he doesn't like me? Oh, and does he know that I know Seth's secret? I'm just gonna tread very lightly just in case. I pulled into the driveway and parked behind a shiny black Mustang convertible. I shook my head and laughed. I didn't realize until now that I had parked next to his car on his first day.

Right before I got out of the car, I had a slight panic attack because I started to wonder if maybe I should have brought something. Well, it's too late now! I thought to myself. I checked my hair in the rearview mirror. Once I caught what I did, I sat back in my seat and clenched my eyes shut. What is wrong with me? I never do things like this.

I got out of the car and walked up to the door. I could feel the butterflies fluttering in my stomach. I took in a breath and let it out, trying to swallow my fear. I don't know why I'm so nervous, it's only Jackson, I thought to myself.

I swallowed hard and knocked on the door.

An elderly man with graying jet-black hair answered the door with a big smile. "So, you must be Veronica." He waved me forward. "Come on in, Seth will be down in a minute." He took my hand. "I'm George. It's so nice to finally meet you. I've heard so much about you for years."

I nodded and smiled kindly. "Thanks. It's nice to meet you, too."

"Would you like to sit down?" he asked.

"Sure." I walked into the living room and sat down on a sofa that sort of resembled the cabin. I started wondering if he made the furniture, too.

The inside was just as breathtaking as the outside. The living room, dining room, and kitchen flowed together in a wide-open floor plan. The staircase leading up to the second floor had the same branch pattern theme in the railings that are on the windows and in the porch railings. The staircase was placed perfectly in the center. I looked around just taking in my surroundings, and I felt oddly comfortable.

"Your house is so beautiful," I told him.

"Thank you, I built it myself. Well I designed it, Seth and I both built it. It took us a few years. It's still something I'm working on." He chuckled. "Maybe, I always will be."

"Well you have a true gift. It's absolutely, gorgeous."

He smiled. "Would you like a glass of iced tea?" he asked.

"Sure." A strange feeling came over me just then, and I shook my head a little. There's that deja vu again.

Seth came down the stairs then, and when I saw him I felt my heart thump against my ribs a couple of times. I started breathing in and out slowly trying to settle my nerves.

"Well, I see you've made yourself at home," he said with a smile.

I stood up. "I'm not too early, am I? You didn't say what time, and I was just guessing really…" I started rambling a little and he put his hand up.

"It's fine. You can come here any time you want." He smiled.

"Oh." I smiled back, that made me blush.

Seth's grandfather came in with my glass of iced tea. "Here you go."

"Thank you." I sat back down on the couch and took a sip. I started thinking about how funny it was, how at home I was already feeling here.

"So, what are you kids gonna do today?" George asked. I just looked over at Seth, I had no clue.

"I think we'll go walking in the Hopyard," Seth said.

"Veronica, are you staying for dinner?" George asked.

"Um, I can if I'm invited." I didn't want to impose.

"Veronica, can you stay for dinner?" Seth smiled.

"Sure."

Seth and I left the house, and started walking down the road towards the park.

"Is that Mustang yours?" I asked him.

"Yes, I bought it about a year ago."

"What year is that?"

"Nineteen seventy-one."

"It's really nice," I told him.

"Thanks." He smiled.

"You want to hear something funny?" I asked him.

"Sure."

"I parked next to you on your first day. I didn't know that was yours."

"That is weird," he replied.

"So what part of Devil's Hopyard are we going to?" I asked.

"I thought we could just go down to the falls, and maybe just follow one of the trails."

"Cool, I love Chapman Falls."

It was a long walk down to the falls, but I didn't notice, nor did I really care. During the walk we talked about school, about friends, some of our interests. I told him about my job, and how much I love working with the kids. I also told him about my plans to become a preschool teacher. He smiled at that. He told me about the various jobs he held in Waterbury, and his love of working on his car. I was so happy. It's been so long since I've felt this good. I hope it never ends.

When we got down to the falls, we climbed down to the bottom and I sat down on a rock along the edge of the water, and he sat down next to me.

"Can I tell you something?" I asked him.

"Sure."

I was staring down at the water. "I beat up Claudette."

"You did what?" He sounded surprised.

"I beat up Claudette, right after you left," I stated again.

He laughed. "Why did you do that?"

"Well, I was a tad...*sensitive* after you left. She called you a freak, and I snapped."

He burst out laughing. "You beat her up for that?"

"Yep. I always hated it when she called you a freak and she knew it. She was just trying to get a reaction out of me, and that day, she definitely got more than she bargained for. I got suspended for two days, but that girl hasn't uttered a peep to me since. It's been nice."

"Wow," he shook his head. "All this time I was so wrapped up in what I was going through, I never realized how any of that had affected you."

"Of course it affected me. You were the only person in my life at the time I could trust and then you were gone. Saying I was devastated would be an understatement."

"I'm so sorry."

I looked at him with narrow brows. "For what?"

"For what you went through after."

"You have nothing to apologize for. None of that was your fault. You didn't do anything bad to me. You couldn't control what happened. You were a kid."

"I still feel bad about it."

"Yeah and I feel bad about it too, it was horrible. But we're together now, so no more feeling bad about anything," I told him.

"Can I tell you something else?" I asked him.

"Sure."

"I don't want to upset you though, it was just something that I observed back then, and I always swore that if I saw you again, I would tell you."

He looked a little worried. "Okay."

"Your mother loved you so much. I know this because I used to watch you with her all the time, and I saw it. Every single time she saw you, her face would light up like she just saw the greatest thing ever, which is so true. Who could blame her? You were so lucky to have a mom as great as she was. But more than that, you could easily see she saw herself as the lucky one because she got to be with you."

He was quiet at first. "Thank you," he said.

"I'm sorry if I was kinda corny. It's just what I saw."

"You weren't." His smile was warm.

"Can I tell you something?" he asked.

"Anything," I felt tingles go down my spine when I said that.

"You were my first friend."

"I'm still your friend," I assured him.

"What I meant was, you were my first and only friend I ever had then."

"How is that even possible? What about when you lived in Florida?" I asked.

"I never had any there either. We moved around so much and I was always so scared all the time. When we moved here, things were still the same. I was so sure that nothing was ever gonna change for me and that I would just never have any friends. I was so miserable. Then one morning you walked into my class and I had this feeling about you. I argued with myself the whole morning about how I was gonna talk to you. So, I just stood there behind you like a dumbass."

I chuckled. "Yeah, I remember."

"You have other friends now, don't you?" I asked.

"I have a few now in Waterbury, but that's it."

"All anyone really needs is one." I looked up and smiled at him. "Well, I'm still glad I bumped into you that day."

"We're always tripping over each other, aren't we?" He chuckled.

"Yeah, I've noticed."

Seth looked at his watch. "We should probably head back, it's already four thirty. I'm sure my grandfather is probably starting to cook dinner."

I got up from the rock and brushed the back of my jeans off. "Alright, let's go."

We started walking back down the road to his house and we were both kinda quiet at first.

"Can I ask what you're thinking about?" he asked breaking the silence.

"Oh, I was just thinking about what I'm doing tonight."

"Why? Do you have plans?" He sounded a little disappointed.

I smiled. "No. I meant, I was trying to figure out, do I try to go home? Or do I just go sleep at my grandparents."

"I bet if I ask you could sleep on our couch," he suggested.

His suggestion sparked a memory and then I started giggling.

"What's so funny?" he asked sounding confused.

"You made me remember something. I didn't get it then, but I do now."

"Tell me."

"Do you remember me asking Mémé if you could sleep over?"

He smirked at me. "Yes."

"I was so confused then why she was saying boys and girls don't have sleepovers."

He raised an eyebrow. "So do you want to sleep over then?"

I playfully smacked his arm. "Seth!"

"What?!" He laughed. "You can't blame a guy for trying!"

Dinner was simple but delicious. George grilled chicken and he made a nice salad. I love being here. They both made me feel so welcomed and I felt so comfortable that I helped George and Seth clean up after dinner.

I was watching Seth and his grandfather while I was helping to clear the table and it was obvious that there's this unspoken sadness between them, and it was heartbreaking to watch. It was clear to me that neither one of them have fully recovered from their loss of Joan. I can't imagine that kind of sudden loss like that ever being an easy thing to deal with.

"Do you want to see my room?" Seth asked me once we were finished.

I swallowed hard. "Sure."

He led the way up the stairs and I followed. "You know I never saw your room back then or even your house," I told him.

He looked back at me and smiled. "Well, I'm showing you now." He turned the knob and opened the door. He waved for me to go ahead of him.

His room looked like any other kid's room. He has a bed and a dresser. He has a stereo with an eight-track player, that's cool. He has some cool band posters—Aerosmith, Led Zeppelin, and Pink Floyd. My favorite though, was the speed limit fifty sign he had right above his headboard. "Hey, I love the street sign."

"Me too...it really brings the whole room together." He laughed.

I went in and sat on his bed. On his nightstand was a framed photo of him and his mother. I picked it up and looked at it for a moment, and then I gently put it back.

"I love your room," I told him. "I don't know if you'll ever see mine."

"Still don't know what you're gonna do yet?" he asked.

I curled my legs up and sat back against his pillows. "I'm probably gonna stay in the cabin again."

"Well, I'll just have to visit you there then." He spoke softly and he gently touched my arm, sending tingles down my spine again.

I took a breath and then exhaled. "You know, I probably should get going," I told him. "I wouldn't want to overstay my welcome."

"That's impossible," he said. I smiled at him.

"Seth, can I give you something to hold for me? Just in case I end up going back home for a while, I obviously can't trust my mother with anything."

"Sure."

"Good, you can follow me out then and I'll give it to you now."

I said goodnight to Seth's grandfather, and I gave him a hug. "Thank you for dinner, and letting me spend the day here."

His smile was warm. "You're welcomed here anytime."

"Thanks." I smiled back.

Seth and I walked out to my car and I climbed in. I reached over into the back seat and rummaged through my duffle bag until I grabbed my music box out.

"I had a feeling this was what you wanted me to hold for you."

"You don't mind, do you? It's just things are so up in the air right now, and she's being such a crazy bitch. Look what she did when she found my money."

He took the box from me. "Don't worry, I'll keep it safe. You can trust me."

I smiled and got into my car. "I know, that's why I gave it to you." I leaned out the window. "Now I have an excuse to come back here."

"Veronica, *you* never need an excuse."

I got to Mémé's around nine and I spent the night in the cabin. I practically passed out when I hit the pillows. When I finally woke up, I saw I had slept until ten o'clock in the morning. I was so relieved. Good, I needed it.

I stayed in bed for a while, thinking about how my world has just flipped upside down so fast this weekend. One second, I was extremely pissed off and so mad at the world, like every other day. Then I was overjoyed and euphoric the next. It feels so good to have that anger suddenly dissolve. I still can't believe he's here. I smiled and stretched just thinking about it. I can't believe how much he's changed! He's no longer that scared chubby little boy that I remember. Now he holds his head up high. Physically he's different, too. If he didn't say anything to me on Friday night I don't think I would have ever recognized him. He's not wearing those dorky striped shirts and corduroys his mom used to dress him in either, he now has his own style. He's leaner now too, and I can't say I didn't notice the muscles under his tee-shirt yesterday. He's definitely no longer chubby little Jackson. Not that I ever saw anything wrong with Jackson. I have to admit though, he does look *really* good.

One thing that is bothering me though, is how nervous he was making me at times.

A few times yesterday, and at the gas station, I found myself feeling anxious when I just asked him simple questions. Then, there was my odd behavior yesterday. I never cared much about what I wear or if my hair was perfect before. Even odder, when we were at Devil's Hopyard and when we were up in his room, several times I was fighting this urge I had to just touch him. I think I'm going crazy.

Maybe I'll go up and see him later today. Too bad I don't have his phone number because then I can check to see if it's okay first. I know Seth and his grandfather said I can come up whenever I want, but I don't want to be a pain and make them sick of me already.

After I did my morning ritual in the cabin, I started up to the house and saw my mother's car in the driveway.

Crap. Now what? What am I going to say to her? *Hey bitch, where's my money?* No, I can't say that. Well, just not in front of Mémé. I'm betting there will be some sucking up from Donna to her mother and then a bunch of apologies. I'm not apologizing for anything. I don't care what that crazy bitch says.

I walked into the kitchen. Mémé, Grandpa, Ray, and Katie were all standing around my mother who was sobbing like a baby at the kitchen table. I had this urge to just stomp my feet. Why can't I just have some breakfast in peace? I wondered.

My mother spun herself around and threw herself at me. "Oh, Sweetie! I've been worried sick!"

I raised an eyebrow. "Really?" I had my doubts.

"Of course, why did you just run away like that?" she sobbed.

"Because, you took my money," I spoke slowly for her, for two reasons. One, so she could understand and process each word. She can be slow sometimes. Reason two, was to control my anger, so I don't just smack her.

Mémé walked over and put her hands on my shoulders. "Honey, all of it was a misunderstanding."

"Really?" I said, as calmly as I could. My tone was oozing with doubt. Of course it was! Isn't that always the way?! I thought to myself sarcastically. I folded my arms. This ought to be good.

"I was going to surprise you with your own bank account!"

"Wow...really?" I hope I sounded impressed. Oh, and I'm not stupid, I added in thought. I heard the *WAS* in there!

"You really didn't have to do that and I would prefer it if you just gave it back," I told her.

"I told you she'd be ungrateful," Ray butted in.

I rolled my eyes. "Mind your own business, Ray." I sighed. "I'm not ungrateful. I just wanted to do this on my own. Can I please have my money back?"

"But honey, I already put it in a savings account for you."

"Really?" Of course they did! They were just toying with me now, and I was growing even more annoyed. "Where's the bank book?"

"Oh, it's at home. Don't worry, I'll give it to you later." *Yeah right,* I thought to myself.

"Uh, huh." I sighed.

"Oh Veronica, I know things between us haven't been that good lately, and I just wanted to do something nice. I was hoping that if I opened this account for you that I was showing you how proud I am that you were able to save up so much money. I just want things to be better between us."

She blew her nose. "Please, just come home." This woman makes no sense.

I sighed. "Fine." She smiled and hugged me, and as a show of good faith I did hug her back. But I couldn't resist rolling my eyes though. Now I feel dirty like I need a shower.

CHAPTER 17

I sat on our living room sofa examining my new bank
book.

Ray was in the recliner, and Katie and Donna were
right next to me. The book's cover had my name on it,
and my mother's. Next to her name it said custodian,
and according to this bank book all the money was in
there. I have to admit, I was surprised.

"What does custodian mean exactly?" I asked.

She was stroking my hair smiling. "Well, you're not
old enough to have an account by yourself yet. It just
means that I'm your mother, and I will help you protect your money," she said.

"Ahhh, I see. *So*…what do I do to put money in?"

"You go down to the bank, fill out a deposit slip, and
give your money and the slip to the bank teller; it's very
easy. I could help you with that if you want me to."

"I think I can figure that part out, Mom." I smiled
and I sucked in a breath. I already knew the answer to
this but I threw caution to the wind and asked anyway.
"So, what do I do if I want to take any money out?"

She patted my knee. "Well then, you and I will go down to the bank together and fill out a withdrawal slip."

I raised my brow slightly. "So, let me see if I understand this. I can go down to the bank by myself all I want to put money in, but I need *you* to help me get my money out?"

"Yes, Sweetie, you need my signature."

I wanted to smack my head against the wall.

"Thanks Mom, this is just great." I tried hard to not sound just really pissed.

"Oh, you're welcome, Sweetie," she sounded so proud of herself.

I'm guessing, I'll probably never see a dime of my money. I had to get away from them all before I explode.

"I'm just gonna go put my stuff away," I told her through my teeth.

"Okay, Sweetie. We're getting pizza for dinner tonight!"

"Cool, thanks Mom." I walked up the stairs to my room and shut the door leaning up against it. I felt trapped. I really want to just get out of here. I seriously debated about just going out the window again. I wonder what Ray did with the rope?

Shockingly, I decided not to go out the window. Instead I ended up spending the rest of the afternoon actually hanging out with Mom, Ray, and Katie. I had neglected to do my homework on Friday because I had figured I wouldn't be here Monday, so I took the time and got that done. Then Mom and Ray bought pizza and soda. I have to admit it was kind of pleasant, and it's not so bad when Mom's sober and in a good mood.

Katie played a few songs that she wrote herself on the piano in the living room, and they were beautiful. Everyone was being nice for a change, and it felt good to just hang around at home. I don't care how nice everyone's being though, I'll never stand Ray.

After dinner, I tried my luck calling Evelyn again. I wanted to see what was going on. Was she mad at me? I was super grouchy the other day, and I should apologize. I didn't mean to take out my aggravation on her directly, but that rumor crap was really pissing me off.

I got lucky it was her that answered. "Hello?"

"Hey Evelyn, its Veronica," I began.

"Hey, where were you all weekend?" she asked.

I thought about telling her where I was, but, in the interest of keeping Seth's secret, I decided it would be better not to yet. Besides, if I told her she would probably freak out asking for way more details than I can really give. "Oh, I just hung around here and at my grandparents'."

"Really, you hung around at home?" she sounded surprised.

"Yeah, Donna is being kinda decent this weekend."

"Hey, I'm sorry if I was being kinda bitchy the other day. I was just in a rotten mood," I told her.

"No problem, I know how you are." She paused briefly. "Are you still going to the dance with Kevin on Friday?"

"Um, well...I was planning on it. Let me ask you a question though, have you heard any rumors about that?"

"No," she answered quickly, and then she became quiet for a moment. "Why? ...have you heard something?"

"Not directly. I was just checking." I heard that pause, and I was wondering who my friends really are. "Do you need a ride to school in the morning?" I asked.

"Actually, Leslie's picking me up."

"Okay, well, see you in school then."

"Bye." She hung up kind of quick.

Well that just figures. That jerk has been talking shit about me behind my back, and to add insult to injury, Evelyn and Leslie knew that. I hate that crap. But more than that, I hate it when your own friends don't have the guts to just tell you to your face what's going on.

When I got to school Monday morning I was really nervous because things are different now. I've got that jackass Kevin, talking shit about me behind my back, so I have that to deal with today. Then, my best friend's here but I have to pretend it's not him. Seth and I never talked about how we were supposed to act or anything. I didn't know what to do. What if I hurt his feelings not talking to him? I wasn't afraid to talk to him before, maybe I should just be careful not to talk to him too much? Oh crap, and I never showed up Friday for detention, and I have her first period.

I went to put my things in my locker and get my stuff for English. I was seriously thinking about skipping that.

"Hey Veronica."

"Hey Evelyn." I leaned back against my locker.

"So, what's new this morning?" she asked.

"Well, I skipped detention on Friday and I have that class first period."

"Ouch." She glanced around. "Have you seen Kevin yet?"

"Nope, not yet. Why, is he looking for me?" I was trying so hard to act like I didn't know anything.

"Probably. He was asking about you this weekend. But no one knew where you were."

"Like I said last night, I was at my grandparents', and then I just hung around home."

"Oh, so I went out with Charles on Saturday..." Evelyn started.

Seth came around the corner just then. He had his leather jacket tossed over his shoulder and was wearing a black Led Zeppelin tee-shirt. As he walked by to go to his locker he glanced over at me and smirked, which caused my heart to thud against my ribs a few times. I was smirking back at him and I glanced down at my feet.

"VERONICA!"

I shook my head and looked at Evelyn. "What?"

"I was trying to tell you about my date with Charles," she sounded annoyed.

"Oh, I'm sorry, I was just spacing out." I took a breath. "So, did you kiss him?"

"Yeah, he's taking me to the dance Friday." She quickly went back to gushing.

"Cool." Thank God, I thought. She didn't seem to notice our little exchange.

When I got to English, he was already sitting at his desk. My nerves got the better of me and I tripped over my own two feet going to my desk. I heard him chuckle, and I smirked and shot him a playful glare.

Ms. Mcgrath came into the room. "So where were you after school on Friday Miss Edwards?" she called out on her way to her desk.

"I was at work."

"I assume you'll be making up that detention after school today then?"

"Nope. I have to work," I said coolly. I heard him chuckle.

"You owe me time, young lady," she stated.

I sighed. "I owe you nothing," I said staring her down.

"You have to serve that detention; do I have to call home?!"

"I missed the garbage can spitting my gum out. That hardly deserves a detention!" I argued back.

"You have quite the attitude problem."

"And you're a dumb bitch!" I heard him burst out laughing.

She gasped. "OUT!"

"*FINE!*" I gathered up my things and headed for the door.

"You'll be happy to know I'll be calling home today, young lady!"

"Whatever!" I said and I slammed the door as I walked out of class...*again.*

The rest of my day up until lunch gratefully was fairly ordinary. I was still in a cranky mood because of first period, so I wasn't really in the mood to eat lunch.

When I entered the cafeteria, I walked over to the table where I normally sit and I just stood there scanning the room. I hadn't seen Kevin all day, and after dealing with that old bitch this morning, I was all warmed up and ready to confront him.

I saw him sitting down at his normal table. He had already gotten his lunch and he was laughing with his friends.

Awe, he looks like he's having a good day. He saw me looking at him and he waved to me. So, I smiled kindly, and waved back.

"Veronica, aren't you gonna sit down?" Evelyn asked.

I glanced over at her. "In a moment. I'm gonna go talk to Kevin first."

She gushed. "Oh."

I casually strolled over to Kevin's table trying hard to keep hold of my cool poker face.

"Hey, sweetheart." He smiled.

I smiled back. "Hello, Kevin." I steadied myself and crossed my arms.

"What's up?" he asked.

"What's up?" I checked my nails, as I repeated his words back to him. "Well now, let me see," I started off as calmly as I could.

"So, I hear you like bragging about our dates?" I asked him as nicely as I could, looking at him straight in the face.

"Of course I do." He was smiling, and he glanced around at the faces at the table.

"So, what you've been telling them is all true then?" I felt my pulse start to quicken.

He looked a little nervous. "Every word," he uttered.

"Oh, really?" I replied. My blood really started to boil and I began shouting, "YOU'VE BEEN TELLING PEOPLE THAT I LET YOU GO TO THIRD BASE?! YOU PATHETIC PIECE OF SHIT!" I shook my finger at him. "YOU KNOW DAMN WELL YOU'VE NEVER BEEN PAST FIRST! AND YOU *CERTAINLY*, WON'T *EVER*, SLIDE HOME!" I was so mad, I grabbed his lunch and dumped it all over his head, and stormed out of the lunch room. I caught sight of Seth out of the corner of my eye on my way out, and his whole body was shaking with laughter.

Evelyn quickly chased after me. "Hey, what was that all about?!" she asked.

I was animated and pointing towards the cafeteria. "That jerk's been telling people that I let him go to third base all the time! And how I told him I'd go all the way with him after the dance!" I was still quite furious.

"Whoa, how'd you find that out?" she asked.

"I have my resources," I was panting, and crossed my arms. "Did you know he was saying that?" I watched her face.

Her eyes were wide with concern. "I didn't know, I swear." She put her arm around me. "He's a jerk."

"I knew there was something just off about that guy," I said, trying to calm down.

"You're still going to the dance, right?"

"The one this Friday?" I shook my head. "I don't know."

"Veronica, you have to go! It'll be fun!" she begged.

I threw my hands up. "Ugh, fine, I'll go!"

"Good, I know you. You're pissed off now, but come Friday, you'll be ready to party."

I laughed. "Just so you know, and you can spread this all you like. Kevin and I never did anything other than kiss on the few dates we had. And he is a terrible kisser. He sounds like a kid sucking down the last bits of his milkshake the whole time." I shuddered.

She laughed. "Don't worry, I'll spread it." We high-fived.

Evelyn went back inside the cafeteria, and I continued walking down the hall. A good part of me wanted to just ditch and blow off the rest of the day, because I was still really aggravated.

I really just need to calm down, and I didn't really know what I wanted to do. I think better and I calm down faster if I'm chewing on a piece of gum. So, I went to my locker and started rummaging through my bag for a piece.

I heard someone lean up against the locker next to me. "You've developed quite the temper in my absence."

I looked up, and Seth was leaning back against the locker smiling ear to ear. He shook his head. "First you beat up Claudette. Then you dump that Kevin guy's lunch all over him!" He laughed. "*Boy*, remind me to never piss you off!"

"I just don't like people talking shit about me, or the people I care about," I stated.

I unwrapped my piece of gum and popped it in my mouth, and just glared at him. He was grinning.

I was still fuming. "I'm glad you find this so funny," I spoke with an attitude. I grabbed my books for my next class.

"So, are you going to the dance on Friday?" he asked.

"I am," I sounded annoyed.

"Veronica, what's the matter?" he asked.

I closed my locker. "Nothing, I'm just really annoyed still."

"Did I do something?" he asked.

"No." I shook my head.

"Then, what's wrong?"

Kids started coming down the hall then and all I could think to say was, "I'm just keeping your secret."

When I got home after work, my mother was waiting at the door for me, and she looked pissed.

She had her arms crossed and started yelling before I got to the door. "You called your English teacher a dumb bitch?!" she questioned.

"Yeah so," I shrugged.

"*So*, she said you're always giving her problems! That you have a bad attitude and you're always disruptive!"

"How am I disruptive?! She picks on me!"

"She also said you owe her assignments!"

"That's because she kicks me outta class before I can hand them in! She's always picking on me! Mom, she hates me!"

She crossed her arms. "I think you're just trying to get away with not doing what you're supposed to be, like always!"

"I am not! I go to school, I work, and I do my homework every day, and I hand it in! That old bat is crazy!" What is wrong with people?

I sighed. "What do you want me to do?"

"Well you can start by apologizing to Ms. Mcgrath tomorrow!"

"No way!" I shouted.

"You have to, and you have to serve that detention, young lady!"

"Like hell I do!" I told her. "All I did was miss the garbage when I spit out my gum. If I serve that detention I'll miss work! I won't miss work!"

"If you don't serve that detention and apologize you are grounded!"

I stomped by her and went up the stairs to my room. "Whatever." I'm not serving that either, I thought.

The rest of my week, for the most part, was uneventful. My first solution for dealing with Ms. Mcgrath was seeing the guidance counselor and trying to switch to another English class, but unfortunately that didn't work. Apparently, all the other English classes are full. So now I'm just skipping that class all together. My logic is, I can read, I can write, and I already speak English. I think we've already beaten that horse to death. I'll just have to make it up at some point before I graduate.

The only part of skipping that class I don't like is having to wait until second period math to see Seth. We haven't hung out all that much but it's already so much more fun with him around. We exchange glances and smirks every time we pass each other in the halls, and no one knows, but us, what we know.

I've always been happy to see Seth for as long as I've known him. But lately I've been noticing him differently, and its scaring me a little.

This morning in math, I glanced over at him and he was leaning back stretching and his shirt popped up exposing his skin a little. I zoned out losing my train of thought and I had that overwhelming urge to touch him, *again*. I'm constantly thinking about that, just touching him. I'm thinking about him a lot, actually more than I should be, and in ways that I never had before, and I'm freaked out. Seth and I are supposed to be best friends. What if I took the chance and told him, and then he didn't feel the same? What if he just wants to be my friend and that's it? I can't and won't mess up being friends with him. I couldn't handle losing him twice.

But then I think, what if he does like me that way? That's when the butterflies start and my whole body tingles. This is what I was talking about all along with Evelyn and she never understood. This is how it should feel when you love someone, I think. I've always loved him and I told him so a long time ago. At the time, I was young and innocent.

But, am I in love with him?

Maybe.

Maybe I always have been, but I didn't understand the feelings until now. At least, it would explain my disinterest in dating I've had over the last few years. How can I date anyone else when I already gave my heart away a long time ago?

When I got home from work the house was empty. I went into the kitchen and helped myself to a little orange juice from the fridge. I then remembered Katie was at a sleepover tonight. So that probably means Mom and Ray went out to the bar, which was good for me, because then there will be nobody here to fight with about me going anywhere.

I went upstairs and took a shower and got dressed for the dance. It wasn't a formal so I just put on a pair of black denim jeans and my favorite dark red halter top, and I blow dried my hair.

When I opened my car door to leave for the dance I found one single red rose on my front seat. I picked it up and put it to my nose, and it smelled nice. I worried for a moment that this may have come from Kevin. I looked around to see if whoever left it was still here, but I didn't see anyone.

I drove myself to the dance alone, and I don't care. I feel very comfortable going stag. I'd rather go alone anyway then go with that creep.

I parked my car, and I went in and paid for my ticket. I started to wonder though if I just wasted my money.

The dance was being held in the gym, and it was decked out in crepe paper everywhere. Honestly, it just looks like a bunch of kids TP'd the gym. There was a cheesy band playing, which in my opinion, I already think sucks. They actually have violins! —it's gonna be a *long* night!

Evelyn, Charles, Leslie, and Paul were already here, and were hanging out in the corner by the food.

"Hey, Veronica's here!" Evelyn sang.

"Yes, now the fun can start!" I sang back, I was trying to sound enthusiastic. Really, I already just wanted to leave.

"Hey Veronica, are you in a better mood tonight?" Paul asked. He was smirking.

"I'm fine," I replied.

"Good, wouldn't want you to throw any of this at me," he snickered and waved his hand at the table.

"Well then, make sure you don't talk shit about me!" I snapped and I crossed my arms.

It better not be like *this* all night, I thought to myself.

I was sitting down in a chair against the wall with Evelyn and Leslie just hanging out.

"So, Leslie, did you come here with a date or are you here stag like me?" I asked trying to be nice and making small talk.

Leslie smiled. "I came here with Paul," she replied.

"Really, is this a date?" I asked. When did that start? I wondered. I felt a little out of the loop.

"Yes. We've only gone out a few times."

"So, it's safe to assume then that things are going well?" I asked.

She smiled warmly and glanced over at Paul who was chatting with Charles. "Yeah, I'd say so."

"Wow...that's great Leslie." I smiled at her.

"Veronica, we're actually on a double date tonight," Evelyn said.

"Oh," now I was feeling like a fifth wheel. Why did they want me to come here tonight then? This wasn't my idea, I thought to myself.

"I don't know if I'm staying for the whole dance," I commented.

"Awe, why not?" Evelyn said.

"Well, I only came because you said it would be fun. But now I'm just feeling like a fifth wheel. You guys are all on a double date. Plus, this band sucks." I smiled and pretended to gag.

Evelyn sat up and suddenly gasped. "OH! MY! GOD!" she yelled.

Leslie and I looked up. "What?" I said.

"Kevin's here, and look who he's with!" I glanced over by the door where Evelyn was looking and I gasped. "He came here with Claudette?" I was shocked. "He told me he hated her," I told the girls.

Leslie put her hands on her hips. "Well, apparently not."

"He's just with her because everyone knows she's easy. He's a slime ball and a half!" Evelyn replied. "He only brought her here to upset you, I bet."

"Well it didn't work, she can have him. I hope she likes making out with milkshake man." I started laughing.

The girls and I went back to talking, but I was miserable. I kept glancing over at the clock. I wonder how long I have to suffer through this so my friends don't think I'm just being a cranky bitch. This so-called dance sucks. All I could think about was leaving.

"Holy crap!" Evelyn said suddenly.

Leslie looked up. "What?"

"That Seth kid's here," she replied.

My heart skipped a beat and I stood up to see. He was standing in the doorway with his arms crossed scanning the room. I quickly sat back down in the chair and I felt my chest start to heave. A panic attack, really?! I'm having a freaking panic attack!

As much as I was denying my feelings all week, I couldn't shake the feeling he might be here for me and I was petrified. I gripped the bottom of the chair and took in very slow, controlled deep breaths, trying to settle myself.

"Veronica, are you alright?" Evelyn asked. "You look a little green."

"I'm fine." Good, I managed to get words out. So far so good, I told myself.

"Evelyn, I think he's coming over here," Leslie said.

"Who?!" I managed to choke out.

I peeked around Leslie and spotted him in the crowd and as soon as we made eye contact he smiled at me and my heart took off racing.

He strolled over very calmly. "Good evening, girls," he spoke to both Evelyn and Leslie.

Evelyn was the only one who said anything. "Hi."

Leslie was still in shock☒she probably thinks Jack the Ripper is here to kill us.

He raised his eyebrow and he held out his hand to me. "Dance with me?" he asked.

I didn't say anything, not that I could at the moment anyway. So, I just smiled softly and took his hand. I held my breath, as I let him lead me out onto the dance floor. He never let go of my hand. He turned and put his other hand on my waist and it made me dizzy. I had to take controlled deep breaths in and out to settle my nerves.

He did look so good tonight. I could tell he stepped out of his comfort zone just a little putting on the dark blue dress shirt. I love the fact that he didn't wear the dress pants and kept the jeans. He must have left his leather jacket in the car. It's also a nice change to see his hair combed out of his face. It makes it that much easier for me to stare at it.

When we started to move I was surprised. I wasn't aware that he knew how to dance.

"Where'd you learn to dance?" I asked.

"My mother," he replied softly.

"Oh." I glanced down feeling a little embarrassed. When I brought my head back up he was looking at me. His green eyes were so intense I almost couldn't look, but at the same time I couldn't look away. I didn't want to.

He brought the hand he was holding in a little closer. He reached down with his thumb and touched my bracelet. "You're still wearing that?"

"Yes." I looked down. I was still a little embarrassed. "Why?"

"Because I promised you I wouldn't take it off," I admitted.

He had a serious look in his eyes. "I remember."

"Are you still wearing mine?"

"Of course." He chuckled. "You fused it on so it would never come off."

I shook my head and chuckled. "I can't believe you remember that."

He leaned in and whispered, "I remember every moment I've ever spent with you."

I felt my cheeks flush.

"Did you like my gift?" he asked.

"Were you the one who left the rose in my car?"

"Yes." He nodded.

I smiled. "I loved it, thank you...I have a question though."

He just looked at me.

"Not that I mind, but how did you know where I live? I never told you."

He smiled. "I looked it up in the phone book."

"Oh." I found myself gushing.

He was glancing over my shoulder. "Your friends are staring at us," he commented.

"Let them," I replied. I didn't care. The two of them have been jumping up and down on my last nerve lately anyway.

"You aren't afraid to be with me?" he asked.

I looked at him with narrow brows. "Have I ever been afraid to be with you?"

He smiled. "No."

He tightened his hold on my waist and pulled me closer. I closed my eyes and I slowly inhaled his scent, which was sweet like honey, with just a hint of leather, which I found to be intoxicating.

He leaned in and skimmed my cheek with his lips to whisper in my ear, "Thank you for keeping my secret."

"Which one?" I asked. I was trembling, I could barely speak.

"All of them," he whispered again.

"I'll always keep them," I whispered back.

Then a thought occurred to me and I chuckled. I pulled back to look at him. "Hey, it's Friday night, why aren't you out at the bar? I'm sure I might get asked that."

He smiled. "*Ahhh*, the night is young." He laughed once, and then he playfully twirled me. He pulled me in close again pressing me up against him.

We danced quietly for a while moving in a slow circle. All that kept running through my mind was, I wonder what it would be like to kiss him.

"Would you go out with me?" he asked suddenly interrupting my thoughts.

My heart pounded against my rib cage in shock, making my chest feel like a pinball machine. I started wondering if he could feel it. I had to take a slow steady breath before I could even answer.

I had to glance down so I could speak. "Do you mean, like a date?" I spoke softly.

Oh God, I thought, please say yes.

"Yeah," he replied coolly.

Of course I wanted to go out with him. I was freaking out now and screaming on the inside. But I played it cool. "Sure."

"Good." I heard him exhale.

"When do you want to go?" I asked. I hope I didn't sound too eager.

"Can we go tomorrow night?" he asked.

"Sure."

The song ended, and he tenderly kissed my cheek. "I'll see you later."

He walked away and I just stood there in a daze. It took me a few minutes before I could put together coherent thoughts that allowed me to walk back over to my friends.

I was in total shock. I slumped down in a chair and sat back.

Evelyn and Leslie both stood over me with their arms crossed and looked at me with concern.

"Veronica, what is going on with you and that Seth kid?" Evelyn asked. She spoke slowly, which was good.

I wasn't totally here yet, and it allowed me a chance to fully process what she asked before I answered her.

My head was spinning. "I have a date with him," I said in a daze. She still had her arms crossed and she looked a little worried. "You have a date with him? Aren't you afraid to go out with him?" she asked.

I shook my head. "Of course not."

"But what about all those things everyone's been saying about him?" Evelyn asked.

"Be realistic, Evelyn. None of that's true."

"Well for your sake I hope your right," Leslie added.

"This time, I know I am," I replied back.

The dance finally ended around ten, and I took my time strolling out to my car trying to avoid some of the traffic that is associated with events such as these. I was in too much of a daze to rush out of here anyway.

I was in no hurry. I was way too happy to be.

When I got to my car, Seth suddenly walked out from behind it and into view.

"Did you change your mind about going to the bar?" I teased him smiling. I leaned up against my door.

"Something like that." He smiled, his eyes were smoldering.

He surprised me coming up close placing his hands on my car, one on each side of me. He leaned in pressing his body against mine, pinning me up against my car. I held my breath. He leaned in slowly and closed his eyes hovering just above my lips. I could feel the warmth of his breath on them and I was shaking. I was the one who closed the gap pressing my lips to his and then I closed my eyes. The moment our lips touched was electric, and I felt something erupt inside my chest. Maybe it was my heart bursting from the pressure? I felt an intense longing and desire that I never felt before. I put my arms around his neck and gripped his collar. I lost all sense of time, and controlled thought. We could have been kissing for an eternity and I wouldn't have noticed and it wouldn't have fazed me either.

I didn't want to stop.

When he finally pulled away his breathing was ragged. "Wow," he whispered.

I was still gripping on to his jacket collar and I couldn't let go.

I opened my eyes and I glanced up at him. "That was a bit better than the last time," I whispered.

He shook his head. "Hey, wait a second." He smirked. "Did you want me to kiss you like that back then?"

"I want you to now," I whispered.

I pulled him closer, and I pressed my lips to his again breathing in his sweet honey-like scent and I felt him tremble. He held me tightly in his arms for a long moment before letting me go.

"I'll pick you up at your house tomorrow night, around six thirty. Is that okay?" he asked.

"I guess."

He looked concerned. "Why? What's wrong with six thirty? Is it too early?"

"No." I looked down.

"Then what's wrong?"

"It's not soon enough," I pouted.

He laughed and kissed my cheek. "I'll see you tomorrow."

The next morning, I woke to the startling sound of dishes smashing.

"GET OUT!" I heard my mother scream and then I heard something hit the wall hard shattering into a million pieces.

"Awe c'mon, cupcake, don't be like that!" I heard Ray yell back. "You're making way too big of a deal out of this!"

I rubbed my eyes. "Oh, what the hell!" I grumbled.

There was a soft knock and my door opened. "Can I hide in here?" Katie asked, as she shut the door and tip-toed over to my bed.

I was still groggy, but I was up now. "Yeah, what's going on?" I asked rubbing my eyes.

"Mom found out Ray's been seeing someone behind her back."

We both jumped when we heard something hit the wall. "You, useless piece of shit! —*get out!*" Donna shouted.

"Stop throwing my stuff!" Ray yelled. "It's not what it looks like! I can explain!"

"How'd she find out?" I asked.

Something else hit the wall downstairs making a loud thud and I jumped.

Katie chuckled. "Ray's girlfriend showed up early this morning and knocked on the door. She told Mom that not only was she having an affair with him, she said he's marrying her."

I gasped.

She grinned and nodded. "Oh, she's having his baby too!"

"Ewe, there's someone willing to marry *and* have a baby with that guy?" I shuddered. "Oh well. Can't say I'm gonna miss him... Bye Ray!"

Katie and I jumped up and ran to the window when we heard the door slam. Ray was running around the front yard picking up his stuff from the front lawn. We watched two shoes fly through the air hitting him in the back.

I turned and raised an eyebrow. "How did I miss her throwing his stuff on the lawn?" I asked chuckling.

"I don't know. She did that first. As soon as Ray's girlfriend left, Mom marched right upstairs and started throwing his stuff out the window. He wasn't even out of bed yet." She was giggling.

It was quiet downstairs now except for the dramatic sobbing. We watched Ray pile his things into his car, get in, and pull out of the driveway.

I glanced at Katie. "When do you think we should go down there?"

"Now is probably a good idea," she suggested.

Katie and I tip-toed down the stairs slowly and as we entered the living room we were surveying the damage.

The living room looked like a bomb went off. All the vases, knick-knacks, and ceramics that we had up on the shelves decorating our home were strewn all over the floor in millions of pieces. I stepped on a piece of glass, cutting my foot and immediately regretted not having my shoes on. I went into the kitchen, grabbed the first-aid kit, and took out a bandage for my foot. Once my foot was bandaged, I grabbed the dust pan and the broom and dragged the garbage can out into the living room.

Donna was on the sofa sobbing, she had her face buried in the pillows.

"Do you want us to help clean up?" Katie asked.

"Oh! You're such a good girl!" Mom said between sobs. "I don't know what I'm going to do!" She wailed. "How can he do this to me? I did everything for him!"

I started sweeping up the broken dishes, loading the dust pan and emptying it into the trash can.

Katie sat down by Donna. "I know, you did everything for him. He's a jerk, Mom, you deserve much better," she said stroking her hair.

Even I agreed with that. "Yeah, I agree with Katie, Mom, that guy was gross," I added.

"Why do these things keep happening to me?!" she yelled.

"Don't worry, Mom. Things will get better," Katie told her as she handed her a tissue.

"Why doesn't he want me?!" Donna sat up. "It's because I'm old!" She threw herself down on the pillows.

"Awe Mom, you're not old!" Katie told her.

"It's because I'm fat then!" she cried.

"You're not fat! He's just a jerk." Katie was rubbing her back.

I finished cleaning up the broken dishes and glass, and sat down in the recliner. I didn't know what to do next. Katie was already comforting Donna and the mess was cleaned up. I can't do anything about the damaged walls though⊠the landlord's gonna be so pissed!

I was starting to get hungry. "Hey, does anyone want me to make breakfast?" I offered.

Donna and Katie shot me an angry glare. "I'm too fat to eat!" My mother cried.

I just put my hands up, defensive. "I was just offering."

Donna rolled over onto her back, and put her hand over her eyes. "Can one of you shut the blinds? I'm getting such a headache."

Katie walked over. "I'll do it, Mom." She pulled the cord on the blinds.

"Please leave me." She sobbed dramatically. "I need to be alone."

Katie and I went back upstairs. I went to my room and she went into hers.

I laid back down on my bed and thought about my morning.

Well at least Ray's gone. That's like the best news ever. I really dislike living here normally, but I disliked it even more when he was here. Maybe things are starting to turn around for me here? Maybe my guardian angel's awake now finally, and actually doing her job?

First, I get to go on a date with Seth later, and then I wake up to my mother kicking Ray out! Okay the date completely trumps Mom kicking Ray out, but a good thing is a good thing!

I turned to my side and stretched across my bed smiling.

Actually, kissing him trumps it even more. I can't believe he kissed me like that! It makes me dizzy just thinking about it. See, this is what I've been going on about to Evelyn. This is how it's supposed to be. When you go out with someone there should be sparks, and feelings, and butterflies in your stomach.

I'm going on a date with Seth tonight! I squealed. I wonder where he's taking me? I wonder what we're doing?

I looked at the clock and it was only two. What am I gonna do in the meantime while I'm waiting for him to pick me up at six thirty? I could go take my shower now and get dressed. That way I'm ready in the event I have to run out of here. God only knows what she's

gonna do later, and there is no way I'm not going out
with Seth tonight.

CHAPTER 18

I checked my hair a dozen times, but I checked the clock more. I swear that sucker is just testing my patience. It's risking its own little life, letting time drag like that. Does it want me to smash it? Why won't the time go by faster when I want it to?! It's five thirty, just an hour to go now.

I've already killed listening to my Aerosmith record. I've played it more times in a row than I can count, and I know if I listen to "Dream On" one more time I'm gonna lose it. I know, it's my own fault! I'm driving myself nuts! But what else can I do to kill the time? I've already bothered Katie a ton, and have zero interest in doing so anymore today. She can be quite catty at times, and listening to her go on and on about her performances can certainly wear on my nerves.

I can't even risk going downstairs yet. If I do, I might disturb Donna and then I might have a problem escaping tonight. Nope, going downstairs right now is not an option.

Why the hell did he say six thirty? Why would he torture me like this? Doesn't he remember how impatient I am? I thought he knew me?

Maybe I'll get lucky and he'll show up early. Maybe I should watch for him from the window.

I wandered over to the window and propped myself up on the radiator.

I watched the driveway for a bit, and then my eyes wandered over to where a few robins had landed. I watched them hopping around the yard in search of worms and bugs. I saw two children, a boy and a girl, riding by on their bikes, and they were laughing. They looked like they were about the age we were when we met. I smiled. I must admit, that was the best thing that has ever happened to me in my life.

My life so far has been loaded with (well in lack of a better term) "crappy people," and my mother has been the queen. I chuckled, "Queen crappy."

Seth has always been kind, giving, honest, and trustworthy. Not one time has he ever been anything else.

I got the urge to glance at the clock. I closed my eyes tight and turned around. I swear if that sucker hasn't moved it's going right out this very window!

I opened my eyes and it said six. Crap! That's it!? Only a half hour went by?

A more positive thinking person might say; "Oh, I only have a half hour to go!" But I tend to lean hard in the opposite direction when I'm impatiently waiting for something I really want.

I moseyed on over to my mirror to check my hair again, it still looks alright. Maybe I should change my top? Maybe it's too much? No, I think it's good. I had decided to wear my white off-the-shoulder blouse. I think it's nice. It slings off to one side. I hardly ever wear it, because it's a little too dressy for most events I attend.

But I think it just might fit the occasion tonight.

I heard the sound of a car rolling across the gravel in the driveway and I ran to the window. I started jumping up and down like a lottery winner running towards the door. "He's here!"

I swung open the door at first and was just about to bolt down the stairs, when I froze remembering the reason for staying upstairs⌧Donna.

I grabbed my overnight bag and carefully tip-toed down the stairs, cursing every creak they made under my breath. Donna was still lying on the couch. She was facing the back snoring. I gently tip-toed by her holding my breath and got to the door. I quietly turned the knob, opened the door, and tip-toed my way out shutting it as quietly as I could.

When I turned around he was already outside of his car leaning against it, arms crossed with a huge smirk on his face. I ran over and skidded to a stop in front of him.

"You look like you're escaping from prison." He chuckled.

I looked back quick. "I am, let's go!"

I jumped into the car and exhaled in relief. He got in and was shaking his head.

"So, what's going on?" he asked, as he was backing out of the driveway.

"You wouldn't," I stopped and shook my head. "I was gonna say you wouldn't believe what happened with her today, but I just realized you would." I laughed.

"So, is your mother being difficult?" he asked.

"Well, this morning she was throwing anything and everything breakable at Ray because he has been cheating on her I guess. She kicked him out too." I did a happy little jiggle in my seat and smiled. "I hated that guy. Well, to make a long story short, she's been all devastated on the couch all day, and if she knew I had plans she would have been such a bitch."

He glanced over. "So, you can't just go out?"

"Sort of."

"What do you mean sort of?" he asked.

"If she's around she tries to get in my way usually, telling me I'm grounded, but I never listen and just leave." I looked over at him and winked.

"What does she ground you for?" he asked.

"Everything, blinking, breathing. She told me the other day I was grounded because I have a bad attitude." I shook my head and chuckled.

I sighed. "I miss the days when she used to just ignore me. At least then I didn't have to go to such drastic measures to get out of the house and she didn't care when I came back. But with Ray around she had to show him that she's this "great mother." He had the nerve to tell me how my mother does everything for me and that I'm ungrateful! She never grounds Katie for anything. I used to just take her shit, but I stopped. I told you a long time ago, she doesn't like me."

"I still can't wrap my head around someone not liking you," he said.

That made me blush.

"So, what will she do when she finds out you're gone?" he asked.

"She locks the door so I can't come back in. The first time she did that I spent the night in my car. That's why Mémé started leaving a cabin open for me. I always bring my overnight bag with me everywhere."

I laughed. "Do you remember the night you spilled your beer on me?"

"I said I was sorry."

"Oh, I don't care about that." I smiled at him. "That night she told me I was grounded for not going to Katie's recital with her and Ray, and while I was in the shower she let the air out of two of my tires. Then her and Ray sat downstairs and said they weren't letting me go anywhere, for my own good." I had a sly grin.

"So, what did you do?" he prompted.

"I snuck into Donna's room and called Evelyn. She brought over some rope and then I climbed out my bedroom window."

He chuckled and his eyes went wide. "I'm so sorry you have to put up with all of that."

I shrugged. "I'm used to it."

"You deserve better," he said softly.

I looked up at him and took in a deep breath and exhaled. Then I smiled at him. "Okay, enough talking about that crap. What are we doing tonight?"

"So, it's safe to assume then that you have no curfew?"

"I would break it if I did." I grinned.

He chuckled. "Good."

We were quiet for a moment, and I just sat back in my seat smiling.

"Can I ask you something?" he asked suddenly.

"Hmmm?"

"Are you freaked out?"

I glanced at him with narrow eyes. "Freaked out? By what?"

"That we're doing this? That you're going out with me." He looked like he was bracing himself.

"Well...yeah...kind of. A part of me is totally scared. You and I have been best friends for so long, and I don't want to ever lose that. I don't think I could take it, and I know I'd probably die at this point if I lost you again. But, then there's this other part of me that kind of... 'knew it all along.'" I smiled and shook my head. "It at least explains why I've been so picky."

He glanced over at me. "Picky?" he questioned.

"Yeah, Evelyn thought I was crazy. Since I've started high school I've had quite a few guys ask me out and I found reasons to say no to every one of them. I just couldn't do it."

"But what about that Kevin guy? Why did you end up saying yes to him?"

"I didn't really. He hangs out with Evelyn's brother so he was around a lot. Evelyn was constantly telling me how crazy I was for turning down half the guys that I did. I started wondering if maybe there was something wrong with me. So, one night we were all hanging out and he and I ended up alone and he kissed me. I tried dating him, but I was constantly telling him how things were never gonna be serious between us. But even just trying that, it was always just all wrong." I shook my head.

He smiled. "Oh."

"Why?" I glanced up at him. "Are *you* freaked out?"

"No, I was more afraid that you were."

"Why would you think that after last night?" I asked raising an eyebrow.

He smiled. "I guess, I just...freaked out."

I smirked. "Well, it's your own fault, you know!"

"What's my fault?" He looked confused.

"You're the one who crossed the line, if you hadn't kissed me like that..." I started to tease him and I shook my head. "You started this whole thing!"

"I couldn't help it, I had to." He glanced over, he looked nervous.

"Me too." I was leaning back in my seat grinning.

"Seth, can't you feel that?" I asked sighing, I was feeling so content.

He glanced down at me. "Feel what?"

"That this is what you and I are supposed to do."

Whoa, I thought. Where did that come from?

He reached over and squeezed my hand. "Yes."

I glanced over at him. "I always just blurt out way too much when I'm with you."

"So what? I like that about you," he replied.

"So, what about you?" I asked turning the spotlight on him. "*My fair share*?" My tone was teasing.

"I briefly dated two different girls. One I met at a party, her name was Andrea. Nice girl, but there was just something missing. It only lasted about a month. The other girl, her name was Mandy. I met her in my biology class. Both ended up being something similar to what you described. I just thought I was doing what I was supposed to be doing."

"Interesting," I replied. "Were they cute?" I asked.

He glanced over at me. "They were both pretty."

I smiled at him and just sat back in my seat relaxing.

"Are you upset?" he suddenly asked.

I looked over at him puzzled. "No, why would I be?"

"Because, I just said I thought two other girls were pretty."

"So what," I shrugged.

"You're not hurt I said that?" He seemed confused.

I shook my head. "No."

He just looked over at me with a worried expression. Like he was expecting some bottom to just drop out suddenly and that I would start freaking out or something.

"Are you confused why I'm not upset?" I asked him.

"A little," he admitted.

"I'm not upset because you didn't say that I wasn't pretty, and you didn't say that they were prettier than me either," I told him. "Plus, I'm here and they're not." I sounded smug.

"You are much more to me than just pretty," he told me.

I smiled at him. "Thank you."

I didn't pay much attention to where we were going so when we arrived at our destination a few minutes later I was a bit confused. "We're at Devil's Hopyard?"

"Yes, why? What were you expecting?"

"I thought you were taking me out to dinner or something," I said.

"I am. We're just not eating at a restaurant... Do you trust me?"

"That's a silly question," I replied.

We pulled into the parking lot across from Chapman Falls and parked. I just sat there at first. I wasn't totally sure what I should do, or what was happening. He stepped out of the car and then came around to my side and opened the door taking my hand to help me out, which caused my cheeks to flush red.

I stood there shivering, as I watched him rummage through his trunk. It's early spring, so it's still chilly here outside at night. I was seriously regretting wearing this top and I know I don't have anything warmer in my bag. I just keep a simple change of clothes in there most of the time, just a tee-shirt and jeans. I should have asked him what he was planning. Then I could have dressed a little warmer; I'm a moron.

He took out a small cooler and placed it on the ground, and then he grabbed a folded blanket and placed it on top. He shut the trunk and looked over at me. "Did I tell you how beautiful you look tonight?"

I blushed. "No."

"You look incredible, actually," he said.

"Thank you." I glanced down at my feet, gushing.

"You must be cold, though."

"I am a little," I replied.

He reopened his trunk and opened a bag and pulled out a red flannel shirt and handed it to me. "This might help."

"Thanks, I'm gonna change in your car." I narrowed my eyes. "No peeking."

He chuckled. "I've already seen what you're like when your mad. I don't want to wear any of this." He pointed to the cooler.

"You're funny," I said sarcastically. Is anyone just gonna let that go?

I got into his car and climbed into the back seat. I figured, I'd have a bit more coverage if I changed in the back. I glanced over at him and his back was towards the car. I pulled off my white top and quickly put my arms through the sleeves of the flannel pulling it closed. However, as I started doing up the buttons I could feel a set of eyes on me. I glanced up with just my eyes and his head was turned slightly. I turned quick and he quickly looked away.

Once I was done changing I stepped out of the car and shut the door. I expected him to turn around but he didn't. I knew it right there⊠he looked.

That put me in a very awkward position. If this was someone else, let's just say for argument sake⊠Kevin. I would definitely lose it and would be cursing him up and down. I'd probably slap him and leave too. But this is Seth. I can't imagine he would just do that because he's a pig. No, I know him, he's not that. So, I just couldn't react the way I normally would, the anger just wasn't there. Yep, this was all new territory.

I took a breath and exhaled. "I'm all set. Thanks for the shirt." I watched his eyes.

He cleared his throat. "No problem. I had a feeling you might need that," he said, his face looked so guilty.

"So, where are we eating?" I asked him.

He picked up the cooler and the blanket. "I thought since you love it so much we could sit over by the falls. There's a nice spot on the side next to the fence on the rocks." I didn't miss him not making eye contact.

I smirked at him, and grabbed the blanket from under his arm. "Well, come on then." I walked across the street.

I spread out the blanket and sat down. "So, what's in the cooler?" I asked.

He knelt down and opened the cooler. "Just a couple of sandwiches and some snacks, Cokes too." I noticed he wasn't looking up at me while he was talking.

"What kind of sandwiches?"

He kept his eyes down. "Ham and cheese, is that okay?"

"Yeah." I sighed.

"Is it gonna be like this the rest of the night?" I asked. I couldn't help the sly smile on my face. It was kinda fun watching him squirm.

He glanced up at me awkwardly. "What do you mean?"

I crossed my arms. "Don't give me that, Seth. You and I both know what I'm talking about."

He handed me a sandwich. "Go ahead and throw it at me, I deserve it."

I started laughing. "I'm way too hungry to throw that sandwich at you."

He held up an apple. "An apple then?"

"Seth, you can relax. I'm not mad."

He exhaled hard like he was holding his breath. "You're not?"

"No, surprisingly." I laughed.

I unwrapped my sandwich and started eating. I was starving. Because of Donna and her crap today I never did get to eat.

It was peaceful while we were eating. It was nice sitting next to the falls at night. I found the sound of the rushing water to be very soothing. The air wasn't too bad either. It was a little chilly, but better now that I was wearing his flannel.

I finished with the sandwich before he did and started going through the cooler to grab a Coke.

"Are you done with the sandwich already?" he asked, he sounded surprised.

"Yeah, I didn't get to eat at all today," I commented.

"Why, not?"

"Because of Donna and all the crap earlier. I got woken up with that shit. I offered to make breakfast but I nearly got my head bit off for even asking. Then she had a headache, and she doesn't allow us to make any noise or be around her when that happens. She gets all crazy if I even try. So, I couldn't go down to the kitchen for anything all day."

He looked at me with concern. "Why didn't you just leave then?"

I smiled. "Because, I was waiting for you."

"I am sorry you had to wait, but I had to work today. And if I had known any of this, I would have just told you to go up to my house and wait for me there." He sounded so serious.

"I'll just do that next time," I assured him.

He placed an apple on top of the cooler and took out his knife from his pocket and swung it around fast to open it, and he cut the apple in half. He handed me half.

"Thanks. Where did you learn to do that?"

He glanced at me funny. "What, this?" He swung it around to close it.

"Yeah."

"A friend of mine at a youth camp my grandfather forced me to go to."

I smiled when he mentioned he had a friend. "Oh, was it fun?"

He shrugged. "It was okay."

What happened before was on my mind still and curiosity got the better of me. "Can I ask you something?"

"Sure."

"Did you see anything?" I watched his face.

He was stiff. "What do you mean?"

I rolled my eyes. "Seth, you know exactly what I mean."

He looked down. "Kinda."

I just nodded. "How much?" I asked prying.

He just kept his eyes down. "I thought you said you weren't upset."

"I'm not." I shook my head a little. I was still shocked at that. "How much did you see?"

He didn't say anything. He just sat there looking down. "Seth, how much?" I pressed.

He took a breath in and exhaled hard. "Not as much as I wanted to," he said abruptly.

I laughed. "Finally!" I threw my hands up and let out a sigh of relief.

He looked at me puzzled. "What?"

"You finally say stuff when you're too scared to! That used to drive me nuts!"

He just made a funny face. "So, you like that then?"

"Yeah."

"Well then, how about I tell you something else?" he sounded a little anxious.

I smiled and I leaned in closer. "Go ahead."

He took in a big breath, held it for a moment, and then I heard him exhale hard before he spoke. "I've had the biggest crush on you since your first day here."

I was surprised. "Really?" I had no idea.

"Yeah, I was obsessed."

"Why didn't you say something?"

"Duh, I was too scared." He became quiet for a moment and was just staring at me.

I just looked back at him trying to read his face. "What?"

"I was debating on telling you more."

I leaned over more cupping my chin in my hands and resting my elbows on the cooler. "Okay, now you have no choice." I smiled.

He closed his eyes, for a moment. "Do you remember that last time we were together, at your grandparents'?"

"Of course I do," I replied.

"Do you remember dragging me down to the stream?"

"Yes." I smiled.

"Do you remember anything you said?" He looked up at me.

I sat back for a moment and I closed my eyes. I could picture the both of us sitting by the stream and I know I was telling him a lot of stuff that day.

"Seth, I remember I said a lot of things to you. You were worrying me a lot at that point. So, you need to be more specific."

He took a breath and exhaled. "You told me that you loved me."

I froze there for a moment, thinking about that day. Of course, I remembered saying that, it was already weighing heavy on my mind all last week. I then had a realization...he kissed me shortly after.

I nodded. "I remember," I said softly.

"That's why I told you that I loved you too and the reason's the same for why I kissed you. I wouldn't have had the guts then otherwise."

"You know I thought about that all day the next day. Then I spent that Monday morning searching for you in the cafeteria."

"What were you going to do?" he asked.

"I remember thinking how I wasn't really ready for anything like that yet. I didn't really know what I was going to say to you. I didn't understand what I was feeling yet. At that time though I always felt kind of," I paused struggling for the right word, "possessive of you. I was always ready to pounce on anyone that did anything mean to you back then."

I started laughing. "Hell, look what I did to Claudette! That girl was such a pain in the ass back then. I'm betting if you had stayed I still would have beaten the crap out of her. After that though, no one said one single bad thing about you to me because they all knew I'd send them to the nurse's office."

He burst out laughing. "You didn't tell me she went to the nurse."

I smiled and shrugged. "Yeah, she did."

He was smiling and he slid over a little closer to me. "Possessive?" he questioned.

I chuckled. "I was nine. I didn't know anything back then except that you were mine," I told him.

He lifted his hand up and caressed my cheek. "I am so sorry I didn't write to you and I'm so sorry I didn't call," he said softly.

I held his hand to my cheek. "I forgive you and I understood. What you went through had to be so hard. I can't even begin to imagine what that must have been like for you." I felt my eyes starting to sting, and I took a breath trying to stay in control. "The hardest part for me was that I knew something was wrong back then. I could feel it. I was worrying every moment you weren't with me. That's why I dragged you down to the stream, to make you talk to me. Then that whole time you and I were talking, I was trying to figure out how to hide you somewhere so no one could touch you. I was so frustrated that I wasn't able to protect you. Then up until now, it was just not knowing if you were okay, or even just where you were."

He leaned in and kissed my lips. "I'm here now," he spoke softly and then he pressed his lips to mine again, and I closed my eyes. I could feel all the pain that I held in from that time starting to dissolve. He moved his hand from my cheek to the nape of my neck holding me there for a moment. He paused briefly and I could feel him quivering. His lips hovering just slightly out of reach. "I love you," he whispered.

"I love you too," I whispered back.

We sat by the falls until the sun came up. It was cooler this morning. The temperature had dropped a little overnight, but I wasn't cold. I was leaning back against his chest, he had tucked me inside his jacket and he kept his arms around me. I could feel the warmth coming from his chest, and I could feel his heartbeat. I was content with the idea of sitting like this forever.

I don't think I've ever seen anything more serene then dawn in the Hopyard. The dew that had settled overnight was beginning to rise up off the moss-covered rocks and the grass, circling up through the trees, and the water cascading down the waterfall was starting to glisten and evaporate in the sun.

We watched two deer quietly wander through at the bottom of the falls stopping to drink from a small pool of water that had collected between some rocks.

The most amazing part of any of it was the person sitting here with his arms around me.

I snuggled in a little closer and I closed my eyes. "I know we should probably consider going back to civilization, but I just don't want to," I said.

"Me neither." He pressed his face into my hair, and kissed my head. "Where am I even bringing you to?"

"Hmm, I guess you can just bring me home so I can get my car. What time is it?"

He pushed back his sleeve to show me his watch. It was six o'clock in the morning. I groaned. "Crap. We have to go now if we want any sort of chance of avoiding Donna."

I turned around and looked at him and my heart started aching at the thought that this had to end.

He started to get up but I crawled towards him and leaned in causing him to lose his balance and fall back. I grabbed him by his jacket and forced him to the ground. I pressed my lips to his holding him here with me just a little longer.

I sat up, and he stayed pinned beneath me on the ground. He placed his hands behind his head and smiled. "So, do I really need to bring you back?"

"Unfortunately," I sighed.

I stood up and held my hand out to help him up.

He surprised me.

When he took it, he pulled me down onto his lap and flipped around quickly pinning me to the ground, making me laugh.

He had me pinned underneath him. He bent down and kissed me with such passion and desperation that made my will from before to ever be able to leave him crumble.

He stopped and tried to sit up and then he started laughing. "Why do you do that?"

I opened my eyes and realized I was clutching his jacket so hard that he couldn't move.

I was in a daze. "I don't know."

It took everything I had to release my hands.

He was staring at me. His smile was warm and glowing. "Come on, let's get you to your car."

I was surprised, but happy to discover, Donna's car missing from the driveway. "Well, looks like Donna took off for the night too," I commented to him when we pulled into the driveway.

"Does she do that a lot?" he asked.

I shrugged. "Mostly when she's upset, but there have been plenty of times where she just left because she felt like it."

"How long does she stay out for?"

"However long she feels like. Sometimes it's a few hours, sometimes a few days." I glanced at him. "Why? Do you want to come in?"

"Can I?"

"Sure, as long as the door's unlocked."

"Don't you have a key?"

"No, she gave one to Katie but wouldn't give one to me, because I'm *too irresponsible*." I chuckled.

He just shook his head. We got out of the car and walked up to the front door.

I looked at him, and put my finger to my lips. "Shhh ...just in case," I whispered. He nodded. I slowly turned the knob and opened the door. I peeked in checking the couch to see if Donna was still on it, she wasn't. I walked inside and held the door for him and then quietly shut it behind him. I slipped off my shoes and picked them up to carry them. I tip-toed over to the kitchen door and peered in and it was empty.

"So far, so good," I said quietly. "Follow me."

"Did you need me to take my shoes off too?" he asked quietly.

I walked over to him. "I only did that in case she was in the kitchen. I'm quieter on my toes."

I walked up the stairs and saw Katie's door was open. I held up my finger and glanced inside and she was gone too.

I let out a sigh of relief. "Looks like they're both gone."

I walked across the hall to my room and turned the knob. "Looks like you get to see my room after all."

I opened the door and stood out of the way letting him walk by and I shut the door behind us. I started thinking; thank God I had picked up in here yesterday while I was trapped. I did have a few of my bras lying on the floor.

He took off his jacket and tossed it onto the floor next to my dresser.

He sat down on my bed, lying himself back against my pillows, and placed his hands behind his head. He had a soft smile and he closed his eyes. I stood at the foot of my bed leaning against my bed post watching him. I found his relaxed, carefree attitude very entertaining. The difference between the kid I knew then and the man I know now is almost like night and day. It's nice to see him so alight, instead of the way he used to be, which was miserable and scared.

He slowly opened his eyes and looked up at me and my heart thumped hard against my ribs.

"How long do you think they're gonna be gone?" he asked.

"It's hard to say. They never tell me when they decide to do anything. One time they went to Maine and never told me they were going and I had the house to myself for four days."

"How long ago was that?"

"That was before Ray. I think I was fourteen."

"Whoa."

I smirked at him. "Why? What are you thinking?" I crossed my arms.

He put a hand on his chest. "I was thinking about taking a nap." He smirked back at me and an eyebrow rose. "Why? What were you thinking?"

I wandered over and laid down on the bed curling up next to him. He curled his arm around me.

I started to feel so grateful that he was okay, and that I was no longer alone. The emotions that began to run through me were overwhelming and I could feel the tears pooling up in my eyes.

"Thank you," I said softly.

"Thank you?" He sounded puzzled. "For what?"

"For coming back." Now the tears were really flowing and I was starting to gasp.

He sat up to look at me. "Veronica what's wrong? Why are you crying?" He sounded worried.

I broke down. "I'm just so relieved that you're really here. I can't tell you how many days and nights I spent wondering if I'd ever see you again. I've just had to live with the pain of that time for so long." I sobbed. "You had always made being here bearable and then when you were gone I was so alone... I'm just so, relieved."

He held me tighter. "I'm not going anywhere, ever again, without you."

I chuckled. "What about when you go to work?"

"It's a store, you can hang out," he said simply.

I wiped my eyes with his flannel. "I can handle you having to go to work, you know. I can survive that."

He laughed lightly and then he glanced over at my alarm clock.

"Do you have somewhere you need to be?" I asked him.

"I promised my grandfather I'd help him with some stuff today, so I do need to go soon."

"Fine." I sulked. "When will I get to see you again?"

"How about I pick you up for school tomorrow?"

"I would love that but I have to work right after school."

"So what, I have to work after school too. I'll just drop you off and pick you up." He shrugged.

I sat up and looked at him. "I guess that's fine. But, I'm staying in your car until second period."

When Seth finally left to go home I was still wired. I started a load of laundry for myself, and then I wrote a nice letter to my father. I apologized to him for not writing sooner and I asked (okay, more like begged) him not to call Mom. I told him how happy I was for him and Linda, and I even told him a little about Seth. I just left out some of the more personal details⊠like how we made out for about twenty minutes on my bed before he had to leave. When I was finished, I tucked the letter in an envelope and stuck it in my bag.

I did my homework and I cleaned the entire house. I figured I would try to be a little nice even though I'm sure my efforts are probably gonna go unappreciated.

I took a shower and I put my pajamas on and then I lied down on my bed. I haven't slept for a good twenty-four hours now. I was wide awake, and all I could do was think about and gush over everything that had happened between us.

I love him, and that's a fact. I can't believe it took me so long to realize when it actually began though. Why didn't I notice that? Was I too young?

I winced at the thought of what might have happened if he didn't come back. Would I have been alone forever? Or would I be stuck miserably in a relationship with someone that I just couldn't connect with? Thank God neither of those things are the case!

CHAPTER 19

I was surprised at myself when I woke up an hour before my alarm was set to go off.

What surprised me even more, was that not only did I want to get up, I was actually happy about it. I've never liked waking up early, ever.

In the past when I woke up early, and I couldn't go back to sleep, I'd be cursing at myself so bad. Then I'd end up being such a bitch all day long, because everything would be even more irritating than normal.

I sang on my way to the bathroom, and while I was in the shower. Then I sang my way around the kitchen looking for something to eat for breakfast.

When I discovered someone ate the last of my Sugar Crisps, and was kind enough to leave me the empty box, instead of the raging fit I normally would throw over such things, I just threw the empty box away and decided to just not bother with breakfast this morning.

It's so bizarre to me feeling this good. I don't think I've gone one day where I didn't get pissed off about something or was just cranky. I can't help wondering in the back of my mind though how long my happiness will last.

I waited by the door for him to arrive and when I saw him pull into the driveway I ran out of the house skipping and bouncing all the way down the front walk, greeting him at his car.

He rolled down his window when he saw me, and I reached my head in and started kissing him before he had a chance to put it in park. He pulled me in onto his lap through the window.

When I finally sat back and smiled at him he started laughing. "Wow, I'm coming here every morning!" he exclaimed.

I grinned and kissed his cheek. "Good morning to you too," I said, sliding over into the passenger seat.

"So, what did you do after I left?" he asked, backing out of the driveway.

"I had a very exciting Sunday," I said smiling. "Yep, I cleaned the whole house and I did my laundry...and I did my homework."

"Sounds like fun," he commented.

"What did you do?" I asked.

"I helped my grandfather start building his workshop on the side of the house. Well, he had it started before I even got there actually." He shook his head.

"That sounds nice. I can't wait to see it."

When we got to school, I could see Evelyn waiting very impatiently over by Leslie's car. I laughed. "Looks like I'm gonna get ambushed."

"Why? Is she waiting to talk to you?" he asked.

I chuckled. "Probably. She knew we were going out on Saturday. She probably wants details. She's kind of a pervert."

He laughed. "What are you gonna tell her?"

I leaned over and hovered just inches away from his lips. "I'm just gonna tell her how incredible I think you are," I whispered. I closed my eyes and kissed his lips. I felt him run his hand up my shoulder to the back of my neck twisting his fingers into my hair.

He pulled away slightly so he could speak. "Incredible?" he questioned.

I was so dazed it took me a moment before I could speak. "Yes."

"Well as long as you tell her how unbelievably beautiful I think you are," he said. I looked into his eyes and they were smoldering.

He sat back against his seat and shook his head clearing it. "Do you really need to skip first period?" he asked.

"Yes, why?"

"It's just gonna be so hard waiting until second period to see you."

He reached over me to grab his books off the floor, and I placed my hands on his head and started running my fingers through his hair. He placed his head in my lap and closed his eyes and I felt him sigh. I just sat there quietly running my fingers through his hair comforting him. "I love you, too," I said softly.

He sat up and glanced over my shoulder and chuckled. "I better go in; your friend looks like she's gonna burst." He kissed me quick and then stepped out of the car.

It only took seconds before there was a knock on my window.

When I looked up, Evelyn was smiling at me. I motioned for her to get in the car and I slid over into his seat.

"Good morning, Evelyn," I greeted her.

"*Well*, good morning Veronica," she sang, shutting the door. "Still avoiding English?" she asked.

"Yep." For as long as I can, I added in thought.

She smiled at me. "So, I see things must have gone well Saturday between you and Seth," she commented.

I rested the back of my head against the seat and smiled at her. "Yeah," I said on an exhale. "He's just so … *Incredible*." I sighed, happily.

She motioned me forward with her hand. "So, spill then. What did you guys do for your date?"

"He took me to Devil's Hopyard, and we had a small picnic next to the falls." I was smiling just thinking about it.

"I like it, it's different. Most guys just take you to the movies or a restaurant. It sounds so romantic, he must you." She smiled. "What time did you get she asked.

was ten of seven when I got home yesterday orning." I smirked.

Her eyes bulged out of her head. "And what did you two do⊠*all night*?!"

I chuckled and smacked her arm. "Not that you perv!"

"I was only teasing," she nudged me with her shoulder, "I do know you better than that. Was Donna pissed?"

"Donna wasn't even home when I got back, and neither was Katie. It was the jewel in the crown of a perfect evening."

"Cool. So, what else happened on your date?"

I smiled at her and sighed. "Not too much. We just ate sandwiches and then just talked most of the night."

"So, you obviously kissed him," she commented.

I glance at her and smiled. "Yes." I couldn't help it, I was glowing.

"Did he make funny noises when you kissed?"

"No." I chuckled.

"Does he smell bad?"

"No, he smells quite good actually."

"So, you mean to tell me you haven't found something wrong with him?"

I shook my head.

"No twitchy eye or extra limb or something?" she poked.

I chuckled. "No."

She dramatically sat back against the door. "Whoa, this is major." I laughed.

"So, do you have your butterflies?" she asked.

"Yes, tons!" I placed my hands on my chest. "Every time I see him my heart feels like it's gonna leap out of my chest, too."

"Well, it's about time!" She gave me a playful shove. "We should all celebrate on Friday at Wicked Riff's. Do you think he'd want to come?"

"Hmm, I don't know. I'll ask him." I looked over at her. "What time is it?"

"It's almost time for second period," she replied.

I did a jiggle in my seat and grabbed my bag. "Come on, let's go in!"

When I got to math class I saw Seth leaning against the wall outside the door. He had his head against the wall and his eyes were closed. I felt the butterflies in my stomach take off causing my head to swirl. I walked over as quietly as I could and stopped right in front of him. He opened his eyes and smiled wide. I reached up onto my toes and put my arms around his neck. He lifted me up off the floor kissing me in his arms. I heard him make a sound as though he just tasted something sweet. I became so swept up in the kiss it took a few coughs and throats clearing from passersby to remind me of where I was.

s the longest class I've ever had to sit through,"
miling.

sed his cheek. "I'm sorry you were suffering. You
always skip with me tomorrow." I smirked at him.

He put me back down on the floor. "That sounds like more fun."

We walked into class holding hands and he sat down at the desk next to me.

"Hey, Evelyn invited us to go out on Friday. Do you want to go?" I asked him.

"Where?"

"Wicked Riff's."

"I have to work until nine, but I'm free after. We can go then if that's okay," he said.

"Sure, we usually go out around that time normally anyway."

"Why don't you go up to my house when you're done with work, and I'll meet you there when I'm done," he suggested.

I smiled at him. "Okay."

Third-period biology sucked. The clock just ticked by slowly, making every second feel like an eternity. Then, I had to suffer through a quiz, which I'm ninety percent sure I flunked, because I couldn't concentrate at all, and all I could think about was when I was going to see him next.

As soon as the bell rang, I took off running down the hall towards the cafeteria. I saw him standing in the middle of the hall, and skidded to a stop at his feet. (I had considered jumping on him, but at the last second, I chickened out. I have a slight fear of pain.) He started laughing, and wrapped his arms around me tightly, kissing my cheek and then skimmed his nose down past my jaw to my collarbone, and I could feel him taking in a deep breath.

He let go and held the cafeteria door open for me. "Where do you want to sit?" I asked him.

"I'll sit wherever you do."

I nudged him. "I have to get a sandwich first, are you coming with me?"

"Yes," he replied taking my hand.

Walking through the cafeteria to the lunch line I caught a few different sets of eyes watching us. The first ones I noticed were of course Evelyn and Leslie, which made sense, they're probably wondering where we're sitting.

The other was Kevin. *Awe, he looks upset*, I thought, sarcastically. Not that I really care one way or the other on that one. That guy can go straight to hell.

When we got up to the front of the line where the food is I grabbed a chicken salad sandwich. "What are you getting?" I asked him.

"I'm not getting anything," he replied.

I just looked at him. "Why not? Aren't you hungry?"

"I am. I just don't bring any money with me."

I grabbed an extra sandwich and two sodas and shot him a glare. "I'm buying, don't argue."

...is hands up. "Never." He smirked.

...m to the table I normally sit at with Evelyn ...slie. Charles and Paul were both sitting there ...I was amused at the thought that this was the first ...ne I was sitting down with them where we all have someone at the same time. I'm no longer the odd ball out.

I pointed starting the introductions. "Seth, this is Evelyn, Charles, Leslie, and Paul. Everyone, this is Seth." I waved my hand down the front of him like a game show hostess. Seth said hi and shook hands with Charles and Paul, and nodded his head towards Evelyn and Leslie, and we both sat down.

Evelyn leaned over the table. "So, what's the verdict? Are you guys coming on Friday night?"

I had my mouth full so I just nodded my head at first until I swallowed. "Yeah, we're coming when Seth gets out of work."

"Cool, it's much more fun when you come," she commented.

"Leslie, are you gonna go this time?" I asked. It was amusing watching her. It looks like she still finds him scary.

"You know that place is not my scene," she said.

Evelyn just waved her hand at her. "Don't mind her, Seth. She just doesn't know how to have a good time... *Now*, your girl Veronica on the other hand," she laughed and then she pointed at me, "*well*, she's a wild child!" she spoke loudly.

I almost choked on my sandwich and then I glared at her. Then I glanced over at Seth out of the corner of my eye checking his reaction.

He was looking at me with a funny grin. "Wild child, huh?" he commented.

"Yeah! You should have seen some of the crazy stuff she's done! It's always an adventure when she goes out! Did she tell you about the last time we went to Wicked Riff's? She climbed out her bedroom window down a freaking rope! She looked like a criminal escaping from prison!"

I sat back in my chair and crossed my arms. She's lucky I'm still chewing on my sandwich right now.

"Yeah, she mentioned it. I would have loved to have seen that," he said.

I sighed and patted his knee. "Well then, stick around. With Donna as my mother anything like that is possible."

"Every single time we go out anywhere, Veronica is a blast! She's loud, and always tells it like it is! She loves going to concerts and parties too, and she loves getting down with me to hard rock," she blurted out.

Seth leaned over, chuckling. "I like her," he commented.

I could feel my face turning red. "Oh Evelyn?" I sang.

She smiled warmly. "Yes dear?"

"Shut up." I smirked.

She started laughing. "I'm just trying to help you out." She winked. Seth was chuckling and he took my hand.

I smirked at her. "How about I help you out too... Miss I-95!"

Her eyes narrowed. "Now you're just playing dirty."

Charles sat up. "What's I-95?"

She shot me a glare and shook her head.

"Charles, maybe you'll get lucky later and she'll show you." I grinned at her.

Now she was beet red. "Evelyn?" I called out.

"What?"

"Don't worry. You know I'd never tell." I smiled at her. I held my hand up and we high-fived.

"I know," she replied. "Love ya, chickee."

"Love ya, too," I said back.

Paul sat up and leaned across the table. "Hey, Seth?"

Seth looked up. "Yeah?"

"I hope you don't mind me asking, but how'd you get that scar on your face?"

I sat there in horror holding my breath and I squeezed Seth's hand. It took everything I had to control the rage that was suddenly boiling under my skin. I wanted to jump across the table and slap Paul across his stupid mouth. That kid's always aggravating me!

I felt Seth take a breath. "Car accident," he said smoothly.

Paul's eyes widened and he just nodded. I let out a sigh of relief. But I was cursing that kid straight to hell in my head.

After lunch, Seth walked me to my locker so I could switch out my books.

"Are you okay?" I asked him.

"Very," he replied.

"That Paul kid is always pushing my buttons," I commented. It came out sounding harsh.

"Did what he ask me upset you?" he asked. He was suddenly pressing me up against my locker.

I pointed up at him. "Possessive, remember?"

He threaded his fingers through my belt loops, and smirked. "Uh huh."

He leaned in and kissed me and then I forgot what I was even saying.

"I'll meet you right here at the end of the day and then I'll take you to work," he said.

"Okay," I said in a daze.

He kissed my cheek and I watched him walk down the hall and turn the corner before I opened my locker to switch out my books.

Someone walked up behind me, but I was in too much of a daze to even notice.

I was horrified when I heard a familiar voice say my name. "Veronica?"

I cringed before I turned around because I knew it was Kevin standing there. This can't be good, I thought.

I crossed my arms. "And what do you want?" I asked. My tone was bossy and I was staring him down.

"So...you and that Chase kid, huh?" he commented with a surly attitude.

"That's none of your business," I snapped at him.

"It is my business! You and I were going out!" he snapped back.

"Hardly!" I yelled.

"You know damn well how I felt! I told you every single stinking date that we ever had that you and I were never gonna be serious! But you just wouldn't listen!" I started pointing at him. "Then you had the nerve to tell people that I was gonna sleep with you? Are you freaking kidding me?!" I was really mad now. I slammed my locker door shut and started walking away. I looked back and he was following me. "God Kevin, *go away*!"

"Yeah, well, I've been seeing Claudette!" he said, trying to throw that in my face.

"Good for you. I'm so happy for you both." I kept walking.

"Thanks," he said in a snotty tone. "Oh, just so you know, her and I already..."

I stopped dead in the hall, and put my hand up cutting him off right there. "Ewe! Please stop! I just ate lunch!"

Seth came back around the corner just then and wound his arm around me. "I could hear you yelling from down the hall." He kept his eyes narrowed on Kevin, and he was rubbing my shoulder. "Are you alright?" he asked me.

"I'm fine." I sighed, sounding annoyed. Kevin and Seth were staring each other down.

Kevin had an angry smirk on his face. "I'll see you later, Veronica."

"It'll be a cold day in hell!" I yelled back at him.

He turned and looked up at Seth and chuckled. "Good luck tapping that one, Chase. That girl's like Fort Knox... I was starting to think she's a lesbian."

My mouth dropped open and I gasped.

In the time it took for Kevin to finish that sentence, Seth grabbed him by his arm, twisted it behind his back, and shoved him up hard against the wall. It was the most amazing thing I'd ever seen! It was like watching a black panther taking down a large buck, he was fast and lethal.

"You want to try saying that again?" Seth spoke calmly into his ear. His naturally deep voice made him sound so dark and intimidating, it was so surreal. He pressed against his arm harder causing Kevin to yelp. "I'm only gonna tell you this once," Seth continued, his voice was very calm and dark. "You ever talk about my girlfriend like that again, and I will break this very arm⊠do you understand me?"

Kevin just nodded, his face was red and he was gasping for air.

"You better remember what I said," his voice sounded so threatening, it wouldn't surprise me if Kevin just soiled himself. Seth released his arm, and Kevin took off down the hall like a dog with his tail between his legs, and I can't say I felt even the slightest bit bad about it.

I was kind of in shock though. Until now, I've never heard Seth call me his girlfriend before so I was kind of in awe of that. Then, in all the years I've known him, I've never seen Seth like that ever. It was impressive. So, I was having a sort of out-of-body experience at that moment. I'm not used to anyone coming to my defense either, so it was a lot to process. I just stood there for a moment assessing what just happened.

"Are you alright?" Seth asked, rubbing my shoulder.

I looked up at him with narrowed brows and chuckled lightly. "Yeah."

"You look like you're scared," he commented.

"I'm not scared." I shook my head.

He looked worried. "Then what's wrong?"

I smiled at him. "Nothing's wrong. I'm just not used to anyone protecting me."

"Are you upset that I did that?" he asked and then pointed down the hall. "I only did that because that guy was outta line."

"Seth, I'm not upset. You forget though, who I am. I was always the one coming to your defense. It's just bizarre to be on the other side of the table."

"Are you upset you didn't get to hit him?" he teased. I laughed at him. "A little," I admitted.

"Would you like me to drag him back?" he teased me again.

"No," I put my arms around his waist, "I'll live."

It was almost impossible leaving him to go to work. But I kissed him, stepped out of his car, put one foot in front of the other, and headed into the building.

It is my other passion. I love my job. How many people go to work every day and can say that? I love working with the kids. My favorite part is just talking with them. I'm always fascinated by the way they think. The unique things they will think up just to explain something. The wild detailed stories that you later find out aren't true. The way they will blurt out the obvious. I find I have a lot in common with them.

Today, I was sitting at the table by the window helping a little girl named Hannah. She's a beautiful blonde girl with rosy red cheeks and little dimples. She's almost four and she's in her own world. She's always talking in her own made up language, she sings in it too. She plays by herself a lot and seems very content doing so. She does occasionally say a few random words, but then she'll start laughing and singing in her own language again.

She loves to color, so I sit and color with her. I talk to her about the pictures she colors and she smiles. She doesn't say this but I can tell she understands everything I say. I keep telling her parents that too, but

I don't think they believe me. I can't say that I blame them. Who am I but some teenage assistant? I've come to the determination that her parents ignore her.

And how might I know this? Because I am an expert on being ignored. My case is different though. My father never ignored me, but my mother did, and still does. I believe she's ignored by both of her parents. I keep these thoughts about Hannah to myself. I can't go upsetting the parents that way. There's really no way of proving that. When her mother comes to pick her up she dotes on her very affectionately, but I can see right through her. She reminds me of my own mother, and she is always the very last parent to show up.

While I was coloring with Hannah I glanced out the window and saw Seth leaning against his car watching me, smiling warmly. I smiled back at him, and then glanced at the clock. It was quarter of six.

I leaned over to Hannah. "Hey, do you see that man outside?" I pointed.

She looked up at me and then looked out the window. I whispered in her ear, "I love him."

She giggled.

"You know girly, it would really make me look good if you said something to me today," I told her.

She looked up at me with a big dimpled smile. "Harmony," she said.

I sat up and gave her a funny look. "Harmony, huh?" I shrugged. "Well, at least you said something."

At five of, Hannah's mom finally came. I picked up our mess, and then I said goodbye to my wonderful boss Glenda, remembering to toss my dad's letter in the outgoing mail pile, like I normally do.

I strolled out to greet him, and he grabbed me up into a big hug and kissed me with serious enthusiasm, like I kissed him this morning.

I climbed into his car. "I hope you don't mind that I put the top down?" he asked, smiling. "It's just so nice today."

"I don't mind at all," I said, smiling back at him.

So, how was work?" he asked me.

"It was good." I held up my hands and smiled. "See?" I had a little green paint left over from an art project. "You can always tell when I've had a good day here, because I end up wearing some of it home." I laughed.

He smiled and grabbed my hand kissing my palm. "The kids must love you," he commented.

I smiled at him. "So how was your afternoon?" I asked.

"Long. I'm just glad it's over," he said.

He started the car. "So, am I taking you home?"

"Yeah." I sighed. "I have a ton of homework."

He shook his head and laughed. "How so? You skip English."

"Well, I still have math, biology, and history," I complained.

He was still chuckling. "So, are you gonna tell me what I-95 is?"

"No," I smirked at him. "I swore to Evelyn that I'd take that to the grave, and never tell anyone. What kind of friend would I be if I couldn't keep a secret?" I laughed. "Knowing Evelyn though, it just might come out anyways."

We pulled out of the parking lot and I settled quietly into my seat. I then heard the faint sound of a song I love coming from the car's speakers. I reached over and turned up the radio; sure enough, "Ramble On" was playing. I got excited and did a little jiggle in my seat and started singing along.

Seth glanced over at me and laughed. "You like Led Zeppelin?" he asked.

I nodded. "Uh yeah, I love them!"

"What other bands do you like?" he asked.

I put my fingers to my lips. "I love Aerosmith, they're my favorite. I have their record at home. I listen to that a ton. I also like Black Sabbath, Deep purple, and Pink Floyd. Pretty much anything that rocks," I said, happily.

I looked over at him. "What kind of music do you like? *Please*...don't say country."

He looked at me like I was crazy. "Don't worry, I don't like country." He winced. "I like the same music you do."

"But what's your favorite band?" I asked.

"Aerosmith," he said quickly.

I narrowed my brows at him. "You're not just saying that are you?"

He chuckled and reached over, popping open the glove box. He had a few eight-track tapes stuffed inside.

I started going through them and I squealed. "You are just too good to be true," I told him.

He had the same Aerosmith album I have, plus the album I wanted, *Get Your Wings*. I popped it into the eight-track player and pressed fast forward until I got to my favorite song on that album, "Train Kept a Rollin."

When the song started off, I sat back in my seat and closed my eyes for a moment feeling the melody. I began grooving along to the sound of the song's mind-altering guitar riff. I love this song, it gets all inside you mingling with your soul, helping you to escape for a while.

I opened my eyes and kicked off my shoes when the beat started up. I put my feet up on the dash and started tapping my toes and my hands singing along.

"Well on a train▢I met a dame,"

"She rather handsome▢we kind of look the same,"

"She was pretty▢from New York City,"

"I'm walkin down that old fair lane,"

"I'm in heat▢I'm in love. But I just couldn't tell her so,"

"I said a train kept a-rollin all night long,"

"Train kept a-rollin all night long,"

"Train kept a-rollin all night long,"

"Train kept a-rollin all night long. With a heave! And a-ho! But I just couldn't tell her so, no, no, no!"

I really started getting into the song swaying back and forth grooving to the rhythm, completely forgetting that I had an audience.

"Well, get along, sweet little woman get along."

"On your way, get along, sweet little woman get along."

"On your way, ⊠I'm in heat, I'm in love. But I just couldn't tell her so, no, no, no."

I caught him out of the corner of my eye smiling, and he kept glancing over.

Not that I'm ever normally, but it was starting to make me feel a little self-conscious.

I looked back at him. "What?"

"I just can't get over how *fantastic* you are!" He was grinning.

I smirked at him with my eyes narrowed. "*Me*?" I was a little surprised.

"Yes, you! The more time I spend with you, the more I want to be with you," he said. He was glowing.

I leaned over and rested my head against his arm. "That's funny...that's how I feel about you too."

I sat up and smiled when I heard my favorite part, Joey Kramer's drum roll going into when the song starts really rockin! I started bopping my head and stomping my feet to the rhythm. I beamed when Seth turned it up.

I ran my fingers through my hair when the guitars started wailing, beckoning my wild child out like a loud siren.

I got excited when the song started really rockin! I shook my hair out and threw my hands up and started dancing in my seat. I smiled wide when I saw Seth dancing in his seat too.

As we were driving down the road, both of us were dancing and rockin in our seats singing really loud.

"Well on a train.⊠I met a dame!"

"She rather handsome.⊠we kind of look the same!"

"She was pretty.⊠From New York City!"

"I'm walkin down that old fair lane!"

"I'm in heat⊠I'm in love! But I just couldn't tell her so!"

"I said a train kept a-rollin all night long!"

"Train kept a-rollin all night long!"

"Train kept a-rollin all night long!"

"Train kept a-rollin all night long! With a heave! And a-ho! But I just couldn't tell her so!"

We pulled into my driveway still singing loudly, and dancing like crazy in our seats with the song still blasting. I was all keyed up now. I was having so much fun. I can't wait to go out with him Friday night now!

"Well, get along, sweet little woman get along!"

"On your way, get along, sweet little woman get along!"

"On your way, ⊠I'm in heat, I'm in love! But I just couldn't tell her so, no, no, no!"

We both looked over at each other when we sang the last lines.

I was so excited. My heart was pounding, and my breathing was rough. I sat there just staring at Seth and he was staring back at me just as lit up as I was. He was grinning ear to ear and I could see his chest heaving from the exertion.

He reached for me knotting his fingers into my hair and pulled me in quickly, kissing me feverishly and with such passion that it bordered aggression. I quickly got to my knees and climbed on top of him gripping his shirt eagerly craving more...I felt him reach down and recline his seat back and I fought with new desires as the song raged on...

He is so amazing! He excites me and he makes me feel so alive! We're way beyond being best friends now! It's official, I know I have found my true other half! We love each other. We protect each other. We can trust each other, and he loves hard rock and will party right along with me! ⊠*Hell yeah*! ⊠I'll never love anyone else, ever!

I can feel it down to my core that he is my soul mate! He's got to be! It's the only thing that explains how alive I feel when I'm with him, and the emptiness I feel when he's not.

How can he not be my soul mate? There's no other explanation that exists!

CHAPTER 20

I was still wrapped in the arms of the most amazing woman the Heavens has ever created. I felt such peace lying with her, such *Harmony*. Nestled in the crook of her arm, I turned my head up to take in the beauty of my only love. She was gazing up at the ceiling; her curls were fanned out across my pillow. She was casually running her fingers up and down my arm, her full lips turned up into the most gorgeous smile.

It was obvious she was enjoying reliving the moments we shared together as much as I was enjoying listening to her tell it. I wish I could remember something, anything, from that time. Just a small piece, to know for certain that this is all really real.

I rolled myself over on top of her, to look into her beautiful brown eyes and she smiled warmly. I smiled back at her and caressed her cheek with my thumb and brushed a curl away from her face with my fingertips.

"What?" she spoke softly.

I leaned in and tenderly kissed her lips. The taste of her sweet lips had my heart bursting and overflowing with such overwhelming affection for her. Her scent had my mind spinning like a crazy top when suddenly it popped into my mind, my one and only memory of her. I held my eyes closed as I pulled away slightly, hovering just out of reach of her lips so I could speak.

"I've been looking for you," I admitted to her suddenly. My nerves were on edge and my heart pounded against my sore ribs. I opened my eyes to check her reaction. She just laid there frozen with confusion in her eyes. It took a moment before she spoke. I think I may have caught her off guard. I held my breath waiting for her to reply.

"What do you mean you've been looking for me?" she asked. Her tone confirmed the confusion.

"I've been dreaming of you," I said, still holding my breath.

"*You have?*" She sounded shocked.

I started to become a little lightheaded and exhaled sharply. My whole body relaxed in relief. Not one time have I ever told that secret to anyone. It felt so good to finally share it with someone, like a weight has been lifted. It seems only fitting that I shared it with her, my dream girl.

"Yes, every night since I was ten," I told her confessing more, I was feeling extraordinary. But my relief was short lived seeing the shock still present in her eyes. I started to become worried that maybe this wasn't normal. "Is that not normal?" I asked her. My pulse raced a little waiting for her response.

She was still running her finger through my hair; her face was frozen with a cautiously placed smile. It seemed like she was carefully thinking about her answer. She sighed, before she spoke. "No, not really. We're not supposed to be able to remember anything about home when we are here," she replied.

I rolled off of her onto my back sighing, sinking against my pillows thinking about her answer. "You did say that there is a reason for everything. Do you think that our love is strong enough, that I was kind of unknowingly remembering it? Like maybe that's why I was dreaming of you?" I asked her.

"What do you mean?" she asked.

"It just feels like it would make a little sense. My subconscious knows what my brain doesn't, and it's been trying to tell me. My aches, my struggles to breathe normally, the dreams," I said clarifying.

She was smiling. "You're definitely on the right track."

I smiled back at her reply.

She rolled over, and kissed my cheek. "It's no wonder you've been so miserable. I don't think anyone realized how much of us you were gonna carry down."

"I didn't mean to do that," I replied. I turned to look into her glowing brown eyes. "And I'm not upset about it. I'm glad I was dreaming about you every night. At least I never had any nightmares."

"True, that is a good thing then." She rolled over suddenly and got to her knees straddling me, pinning me down on the bed and smiling. Her eyes were suddenly lit up. "So, what was your dream about? Did you have the same one over and over, or were they different?"

I smiled at her. "I've had the same dream over and over since I was ten. Except for last night, that one was different."

"That one was different?" She smirked. "How?"

"Well, in all of them before I could always just see you. But the one I had last night was more real. I could feel you, smell you, taste you, it was..." I struggled for the right words. "Well, like Heaven."

She chuckled. "That one may have been my fault," she confessed.

I playfully narrowed my eyes at her. "How was that your fault?"

"I told you, I've been here for a while. I was there that night at the hospital after they brought you in, and I stayed with you the whole time making sure you were going to be alright. Then, I followed you here and kept an eye on you. Like I said before, I was trying to figure out how to approach you without scaring you. Last night you were lying here and you looked so peaceful and I couldn't resist leaning in to breathe in your sweet honey scent...I got a little carried away."

I was glowing inside and out. I know if the role was reversed and she was here and I had stayed behind, I wouldn't be able to resist her either. I threaded my fingers with hers and chuckled. "Well, at least that explains why it seemed so real."

She was smiling. "I never expected you to kiss me back the way you did. It kinda surprised me at first. That's when I decided to show myself to you." She leaned down getting inches away from my face. "Tell me about the other one," she whispered.

"I'm standing in a dark room. The room starts to lighten up and I realize that I'm standing in a doorway holding a large bouquet of flowers, and I can see you sitting at a table but your back is to me. You and I are naked, but I don't even notice that I am until I give you the flowers. I freak out because I figure out I'm naked and I run back towards the door and then you chase after me. You and I stand there just staring at each other smiling until the doorway closes on us. That's it."

"*Oooh*, interesting," she began grazing her lips with mine, "so we don't even kiss?" she asked just above whispering.

"It's never that I don't want to," I whispered back. I reached up combing my fingers into her soft curls, pulling her in quickly, desperate for her lips on mine. I rolled her to her back and I held her in my arms breathing her in, savoring my time with her.

I started casually running my lips along her neck up under her ear breathing in her sweet scent that is heavy in her beautiful brown curls. I just couldn't help myself. I can't seem to get enough of her powerful fragrance. It's intoxicating and it radiates throughout me making me feel so alive.

I heard her moan softly with desire, and she turned suddenly molding her full sweet lips to mine. I felt her casually wrap her leg around mine and she was intensely gripping my tee-shirt. I pulled back a little to look up at her beautiful face. "So what else happened?"

She glanced over at my alarm clock. It was three in the morning. "You must be tired," she stated.

I nuzzled my face against her neck again kissing her softly and breathing in her sweet floral scent. "Nope," I mumbled.

"It's really late for you. You need to sleep," she said, insisting.

I looked up at her. "How can I bother with something so trivial, when my time with you is so limited?"

"I love you too, but I'm not going anywhere yet." She was running her fingers through my hair sending waves of pleasure straight to my heart. "I told you I'd be here long enough to make sure you are alright and explain things to you. We can pause so you can sleep, and I'll tell you more when you wake up."

I smirked at her. "Are you telling me to go to sleep?"

She chuckled. "I would never tell you what to do. I just don't want you falling asleep while I'm telling you the best parts."

I sighed in defeat. "What are you gonna do while I'm sleeping?"

"I'm gonna stay right here with you." She raised an eyebrow. "Maybe I'll do some things to improve your dreams." She was grinning.

"Mmmm, that sounds good." I rolled to my side, laying my head on the pillow so I was facing her; I took her hand in mine and I let myself yawn. "I love you," I reminded her.

She was combing my hair out of my face and she kissed my cheek. "I love you, too. Sweet dreams, my love. I'll be right here when you wake up, and I'll tell you more of our story."

I closed my eyes allowing my body to succumb to the fatigue I was feeling, lying alongside the most amazing woman in existence. I'm overjoyed that she is mine.

Epilogue

As Curtis Parker sleeps, memories tucked deep within his subconscious from his previous life are beginning to break through the barrier, and are bubbling to the surface...

I scooped her up into my arms, and carried her into the motel room.

She placed her arms around my neck, and smiled softly. "I thought you're supposed to wait until after we get married to carry me?"

"As far as I'm concerned, you and I already are," I replied to her just above a whisper. I set her down on her feet. "I'm gonna go get the bags."

"Okay, I'll help you," she said.

I put my hand up. "Nope, I'll do it," I insisted. There was no way I was gonna make her do that knowing she may still be suffering a little after what that asshole did to her. She seems alright on the surface, but I didn't want to take that chance. She's constantly taking care of me, and she's so independent. Insisting all the time that she is so tough. A human being can only take so much. She's always doing everything herself. It's about time someone stepped in, and spoiled her the way she deserves.

I went back to the car and grabbed all of the bags out of the trunk, placing them on the ground. I closed the trunk of my car and made sure the doors were all locked up for the night. I don't know this area very well, and I didn't want to take any chances so far from home. I picked up the bags and headed back to the room. There really weren't so many bags that I needed her help carrying them anyways. I did need her help with the door though.

She opened the door for me, and I set the bags down by the little table. I was already feeling like this was it. That we were married and that I can protect her forever. At the same time, it felt weird. There was this awkward silence lingering in the room, and it worried me. I was wondering if she was feeling it too.

She sat down on the edge of the bed and kicked off her shoes. I sat down next to her, and did the same thing.

"What time do you want to head out tomorrow?" I asked trying to fill the awkward silence.

"Um...how about we just leave when we feel like?" She shrugged. "Unless, you're keeping a set schedule."

"Okay." I glanced down at the floor. "Why is this weird?" I asked her.

She let out a sigh of relief. "I don't know." We both started laughing.

"Maybe it's just because you and I have never been out on our own like this before?" she suggested. She placed her hand on my cheek. "It doesn't feel wrong. I know we're doing the right thing."

I let out a sigh of relief. "So, you still want to marry me then?"

She smiled softly and nodded her head. "As far as I'm concerned, you and I already are."

She leaned in, closing her eyes, and kissed my lips. I suddenly had an idea, which might ease the tension a little. I had a gift for her tucked away in my bag. I was gonna wait until after we got married, but I decided to give it to her now. I gently pulled away and smiled at her. "I have something for you."

She sat back and smiled. "I already have everything I ever wanted."

I got up from the bed and started digging through my bag. "I was saving this for after our wedding, but I want to give it to you now instead."

"You don't have to give it to me now," she said, "I don't mind waiting."

I turned to glance back at her with a raised brow. "*You*, don't mind waiting?" I was surprised. Usually, she's kind of impatient.

She smirked. "I don't mind because I already have you. I don't need anything else."

She makes me so happy. She is far more than I deserve. "Well that's too bad. I'm giving it to you now," I informed her.

I sat down on the bed next to her, and handed her a black rectangular felt covered box and kissed her cheek.

When she flipped open the lid she gasped. Nestled against white satin was a beautiful silver necklace I had made special for her. The pendant was two hearts linked together like a link of a chain. The first heart had a small link in the center where it was secured to a sliver chain. The heart that was linked to it hung on its side off one of the curves and was resting in the V of the first heart. Both hearts were covered on one side with small diamonds.

"I had that made for you back in May. I got the idea from the lid to your music box." My tone was soft.

I turned over the little pendant. "See, it's you and me." On the back side, my name was on the top heart and hers was on the bottom one.

She sat there speechless, and tears were pooling in her eyes. She wiped her cheek and kissed me. "This is the most beautiful necklace I've ever seen in my life, and you are beyond amazing for even thinking of something like this." She placed her hand on my cheek and caressed it with her thumb. "How did I ever get so lucky?" she asked me.

I smiled and shrugged. "I ask myself that exact same question every single moment I get to be with you."

She handed me the box. "Would you help me put it on?"

"Sure." I took the necklace out of the box and un-did the clasp. She turned around and held her hair up while I secured her necklace in place. I watched her touch the pendent gently feeling it in between her fingers and she smiled. "Thank you," she said.

I swept her hair to the side and kissed her neck down by her collarbone. "You're welcome," I whispered, as I began gently gliding my lips up her neck.

"I love you," she said, her voice quivering a little as she spoke.

"I love you, too."

Made in the USA
Middletown, DE
19 January 2018